Francis Turner Palgrave

The Treasury of Sacred Song

Selected From the English Lyrical Poetry of Four Centuries

Francis Turner Palgrave

The Treasury of Sacred Song
Selected From the English Lyrical Poetry of Four Centuries

ISBN/EAN: 9783744766739

Printed in Europe, USA, Canada, Australia, Japan

Cover: Foto ©Andreas Hilbeck / pixelio.de

More available books at **www.hansebooks.com**

THE
TREASURY OF SACRED SONG

F. T. PALGRAVE

F. T. PALGRAVE

LONDON: HENRY FROWDE

OXFORD UNIVERSITY PRESS WAREHOUSE

AMEN CORNER, E.C.

Thirteenth Thousand

THE TREASURY OF SACRED SONG

SELECTED FROM THE

ENGLISH LYRICAL POETRY
OF FOUR CENTURIES

WITH NOTES EXPLANATORY AND BIOGRAPHICAL

BY

FRANCIS T. PALGRAVE

PROFESSOR OF POETRY IN THE UNIVERSITY OF OXFORD

Ex Ipso et per Ipsum et in Ipso

Oxford

AT THE CLARENDON PRESS

MDCCCXC

—ἐπάμεροι· τί δέ τις; τί δ' οὔ τις; σκιᾶς ὄναρ
ἄνθρωπος. ἀλλ' ὅταν αἴγλα διόσδοτος ἔλθῃ,
λαμπρὸν φέγγος ἔπεστιν ἀνδρῶν καὶ μείλιχος αἰών—

PREFACE

To offer poetry for poetry's sake has been my first aim and leading principle in fulfilling the task with which the authorities of the Clarendon Press have honoured me. Hence it is probable that many poems which would be justly expected when the object of a selection is direct usefulness, spiritual aid and comfort, or (to put it in one word) edification, will here be found absent. And this deficiency, I fear, will be felt even by readers who are not satisfied with religious verse, however good its intention, unless it be clothed in the veil of beauty. For verse of this kind, hymns in particular, beyond any other modes of poetry, hold a special place in the hearts of men ; so closely intertwined with the predilections of childhood, with the memories of the home or the church of our youth, with the voices no longer heard on this side the grave, that they have a charm for us beyond criticism,—a spell which is none the less irresistible because it is not cast over us by their own proper magic.

Yet if my aim—an aim in collections of sacred song rarely avowed or followed—to present poetry for poetry's sake, has not here altogether been missed through my own want of taste or discernment, may it not be hoped that the final end and object of all the Fine Arts, and Poetry as the queen of them,—permanent pleasure, elevation and enlightenment of the soul,—to return to the word, edification in the highest sense,—will be secured more effectually and more enduringly, through the subtle, yet powerful aid of melody in words, and beauty in form? It is confessedly thus when Music or Painting are concerned ; the better and finer the art, the more exquisite the pleasure, the more penetrating, the more vivifying, the impression. From this point of view, we may agree with the poet, 'Beauty is truth, truth beauty.' And so far from being alien or opposed to piety, these great gifts of God to man nowhere else have a more fitting place or a loftier function. Nowhere is the power and magic of poetry as an art more naturally in place or better employed than when her inspiring Muses are Faith, Hope, and Love,—when her subjects are those incomparably highest and most vital interests to mankind, which may be briefly summed up as right conduct here, and its reward hereafter.

If, however, the rule of choice which I have tried to follow be theoretically valid, the argument has to be met, that by its very nature, through its general aim and its often imperfect quality as art,—Sacred Poetry rarely deserves the honour of that great name. And there is a large element of truth in this objection. The aim at direct usefulness to the individual or to the Church has unquestionably led to the neglect of Poetry in religious verse; and Art, we may truly say, has here revenged herself upon Religion. The most weighty of these adverse criticisms is the often-quoted verdict of Dr. Johnson. 'Poetry,' he says, 'loses its lustre and its power, because it is applied to the decoration of something more excellent than itself. All that pious verse can do is to help the memory, and delight the ear, and for these purposes it may be very useful; but it supplies nothing to the mind. The ideas of Christian Theology are too simple for eloquence, too sacred for fiction, and too majestick for ornament.' Johnson is a judge whose native good sense, sincerity, and alertness of mind, render disregard of his decisions impossible without folly. Yet we cannot concede to him, in this matter, the infallibility which, (when that great debater had 'tossed and gored' his antagonists), he would laughingly disclaim for himself. His argument seems arbitrarily to confine the range and the capability of religious verse, as it will be found represented in this selection: and it is also a view coloured by the unalloyed seriousness—the gloom—of the great writer's own deeply felt religious faith; possibly, also, by the fact that he was writing at a period when our sacred song was wellnigh confined to hymns. And although with certain singular gifts as a critic of poetry, Johnson was not in advance of his day. Many of the poets who lived before the modern manner had established itself, he appears to have read or valued but little: with Habington or Herbert, for example, I am not aware that he shows any sympathetic acquaintance; while Vaughan, from his own time to ours, was almost wholly forgotten.

It is however undeniable that if, (with some later critics), we inaccurately group all sacred verse under the single section of hymns in the popular sense of the word, the Religious lyric, in comparison with the Secular, (epithets which I use perforce in default of better), will be found largely inferior in poetical charm. But the argument in this form is sophistical. Secular verse covers many provinces; manners, incident, love, landscape,—the vast sphere of drama;—in a word, all the many-coloured romance of life. Sacred verse can hardly go beyond one province: to expect masterpieces in our field approximately numerous as those in the secular lyric is unreasonable. Even more unreasonable is it, when of this single province a district only is chosen out for censure, and treated as the whole domain. Hymns, wellnigh limited to the functions of prayer and of praise, are precisely that region in which a practical aim is naturally, almost inevitably predominant. The writers, (not to dwell upon the imperfect training of many among them), have hence far too frequently and easily made the sacrifice of pleasure to usefulness, of beauty to edification. But it should also be remembered that hymns, in this respect, are subject to the common penalty, the inferiority in art, inherent in all didactic verse; although with a more pressing and powerful excuse than didactic verse can offer for its inevitable prosaicism.

Yet I hope that an answer, far more pleasant and convincing than any argument,—is offered to these objections by the following anthology. If indeed the limitations of its sphere be considered, the triteness of some inevitable motives, the insuperable loftiness of others, it seems to the Editor that English lyrical religious poetry fairly—perhaps fully—holds its own: that Urania has her legitimate throne beside her sister Muses of song. And should this opinion appear partial to my readers, let me plead that I have turned over many thousand pages in my search, as an excuse—if not a justification—for partiality.

A few details remain for notice. Translations, as even when at the best, (by a law of nature, may I not call it?) hardly ever reaching excellence as poetry, or reaching it only for a moment, are here excluded. But paraphrases,—a style for centuries frequent in religious verse,—have been regarded as entitled to a measure of admission, when executed with such freedom and spirit, as to take rank with original inventions.

A book planned for popular use half defeats its own object by adherence to unfamiliar modes of spelling. But whilst in this respect modernizing the diction, I have carefully followed the best text easily accessible;—here, again, judging reference in every case to original editions not essential to the purpose of the volume. No verbal changes whatever have been made: but I have freely allowed such omissions as might appear to bring a poem to a closer unity in idea, or a more equably sustained excellence in poetry:—a freedom for which I shall hope forgiveness, at least from readers who accept the leading principle of the selection. And if the notes added upon obsolete words and phrases appear to any too numerous, I would plead that Poetry,—especially in this age of facile prose—requires every assistance to attract and hold her audience. Better that fifty should find an explanation superfluous, than one find a difficulty unsolved.

Longer explanatory remarks have been reserved for the final notes: in which, also, (supported by the example of Archbishop Trench in his excellent *Household Book of English Poetry*), I have added a few indications of peculiar poetical merit. To separate a poet's serious work from his personality, as Goethe once remarked, is simply impossible. The brief biographies inserted, (which exclude our well-known master-singers, and those still living), will, therefore, it is hoped, satisfy, in a fair degree, the natural desire for some acquaintance with the lives of those whose best and deepest thoughts are here before us. Even when only a few bare facts have been recorded or noticed, they can hardly fail to throw over the verse some light and interest. But greater space has been given to those writers whose public career or personal modes of thought, (in particular when remote from present fashions), have given a special colour to their poetry.

A chronological arrangement,—so far as chronology is possible, where the actual dates of composition are rarely known,—has been generally kept in view. But poems of cognate character, whether in style or in thought, have been often grouped together.

Thanks are due to the unvaried kindness with which owners of copyright have conceded the privilege of reprinting. Amongst these it is proper to specify,—in case of Lord Tennyson, permission given by Messrs. Macmillan:—by Messrs. Parker and Messrs. Burns, for pieces from Keble's Miscellaneous Poems, and Father Faber's Hymns, respectively:—for Archbishop Trench and Mr. Barnes, from Messrs. K. Paul;—Mr. Lyte, Messrs. Rivingtons;—Dr. Bonar, Mr. J. Nisbet.

The aim of this little book, let me repeat, is to offer such lyrical sacred song, and such only, as shall be instinctively felt worthy the august name of Poetry. And as I have also attempted to present here all such pieces known to me as reach a certain standard of excellence, a comparatively large space has been necessarily given to three or four poets who combined high genius with a considerable bulk of suitable work :—whilst the limits of size have compelled me to omit verse of simply moral quality, however pure and lofty, and thus intrinsically religious.

It is, however, the inevitable—perhaps the unfortunate—lot of a selection framed upon these lines, that whether poetical merit or spiritual value be regarded, the selector's own personal tastes and opinions cannot be excluded; and in such matters it is difficult to keep perfectly true the balance of the soul. On the point of merit I can only plead an honest endeavour to shut out all mere individual predilections, and to form the decision by a wide and comparative research through this region of our literature during the last four centuries. But in reference to the different aspects of religion here presented, my task has been aided signally by the wide-embracing charity, the Catholic spirit (as embodied in the Creeds), natural to Poetry as part of her very essence. This has been well expressed by Mr. C. J. Abbey in his valuable essay upon the English Sacred Poetry of the eighteenth century. 'It may be said to be the peculiar privilege of hymn-writers that to a great extent they write, not for any one society of Christians, but for the Church at large. Men whose theological views contrast most strongly meet on common ground when they express in verse the deeper aspirations of the heart, and the voice of Christian praise.'—In a word, whilst severity has been aimed at, where Poetry as an art is concerned,—in regard to the religious quality of the verse selected, my rule has been that which Dante describes as given by S. Peter to the Angel at the gate of the Mount of Purgatory,

> —ch' io erri
> Anzi ad aprir, che a tenerla serrata.

F. T. P.

LITTLE PARK
LYME REGIS:
MAY 1889

The Treasury of Sacred Song

Book First

I

CHRIST'S NATIVITY

NOW gladdeth every living creáture,
   With bliss and comfortable gladnéss,
The heaven's King is clad in our natúre,
Us from the death with ransom to redress;
The lamp of joy, that chases all darknéss,
Ascended is to be the world's[1] light,
From every bale[2] our boundés[3] for to bliss,
Born of the glorious Virgin Mary bright.

Above the radiant heaven ethereal,
The Court of Stars, the course of sun and moon,
The potent Prince of Joy Imperial,
The high surmounting Emperor abone[4],
Is coming from His mighty Father's throne
In[5] earth, with an inestimable light,
And praised[6] of angels with a sweet intone;
Born of the glorious Virgin Mary bright.

Who ever in earth heard so blythe a story,
Or tidings of so great felicity?
As how the garthé[7] of all grace and glory,
For love and mercy hath ta'en humanity;
Maker of angels, man, earth, heaven, and sea,
And t' overcome our foe, and put to flight,
Is coming a babe, full of benignity,
Born of the glorious Virgin Mary bright.

The sovereign senior of all celsitude[8],
That sits above the order'd Cherabin,
Which all things creat, and all things does include,
That never end shall, never did begin,
But[9] Whom is naught, from Whom no time does rin[10],
With Whom all good is, with Whom is every wight,
Is with His wounds come for to wash our sin;
Born of the most chaste Virgin Mary bright.

W. Dunbar

[1] *world's*, a dissyllable   [2] *bale*, sorrow   [3] *boundes*, apparently boundaries
of the earth   [4] *abone*, above   [5] *in* earth, to   [6] after *praised*, *is* omitted
[7] *garthe*, literally *garden*; that which contains   [8] *celsitude* height   [9] *but*,
without   [10] *rin*, run

II

YOUTH

WHEN I look back, and in myself behold
  The wandering ways, that youth could not descry:
And mark'd the fearful course that youth did hold,
And met in mind each step youth stray'd awry;
My knees I bow, and from my heart I call,
O LORD, forget these faults and follies all!

For now I see, how void youth is of skill,
I see also his prime time and his end:
I do confess my faults and all my ill,
And sorrow sore, for that I did offend.
And with a mind repentant of all crimes
Pardon I ask for youth, ten thousand times.

The humble heart hath daunted the proud mind;
Eke wisdom hath given ignorance a fall:
And wit hath taught, that[1] folly could not find,
And age hath youth her subject and her thrall.
Therefore I pray, O LORD of life and truth,
Pardon the faults committed in my youth.

Thou that didst grant the wise king his request:
Thou that in Whale Thy prophet didst preserve:
Thou that forgav'st the wounding of Thy breast:
Thou that didst save the thief in state to sterve[2]:
Thou only GOD, the giver of all grace:
Wipe out of mind the path of youth's vain race.

Thou that, by power, to life didst raise the dead:
Thou that of grace restor'st the blind to sight:
Thou that for love, Thy life and love out-bled:
Thou that of favour mad'st the lame go right:
Thou that canst heal, and help in all assays,
Forgive the guilt, that grew in youth's vain ways.

And now since I, with faith and doubtless mind,
Do fly to Thee by prayer, to appease Thy ire:
And since that Thee I only seek to find,
And hope, by faith, to attain my just desire;
LORD, mind no more youth's error and unskill,
And able age to do Thy holy will.

T. Lord Vaux

---

[1] *that*, that which   [2] *sterve*, die

III

LIFE AND DEATH

THE pleasant years that seem, so swift that run:
   The merry days to end, so fast that fleet:
The joyful nights, of which day dawns so soon:
The happy hours, which mo[1] do miss, than meet,
Do all consume, as snow against the sun:
And death makes end of all, that life begun.

Since death shall dure, till all the world be waste:
What meaneth man to dread death then so sore?
As man might make[2], that life should alway last,
Without regard[3], the LORD hath led before
The dance of death, which all must run on row:
Though how, or when, the LORD alone doth know.

If man would mind, what burdens life doth bring:
What grievous crimes to GOD he doth commit:
What plagues, what pangs, what perils thereby spring:
With no sure hour in all his days to sit:
He would sure think, as with great cause I do:
The day of death were better of the two.

Death is a port, whereby we pass to joy:
Life is a lake, that drowneth all in pain:
Death is so dear, it ceaseth all annoy:
Life is so lewd[4], that all it yields is vain.
And as, by life, to bondage man is brought:
E'en so likewise by death was freedom wrought.

                                   Anon.

[1] *mo*, more   [2] *make*, apparently, desire or aim   [3] *regard*, regarding that   [4] *lewd*, foolish

IV

AN HYMN OF HEAVENLY LOVE

LOVE, lift me up upon thy golden wings,
   From this base world unto thy heaven's height,
Where I may see those admirable things
Which there thou workest by thy sovereign might,
Far above feeble reach of earthly sight,
That I thereof an heavenly Hymn may sing
Unto the GOD of Love, high heaven's King.

Many lewd lays (ah! woe is me the more!)
In praise of that mad fit which fools call love,
I have in th' heat of youth made heretofore,
That in light wits did loose affection move;
But all those follies now I do reprove,
And turnéd have the tenor of my string,
The heavenly praises of true love to sing.

And ye that wont with greedy vain desire
To read my fault, and, wondering at my flame,
To warm yourselves at my wide sparkling fire,
Sith now that heat is quenchéd, quench my blame,
And in her ashes shroud my dying shame;
For who my passéd follies now pursues,
Begins his own, and my old fault renews.

Before this world's great frame, in which all things
Are now contain'd, found any being-place,
Ere flitting Time could wag his eyas[1] wings
About that mighty bound which doth embrace
The rolling Spheres, and parts their hours by space,
That High Eternal Power, which now doth move
In all these things, moved in Itself by love.

It loved Itself, because Itself was fair;
(For fair is loved;) and of Itself begot,
Like to Itself, His eldest Son and heir,
Eternal, pure, and void of sinful blot,
The firstling of His joy, in Whom no jot
Of love's dislike or pride was to be found,
Whom He therefore with equal honour crown'd.

With Him he reign'd, before all time prescribed,
In endless glory and immortal might,
Together with that Third from Them derived,
Most wise, most holy, most almighty Spright!
Whose kingdom's throne no thought of earthly wight
Can comprehend, much less my trembling verse
With equal words can hope it to rehearse.

Yet, O most blesséd Spirit! pure lamp of light,
Eternal spring of grace and wisdom true,
Vouchsafe to shed into my barren spright
Some little drop of Thy celestial dew,
That may my rhymes with sweet infuse imbrue[2],
And give me words equal unto my thought,
To tell the marvels by Thy mercy wrought.

Yet being pregnant still with powerful grace,
And full of fruitful love, that loves to get
Things like Himself, and to enlarge His race,
His second brood, though not in power so great,
Yet full of beauty, next He did beget
An infinite increase of Angels bright,
All glistering glorious in their Maker's light.

To them the heaven's illimitable height
(Not this round heaven, which we from hence behold,
Adorn'd with thousand lamps of burning light,
And with ten thousand gems of shining gold,)
He gave as their inheritance to hold,
That they might serve Him in eternal bliss,
And be partakers of those joys of His.

There they in their trinal triplicities [3]
About Him wait, and on His will depend,
Either with nimble wings to cut the skies,
When He them on his messages doth send,
Or on His own dread presence to attend,
Where they behold the glory of His light,
And carol Hymns of love both day and night.

Both day, and night, is unto them all one;
For He His beams doth still to them extend,
That darkness there appeareth never none;
Ne hath their day, ne hath their bliss, an end,
But there their termless time in pleasure spend;
Ne ever should their happiness decay,
Had not they dared their Lord to disobey.

But pride, impatient of long resting peace,
Did puff them up with greedy bold ambition,
That they 'gan cast their state how to increase
Above the fortune of their first condition,
And sit in God's own seat without commission:
The brightest Angel, ev'n the Child of Light,
Drew millions more against their God to fight.

Th' Almighty, seeing their so bold assay,
Kindled the flame of His consuming ire,
And with His only breath them blew away
From heaven's height, to which they did aspire,
To deepest hell, and lake of damnéd fire,
Where they in darkness and dread horror dwell,
Hating the happy light from which they fell.

So that next offspring of the Maker's love,
Next to Himself in glorious degree,
Degendering[4] to hate, fell from above
Through pride, (for pride and love may ill agree),
And now of sin to all ensample be:
How then can sinful flesh itself assure,
Since purest Angels fell to be impure?

But that Eternal Fount of love and grace,
Still flowing forth His goodness unto all,
Now seeing left a waste and empty place
In His wide Palace, through those Angels' fall,
Cast to supply the same, and to enstall
A new unknowen Colony therein,
Whose root from earth's base groundwork should begin.

Therefore of clay, base, vile, and next to nought,
Yet form'd by wondrous skill, and by His might,
According to an heavenly pattern wrought,
Which He had fashion'd in His wise foresight,
He man did make, and breathed a living spright
Into his face most beautiful and fair,
Endued with wisdom's riches, heavenly, rare.

Such He him made, that he resemble might
Himself, as mortal thing immortal could;
Him to be Lord of every living wight
He made by love out of His own like mould,
In whom He might His mighty Self behold;
For Love doth love the thing beloved to see,
That like itself in lovely shape may be.

But man, forgetful of his Maker's grace
No less than Angels whom he did ensue,[5]
Fell from the hope of promised heavenly place,
Into the mouth of death, to sinners due,
And all his offspring into thraldom threw,
Where they for ever should in bonds remain
Of never-dead yet ever-dying pain;

Till that great LORD of Love, which him at first
Made of mere love, and after likéd well,
Seeing him lie like creature long accurst
In that deep horror of despairéd hell,
Him, wretch, in dool[6] would let no longer dwell,
But cast[7] out of that bondage to redeem,
And pay the price, all were[8] his debt extreme.

Out of the bosom of eternal bliss,
In which He reignéd with His glorious Sire,
He down descended, like a most demiss [9]
And abject thrall, in flesh's frail attire,
That He for him might pay sin's deadly hire,
And him restore unto that happy state
In which he stood before his hapless fate.

In flesh at first the guilt·committed was,
Therefore in flesh it must be satisfied;
Nor Spirit, nor Angel, though they man surpass,
Could make amends to God for man's misguide [10],
But only man himself, who self did slide:
So, taking flesh of sacred Virgin's womb,
For man's dear sake He did a man become.

And that most blesséd Body, which was born
Without all blemish or reproachful blame,
He freely gave to be both rent and torn
Of cruel hands, who with despiteful shame
Reviling Him, that them most vile became [11],
At length Him nailéd on a gallow-tree,
And slew the Just by most unjust decree.

O huge and most unspeakable impression
Of love's deep wound, that pierced the piteous heart
Of that dear Lord with so entire affection,
And, sharply launching [12] every inner part,
Dolours of death into His soul did dart,
Doing Him die that never it deserved,
To free His foes, that from His hest [13] had swerved!

What heart can feel least touch of so sore launch,
Or thought can think the depth of so dear wound?
Whose bleeding source their streams yet never staunch,
But still do flow, and freshly still redound [14],
To heal the sores of sinful souls unsound,
And cleanse the guilt of that infected crime
Which was enrooted in all fleshly slime.

O blesséd Well of Love! O Flower of Grace!
O glorious Morning-Star! O Lamp of Light!
Most lively image of Thy Father's face,
Eternal King of Glory, Lord of Might,
Meek Lamb of God, before all worlds behight [15],
How can we Thee requite for all this good?
Or what can prize [16] that Thy most precious blood?

Yet nought Thou ask'st in lieu of all this love,
But love of us, for guerdon of Thy pain:
Ay me! what can us less than that behove?[17]
Had He required life of us again,
Had it been wrong to ask His own with gain?
He gave us life, He it restoréd, lost;
Then life were least, that us so little cost.

But He our life hath left unto us free,
Free that was thrall, and blesséd that was bann'd;
Ne ought demands but that we loving be,
As He Himself hath loved us afore-hand,
And bound thereto with an eternal band,
Him first to love that us so dearly bought,
And next our brethren, to His image wrought.

Him first to love great right and reason is,
Who first to us our life and being gave,
And after, when we faréd had amiss,
Us wretches from the second death did save;
And last, the food of life, which now we have,
Even He Himself, in His dear Sacrament,
To feed our hungry souls, unto us lent.

Then next, to love our brethren, that were made
Of that self mould, and that self Maker's hand,
That we,[18] and to the same again shall fade,
Where they shall have like heritage of land,[19]
However here on higher steps we stand,
Which also were with self-same price redeem'd
That we, however of us light esteem'd.

And were they not, yet since that loving Lord
Commanded us to love them for His sake,
Ev'n for His sake, and for His sacred word,
Which in His last bequest He to us spake,
We should them love, and with their needs partake;
Knowing that, whatsoe'er to them we give,
We give to Him by Whom we all do live.

Such mercy He by His most holy rede[20]
Unto us taught, and to approve it true,
Ensampled it by His most righteous deed,
Shewing us mercy, (miserable crew!)
That we the like should to the wretches shew,
And love our brethren; thereby to approve
How much, Himself that lovéd us, we love.

Then rouse thyself, O Earth! out of thy soil,
In which thou wallowest like to filthy swine,
And dost thy mind in dirty pleasures moyle,[21]
Unmindful of that dearest LORD of thine;
Lift up to Him thy heavy clouded eyne,
That thou His sovereign bounty may'st behold,
And read, through Love, His mercies manifold.

Begin from first, where He encradled was
In simple cratch, wrapt in a wad of hay,
Between the toilful Ox and humble Ass,
And in what rags, and in how base array,
The glory of our heavenly riches lay,
When Him the silly[22] Shepherds came to see,
Whom greatest Princes sought on lowest knee.

From thence read on the story of His life,
His humble carriage, His unfaulty ways,
His canker'd foes, His fights, His toil, His strife,
His pains, His poverty, His sharp assays,
Through which He past His miserable days,
Offending none, and doing good to all,
Yet being maliced[23] both of great and small.

And look at last, how of most wretched wights
He taken was, betray'd and false accused;
How with most scornful taunts, and fell despites,
He was reviled, disgraced, and foul abused;
How scourged, how crown'd, how buffeted, how bruised;
And lastly, how 'twixt robbers crucified,
With bitter wounds through hands, through feet, and side!

Then let thy flinty heart, that feels no pain,
Empiercéd be with pitiful remorse,
And let thy bowels bleed in every vein,
At sight of His most sacred-heavenly corse,
So torn and mangled with malicious force;
And let thy soul, whose sins His sorrows wrought,
Melt into tears, and groan in grievéd thought.

With sense whereof, whilst so thy soften'd spirit
Is inly touch'd, and humbled with meek zeal
Through meditation of His endless merit,
Lift up thy mind to th' Author of thy weal,
And to His sovereign mercy do appeal;
Learn Him to love, that lovéd thee so dear,
And in thy breast His blesséd image bear.

With all thy heart, with all thy soul and mind,
Thou must Him love and His behests embrace;
All other loves, with which the world doth blind
Weak fancies, and stir up affections base,
Thou must renounce and utterly displace,
And give thyself unto Him full and free,
That full and freely gave Himself to thee.

Then shalt thou feel thy spirit so possest,
And ravish'd with devouring great desire
Of His dear Self, that shall thy feeble breast
Inflame with love, and set thee all on fire
With burning zeal, through every part entire,
That in no earthly thing thou shalt delight,
But in His sweet and amiable sight.

Thenceforth all world's desire will in thee die,
And all earth's glory, on which men do gaze,
Seem dirt and dross in thy pure-sighted eye,
Compared to that Celestial Beauty's blaze,
Whose glorious beams all fleshly sense doth daze
With admiration of their passing light,
Blinding the eyes, and lumining the spright.

Then shall thy ravish'd soul inspired be,
With heavenly thoughts far above human skill,
And thy bright radiant eyes shall plainly see
Th' Idea of His pure glory present still
Before thy face, that all thy spirits shall fill
With sweet enragement[24] of celestial Love,
Kindled through sight of those fair things above.

E. Spenser

[1] *eyas*, new-fledged　　[2] *infuse imbrue*, colour with infusion　　[3] See Note
[4] *degendering*, degenerating　　[5] *ensue*, follow after　　[6] *dool*, sorrow　　[7] *cast*,
considered how　[8] *all were*, although it were　　[9] *demiss*, submissive　　[10] *misguide*, sin　　[11] *became*, suited　　[12] *launching*, lancing　　[13] *hest*, command
[14] *redound*, flow freely　　[15] *behight*, ordained　　[16] *prize*, equal in value
[17] *behove*, profit　　[18] *that we* [were]　　[19] *land*, the grave　　[20] *rede*, counsel
[21] *moyle*, defile　　[22] *silly*, simple　　[23] *maliced*, evilly regarded　　[24] *enragement*, rapture

V -

ETERNAL LOVE

LEAVE me, O Love, which reachest but to dust;
　　And thou, my mind, aspire to higher things;
Grow rich in that which never taketh rust;
Whatever fades, but fading pleasure brings.

Draw in thy beams, and humble all thy might
To that sweet yoke where lasting freedoms be;
Which breaks the clouds, and opens forth the light,
That doth both shine, and give us sight to see.

O take fast hold; let that light be thy guide
In this small course which birth draws out to death,
And think how ill becometh him to slide,
Who seeketh heaven, and comes of heavenly breath.

Then farewell, world; thy uttermost I see:
Eternal Love, maintain Thy life in me.

P. Sidney

VI

SOUL AND BODY

POOR Soul, the centre of my sinful earth,
   [Fool'd by][1] these rebel powers that thee array,
Why dost thou pine within and suffer dearth,
Painting thy outward walls so costly gay?

Why so large cost, having so short a lease,
Dost thou upon thy fading mansion spend?
Shall worms, inheritors of this excess,
·Eat up thy charge? is this thy body's end?

Then, soul, live thou upon thy servant's loss,
And let that pine to aggravate thy store;
Buy terms divine in selling hours of dross;
Within be fed, without be rich no more:

So shalt thou feed on Death, that feeds on men,
And Death once dead, there's no more dying then.

W. Shakespeare

[1] *Fool'd by*: others conjecture *foil'd by*

VII

A PRAYER

O MIGHTY God, Which for us men
   Didst suffer on the Cross
The painful pangs of bitter death,
   To save our souls from loss,
I yield Thee here most hearty thanks,
   In that Thou dost vouchsafe,
Of me most vile and sinful wretch,
   So great regard to have.

Alas, none ever had more cause
　To magnify Thy name,
Than I, to whom Thy mercies shew'd
　Do witness well the same.
So many brunts[1] of fretting foes
　Who ever could withstand,
If Thou had'st not protected me,
　With Thy most holy hand?
A thousand times in shameful sort
　My sinful life had ended,
If by Thy gracious goodness, LORD,
　I had not been defended.
In stinking pools of filthy vice
　So deeply was I drown'd,
That none there was but Thee alone,
　To set my foot on ground.
When as the fiend had led my soul
　E'en to the gates of hell,
Thou call'dst me back, and dost me choose
　In heaven with Thee to dwell:—
Let furies now fret on their fill,
　Let Satan rage, and roar,
As long as Thou art on my side,
　What need I care for more?

H. Gifford

1 *brunts*, assaults

VIII

THE BIBLE

HERE is the spring where waters flow,
　　To quench our heat of sin;
Here is the tree where truth doth grow
　　To lead our lives therein;
Here is the judge that stints[1] the strife
　　When men's devises fail:
Here is the bread that feeds the life
　　Which death cannot assail.
The tidings of salvation dear
　　Comes to our ears from hence;
The fortress of our faith is here;
　　The shield of our defence.
Then be not like the hog that hath
　　A pearl at his desire,

And takes more pleasure in the trough
    And wallowing in the mire.
Read not this book in any case
    But with a single eye:
Read not, but first desire GOD's grace,
    To understand thereby.
Pray still in faith with this respect
    To fructify therein;
That knowledge may bring this effect,
    To mortify thy sin.
Then happy thou in all thy life,
    Whatso to thee befalls;
Yea, doubly happy shalt thou be
    When GOD by death thee calls.

Anon.

[1] *stints*, stays

IX

A CAROL

SWEET Music, sweeter far
    Than any song is sweet:
Sweet Music heavenly rare,
    Mine ears, (O peers[1]) doth greet.
Yon gentle flocks, whose fleeces, pearl'd with dew,
Resemble heaven, whom golden drops make bright:
Listen, O listen, now;—O not to you
Our pipes make sport to shorten weary night:—
    But voices most divine
    Make blissful harmony:
    Voices that seem to shine,
    For what else clears the sky?
Tunes can we hear, but not the singers see;
The tunes divine, and so the singers be.

    Lo, how the firmament
    Within an azure fold
    The flock of stars hath pent,
    That we might them behold.
Yet from their beams proceedeth not this light,
Nor can their crystals such reflection give.
What then doth make the element[2] so bright?
The heavens are come down upon earth to live.

But hearken to the song:
Glory to glory's King,
And peace all men among,
These queristers do sing.
Angels they are, as also (Shepherds) He,
Whom in our fear we do admire to see.

Let not amazement blind
Your souls, (said he) annoy:
To you and all mankind,
My message bringeth joy.
For lo! the world's great Shepherd now is born,
A blesséd babe, an infant full of power:
After long night, up-risen is the morn,
Renowning Bethlem in the Savíour.
Sprung is the perfect day,
By prophets seen afar:
Sprung is the mirthful May,
Which Winter cannot mar.
In David's city doth this Sun appear,
Clouded in flesh;—yet, Shepherds! sit we here.

E. Bolton

[1] *peers*, mates   ·   [2] *element*, ethereal sky

X

THE BURNING BABE

AS I in hoary Winter's night stood shivering in the snow,
    Surprised I was with sudden heat, which made my heart
      to glow;
And lifting up a fearful eye to view what fire was near,
A pretty Babe all burning bright, did in the air appear;
Who, scorchéd with excessive heat, such floods of tears did shed,
As though His floods should quench His flames which with His
      tears were fed;
Alas! quoth He, but newly born, in fiery heats I fry[1],
Yet none approach to warm their hearts or feel My fire but I!
My faultless breast the furnace is, the fuel wounding thorns,
Love is the fire, and sighs the smoke, the ashes shame and scorns;
The fuel Justice layeth on, and Mercy blows the coals;
The metal in this furnace wrought are men's defiléd souls,
For which, as now on fire I am, to work them to their good,
So will I melt into a bath to wash them in My blood.
—With this He vanish'd out of sight, and swiftly shrunk away,—
And straight I calléd unto mind that it was Christmas-day.

R. Southwell

[1] *fry*, used of old for *burn*

XI

A CHILD MY CHOICE

LET folly praise that[1] fancy loves, I praise and love that Child
   Whose heart no thought, Whose tongue no word, Whose
     hand no deed defiled.
I praise Him most, I love Him best, all praise and love is His;
While Him I love, in Him I live, and cannot live amiss.
Love's sweetest mark, laud's highest theme, man's most desired
     light,
To love Him life, to leave Him death, to live in Him delight.
He mine by gift, I His by debt, thus each to other due,
First friend He was, best friend He is, all times will try Him true.
Though young, yet wise, though small, yet strong; though man,
     yet GOD He is;
As wise He knows, as strong He can, as GOD He loves to bliss.
His knowledge rules, His strength defends, His love doth cherish
     all;
His birth our joy, His life our light, His death our end of thrall.
Alas! He weeps, He sighs, He pants, yet do His angels sing;
Out of His tears, His sighs and throbs, doth bud a joyful spring.
Almighty Babe, Whose tender arms can force all foes to fly,
Correct my faults, protect my life, direct me when I die!

[1] *that*, what

XII

O THAT I HAD WINGS LIKE A DOVE

O GRACIOUS GOD, O Saviour sweet,
   O JESUS, think on me,
And suffer me to kiss Thy feet,
   Though late I come to Thee.

Behold, dear LORD, I come to Thee
   With sorrow and with shame,
For when Thy bitter wounds I see,
   I know I caused the same.

Sweet JESU, who shall lend me wings
   Of peace and perfect love,
That I may rise from earthly things
   To rest with Thee above?

For sin and sorrow overflow
　All earthly things so high,
That I can find no rest below,
　But unto Thee I fly.

Wherefore my soul doth loathe the things
　Which gave it once delight,
And unto Thee, the King of kings,
　Would mount with all her might.

And yet the weight of flesh and blood
　Doth so my wings restrain,
That oft I strive and gain no good,
　But rise, to fall again.

Yet when this fleshly misery
　Is master'd by the mind,
I cry, 'avaunt, all vanity':
　And 'Satan, stand behind.'

So thus, sweet LORD, I fly about
　In weak and weary case
Like the lone dove which Noah sent [out],
　And found no resting place.

My weary wings, sweet JESU, mark,
　And when Thou thinkest best
Stretch forth Thy arm from out the ark,
　And take me to Thy rest.

Anon.

XIII

HEAVENLY Messias, (sweet anointed King,
　Whose glory round about the world doth reach,
　Which every beast, plant, rock, and river teach,
And airy birds like Angels ever sing,

And every gale of wind in gusts doth bring,
　And every man with reason ever preach),
　Behold, behold that lamentable breach,
Which (my distresséd conscience to sting)

False spiteful Satan in my soul doth make:
　Oh, (sweet Messias), lend some gracious oil
To cure that wound, e'en for Thy mercy's sake:
　Lest (by that breach) Thy temple he despoil.

Help, help; my conscience thither him doth lead;
And he will come, if Thou bruise not his head.

B. Barnes

XIV

WHO to the golden Sun's long restless race
   Can limits set? What vessel can comprise
  The swelling winds? what cunning can devise
(With quaint Arithmetic) in steadfast place

To number all the stars in heaven's paláce?
  What cunning Artist ever was so wise,
  Who, (by the stars and planets), could advise
Of all adventures the just course and case?

Who measured hath the waters of the seas?
  Who ever (in just balance) poised the air?
As no man ever could the least of these
  Perform with human labour, strength and care,

So who shall strive in volumes to contain
God's praise ineffable, contends in vain.

XV

TRIUMPHANT conqueror of death and hell,
  Behold what legions (though in vain) conspire,
  Thy Temple militant to set on fire,
And Saints which in Thy sanctuary dwell

To burn, whilst they against Thy power rebel:
  See how like bloody tyrants they desire
  Ambitiously to rise, and mount up higher,
Like Lucifer which to perdition fell.

Their forces are addrest against Thy Saints,
  Break thou their bows, knap Thou their spears in sunder:
I know their spirit at Thy presence faints,
  Against their Cannon plant Thy dreadful thunder,

Thy thunderbolts against their bullets dash,
And on their beavers[1] bright let lightning flash.

[1] beaver, helmet

XVI

HIERUSALEM, my happy home,
  When shall I come to thee?
When shall my sorrows have an end,
  Thy joys when shall I see?

C

O happy harbour of the Saints!
  O sweet and pleasant soil!
In thee no sorrow may be found,
  No grief, no care, no toil.

There lust and lucre cannot dwell,
  There envy bears no sway;
There is no hunger, heat, nor cold,
  But pleasure every way.

Thy walls are made of precious stones,
  Thy bulwarks diamonds square;
Thy gates are of right orient pearl,
  Exceeding rich and rare.

Thy turrets and thy pinnacles
  With carbuncles do shine;
Thy very streets are paved with gold,
  Surpassing clear and fine.

Ah, my sweet home, Hierusalem,
  Would God I were in thee!
Would God my woes were at an end,
  Thy joys that I might see!

Thy gardens and thy gallant walks
  Continually are green,
There grows such sweet and pleasant flowers
  As nowhere else are seen.

Quite through the streets, with silver sound,
  The flood of Life doth flow;
Upon whose banks on every side
  The wood of Life doth grow.

There trees for evermore bear fruit,
  And evermore do spring;
There evermore the angels sit,
  And evermore do sing.

Our Lady sings *Magnificat*
  With tones surpassing sweet;
And all the virgins bear their part,
  Sitting about her feet.

Hierusalem, my happy home,
  Would God I were in thee!
Would God my woes were at an end,
  Thy joys that I might see!

Anon.

XVII

THOU hast made me, and shall Thy work decay?
  Repair me now; for now mine end doth haste,
  I run to Death, and Death meets me as fast,
And all my pleasures are like yesterday.

I dare not move my dim eyes any way,
  Despair behind, and Death before doth cast
  Such terror, and my feeble flesh doth waste
By sin in it, which it towards Hell doth weigh:

Only Thou art above, and when towards Thee
  By Thy leave I can look, I rise again;
But our old subtle foe so tempteth me,
  That not one hour myself I can sustain:

Thy grace may wing me to prevent his art,
And Thou like adamant[1] draw mine iron heart.

J. Donne

[1] *adamant*, magnet

XVIII

AS due by many titles, I resign
  Myself to Thee, O GOD. First, I was made
  By Thee and for Thee, and when I was decay'd,
Thy blood bought that the which before was Thine;

I am Thy son, made with Thyself to shine,
  Thy servant, whose pains Thou hast still repaid,
  Thy sheep, Thine image, and, till I betray'd
Myself, a temple of Thy Spirit divine.

Why doth the devil, then, usurp on me?
  Why doth he steal, nay ravish that's Thy right?
  Except Thou rise, and for Thine own work fight,
Oh, I shall soon despair, when I do see

That Thou lov'st mankind well, yet will not choose me,
And Satan hates me, yet is loth to loose me.

XIX

AT the round earth's imagined corners blow
  Your trumpets, Angels; and arise, arise
  From death, you numberless infinities
Of souls, and to your scatter'd bodies go,

All whom the Flood did, and Fire shall, o'erthrow;
  All whom Death, war, age, agues, tyrannies,
  Despair, law, chance hath slain; and you whose eyes
Shall behold God, and never taste death's woe;—

But let them sleep, Lord, and me mourn a space;
  For if above all those my sins abound,
'Tis late to ask abundance of Thy grace,
  When we are there. Here on this lowly ground

Teach me how to repent; for that's as good
As if Thou'dst seal'd my pardon with my blood.

XX

A HYMN TO GOD THE FATHER

WILT Thou forgive that sin where I begun,
    Which was my sin, though it were done before?
Wilt Thou forgive that sin, through which I run
  And do run still, though still I do deplore?
    When Thou hast done, Thou hast not done;
        For I have more.

Wilt Thou forgive that sin which I have won
  Others to sin, and made my sins their door[1]?
Wilt Thou forgive that sin which I did shun
  A year or two, but wallow'd in, a score?
    When Thou hast done, Thou hast not done;
        For I have more.

I have a sin of fear, that when I have[2] spun
  My last thread, I shall perish on the shore;
But swear by Thyself, that at my death Thy Son
  Shall shine, as He shines now and heretofore:
    And having done that, Thou hast done;
        I fear no more.

[1] *door:* by which others entered into sin   [2] pronounce *I've*

XXI

LO, when back mine eye,
    Pilgrim-like I cast,
  What fearful ways I spy,
Which, blinded, I securely past!

But now heaven hath drawn
  From my brows that night;
As when the day doth dawn,
So clears my long-imprison'd sight.

  Straight the Caves of Hell
    Dress'd with flowers I see,
  Wherein False Pleasures dwell,
That, winning most, most deadly be.

  Throngs of maskéd fiends,
    Wing'd like angels, fly;
  E'en in the gates of friends,
In fair disguise black dangers lie.

  Straight to heaven I raised
    My restoréd sight,
  And with loud voice I praised
The Lord of ever-during light.

  And since I had stray'd
    From His ways so wide,
  His grace I humbly pray'd
Henceforth to be my guard and guide.

T. Campion

XXII

VIEW me, Lord, a work of Thine!
  Shall I then lie drown'd in night?
Might Thy grace in me but shine,
I should seem made all of light.

But my soul still surfeits so
On the poison'd baits of sin,
That I strange and ugly grow;
All is dark and foul within.

Cleanse me, Lord, that I may kneel
At Thine altar, pure and white:
They that once Thy mercies feel,
Gaze no more on earth's delight.

Worldly joys, like shadows, fade
When the heavenly light appears;
But the covenants Thou hast made,
Endless, know nor days nor years.

In Thy Word, Lord, is my trust,
To Thy mercies fast I fly;
Though I am but clay and dust,
Yet Thy grace can lift me high!

XXIII

SEEK the Lord, and in His ways persével!
   O faint not, but as eagles fly,
   For His steep hill is high!
Then striving gain the top and triumph ever!

When with glory there thy brows are crownéd,
   New joys so shall abound in thee,
   Such sights thy soul shall see,
That worldly thoughts shall by their beams be drownéd.

Farewell, World, thou mass of mere confusion!
   False light, with many shadows dimm'd!
   Old witch, with new foils trimm'd!
Thou deadly sleep of soul, and charm'd illusion!

I the King will seek, of kings adoréd;
   Spring of light; tree of grace and bliss,
   Whose fruit so sovereign is
That all who taste it are from death restoréd.

XXIV

TO music bent is my retired mind,
   And fain would I some song of pleasure sing;
But in vain joys no comfort now I find;
From heavenly thoughts all true delight doth spring:
Thy power, O God, Thy mercies to record,
Will sweeten every note and every word.

All earthly pomp or beauty to express
Is but to carve in snow, on waves to write;
Celestial things, though men conceive them less,
Yet fullest are they in themselves of light:
Such beams they yield as know no means to die;
Such heat they cast as lifts the spirit high.

XXV

NEVER weather-beaten sail more willing bent to shore,
   Never tired pilgrim's limbs affected slumber more,
Than my wearied sprite now longs to fly out of my troubled
    breast.
O come quickly, sweetest Lord, and take my soul to rest!

Ever blooming are the joys of heaven's high Paradise,
Cold age deafs not there our ears nor vapour dims our eyes:
Glory there the sun outshines; whose beams the Blesséd
    only see.
O come quickly, glorious Lord, and raise my sprite to Thee!

XXVI

LET not the sluggish sleep
  Close up thy waking eye,
Until with judgment deep
  Thy daily deeds thou try :
He that one sin in conscience keeps
  When he to quiet goes,
More vent'rous is than he that sleeps
  With twenty mortal foes !

Anon.

XXVII

IF I could shut the gate against my thoughts
  And keep out sorrow from this room within,
Or memory could cancel all the notes
  Of my misdeeds, and I unthink my sin :
How free, how clear, how clean my soul should lie,
Discharged of such a loathsome company !

Or were there other rooms without my heart
  That did not to my conscience join so near,
Where I might lodge the thoughts of sin apart
  That I might not their clamorous crying hear,
What peace, what joy, what ease should I possess,
Freed from their horrors that my soul oppress !

But, O my Saviour, Who my refuge art,
  Let Thy dear mercies stand 'twixt them and me,
And be the wall to separate my heart
  So that I may at length repose me free ;
That peace, and joy, and rest may be within,
And I remain divided from my sin.

Anon.

XXVIII

THE NATIVITY

I SING the Birth was born to-night,
  The Author both of life and light ;
    The angels so did sound it :—
And like the ravish'd shepherds said,
Who saw the light, and were afraid,
    Yet search'd, and true they found it.

The Son of God, the eternal King,
That did us all salvation bring,
    And freed the soul from danger;
He whom the whole world could not take,
The Word, which heaven and earth did make,
    Was now laid in a manger.

What comfort by Him do we win,
Who made Himself the price of sin,
    To make us heirs of glory!
To see this Babe, all innocence,
A martyr born in our defence!—
    Can man forget this story?

            B. Jonson

XXIX

HEAR me, O God!
    A broken heart
    Is my best part:
Use still Thy rod,
    That I may prove
    Therein Thy love.

If Thou hadst not
    Been stern to me,
    But left me free,
I had forgot
    Myself and Thee.

For sin's so sweet,
    As minds ill bent
    Rarely repent,
Until they meet
    Their punishment.

XXX

DEATH'S LAST WILL

MORE oft than once Death whisper'd in mine ear,
    Grave what thou hears in diamond and gold,
I am that monarch whom all monarchs fear,
Who hath in dust their far-stretch'd pride uproll'd;

All, all is mine beneath moon's silver sphere,
And nought, save virtue, can my power withhold:
This, not believed, experience true thee told,
By danger late when I to thee came near.

As bugbear then my visage I did show,
That of my horrors thou right use might'st make,
And a more sacred path of living take :—
Now still walk arméd for my ruthless blow:

Trust flattering life no more, redeem time past,
And live each day as if it were thy last.

W. Drummond

XXXI

HYPOCRISY

AS are those apples, pleasant to the eye,
 But full of smoke within, which use to grow
Near that strange lake, where GOD pour'd from the sky
Huge showers of flames, worse flames to overthrow;

Such are their works that with a glaring show
Of humble holiness, in virtue's dye
Would colour mischief, while within they glow
With coals of sin, though none the smoke descry.

Ill is that angel which erst fell from heaven,
But not more ill than he, nor in worse case,
Who hides a traitorous mind with smiling face,
And with a dove's white feather masks a raven.

Each sin some colour hath it to adorn;
Hypocrisy, almighty GOD doth scorn.

XXXII

MAN'S KNOWLEDGE

BENEATH a sable veil and shadows deep
 Of unaccessible and dimming light,
In silence, ebon clouds more black than night,
The world's great King His secrets hid doth keep:

Through those thick mists, when any mortal wight
Aspires, with halting pace and eyes that weep,
To pore, and in His mysteries to creep,
With thunders He and lightnings blasts their sight.

O Sun invisible, that dost abide
Within Thy bright abysms, most fair, most dark,
Where with Thy proper rays Thou dost Thee hide!
O ever-shining, never full-seen mark!

To guide me in life's night Thy light me show;—
The more I search, of Thee the less I know.

XXXIII

SAINT JOHN BAPTIST

THE last and greatest Herald of heaven's King,
   Girt with rough skins, hies to the deserts wild,
Among that savage brood the woods forth bring,
Which he than man more harmless found and mild:

His food was locusts, and what young doth spring,
With honey that from virgin hives distill'd;
Parch'd body, hollow eyes, some uncouth thing
Made him appear, long since from earth exiled.

There burst he forth: 'All ye, whose hopes rely
On God, with me amidst these deserts mourn;
Repent, repent, and from old errors turn.'
Who listen'd to his voice, obey'd his cry?

Only the echoes, which he made relent,
Rung from their marble caves, 'Repent, repent!'

XXXIV

SOUL, which to hell wast thrall,
   He, He for thine offence
Did suffer death, Who could not die at all.
O sovereign excellence!
O life of all that lives!
Eternal bounty, which all goodness gives!
How could Death mount so high?
No wit this point can reach;
Faith only doth us teach,
For us He died, at all Who could not die.

XXXV

URBS COELESTIS IERUSALEM

JERUSALEM, that place divine,
   The vision of sweet peace is named;
In heaven her glorious turrets shine,
Her walls of living stone are framed;
While Angels guard her on each side,
Fit company for such a bride.

She, deck'd in new attire from heaven,
Her wedding chamber, now descends,
Prepared in marriage to be given
To CHRIST, on Whom her joy depends.
Her walls, wherewith she is enclosed,
And streets are of pure gold composed.

The gates adorn'd with pearls most bright
The way to hidden glory show,
, And thither by the blesséd might
Of faith in JESUS' merits go
All those who are on earth distress'd,
Because they have CHRIST's name profess'd.

These stones the workmen dress and beat
Before they throughly polish'd are;
Then each is in his proper seat
Establish'd by the Builder's care,
In this fair frame to stand for ever,
So join'd that them no force can sever.

To GOD, Who sits in highest seat,
Glory and power given be;
To Father, Son, and Paraclete,
Who reign in equal dignity;
Whose boundless power we still adore,
And sing Their praise for evermore.

XXXVI

THE FAREWELL

METHINKS I draw but sickly breath:
    Who knows but I
Before next night may sleeping lie,
    Rock'd in the arms of death?

The swift-foot minutes pass away;
    For Time hath wings,
That flag not for the breath of kings,
    Nor brook the least delay.

And what a parcel of my sand
    Is yet to pass,
Or what may break the crazy glass,
    How shall I understand?

Then, base delights and dunghill joys!
    Farewell, adieu!
While yet I live I'm dead to you,
    And such-like toys.

I would not longer own a thought
    That crawls so low,
Or lavish out my wishes so
    In quest of less than nought.

My soul is wing'd with quick desires
    To pass the sky;
Nothing below what is most high
    Allays those noble fires.

LORD, as the kindling is from Thee,
    So Thine the breath
That must continue it, till death
    Be dead and cease to be.

Anon.

XXXVII

INTROIT

MY God, where is that ancient heat towards Thee
    Wherewith whole shoals of martyrs once did burn,
Besides their other flames! Doth poetry
    Wear Venus' livery! only serve her turn?

Why are not sonnets made of Thee? and lays
    Upon Thine altar burnt? Cannot Thy love
Heighten a spirit to sound out Thy praise
    As well as any She? Cannot Thy Dove

Outstrip their Cupid easily in flight?
    Or, since Thy ways are deep, and still the same,
    Will not a verse run smooth that bears Thy name?
Why doth that fire, which by Thy power and might

    Each breast does feel, no braver fuel choose
    Than that, which one day worms may chance refuse?

G. Herbert

XXXVIII

ANTIPHON

Cho. LET all the world in every corner sing
              My GOD and King,

  Vers. The heavens are not too high
    His praise may thither fly;
    The earth is not too low
    His praises there may grow.

Cho. Let all the world in every corner sing
              My GOD and King.

Vers. The Church with psalms must shout,
    No door can keep them out :
    But, above all, the heart
    Must bear the longest part.

Cho. Let all the world in every corner sing
        My God and King.

XXXIX

A TRUE HYMN

MY Joy, my Life, my Crown !
    My heart was meaning[1] all the day,
      Somewhat it fain would say,
And still it runneth muttering up and down
With only this, My Joy, my Life, my Crown !

    Yet slight not these few words ;
  If truly said, they may take part
    Among the best in art :
The fineness which a hymn or psalm affords
Is, when the soul unto the lines accords.

    He who craves all the mind,
And all the soul, and strength, and time,
    If the words only rhyme,
Justly complains that somewhat is behind
To make His verse, or write a hymn in kind.

    Whereas, if th' heart be moved,
Although the verse be somewhat scant,
    God doth supply the want ;
As when th' heart says, sighing to be approved,
' O, could I love ! ' and stops,—God writeth, ' Loved.'

    [1] *meaning,* intending a good matter

XL

SIN

LORD, with what care hast Thou begirt us round !
    Parents first season us ; then schoolmasters
  Deliver us to laws ; they send us bound
To rules of reason, holy messengers,

Pulpits and Sundays, sorrow dogging sin,
  Afflictions sorted, anguish of all sizes,
    Fine nets and stratagems to catch us in,
Bibles laid open [1], millions of surprises,

Blessings beforehand, ties of gratefulness,
 The sound of glory ringing in our ears;
 Without, our shame; within, our consciences;
Angels and grace, eternal hopes and fears :—

 Yet all these fences and their whole array
 One cunning bosom-sin blows quite away. ʼ

  [1] *Bibles* ... the first text seen was taken as a sign

XLI

CHURCH MONUMENTS[1]

WHILE that my soul repairs to her devotion,
 Here I intomb my flesh, that it betimes
May take acquaintance of this heap of dust;
To which the blast of Death's incessant motion,
 Fed with the exhalation of our crimes,
Drives all at last. Therefore I gladly trust

My body to this school, that it may learn
To spell his elements, and find his birth
Written in dusty heraldry and lines :
Which dissolution sure doth best discern,
Comparing dust with dust, and earth with earth.
These laugh at jet and marble, put for signs,

To sever the good fellowship of dust,
And spoil the meeting. What shall point out them
When they shall bow, and kneel, and fall down flat
To kiss those heaps, which now they have in trust?
Dear flesh, while I do pray, learn here thy stem
And true descent, that, when thou shalt grow fat,

And wanton in thy cravings, thou may'st know,
That flesh is but the glass which holds the dust
That measures all our time; which also shall
Be crumbled into dust. Mark here below
How tame these ashes are, how free from lust—
That thou mayst fit thyself against thy fall.

  [1] See Note

XLII

THE CHURCH FLOOR

MARK you the floor? that square and speckled stone,
 Which looks so firm and strong,
    Is PATIENCE:

And the other black and grave, wherewith each one
    Is checker'd all along,
             HUMILITY:

The gentle rising, which on either hand
    Leads to the quire above,
             Is CONFIDENCE:

But the sweet cement, which in one sure band
    Ties the whole frame, is LOVE
             And CHARITY.

XLIII

SUNDAY

O DAY most calm, most bright,
    The fruit of this, the next world's bud,
The indorsement of supreme delight,
Writ by a Friend, and with His blood;
The couch of Time, Care's balm and bay;
The week were dark but for thy light;
    Thy torch doth show the way.

    Sundays the pillars are,
On which Heaven's Palace archéd lies:
The other days fill up the spare
And hollow room with vanities:
They are the fruitful beds and borders
In GOD's rich garden: that[1] is bare
    Which parts their ranks and orders.

    The Sundays of man's life,
Threaded together on Time's string,
Make bracelets to adorn the Wife
Of the eternal glorious King:
On Sunday Heaven's gate stands ope;
Blessings are plentiful and rife,
    More plentiful than hope.

    Thou art a day of mirth;
And where the week-days trail on ground,
Thy flight is higher, as thy birth:
O let me take thee at the bound,
Leaping with thee from seven to seven,
Till that we both, being toss'd from Earth,
    Fly hand in hand to Heaven!

       [1] *that is bare*, the week-days

XLIV

CHRISTMAS

ALL after pleasures as I rid one day,
  My horse and I, both tired, body and mind,
With full cry of affections, quite astray;
I took up in the next inn I could find.

There when I came, Whom found I but my dear,
  My dearest Lord, expecting till the grief
Of pleasures brought me to Him, ready there
To be all passengers' most sweet relief.

O Thou, Whose glorious yet contracted light,
  Wrapt in Night's mantle, stole into a manger;
  Since my dark soul and brutish, is Thy right,—
To Man, of all beasts, be not Thou a stranger:

  Furnish and deck my soul, that Thou may'st have
  A better lodging than a rack or grave.

XLV

AFFLICTION[1]

WHEN first Thou didst entice to Thee my heart,
    I thought the service brave :
So many joys I writ down for my part,
    Besides what I might have
Out of my stock of natural delights,
Augmented with Thy gracious benefits.

What pleasures could I want, whose King I served,
    Where joys my fellows were ?
Thus argued into hopes, my thoughts reserved
    No place for grief or fear;
Therefore my sudden soul caught at the place,
And made her youth and fierceness seek Thy face.

At first Thou gav'st me milk and sweetnesses;
    I had my wish and way;
My days were strew'd with flowers and happiness;
    There was no month but May.
But with my years sorrow did twist and grow,
And made a party unawares for woe.

My flesh began unto my soul in pain,
    Sicknesses cleave my bones,
Consuming agues dwell in every vein,
    And tune my breath to groans :
Sorrow was all my soul; I scarce believed,
Till grief did tell me roundly, that I lived.

When I got health, Thou took'st away my life
    And more—for my friends die :
My mirth and edge was lost, a blunted knife
    Was of more use than I :
Thus, thin and lean, without a fence or friend,
I was blown through with every storm and wind.

Yet, lest perchance I should too happy be
    In my unhappiness,
Turning my purge to food, Thou throwest me
    Into more sicknesses.
Thus doth Thy power cross-bias me, not making
Thine own gift good, yet me from my ways taking.

Now I am here, what Thou wilt do with me
    None of my books will show;
I read, and sigh, and wish I were a tree—
    For sure, then, I should grow
To fruit or shade; at least, some bird would trust
Her household to me, and I should be just.

Yet, though Thou troublest me, I must be meek;
    In weakness must be stout.
Well, I will change the service, and go seek
    Some other master out.
Ah, my dear God, though I am clean forgot,
Let me not love Thee, if I love Thee not.

[1] See Note

XLVI

DENIAL

WHEN my devotions could not pierce
    Thy silent ears,
Then was my heart broken, as was my verse;
    My breast was full of fears
    And disorder ;

My bent thoughts, like a brittle bow,
    Did fly asunder;
Each took his way; some would to pleasures go,
    Some to the wars and thunder
    Of alarms.

As good go anywhere, they say,
　　　As to benumb
Both knees and heart, in crying night and day,
　　'Come, come, my GOD, O come!'
　　　But no hearing.

O that Thou shouldst give dust a tongue
　　　To cry to Thee,
And then not hear it crying!　All day long
　　　My heart was in my knee,
　　　But no hearing.

Therefore my soul lay out of sight,
　　　Untuned, unstrung;
My feeble spirit, unable to look right,
　　　Like a nipt blossom, hung
　　　Discontented.

O, cheer and tune my heartless breast,
　　　Defer no time;
That so Thy favours granting my request,
　　　They and my soul may chime,
　　　And mend my rhyme.

XLVII

VIRTUE

SWEET day, so cool, so calm, so bright—
　　The bridal of the earth and sky;
The dew shall weep thy fall to-night;
　　　For thou must die.

Sweet rose, whose hue angry and brave[1]
Bids the rash gazer wipe his eye,
Thy root is ever in its grave,
　　　And thou must die.

Sweet spring, full of sweet days and roses,
A box where sweets compacted lie,
My music shows ye have your closes,
　　　And all must die.

Only a sweet and virtuous soul,
Like season'd timber, never gives[2];
But though the whole world turn to coal,
　　　Then chiefly lives.

---

[1] *angry and brave*, piercing and dazzlingly splendid　　　[2] *gives*, yields

XLVIII

UNKINDNESS

L ORD, make me coy and tender to offend:
  In friendship, first I think, if that agree
          Which I intend,
    Unto my friend's intent and end;
I would not use a friend as I use Thee.

If any touch my friend or his good name,
It is my honour and my love to free
          His blasted fame
    From the least spot or thought of blame:
I could not use a friend as I use Thee.

My friend may spit upon my curious floor;
Would he have gold? I lend it instantly;
          But let the poor,
    And Thou within them, starve at door—
I cannot use a friend as I use Thee.

When that my friend pretendeth to[1] a place,
I quit my interest, and leave it free;
          But when Thy grace
    Sues for my heart, I Thee displace;
Nor would I use a friend as I use Thee.

Yet can a friend what Thou hast done fulfil?
O, write in brass: 'My GOD upon a tree
          His blood did spill,
    Only to purchase my good will:'
Yet use I not my foes as I use Thee.

1 *pretendeth to*, seeks

XLIX

MORTIFICATION

H OW soon doth man decay!
  When clothes are taken from a chest of sweets
To swaddle infants, whose young breath
          Scarce knows the way,
Those clouts are little winding-sheets,
Which do consign and send them unto Death.

    When boys go first to bed,
They step into their voluntary graves;
    Sleep binds them fast, only their breath
          Makes them not dead;
Successive nights, like rolling waves,
Convey them quickly who are bound for Death.

When Youth is frank and free,
And calls for music, while his veins do swell,
  All day exchanging mirth and breath
        In company,
That music summons to the knell
Which shall befriend him at the house of Death.

When man grows staid and wise,
Getting a house and home, where he may move
  Within the circle of his breath,
        Schooling his eyes;
That dumb enclosure maketh love
Unto the coffin that attends his death.

When Age grows low and weak,
Marking his grave, and thawing every year,
  Till all do melt, and drown his breath
        When he would speak,
A chair or litter shows[1] the bier
Which shall convey him to the house of Death.

Man, ere he is aware,
Hath put together a solemnity,
  And drest his hearse, while he has breath
        As yet to spare;
Yet, LORD, instruct us so to die
That all these dyings may be LIFE in DEATH.

1 *shows*, prefigures

L

MISERY

LORD, Let the angels praise Thy name;
  Man is a foolish thing, a foolish thing;
Folly and sin play all his game;
His house still burns; and yet he still doth sing:
      Man is but grass,
      He knows it; 'fill the glass.'

They quarrel[1] Thee, and would give over
The bargain made to serve Thee; but Thy love
  Holds them unto it, and doth cover
Their follies with the wings of Thy mild Dove,
      Not suffering those
      Who would, to be Thy foes.

Man cannot serve Thee : let him go
And serve the swine—there, there is his delight :
  He doth not like this virtue, no;
Give him his dirt to wallow in all night;
                'These preachers make
           His head to shoot and ache.'

O foolish man ! where are thine eyes?
How hast thou lost them in a crowd of cares !
  Thou pull'st the rug [2], and wilt not rise,
No, not to purchase the whole pack of stars :
                'There let them shine,
           Thou must go sleep, or dine.'

The bird that sees a dainty bower
Made in the tree where she was wont to sit,
  Wonders and sings, but not His power
Who made the arbour : this exceeds her wit.
                But Man doth know
           The spring whence all things flow :

And yet, as though he knew it not,
His knowledge winks, and lets his humours reign ;
  They make his life a constant blot,
And all the blood of God to run in vain.
                Ah, wretch ! what verse
         . Can thy strange ways rehearse ?

[1] *quarrel*, used actively   [2] *rug*, apparently, counterpane

LI

THE QUIP [1]

THE merry World did on a day
  With his train-bands [2] and mates agree
To meet together where I lay,
And all in sport to jeer at me.

First Beauty crept into a rose;
Which when I pluck'd not, 'Sir,' said she,
'Tell me, I pray, whose hands are those?'
But Thou shalt answer, LORD, for me.

Then Money came, and chinking still,
'What tune is this, poor man?' said he;
'I heard in music you had skill :'
But Thou shalt answer, LORD, for me.

Then came brave Glory puffing by
In silks that whistled, who but he !
He scarce allow'd me half an eye :
But Thou shalt answer, LORD, for me.

Then came quick Wit and Conversation,
And he would needs a comfort be,
And, to be short, make an oration:
But Thou shalt answer, LORD, for me.

Yet when the hour of Thy design
To answer these fine things shall come,
Speak not at large; say, 'I am Thine,'
And then they have their answer home.

    [1] *Quip*, smart turn, repartee   [2] *train-bands*, militia

LII

TIME

MEETING with Time, 'Slack thing,' said I,
   'Thy scythe is dull; whet it, for shame.'
'No marvel, sir,' he did reply,
'If it at length deserve some blame;
   But where one man would have me grind it,
   Twenty for one too sharp do find it.'

'Perhaps some such of old did pass,
Who above all things loved this life;
To whom thy scythe a hatchet was,
Which now is but a pruning knife.
   CHRIST's coming hath made man thy debtor,
   Since by thy cutting he grows better.

'And in His blessing thou art blest;
For where thou only wert before
An executioner at best,
Thou art a gardener now; and more,
   An usher to convey our souls
   Beyond the utmost stars and poles.

'And this is that makes life so long,
While it detains us from our GOD;
E'en pleasures here increase the wrong,
And length of days lengthens the rod.
   Who wants the place where GOD doth dwell,
   Partakes already half of hell.

'Of what strange length must that needs be,
Which e'en eternity excludes!'
Thus far Time heard me patiently;
Then chafing said: 'This man deludes;
   What do I here before his door?
   He doth not crave less time, but more.'

LIII

PEACE

SWEET Peace, where dost thou dwell,—I humbly crave,
    Let me once know?
  I sought thee in a secret cave,
    And ask'd if Peace were there.
A hollow wind did seem to answer, 'No;
    Go seek elsewhere.'

I did; and going did a rainbow note:
    Surely, thought I,
  This is the lace of Peace's coat:
    I will search out the matter.
But while I look'd, the clouds immediately
    Did break and scatter.

Then went I to a garden, and did spy
    A gallant flower,—
  The Crown Imperial. Sure, said I,
    Peace at the root must dwell.
But when I digg'd, I saw a worm devour
    What show'd so well.

At length I met a reverend good old man;
    Whom when for Peace
  I did demand, he thus began:
    'There was a Prince of old
At Salem dwelt, Who lived with good increase
    Of flock and fold.

'He sweetly lived; yet sweetness did not save
    His life from foes.
  But after death out of His grave
    There sprang twelve stalks of wheat;
Which many wondering at, got some of those
    To plant and set.

'It prosper'd strangely, and did soon disperse
    Through all the earth;
  For they that taste it do rehearse
    That virtue lies therein:
A secret virtue, bringing peace and mirth
    By flight of sin.

'Take of this grain, which in my garden grows,
    And grows for you:
  Make bread of it; and that repose
    And peace, which everywhere
With so much earnestness you do pursue,
    Is only there.'

LIV

MAN'S MEDLEY

HARK how the birds do sing
      And woods do ring :
All creatures have their joy, and man hath his.
      Yet if we rightly measure,
        Man's joy and pleasure
Rather hereafter than in present is.

      To this life things of sense
        Make their pretence ;
In the other Angels have a right by birth :
      Man ties them both alone,
        And makes them one,
With the one hand touching Heaven, with the other earth.

      Not that he may not here
        Taste of the cheer ;
But as birds drink, and straight lift up their head,
      So must he sip, and think
        Of better drink
He may attain to after he is dead.

      But as his joys are double,
        So is his trouble :
He hath two winters, other things but one ;
      Both frosts and thoughts do nip
        And bite his lip ;
And he of all things fears two deaths alone.

      Yet ev'n the greatest griefs
        May be reliefs,
Could he but take them right and in their ways.
      Happy is he whose heart
        Hath found the art
To turn his double pains to double praise !

LV

VANITY

THE fleet astronomer can bore
   And thread the spheres with his quick-piercing mind;
He views their stations, walks from door to door,
      Surveys, as if he had design'd
To make a purchase there ; he sees their dances,
      And knoweth long before
Both their full-eyed aspécts[1] and secret glances.

The nimble diver with his side
Cuts through the working waves, that he may fetch
His dearly-earnéd pearl; which GOD did hide
    On purpose from the venturous wretch,
That He might save his life, and also hers
    Who with excessive pride
Her own destruction and his danger wears.

The subtle chymick can divest
And strip the creature naked, till he find
The callow principles[1] within their nest:
    There he imparts to them his mind,
Admitted to their bed-chamber, before
    They appear trim and drest
To ordinary suitors at the door.

What hath not man sought out and found,
But his dear GOD? Who yet His glorious law
Embosoms in us, mellowing the ground
    With showers and frosts, with love and awe;
So that we need not say, Where's this command?
    —Poor man, thou searchest round
To find out death, but missest life at hand!

1 *aspects, callow principles,* see Note

LVI

THE PILGRIMAGE

I TRAVELL'D on, seeing the hill, where lay
    My expectation.
    A long it was and weary way:
    The gloomy cave of Desperation
I left on the one, and on the other side
    The rock of Pride.

And so I came to Fancy's meadow, strow'd
    With many a flower:
    Fain would I here have made abode,
    But I was quicken'd by my hour.
So to Care's copse I came, and there got through
    With much ado.

That led me to the wild of Passion, which
    Some call the wold;
    A wasted place, but sometimes rich.
    Here I was robb'd of all my gold,
Save one good angel[1], which a friend had tied
    Close to my side.

At length I got unto the gladsome hill,
      Where lay my hope,
Where lay my heart; and climbing still,
      When I had gain'd the brow and top,
A lake of brackish waters on the ground
      Was all I found.

With that abash'd and struck with many a sting
      Of swarming fears,
I fell and cried, 'Alas, my King,
      Can both the way and end be tears!'
Yet taking heart, I rose, and then perceived
      I was deceived.

My hill was further: so I flung away,
      Yet heard a cry
Just as I went, 'None goes that way
      And lives.' 'If that be all,' said I,
'After so foul a journey death is fair,
      And but a chair[2].'

[1] *angel*, also a coin   [2] *chair*, presumably, a restful *litter*

LVII

PRAISE

KING of glory, King of peace,
      I will love Thee;
And that love may never cease,
      I will move Thee.

Thou hast granted my request,
      Thou hast heard me;
Thou didst note my working breast,
      Thou hast spared me.

Wherefore with my utmost art
      I will sing Thee,
And the cream of all my heart
      I will bring Thee.

Though my sins against me cried,
      Thou didst clear me;
And alone, when they replied,
      Thou didst hear me.

Seven whole days, not one in seven,
      I will praise Thee;
In my heart, though not in Heaven,
      I can raise Thee.

Thou grew'st soft and moist with tears,
            Thou relentedst,
And when Justice call'd for fears,
            Thou dissentedst.

Small it is, in this poor sort
            To enrol Thee;
E'en eternity is too short
            To extol Thee.

LVIII

LONGING

WITH sick and famish'd eyes,
     With doubling knees, and weary bones,
        To Thee my cries,
        To Thee my groans,
To Thee my sighs, my tears ascend:
           No end?

My throat, my soul is hoarse;
My heart is wither'd like a ground
        Which Thou dost curse;
        My thoughts turn round,
And make me giddy: LORD, I fall,
           Yet call.

Bowels of pity, hear;
LORD of my soul, love of my mind,
        Bow down Thine ear;
        Let not the wind
Scatter my words, and in the same
           Thy name.

Look on my sorrows round;
Mark well my furnace. O, what flames,
        What heats abound!
        What griefs, what shames!
Consider, LORD; LORD, bow thine ear,
           And hear!

LORD JESU, Thou didst bow
Thy dying head upon the tree;
        O, be not now
        More dead to me.
LORD, hear. Shall He that made the ear
           Not hear?

> To Thee help appertains:
> Hast Thou left all things to their course,
> And laid the reins
> Upon the horse?
> Is all lock'd? hath a sinner's plea
>   No key?
>
> Thou tarriest, while I die,
> And fall to nothing: Thou dost reign,
> And rule on high,
> While I remain
> In bitter grief; yet am I styled
>   Thy child.
>
> My Love, my Sweetness, hear:
> By these Thy feet, at which my heart
> Lies all the year,
> Pluck out Thy dart,
> And heal my troubled breast, which cries,
>   Which dies.

LIX

THE BAG

AWAY, despair! my gracious LORD doth hear;
 Though winds and waves assault my keel,
He doth preserve it; He doth steer,
Ev'n when the boat seems most to reel.
Storms are the triumph of His art;
Well may He close His eyes, but not His heart.

Hast thou not heard that my LORD JESUS died?
 Then let me tell thee a strange story:
 The GOD of power, as He did ride
 In His majestic robes of glory,
 Resolved to 'light, and so one day
He did descend, undressing all the way.

The stars His tire of light and rings obtain'd,
 The cloud His bow, the fire His spear,
 The sky His azure mantle gain'd;
 And when they ask'd what He would wear,
 He smiled, and said as He did go,
He had new clothes a-making here below.

When He was come, as travellers are wont,
 He did repair unto an inn.
 Both then, and after, many a brunt
 He did endure to cancel sin ;
 And having given the rest before,
Here He gave up His life to pay our score.

But as He was returning, there came one
 That ran upon Him with a spear.
 He, who came hither all alone,
 Bringing nor man, nor arms, nor fear,
 Received the blow upon His side,
And straight He turn'd, and to His brethren cried,

' If ye have anything to send or write—
 I have no bag, but here is room—
 Unto My Father's hands and sight,
 Believe Me, it shall safely come.
 That I shall mind what you impart,
Look, you may put it very near my-heart.

' Or if hereafter any of My friends
 Will use Me in this kind, the door
 Shall still be open ; what he sends
 I will present, and somewhat more,
 Not to his hurt : sighs will convey
Anything to Me.' Hark, Despair, away !

LX

THE PULLEY

WHEN God at first made Man,
  Having a glass of blessings standing by,
' Let us,' said He, ' pour on him all we can ;
Let the world's riches, which disperséd lie,
  Contract into a span.'

  So strength first made a way ;
Then beauty flow'd, then wisdom, honour, pleasure :
When almost all was out, God made a stay,
Perceiving that, alone of all His treasure,
  Rest in the bottom lay.

  ' For if I should,' said He,
' Bestow this jewel also on My creature,
He would adore My gifts instead of Me,
And rest in Nature, not the God of Nature ;
  So both should losers be.

'Yet let him keep the rest,
But keep them with repining restlessness;
Let him be rich and weary, that at least,
If goodness lead him not, yet weariness
    May toss him to My breast.'

LXI

THE FLOWER

HOW fresh, O Lord, how sweet and clean
  Are Thy returns! e'en as the flowers in Spring,
To which, besides their own demesne,
The late-past frosts tributes of pleasure bring;
    Grief melts away
    Like snow in May,
As if there were no such cold thing.

Who would have thought my shrivell'd heart
Could have recover'd greenness? It was gone
  Quite underground; as flowers depart
To see their mother-root, when they have blown,
    Where they together
    All the hard weather,
Dead to the world, keep house unknown.

These are Thy wonders, Lord of power,
Killing and quickening, bringing down to Hell
  And up to Heaven in an hour;
Making a chiming of a passing bell.
    We say amiss,
    This or that is;
Thy Word is all, if we could spell.

O that I once past changing were,
Fast in Thy Paradise, where no flower can wither!
  Many a Spring I shoot up fair,
Offering at Heaven, growing and groaning thither;
    Nor doth my flower
    Want a Spring-shower,
My sins and I joining together.

But while I grow in a straight line,
Still upwards bent, as if Heaven were mine own,
  Thy anger comes, and I decline:
What frost to that? what pole is not the zone
    Where all things burn,
    When Thou dost turn,
And the least frown of Thine is shown?

And now in age I bud again,
After so many deaths I live and write;
  I once more smell the dew and rain,
And relish versing: O my only Light,
        It cannot be
        That I am he
On whom Thy tempests fell all night.

These are Thy wonders, LORD of love,
To make us see we are but flowers that glide;
  Which when we once can find and prove,
Thou hast a garden for us where to bide.—
        Who would be more,
        Swelling through store,
Forfeit their Paradise by their pride.

See Note

LXII

THE GLANCE

WHEN first Thy sweet and gracious eye
    Vouchsafed, e'en in the midst of youth and night,
To look upon me, who before did lie
      Weltering in sin,
  I felt a sugar'd strange delight,
Passing all cordials made by any art,
Bedew, embalm, and overrun my heart,
      And take it in.

  Since that time many a bitter storm
My soul hath felt, ev'n able to destroy,
Had the malicious and ill-meaning harm
      His swing and sway;
  But still Thy sweet original joy
Sprung from Thine eye, did work within my soul,
And surging griefs, when they grew bold, control,
      And got the day.

  If Thy first glance so powerful be—
A mirth[1] but open'd, and seal'd up again—
What wonders shall we feel when we shall see
      Thy full-eyed love!
  When Thou shalt look us out of pain,
And one aspect of Thine spend in delight
More than a thousand suns disburse in light,
      In Heaven above!

[1] *mirth*, joy; as in St. 2

LXIII

THE FOIL

IF we could see below
 The sphere of Virtue and each shining grace,
  As plainly as that above doth show,
This were the better sky, the brighter place.

 God hath made stars the foil
To set-off virtues, griefs to set-off sinning;
 Yet in this wretched world we toil,
As if grief were not foul, nor virtue winning.

LXIV

THE POSY

LET wits contest,
 And with their words and posies windows fill;
  'Less than the least
Of all Thy mercies,' is my posy still.

 This on my ring,
This by my picture, in my book I write;
  Whether I sing,
Or say, or dictate, this is my delight.

 Invention, rest;
Comparisons, go play; wit, use thy will;
  'Less than the least
Of all God's mercies' is my posy still.

LXV

A WREATH

A WREATHÉD garland of deservéd praise,
 Of praise deservéd, unto Thee I give,
I give to Thee, Who knowest all my ways,
My crookéd winding ways, wherein I live—

Wherein I die, not live; for life is straight,
Straight as a line, and ever tends to Thee—
To Thee, Who art more far above deceit,
Than deceit seems above simplicity.

Give me simplicity, that I may live;
So live and like, that I may know Thy ways;
Know them and practise them; then shall I give,
For this poor wreath, give Thee a crown of praise.

LXVI

DISCIPLINE

THROW away Thy rod,
　Throw away Thy wrath;
　　　O my GOD,
Take the gentle path.

For my heart's desire
Unto Thine is bent;
　　　I aspire
To a full consent.

Though I fail, I weep;
Though I halt in pace,
　　　Yet I creep
To the throne of grace.

Then let wrath remove;
Love will do the deed;
　　　For with love
Stony hearts will bleed.

Love is swift of foot;
Love's a man of war,
　　　And can shoot,
And can hit from far.

Who can 'scape his bow?
That which wrought on Thee,
　　　Brought Thee low,
Needs must work on me.

Throw away Thy rod:
Though man frailties hath,
　　　Thou art GOD;
Throw away Thy wrath.

LXVII

THE ELIXIR

TEACH me, my GOD and King,
　In all things Thee to see,
And what I do in anything,
　To do it as for Thee.

All may of Thee partake :
Nothing can be so mean
Which with his tincture[1], For Thy sake,
Will not grow bright and clean.

A servant with this clause
Makes drudgery divine ;
Who sweeps a room as for Thy laws,
Makes that and the action fine.

This is the famous stone
That turneth all to gold ;
For that which God doth touch and own
Cannot for less be told[2].

[1] *his tincture*, see Note   [2] *told*, reckoned

LXVIII

DEATH

DEATH, thou wast once an uncouth hideous thing,
Nothing but bones,
The sad effect of sadder groans :
Thy mouth was open, but thou couldst not sing.

For we consider'd thee as at some six
Or ten years hence,
After the loss of life and sense ;
Flesh being turn'd to dust, and bones to sticks.

We look'd on this side of thee, shooting short,
Where we did find
The shells of fledge-souls left behind ;
Dry dust, which sheds no tears, but may extort.

But since our Saviour's death did put some blood
Into thy face,
Thou art grown fair and full of grace,
Much in request, much sought for, as a good.

For we do now behold thee gay and glad,
As at doomsday,
When souls shall wear their new array,
And all thy bones with beauty shall be clad.

Therefore we can go die as sleep, and trust
Half that we have
Unto an honest faithful grave,
Making our pillows either down, or dust.

LXIX

LOVE

LOVE bade me welcome; yet my soul drew back,
    Guilty of dust and sin.
But quick-eyed Love, observing me grow slack
    From my first entrance in,
Drew nearer to me, sweetly questioning,
    If I lack'd anything.

'A guest,' I answer'd, 'worthy to be here :'
    Love said, 'You shall be he.'
'I, the unkind, ungrateful? Ah, my dear,
    I cannot look on Thee.'
Love took my hand, and smiling, did reply,
    'Who made the eyes but I?'

'Truth, Lord, but I have marr'd them; let my shame
    Go where it doth deserve.'
'And know you not,' says Love, 'who bore the blame?'
    'My dear, then I will serve.'
'You must sit down,' says Love, 'and taste my meat.'
    So I did sit and eat.

LXX

IESU

IESU is in my heart; His sacred name
    Is deeply carvéd there : but th' other week
A great affliction broke the little frame,
Ev'n all to pieces; which I went to seek :
And first I found the corner where was I,
After, where ES, and next where U was graved.
When I had got these parcels, instantly
I sat me down to spell them, and perceived
That to my broken heart He was *I ease you*,
    And to my whole is IESU.

LXXI

COMFORT IN EXTREMITY

ALAS! my Lord is going,
        Oh my woe!
It will be mine undoing;
        If He go,

I 'll run and overtake Him;
    If He stay,
I 'll cry aloud, and make Him
    Look this way.
 O stay, my LORD, my Love, 'tis I;
 Comfort me quickly, or I die.

'Cheer up thy drooping spirits;
    I am here.
Mine all-sufficient merits
    Shall appear
Before the throne of glory
    In thy stead:
I 'll put into thy story
    What I did.
 Lift up thine eyes, sad soul, and see
 Thy Saviour here. Lo, I am He.'

Alas! shall I present
    My sinfulness
To Thee? Thou wilt resent
    The loathsomeness.
'Be not afraid, I 'll take
    Thy sins on Me,
And all My favour make
    To shine on thee.'
 LORD, what Thou 'lt have me, Thou must make me.
 'As I have made thee now, I take thee.'
        C. Harvey

LXXII

DEUS DEUS MEUS

WHAT am I who dare call Thee, GOD!
 And raise my fancy to discourse Thy power?
To whom dust is the period,
Who am not sure to farm[1] this very hour?
 For how know I the latest sand
In my frail glass of life, doth not now fall?
 And while I thus astonish'd stand
I but prepare for my own funeral?
 Death doth with man no order keep:
It reckons not by the expense[2] of years,
 But makes the Queen and beggar weep,
And ne'er distinguishes between their tears.

He who the victory doth gain
Falls as he him pursues, who from him flies,
 And is by too good fortune slain :
The lover in his amorous courtship dies :
 The statesman suddenly expires
While he for others ruin doth prepare :
 And the gay Lady while she admires
Her pride, and curls in wanton nets her hair.
 No state of man is fortified
'Gainst the assault of th' universal doom :
 But who the Almighty fear, deride
Pale Death, and meet with triumph in the tomb.

W. Habington

¹ *farm*, possess or rent: (see LXXV, St. 6) ² *expense*, expenditure

LXXIII

SOLUM MIHI SUPEREST SEPULCHRUM

WELCOME, thou safe retreat !
 Where th' injured man may fortify
'Gainst the invasions of the great :
Where the lean slave, who th' oar doth ply,
Soft as his admiral may lie.

 Great statist ! 'tis your doom,
Though your designs swell high and wide,
To be contracted in a tomb !
And all your happy cares provide
But for your heir authórized pride.

 Nor shall your shade delight
I' th' pomp of your proud obsequies :
And should the present flattery write
A glorious epitaph, the wise
Will say, ' The poet's wit here lies.'

 How reconciled to fate
Will grow the aged villager,
When he shall see your funeral state !
Since death will him as warm inter
As you in your gay sepulchre.

 The great decree of GOD
Makes every path of mortals lead
To this dark common period.
For what by-ways soe'er we tread,
We end our journey 'mong the dead.

LXXIV

LAUDATE DOMINUM DE CAELIS

YOU Spirits! who have thrown away
     That envious weight of clay,
Which your celestial flight denied:
Who by your glorious troops supply
     The wingéd Hierarchy,
So broken in the Angels' pride!

O you! whom your Creator's sight
     Inebriates with delight!
Sing forth the triumphs of His name
All you enamour'd souls! agree
     In a loud symphony,
To give expressions to your flame!

To Him, His own great works relate,
     Who deign'd to elevate
You 'bove the frailty of your birth:
Where you stand safe from that rude war,
     With which we troubled are
By the rebellion of our earth.

While a corrupted air beneath
     Here in this world we breathe,
Each hour some passion us assails:
Now lust casts wild-fire in the blood,
     Or that it may seem good,
Itself in wit or beauty veils.

Then envy circles us with hate,
     And lays a siege so streight,
No heavenly succour enters in:
But if revenge admittance find,
     For ever hath the mind
Made forfeit of itself to sin.

Assaulted thus, how dare we raise
     Our minds to think His praise,
Who is eternal and immense?
How dare we force our feeble wit
     To speak Him infinite,
So far above the search of sense!

O you! who are immaculate
     His name may celebrate
In your soul's bright expansión:
You whom your virtues did unite
     To His perpetual light,
That even with Him you now shine one.

LXXV

RECOGITABO TIBI OMNES ANNOS MEOS

TIME! where didst thou those years inter
  Which I have seen decease?
My soul's at war, and truth bids her
Find out their hidden sepulchre,
  To give her troubles peace.

Pregnant with flowers doth not the Spring
  Like a late bride appear?
Whose feather'd music [1] only bring
Caresses, and no requiem sing
  On the departed year?

The Earth, like some rich wanton heir
  Whose parents coffin'd lie,
Forgets it once look'd pale and bare,
And doth for vanities prepare,
  As the Spring ne'er should die.

The present hour, flatter'd by all,
  Reflects not on the last;
But I, like a sad factor[2], shall
To account my life each moment call,
  And only weep the past.

My memory tracks each several way
  Since reason did begin
Over my actions her first sway:
And teacheth me that each new day
  Did only vary sin.

Poor bankrupt Conscience! where are those
  Rich hours but farm'd to thee?
How carelessly I some did lose,
And other to my lust dispose,
  As no rent-day should be!

I have infected with impure
  Disorders my first years.
But I'll to penitence inure
Those that succeed. There is no cure
  Nor antidote but tears.

---

[1] *music,* used here plurally for *musicians*   [2] *factor,* business-manager

LXXVI

NOX NOCTI INDICAT SCIENTIAM

WHEN I survey the bright
            Celestial sphere;
So rich with jewels hung, that Night
Doth like an Ethiop bride appear:

My soul her wings doth spread
            And heaven-ward flies,
The Almighty's mysteries to read
In the large volumes of the skies.

For the bright firmament
            Shoots forth no flame
So silent, but is eloquent
In speaking the Creator's name.

No unregarded star
            Contracts its light
Into so small a character,
Removed far from our human sight,

But if we steadfast look
            We shall discern
In it, as in some holy book,
How man may heavenly knowledge learn.

It tells the conqueror,
            That far-stretch'd power,
Which his proud dangers traffic for,
Is but the triumph of an hour:

That from the farthest North,
            Some nation may,
Yet undiscover'd, issue forth,
And o'er his new-got conquest sway:

Some nation yet shut in
            With hills of ice
May be let out to scourge his sin,
Till they shall equal him in vice.

And then they likewise shall
            Their ruin have;
For as yourselves your empires fall,
And every kingdom hath a grave.

Thus those celestial fires,
    Though seeming mute,
The fallacy of our desires
And all the pride of life confute:—

For they have watch'd since first
    The World had birth:
And found sin in itself accurst,
And nothing permanent on Earth.

LXXVII

SHOW me more love, my dearest LORD;
    Oh turn away Thy clouded face,
Give me some secret look or word
That may betoken love and grace;
No day or time is black to me
But that wherein I see not Thee.
Show me more love: a clouded face
Strikes deeper than an angry blow;
Love me and kill me by Thy grace,
I shall not much bewail my woe.
      But even to be
      In heaven unloved of Thee,
Were hell in heaven for to see.
Then hear my cry and help afford:
Show me more love, my dearest LORD!

Show me more love, my dearest LORD,—
I cannot think, nor speak, nor pray;
Thy work stands still, my strength is stored
In Thee alone. Oh come away,
Show me Thy beauties, call them mine,
My heart and tongue will soon be Thine.
Show me more love; or if my heart
Too common be for such a guest,
Let Thy good Spirit, by Its art,
Make entry and put out the rest;
      For 'tis Thy nest.
      Then he's of heaven possest,
      That heaven hath in his breast.
Then hear my cry, and help afford;
Show me more love, my dearest LORD!

Anon.

LXXVIII

THE INVITATION

LORD, what unvalued pleasures crown'd
    The days of old;
When Thou wert so familiar found,
    Those days were gold;—

When Abram wish'd Thou couldst afford
    With him to feast;
When Lot but said, 'Turn in, my LORD,'
    Thou wert his guest.

But, ah! this heart of mine doth pant,
    And beat for Thee;
Yet Thou art strange, and wilt not grant
    Thyself to me.

What, shall Thy people be so dear
    To Thee no more?
Or is not heaven to earth as near
    As heretofore?

The famish'd raven's hoarser cry
    Finds out Thine ear;
My soul is famish'd, and I die
    Unless Thou hear.

O Thou great ALPHA! King of kings!
    Or bow to me,
Or lend my soul seraphic wings,
    To get to Thee.

Anon.

LXXIX

D. O. M.

ETERNAL Mover, whose diffuséd glory,
    To show our grovelling reason what Thou art,
Unfolds itself in clouds of nature's story,
    Where Man, Thy proudest creature, acts his part;
Whom yet, alas, I know not why, we call
The world's contracted sum, the little all;

For what are we but lumps of walking clay?
    Why should we swell? whence should our spirits rise?
Are not brute beasts as strong, and birds as gay,—
    Trees longer lived, and creeping things as wise?
Only our souls were left an inward light,
To feel our weakness, and confess Thy might.

Thou then, our strength, Father of life and death,
    To whom our thanks, our vows, ourselves we owe,
From me, Thy tenant of this fading breath,
    Accept those lines which from Thy goodness flow;
And Thou, that wert Thy regal Prophet's muse,
Do not Thy praise in weaker strains refuse!

Let these poor notes ascend unto Thy throne,
    Where majesty doth sit with mercy crown'd,
Where my Redeemer lives, in Whom alone
    The errors of my wandering life are drown'd:
Where all the choir of Heaven resound the same,
That only Thine, Thine is the saving Name!

Well, then, my soul, joy in the midst of pain;
    Thy CHRIST, that conquer'd Hell, shall from above
With greater triumph yet return again,
    And conquer His own justice with His love;
Commanding earth and seas to render those
Unto His bliss, for whom He paid His woes.

Now have I done; now are my thoughts at peace;
    And now my joys are stronger than my grief:
I feel those comforts, that shall never cease,
    Future in hope, but present in belief;
Thy words are true, Thy promises are just,
And Thou wilt find Thy dearly-bought in dust!

                           H. Wotton

LXXX

RISE, O my soul! with thy desires to heaven,
    And with divinest contemplation use
Thy time, where Time's eternity is given,
    And let vain thoughts no more thy thoughts abuse;
But down in [midnight] darkness let them lie;
So live thy better, let thy worse thoughts die!

And thou, my soul, inspired with holy flame,
    View and review, with most regardful eye,
That holy Cross, whence thy salvation came,
    On which thy Saviour and thy sin did die!

For in that sacred object is much pleasure,
And in that Saviour is my life, my treasure.

To thee, O Jesu! I direct my eyes;
  To Thee my hands, to Thee my humble knees;
To Thee my heart shall offer sacrifice;
  To Thee my thoughts, Who my thoughts only sees:
To Thee myself,—myself and all I give;
To Thee I die; to Thee I only live!

Anon.

LXXXI

ON THE MORNING OF CHRIST'S NATIVITY

THIS is the month, and this the happy morn,
  Wherein the Son of Heaven's eternal King,
Of wedded Maid and Virgin Mother born,
Our great redemption from above did bring;
For so the holy sages once did sing,
  That He our deadly forfeit should release,
And with His Father work us a perpetual peace.

That glorious Form, that light unsufferable,
And that far-beaming blaze of majesty,
Wherewith He wont at Heaven's high council-table
To sit the midst of Trinal Unity,
He laid aside; and, here with us to be,
  Forsook the courts of everlasting day,
And chose with us a darksome house of mortal clay.

Say, Heavenly Muse, shall not thy sacred vein
Afford a present to the Infant God?
Hast thou no verse, no hymn, or solemn strain,
To welcome Him to this His new abode,
Now while the heaven, by the sun's team untrod,
  Hath took no print of the approaching light,
And all the spangled host keep watch in squadrons bright?

See how from far upon the eastern road
The star-led wizards haste with odours sweet!
Oh run, prevent them with thy humble ode,
And lay it lowly at His blessèd feet;
Have thou the honour first thy Lord to greet,
  And join thy voice unto the angel quire,
From out His secret altar touch'd with hallow'd fire.

THE HYMN

It was the winter wild,
While the heaven-born Child
   All meanly wrapt in the rude manger lies;
Nature, in awe to Him,
Had doff'd her gaudy trim,
   With her great Master so to sympathize:
It was no season then for her
To wanton with the Sun, her lusty paramour.

Only with speeches fair
She woos the gentle air
   To hide her guilty front with innocent snow,
And on her naked shame,
Pollute with sinful blame,
   The saintly veil of maiden white to throw;
Confounded, that her Maker's eyes
Should look so near upon her foul deformities.

But He, her fears to cease,
Sent down the meek-eyed Peace;
   She, crown'd with olive green, came softly sliding
Down through the turning sphere[1]
His ready harbinger,
   With turtle wing the amorous clouds dividing,
And waving wide her myrtle wand,
She strikes a universal peace through sea and land.

No war, or battle's sound,
Was heard the world around;
   The idle spear and shield were high uphung;
The hookéd chariot stood,
Unstain'd with hostile blood;
   The trumpet spake not to the arméd throng;
And kings sat still with awful eye,
As if they surely knew their sovran LORD was by.

But peaceful was the night,
Wherein the Prince of Light
   ·His reign of peace upon the earth began:
The winds with wonder whist[2]
Smoothly the waters kiss'd,
   Whispering new joys to the mild Oceán;
Who now hath quite forgot to rave,
While birds of calm sit brooding on the charméd wave.

The stars with deep amaze
Stand fix'd in steadfast gaze,
   Bending one way their precious influence;
And will not take their flight,
For all the morning light,
   Or Lucifer[3] that often warn'd them thence;
But in their glimmering orbs did glow,
Until their Lord Himself bespake, and bid them go.

And though the shady gloom
Had given day her room,
   The Sun himself withheld his wonted speed,
And hid his head for shame,
As his inferior flame
   The new-enlighten'd world no more should need:
He saw a greater Sun appear
Than his bright throne or burning axletree could bear.

The shepherds on the lawn,
Or ere the point of dawn,
   Sat simply chatting in a rustic row;
Full little thought they than[4],
That the mighty Pan[5]
   Was kindly come to live with them below;
Perhaps their loves, or else their sheep,
Was all that did their silly[6] thoughts so busy keep.

When such music sweet
Their hearts and ears did greet,
   As never was by mortal finger strook;
Divinely-warbled voice
Answering the stringéd noise,
   As all their souls in blissful rapture took:
The air, such pleasure loth to lose,
With thousand echoes still prolongs each heavenly close.

Nature that heard such sound
Beneath the hollow round
   Of Cynthia's[7] seat, the airy region thrilling,
Now was almost won
To think her part was done,
   And that her reign had here its last fulfilling;
She knew such harmony alone
Could hold all Heaven and Earth in happier union.

At last surrounds their sight
A globe of circular light,
   That with long beams the shame-faced night array'd:

The helmèd Cherubim,
And sworded Seraphim,
  Are seen in glittering ranks with wings display'd,
Harping in loud and solemn quire
With unexpressive[8] notes to Heaven's new-born Heir.

Such music (as 'tis said)
Before was never made,
  But when of old the Sons of Morning sung,
While the Creator great
His constellations set,
  And the well-balanced World on hinges hung,
And cast the dark foundations deep,
And bid the weltering waves their oozy channel keep.

Ring out, ye crystal spheres!
Once bless our human ears,
  (If ye have power to touch our senses so,)
And let your silver chime
Move in melodious time,
  And let the bass of Heaven's deep organ blow;
And with your ninefold harmony
Make up full consort[9] to the angelic symphony.

For if such holy song
Enwrap our fancy long,
  Time will run back and fetch the Age of Gold,
And speckled Vanity
Will sicken soon and die,
  And leprous Sin will melt from earthly mould,
And Hell itself will pass away,
And leave her dolorous mansions to the peering day.

Yea, Truth and Justice then
Will down return to men,
  Orb'd in a rainbow; and, like glories wearing,
Mercy will sit between,
Throned in celestial sheen,
  With radiant feet the tissued clouds down steering;
And Heaven, as at some festival,
Will open wide the gates of her high palace-hall.

But wisest Fate says No,
This must not yet be so:
  The Babe lies yet in smiling infancy
That on the bitter Cross
Must redeem our loss;
  So both Himself and us to glorify:

Yet first, to those ychain'd in sleep,
The wakeful trump of doom must thunder through the deep,

With such a horrid clang
As on Mount Sinai rang,
   While the red fire and smouldering clouds out-brake:
The aged Earth aghast,
With terror of that blast,
   Shall from the surface to the centre shake;
When, at the world's last session,
The dreadful Judge in middle air shall spread His throne.

And then at last our bliss
Full and perfect is,—
   But now begins; for from this happy day
The old Dragon under ground
In straiter limits bound,
   Not half so far casts his usurpéd sway,
And, wroth to see his kingdom fail,
Swinges the scaly horror of his folded tail.

The oracles are dumb,
No voice or hideous hum
   Runs through the archéd roof in words deceiving:
Apollo from his shrine
Can no more divine,
   With hollow shriek the steep of Delphos leaving.
No nightly trance, or breathéd spell,
Inspires the pale-eyed priest from the prophetic cell.

The lonely mountains o'er,
And the resounding shore,
   A voice of weeping heard and loud lament;
From haunted spring and dale,
Edged with poplar pale,
   The parting Genius is with sighing sent;
With flower-inwoven tresses torn
The Nymphs in twilight shade of tangled thickets mourn.

In consecrated earth,
And on the holy hearth,
   The Lars and Lemurés moan with midnight plaint;
In urns and altars round,
A drear and dying sound
   Affrights the Flamens at their service quaint;
And the chill marble seems to sweat,
While each peculiar Power foregoes his wonted seat.

Peor and Baälim
Forsake their temples dim,
  With that twice batter'd god of Palestine;
And mooned Ashtaroth,
Heaven's queen and mother both,
  Now sits not girt with tapers' holy shine;
The Libyc Hammon shrinks his horn,
In vain the Tyrian maids their wounded Thammuz mourn.

And sullen Moloch, fled,
Hath left in shadows dread
  His burning idol all of blackest hue;
In vain with cymbals' ring
They call the grisly king,
  In dismal dance about the furnace blue;
The brutish gods of Nile as fast,
Isis, and Orus, and the dog Anubis, haste.

Nor is Osiris seen
In Memphian grove or green,
  Trampling the unshower'd[10] grass with lowings loud
Nor can he be at rest
Within his sacred chest,
  Nought but profoundest Hell can be his shroud;
In vain with timbrell'd anthems dark
The sable-stoléd sorcerers bear his worshipp'd ark.

He feels from Juda's land
The dreaded Infant's hand;
  The rays of Bethlehem blind his dusky eyn;
Nor all the gods beside,
Longer dare abide,
  Nor Typhon huge ending in snaky twine:
Our Babe, to show His Godhead true,
Can in His swaddling bands control the damnéd crew.

So when the sun in bed,
Curtain'd with cloudy red,
  Pillows his chin upon an orient wave,
The flocking shadows pale
Troop to the infernal jail;
  Each fetter'd ghost slips to his several grave;
And the yellow-skirted Fays
Fly after the night-steeds, leaving their moon-loved maze.

—But see! the Virgin blest
Hath laid her Babe to rest:—

Time is our tedious song should here have ending;
Heaven's youngest-teeméd[11] star
Hath fix'd her polish'd car,
   Her sleeping LORD with handmaid lamp attending:
And all about the courtly stable
Bright harness'd[12] Angels sit in order serviceable.

                          J. Milton

[1] *turning sphere*, of the Universe   [2] *whist*, hushed   [3] *Lucifer*, the Morning Star   [4] *than*, then   [5] *Pan*, used here for God   [6] *silly*, simple   [7] *Cynthia*, the Moon   [8] *unexpressive*, inexpressible   [9] *consort*, concert   [10] *unshower'd*, watered by Nile only   [11] *teeméd*, born   [12] *harness'd*, armoured

LXXXII

UPON THE CIRCUMCISION

YE flaming Powers, and wingéd warriors bright,
   That erst with music, and triumphant song,
First heard by happy watchful shepherds' ear,
So sweetly sung your joy the clouds along
Through the soft silence of the listening night;
Now mourn; and if[1], sad share with us to bear,
Your fiery essence can distil no tear,
Burn in your sighs, and borrow
Seas wept from our deep sorrow:
He Who with all Heaven's heraldry whilere
Enter'd the world, now bleeds to give us ease;
Alas, how soon our sin
   Sore doth begin
     His Infancy to seize!
O more exceeding love, or law more just!
Just law indeed, but more exceeding love!
For we by rightful doom remediless
Were lost in death, till He that dwelt above
High throned in secret bliss, for us frail dust
Emptied His glory, even to nakedness;
And that great covenant which we still transgress
Entirely satisfied,
And the full wrath beside
Of vengeful justice bore for our excess,
And seals obedience first with wounding smart
This day; but O! ere long
Huge pangs and strong
   Will pierce more near His heart.

        [1] See Note

LXXXIII

ON TIME

FLY, envious Time, till thou run out thy race;
   Call on the lazy leaden-stepping Hours,
Whose speed is but the heavy plummet's pace;
And glut thyself with what thy womb devours,
Which is no more than what is false and vain,
And merely mortal dross;
So little is our loss,
So little is thy gain!
For when as each thing bad thou hast entomb'd,
And last of all thy greedy self consumed,
Then long Eternity shall greet our bliss
With an individual kiss;
And joy shall overtake us as a flood:
When every thing that is sincerely good
And perfectly divine,
With Truth, and Peace, and Love, shall ever shine
About the supreme Throne
Of Him, t' Whose happy-making sight alone
When once our heavenly-guided soul shall climb,
Then, all this earthy grossness quit,
Attired with stars, we shall for ever sit,
Triumphing over Death, and Chance, and thee, O Time!

LXXXIV

AT A SOLEMN MUSIC

BLEST pair of Sirens, pledges of Heaven's joy,
   Sphere-born harmonious Sisters, Voice and Verse,
Wed your divine sounds, and mixt power employ,
Dead things with inbreathed sense able to pierce;
And to our high-raised phantasy present
That undisturbéd song of pure concent[1],
Aye sung before the sapphire-colour'd Throne
To Him that sits thereon,
With saintly shout and solemn jubilee;
Where the bright Seraphim in burning row
Their loud uplifted Angel-trumpets blow,
And the Cherubic host in thousand quires
Touch their immortal harps of golden wires,
With those just Spirits that wear victorious palms,
Hymns devout and holy psalms
Singing everlastingly:

That we on Earth, with undiscording voice,
May rightly answer that melodious noise;
As once we did, till disproportion'd sin
Jarr'd against nature's chime, and with harsh din
Broke the fair music that all creatures made
To their great LORD, Whose love their motion sway'd
In perfect diapason, whilst they stood
In first obedience, and their state of good.
O may we soon again renew that song,
And keep in tune with Heaven, till GOD ere long
To His celestial consort [2] us unite,
To live with Him, and sing in endless morn of light.

    [1] *concent* symphony   [2] *consort*, concert

LXXXV

ON HIS BLINDNESS

WHEN I consider how my light is spent,
   Ere half my days, in this dark world and wide,
And that one talent, which is death to hide,
Lodged with me useless,—though my soul more bent

To serve therewith my Maker, and present
   My true account, lest He, returning, chide,—
'Doth GOD exact day-labour, light denied?'
I fondly ask: But Patience, to prevent

That murmur, soon replies, 'GOD doth not need
   Either man's work or His own gifts: Who best
     Bear His mild yoke, they serve Him best: His state
Is Kingly: Thousands at His bidding speed,
   And post o'er land and ocean without rest:
     They also serve who only stand and wait.'

LXXXVI

LIFE AND DEATH

FRAIL Life! in which, through mists of human breath
   We grope for truth, and make our progress slow,
Because by passion blinded; till, by death
Our passions ending, we begin to know.

O reverend Death! whose looks can soon advise
E'en scornful youth, whilst priests their doctrine waste;
Yet mocks us too; for he does make us wise,
When by his coming our affairs are past.

O harmless Death! whom still the valiant brave,
The wise expect, the sorrowful invite,
And all the good embrace, who know the grave
A short dark passage to eternal light.

W. Davenant

LXXXVII

EVENING HYMN

THOU Whose nature cannot sleep,
  On my temples sentry keep!
Guard me 'gainst those watchful foes,
Whose eyes are open while mine close;
Let no dreams my head infest,
But such as Jacob's temples blest.
While I do rest, my soul advance;
Make me to sleep a holy trance,
That I may, my rest being wrought,
Awake into some holy thought;
And with as active vigour run
My course as doth the nimble sun.
Sleep is a death; Oh! make me try,
By sleeping, what it is to die:
And as gently lay my head'
On my grave, as now my bed.
Howe'er I rest, great GOD, let me
Awake again at last with Thee.
And thus assured, behold I lie
Securely, or to wake or die.

T. Browne

LXXXVIII

PSALM FOR CHRISTMAS DAY

FAIREST of morning lights appear,
  Thou blest and gaudy day [1],
On which was born our Saviour dear;
  Arise and come away!

This day prevents His day of doom;
  His mercy now is nigh;
The mighty GOD of Love is come,
  The Dayspring from on high!

Behold the great Creator makes
  Himself an house of clay,
A robe of Virgin-flesh He takes
  Which He will wear for aye.

Hark, hark, the wise Eternal Word
  Like a weak infant cries:
In form of servant is the Lord,
  And God in cradle lies.

This wonder struck the world amazed,
  It shook the starry frame;
Squadrons of Spirits stood and gazed,
  Then down in troops they came.

Glad Shepherds ran to view this sight;
  A quire of Angels sings;
And eastern Sages with delight
  Adore this King of kings.

Join then, all hearts that are not stone,
  And all our voices prove,
To celebrate this Holy One,
  The God of peace and love.

T. Pestel

¹ *gaudy day*, festival

LXXXIX

A PSALM FOR SUNDAY NIGHT

O SING the glories of our Lord;
  His grace and truth resound,
And His stupendous acts record,
  Whose mercies have no bound!

He made the all-informing light
  And hosts of Angels fair;
'Tis He with shadows clothes the night,
  He clouds or clears the air.

Those restless skies with stars enchased
  He on firm hinges set;
The wave-embracéd earth He placed
  His hanging cabinet.

We in His summer-sunshine stand,
  And by His favour grow;
We gather what His bounteous hand
  Is pleaséd to bestow.

When He contracts His brow, we mourn,
  And all our strength is vain;
To former dust in death we turn,
  Till He inspire again.

XC

THE WHITE ISLAND

IN this world, (the Isle of Dreams),
  While we sit by sorrow's streams,
Tears and terrors are our themes
          Reciting :

But when once from hence we fly,
More and more approaching nigh
Unto young Eternity
          Uniting :

In that whiter Island, where
Things are evermore sincere;
Candour [1] here, and lustre there
          Delighting :

There no monstrous fancies shall
Out of Hell an horror call,
To create (or cause at all)
          Affrighting.

There in calm and cooling sleep
We our eyes shall never steep;
But eternal watch shall keep,
          Attending [2]

Pleasures, such as shall pursue
Me immortalized, and you ;
And fresh joys, as never too
          Have ending.

                R. Herrick

[1] *candour*, whiteness   [2] *attending*, waiting for

XCI

DEATH

THOU bidst me come away,
  And I 'll no longer stay,
Than for to shed some tears
For faults of former years ;

And to repent some crimes,
Done in the present times:
And next, to take a bit
Of Bread, and Wine with it:
To d'on[1] my robes of love,
Fit for the place above;
To gird my loins about
With charity throughout;
And so to travel hence
With feet of innocence:—
These done, I 'll only cry
'GOD mercy'; and so die.

[1] *d'on*, so spelt for *do on*

XCII

ETERNITY

O YEARS! and Age! Farewell:
    Behold I go,
    Where I do know
Infinity to dwell.

And these mine eyes shall see
    All times, how they
    Are lost i' the Sea
Of vast Eternity.

Where never Moon shall sway
    The Stars; but she,
    And Night, shall be
Drown'd in one endless Day.

XCIII

GRACE FOR A CHILD

WHAT GOD gives, and what we take,
    'Tis a gift for Christ His sake:
Be the meal of beans and pease,
GOD be thank'd for those and these:
Have we flesh, or have we fish,
All are fragments from His dish.
He His Church save, and the King,
And our Peace here, like a Spring,
Make it ever flourishing.

XCIV

A THANKSGIVING TO GOD FOR HIS HOUSE

LORD, Thou hast given me a cell
    Wherein to dwell;
A little house, whose humble roof
    Is weather-proof;
Under the spars of which I lie
    Both soft, and dry;
Where Thou my chamber for to ward
    Hast set a Guard
Of harmless thoughts, to watch and keep
    Me, while I sleep.
Low is my porch, as is my Fate,
    Both void of state;
And yet the threshold of my door
    Is worn by the poor,
Who thither come, and freely get
    Good words, or meat:
Like as my Parlour, so my Hall
    And Kitchen's small:
A little Buttery, and therein
    A little Bin,
Which keeps my little loaf of Bread
    Unchipt, unflead [1]:
Some brittle sticks of thorn or briar
    Make me a fire,
Close by whose living coal I sit,
    And glow like it.
LORD, I confess too, when I dine,
    The Pulse is Thine,
And all those other bits, that be
    There placed by Thee;
The Worts, the Purslain, and the mess
    Of water-cress,
Which of Thy kindness Thou hast sent;
    And my content
Makes those, and my belovéd Beet,
    To be more sweet.
'Tis Thou that crown'st my glittering Hearth
    With guiltless mirth;
And giv'st me Wassail-bowls to drink,
    Spiced to the brink.
Lord, 'tis Thy plenty-dropping hand
    That soils [2] my land;
And giv'st me, for my bushel sown,
    Twice ten for one:

Thou mak'st my teeming Hen to lay
    Her egg each day:
Besides my healthful Ewes to bear
    Me twins each year:
The while the conduits of my Kine
    Run Cream, (for Wine.)
All these, and better, Thou dost send
    Me, to this end,
That I should render, for my part,
    A thankful heart;
Which, fired with incense, I resign,
    As wholly Thine;
But the acceptance,—that must be,
    My Christ, by Thee.

¹ *unflead*, may be, unmouldy, or, unchipped ² *soils*, manures

XCV

LITANY

IN the hour of my distress,
  When temptations me oppress,
And when I my sins confess,
    Sweet Spirit comfort me!

When I lie within my bed,
Sick in heart and sick in head,
And with doubts discomforted,
    Sweet Spirit comfort me!

When the house doth sigh and weep,
And the world is drown'd in sleep,
Yet mine eyes the watch do keep;
    Sweet Spirit comfort me!

When the artless Doctor sees
No one hope, but of his fees,
And his skill runs on the lees;
    Sweet Spirit comfort me!

When his potion and his pill
Has or none, or little skill,
Meet for nothing, but to kill;
    Sweet Spirit comfort me!

When the passing-bell doth toll,
And the Furies in a shoal
Come to fright a parting soul;
    Sweet Spirit comfort me!

When the tapers now burn blue,
And the comforters are few,
And that number more than true;
   Sweet Spirit comfort me!

When the Priest his last hath pray'd,
And I nod to what is said,
'Cause my speech is now decay'd;
   Sweet Spirit comfort me!

When (GOD knows) I'm toss'd about,
Either with despair, or doubt;
Yet before the glass be out,
   Sweet Spirit comfort me!

When the Tempter me pursu'th
With the sins of all my youth,
And half damns me with untruth;
   Sweet Spirit comfort me!

When the Judgment is reveal'd,
And that open'd which was seal'd,
When to Thee I have appeal'd;—
   Sweet Spirit comfort me!

XCVI

ON EASTER DAY

EACH thing below here hath its day,
 As in the Proverb's said;
And so it comes to pass that they [1]
 Conquer are Conqueréd.
For He who for man's fault assign'd
 Death, and a Grave's reward,
Was pleased those bands for to unbind,
 And so Himself not spared;
But issuing forth His heavenly throne,
 Vouchsafes the earth to bless,
And became here a little One,
 To make our crimes go less:
Not that our disobedience can
 In weight or measure shrink,
But that this Great Physicián
 Before us takes the drink,
That bitter potión we had
 Deserved to quaff; and thus
He weeps Himself, and becomes sad
 To purchase joy for us.

And more than so : for everyone
    Will for his friend lay down
Some spark of love : but He alone
    His enemies to crown
Refused not Death ; so deep from high
    His mercies did extend ;
And if you ask the reason why,
    'Twas mere for Mercy's end.
Yet that grim Death and mouldy Grave
    No longer be His prison
Than He Himself alone would have,
    He bides not there, but 's risen.
And if we would as Conquerors rise
    With Him who vanquish'd those,
We must not fear, where danger lies,
    For Him all to expose,
But though the grave do open stand
    And persecutions reign
At Hell's desire and Death's command,
    Look on our Sovereign.
His Banner doth present the Cross
    He bore, and bare Him too
For us ; and we must count it loss
    To fail what He did do.
Thus Sin and Hell, the Grave and Death,
    Must quit the field and fly,
Whilst, in contempt of borrow'd breath,
    We'd live Eternally.
—Thrice happy day, whereon the Sun
    Of Righteousness did rise,
And such a glorious conquest won,
    By being our Sacrifice !
And as unhappy he, that shall
    Not find the white[2] and best
Of Stones, to mark the same withal,
    And prize 't above the rest.

                    M. Lord Westmoreland

[1] *they* [who]   [2] *white,* put for *whitest*

XCVII

ON JUSTICE AND MERCY

JUSTICE doth call for vengeance on my sins,
    And threatens death as guerdon for the same ;
Mercy to plead for pardon then begins,
    With saying, CHRIST hath undergone the shame.

Justice shews me an angry GOD offended,
  And Mercy shews a Saviour crucified:
Justice says, I that sinn'd must be condemnéd:
  Mercy replies, CHRIST for my sins hath died.
Grim Justice threats with a revengeful rod:
Meek Mercy shews me an appeaséd GOD.
  LORD! though my sins make me for Justice fit,
  Through CHRIST let Mercy triumph over it.

Anon.

XCVIII

PEACE

I SOUGHT for Peace, but could not find;
  I sought it in the city,
But they were of another mind,—
    The more's the pity.
I sought for Peace of country swain,
  But yet I could not find;
So I, returning home again,
    Left Peace behind.
Sweet Peace, where dost thou dwell? said I;—
  Methought a voice was given,
'Peace dwelt not here, long since did fly
    To GOD in heaven.'
Thought I, this echo is but vain,
  To folly 'tis of kin;
Anon, I heard it tell me plain,
    'Twas kill'd by sin.
Then I believed the former voice,
  And rested well content;
Laid down and slept, rose, did rejoice,
    And then to Heaven went.
There I enquired for Peace, and found it true:—
An heavenly plant it was, and sweetly grew.

Anon.

XCIX

SONG OF THE EMIGRANTS IN BERMUDA

WHERE the remote Bermudas ride
  In the ocean's bosom unespied,
From a small boat that row'd along
The listening winds received this song:
'What should we do but sing His praise
That led us through the watery maze

Where He the huge sea-monsters wracks,
That lift the deep upon their backs,
Unto an isle so long unknown,
And yet far kinder than our own?
He lands us on a grassy stage,
Safe from the storms, and prelate's rage:
He gave us this eternal Spring
Which here enamels everything,
And sends the fowls to us in care
On daily visits through the air.
He hangs in shades the orange bright
Like golden lamps in a green night,
And does in the pomegranates close
Jewels more rich than Ormus shows:
He makes the figs our mouths to meet,
And throws the melons at our feet;
But apples plants of such a price,
No tree could ever bear them twice.
With cedars chosen by His hand
From Lebanon He stores the land;
And makes the hollow seas that roar
Proclaim the ambergris on shore.
He cast (of which we rather boast)
The Gospel's pearl upon our coast;
And in these rocks for us did frame
A temple where to sound His name.
O let our voice His praise exalt
Till it arrive at Heaven's vault,
Which thence (perhaps) rebounding, may
Echo beyond the Mexique bay!'
—Thus sung they in the English boat
A holy and a cheerful note:
And all the way, to guide their chime,
With falling oars they kept the time.

A. Marvell

C

THE CORONET

WHEN for the thorns with which I long, too long,
    With many a piercing wound,
      My Saviour's head have crown'd,
I seek with garlands to redress that wrong:
    Through every garden, every mead,
I gather flowers—(my fruits are only flowers),
    Dismantling all the fragrant towers [1]
That once adorn'd my shepherdesse's head:

And now, when I have summ'd up all my store,
    Thinking, (so I myself deceive),
    So rich a chaplet thence to weave
As never yet the King of Glory wore:
    Alas! I find the Serpent old,
    That, twining-in his speckled breast,
    About the flowers disguised, does fold
    With wreaths of fame and interest.
Ah, foolish man, that would'st debase with them,
And mortal glory, Heaven's diadem!
—But Thou Who only could'st the Serpent tame,
Either his slippery knots at once untie,
And disentangle all his winding snare;
Or shatter too, with him, my curious frame[2],
And let these wither—so that he may die—
Though set with skill, and chosen out with care:
That they, while Thou on both their spoils dost tread,
May crown Thy feet, that could not crown Thy head.

[1] *towers*, garlands to crown a girl   [2] *frame*, his own ingenious poetry

CI

To my most merciful, my most loving, and dearly-loved REDEEMER,
the ever-blessed, the only HOLY and JUST ONE,
JESUS CHRIST,
The Son of the living God, and the Sacred Virgin Mary.

DEAR LORD, 'tis finish'd! and now he
    That copied it, presents it Thee.
'Twas Thine first, and to Thee returns,
From Thee it shined, though here it burns.
If the sun rise on rocks, is 't right,
To call it their inherent light?
No, nor can I say, this is mine,—
For, dearest JESUS, 'tis all Thine,
As Thy clothes,—when Thou with clothes wert clad—
Both light from Thee, and virtue had;
And now—as then—within this place
Thou to poor rags dost still give grace.

My dear Redeemer, the world's light,
And life too, and my heart's delight!
For all Thy mercies and Thy truth,
Shew'd to me in my sinful youth,
For my sad failings and my wild
Murmurings at Thee, when most mild;

For all my secret faults, and each
Frequent relapse and wilful breach,
For all designs meant against Thee,
And every publish'd vanity
Which Thou divinely hast forgiven,
While Thy blood wash'd me white as Heaven,—
I nothing have to give to Thee,
But this Thy own gift, given to me.
Refuse it not! for now Thy token
Can tell Thee where a heart is broken.

                 H. Vaughan

CII

THE RETREAT

HAPPY those early days, when I
    Shined in my Angel-infancy!
Before I understood this place
Appointed for my second race,
Or taught my soul to fancy ought
But a white celestial thought;
When yet I had not walk'd above
A mile or two from my first Love,
And looking back—at that short space—
Could see a glimpse of His bright face :—
When on some gilded cloud, or flower,
My gazing soul would dwell an hour,
And in those weaker glories spy
Some shadows of eternity :—
Before I taught my tongue to wound
My Conscience with a sinful sound,
Or had the black art to dispense
A several sin to every sense,
But felt through all this fleshly dress
Bright shoots of everlastingness.

  O how I long to travel back,
And tread again that ancient track!
That I might once more reach that plain
Where first I left my glorious train[1];
From whence the enlighten'd spirit sees
That shady City of Palm-trees.
But ah! my soul with too much stay
Is drunk, and staggers in the way!
Some men a forward motion love,
But I by backward steps would move;
And when this dust falls to the urn,
In that state I came, return.

            [1] See Note

CIII

CHILDHOOD

I CANNOT reach it; and my striving eye
  Dazzles at it, as at eternity.
    Were now that Chronicle alive,
Those white[1] designs which children drive[2],
And the thoughts of each harmless hour,
With their content, too, in my power,
Quickly would I make my path even,
And by mere playing go to Heaven.

Dear, harmless age! the short, swift span
Where weeping Virtue parts with man;
Where love without lust dwells, and bends
What way we please without self-ends.

An age of mysteries! which he
Must live twice[3] that would God's face see;
Which angels guard, and with it play;—
Angels! which foul men drive away.

How do I study now, and scan
Thee more than e'er I studied man,
And only see through a long night
Thy edges and Thy bordering light!
O for Thy centre and mid-day!
For sure that is the narrow way.[4]

[1] *white*, innocent   [2] *drive*, pursue   [3] See S. John; iii, 3
[4] Apparently, O that I knew how to carry childhood through later life

CIV

O LET me climb
    When I lie down! The pious soul by night
Is like a clouded star, whose beams, though said
     To shed their light
     Under some cloud,
     Yet are above,
     And shine and move
    Beyond that misty shroud.
     So in my bed,
—That curtain'd grave,—though sleep, like ashes, hide
My lamp and life,—both shall in Thee abide.

CV

RULES AND LESSONS

WHEN first thy eyes unveil, give thy soul leave
  To do the like; our bodies but forerun
The spirit's duty. True hearts spread, and heave
Unto their GOD, as flowers do to the sun.
 Give Him thy first thoughts then; so shalt thou keep
 Him company all day, and in Him sleep.

Yet never sleep the sun up;—Prayer should
Dawn with the day. There are set, awful hours
'Twixt Heaven, and us. The manna was not good
After sun-rising; fair[1]-day sullies flowers.
 Rise to prevent the sun; sleep doth sins glut,
 And Heaven's gate opens, when this world's is shut.

Walk with thy fellow-creatures: note the hush
And whispers amongst them. There's not a spring,
Or leaf but hath his morning-hymn; Each bush
And oak doth know I AM. Canst thou not sing?
 O leave thy cares and follies! go this way,
 And thou art sure to prosper all the day.

To heighten thy devotions, and keep low
All mutinous thoughts, what business e'er thou hast,
Observe GOD in His works; here fountains flow,
Birds sing, beasts feed, fish leap, and th' earth stands fast;
 Above are restless motions, running lights,
 Vast circling azure, giddy clouds, days, nights.

When Seasons change, then lay before thine eyes
His wondrous method; mark the various scenes
In heaven; hail, thunder, rain-bows, snow, and ice,
Calms, tempests, light, and darkness, by His means;
 Thou canst not miss His praise; each tree, herb, flower
 Are shadows of His wisdom, and His power.

   [1] *fair*, in original text (1650), *far*

CVI

SON-DAYS[1]

BRIGHT shadows of true Rest! some shoots of bliss;
  Heaven once a week;
The next world's gladness prepossest in this;
  A day to seek;

Eternity in time; the steps by which
We climb above all ages; Lamps that light
Man through his heap of dark days; and the rich
And full redemption of the whole week's flight!

The pulleys[2] unto headlong man; Time's bower;
　　　　　The narrow way;
Transplanted Paradise; God's walking hour,
　　　　　The cool o' th' day:

The Creature's jubilee; God's parle with dust;
Heaven here; Man[3] on those hills of myrrh, and flowers;
Angels descending; the returns of trust;
A gleam of glory, after six-days-showers!

> [1] *Son-days*, so spelt here, probably only for *Sundays*
> [2] *pulleys*, ropes to restrain or guide　　　　　[3] See Note

CVII

THE FAVOUR

O THY bright looks! Thy glance of love
　　Shown, and but shown, me from above!
Rare looks! that can dispense such joy
As without wooing wins the coy,
And makes him mourn, and pine and die,
Like a starved eaglet for Thine eye.
Some kind herbs here, though low and far,
Watch for and know their loving star.
O let no star compare with Thee!
Nor any herb out-duty me!
So shall my nights and mornings be
Thy time to shine, and mine to see.

CVIII

THE BOOK

ETERNAL God! Maker of all
　　That have lived here since the Man's fall!
The Rock of Ages! in whose shade
They live unseen, when here they fade;

Thou knew'st this paper, when it was
Mere seed, and after that, but grass;
Before 'twas drest or spun; and when
Made linen, who did wear it then:
What were their lives, their thoughts and deeds,
Whether good corn, or fruitless weeds.

Thou knew'st this tree, when a green shade
Cover'd it, since a cover[1] made,
And where it flourish'd, grew, and spread,
As if it never should be dead.

Thou knew'st this harmless beast, when he
Did live and feed by Thy decree
On each green thing; then slept, well-fed—
Clothed with this skin, which now lies spread
A covering o'er this aged book,
Which makes me wisely weep, and look
On my own dust; mere dust it is,
But not so dry and clean as this.
Thou knew'st and saw'st them all, and though
Now scatter'd thus, dost know them so.

O knowing, glorious Spirit! when
Thou shalt restore trees, beasts and men,
When Thou shalt make all new again,
Destroying only death and pain,
Give him amongst Thy works a place,
Who in them loved and sought Thy face!

[1] *cover*, literal *boards*

CIX

TO THE HOLY BIBLE

O BOOK! Life's guide! how shall we part,
　　And thou so long seized[1] of my heart?
Take this last kiss; and let me weep
True thanks to thee before I sleep.

Thou wert the first put in my hand
When yet I could not understand,
And daily didst my young eyes lead
To letters, till I learnt to read.
But as rash youths, when once grown strong,
Fly from their nurses to the throng,
Where they new consorts choose, and stick
To those till either hurt or sick;
So with that first light gain'd from thee
Ran I in chase of vanity,
Cried[2] dross for gold, and never thought
My first cheap book[3] had all I sought.
Long reign'd this vogue; and thou, cast by,
With meek, dumb looks didst woo mine eye,

And oft left open, would'st convey
A sudden and most searching ray
Into my soul, with whose quick touch
Refining still[3], I struggled much.
By this mild art of love at length
Thou overcam'st my sinful strength,
And having brought me home, didst there
Shew me that pearl I sought elsewhere,—
Gladness, and peace, and hope, and love,
The secret favours of the Dove[4];
Her quickening kindness, smiles and kisses,
Exalted pleasures, crowning blisses,
Fruition, union, glory, life,
Thou didst lead to, and still all strife.
Living, thou wert my soul's sure ease,
And dying mak'st me go in peace:—
Thy next effects no tongue can tell;
Farewell, O book of GOD! farewell!

[1] *seized*, legal term for *possessed of* [2] *cried*, cried up
[3] See Note [4] *the Dove*, the Holy Spirit

CX

RIGHTEOUSNESS

FAIR, solitary path! whose blessèd shades
 The old, white prophets planted first and drest;
Leaving for us—whose goodness quickly fades,—
 A shelter all the way, and bowers to rest;

Who is the man that walks in thee? who loves
 Heaven's secret solitude, those fair abodes,
Where turtles build, and careless sparrows move,
 Without to-morrow's evils and future loads?

Who hath the upright heart, the single eye,
 The clean, pure hand, which never meddled pitch?
Who sees invisibles, and doth comply[1]
 With hidden treasures that make truly rich?

He that doth seek and love
The things above,
Whose spirit ever poor, is meek and low;
Who simple still and wise,
Still homewards flies,
Quick to advance, and to retreat most slow.

Whose acts, words, and pretence,
Have all one sense,
One aim and end; who walks not by his sight;
Whose eyes are both put out,
And goes about
Guided by faith, not by exterior light.

Who spills no blood, nor spreads
Thorns in the beds
Of the distrest, hasting their overthrow;
Making the time they had
Bitter and sad,
Like chronic pains[2], which surely kill, though slow.

Who knows Earth nothing hath
Worth love or wrath,
But in his Hope and Rock is ever glad:
Who seeks and follows peace,
When with the ease
And health of conscience it is to be had.

Who bears his cross with joy,
And doth employ
His heart and tongue in prayers for his foes;
Who lends, not to be paid,—
And gives full aid
Without that bribe which usurers impose.

Who never looks on[3] Man
Fearful and wan,
But firmly trusts in GOD; The great man's measure,
Though high and haughty, must
Be ta'en in dust;
But the good man is GOD's peculiar treasure.

—Who doth thus, and doth not
These good deeds blot
With bad, or with neglect; and heaps not wrath
By secret filth, nor feeds
Some snake, or weeds,
Cheating himself;—That man walks in this path.

---

[1] *comply*, accord with   [2] Misprinted *prayers* (Grosart)
[3] *looks on*, regards

CXI

ANGUISH

MY God and King! to Thee
    I bow my knee;
I bow my troubled soul, and greet
With my foul heart Thy holy feet.
Cast it[1], or tread it! it shall do
Ev'n what Thou wilt, and praise Thee too.

    My God, could I weep blood,
        Gladly I would;
Or if Thou wilt give me that art,
Which through the eyes pours out the heart,
I will exhaust it all, and make
Myself all tears, a weeping lake.

    O! 'tis an easy thing
        To write and sing;
But to write true, unfeignéd verse
Is very hard! O God, disperse
These weights, and give my spirit leave
To act as well as to conceive!

    O my God, hear my cry;
        Or let me die!

[1] *cast it*, [away]

CXII

THE AGREEMENT

O GOD! I know and do confess
    My sins are great and still prevail:
Most heinous sins and numberless!
    But Thy compassions cannot fail:—
        If Thy sure mercies can be broken,
        Then all is true my foes have spoken.

But while Time runs, and after it
    Eternity, which never ends,
Quite through them both, still infinite,
    Thy Covenant by CHRIST extends;
        No sins of frailty, nor of youth,
        Can foil His merits, and Thy truth.

Wherefore with tears—tears by Thee sent—
  I beg my faith may never fail!
And when in death my speech is spent,
  O let that silence then prevail!
    O chase in that cold calm my foes,
    And hear my heart's last private throes!

CXIII

THE REVIVAL

UNFOLD! unfold! Take in His light,
  Who makes thy cares more short than night.
The joys which with His day-star rise
He deals to all but drowsy eyes;
And, what the men of this world miss,
Some drops and dews of future bliss.

  Hark! how the winds have changed their note!
And with warm whispers call thee out;
The frosts are past, the storms are gone,
And backward life at last comes on.
The lofty groves in express joys
Reply unto the turtle's voice;
And here in dust and dirt, O here
The lilies of His love appear!

CXIV

THE WREATH

SINCE I in storms used most to be,
  And seldom yielded flowers,
    How shall I get a wreath for Thee
From those rude, barren hours?
The softer dressings of the Spring,
  Or Summer's later store,
I will not for Thy temples bring,
  Which thorns, not roses, wore.

But a twined wreath of grief and praise,
Praise soil'd with tears, and tears again
Shining with joy, like dewy days,
This day I bring for all Thy pain;
Thy causeless pain! and, sad as death,
Which sadness breeds in the most vain,

—O not in vain—now beg Thy breath,
Thy quickening breath, which gladly bears
Through saddest clouds to that glad place,
Where cloudless quires sing without tears,
Sing Thy just praise, and see Thy face.

CXV

THE ECLIPSE

WHITHER, O whither didst thou fly!
    When did I grieve Thine holy eye,
When Thou didst mourn to see me lost,
And all Thy care and counsels crost?
O do not grieve, where'er Thou art!
Thy grief is an undoing smart,
Which doth not only pain, but break
My heart, and makes me blush to speak.
Thy anger I could kiss, and will;
But—O—Thy grief, Thy grief, doth kill!

CXVI

THE MEN OF WAR [1]

'IF any have an ear'
    Saith holy John, 'then let him hear!
He, that into captivity
Leads others, shall a captive be.
Who with the sword doth others kill,
A sword shall his blood likewise spill.
Here is the patience of the saints,
And the true faith, which never faints.'

For in this bright, instructing verse
Thy saints are not the conquerers,
But patient, meek, and overcome
Like Thee, when set at nought and dumb.
Armies Thou hast in Heaven, which fight
And follow Thee, all clothed in white;
But here on Earth—though Thou hadst need—
Thou wouldst no legions, but wouldst bleed.
The sword wherewith Thou dost command
Is in Thy mouth, not in Thy hand;
And all Thy saints do overcome
By Thy blood, and their martyrdom.

But seeing soldiers long ago
Did spit on Thee, and smote Thee too ;
Crown'd Thee with thorns, and bow'd the knee,
But[2] in contempt, as still we see,
I 'll marvel not at aught they do,
Because they used my Saviour so ;
Since of my LORD they had their will,
Thy servant must not take it ill.

Dear JESUS, give me patience here,
And faith to see my crown as near,
And almost reach'd, because 'tis sure
If I hold fast, and slight the lure.
Give me humility and peace,
Contented thoughts, innoxious ease,
A sweet, revengeless, quiet mind,
And to my greatest haters, kind.
Give me, my GOD! a heart as mild
And plain, as when I was a child.
That when Thy throne is set, and all
These conquerors before it fall,
I may be found—preserved by Thee—
Amongst that chosen company,
Who by no blood—here—overcame,
But the blood of the Blesséd Lamb.

[1] See Note   [2] *but*, only

CXVII

PEACE

MY soul, there is a country
   Far beyond the stars,
Where stands a wingéd sentry
   All skilful in the wars :
There above noise, and danger,
   Sweet Peace sits crown'd with smiles,
And One born in a manger
   Commands the beauteous files[1].
He is thy gracious Friend,
   And—O my soul awake !—
Did in pure love descend,
   To die here for thy sake.
If thou canst get but thither,
   There grows the flower of Peace,
The Rose that cannot wither,
   Thy fortress, and thy ease.

Leave then thy foolish ranges,
    For none can thee secure,
But One, Who never changes,
    Thy GOD, thy life, thy cure.

[1] *files*, of the heavenly host

CXVIII

CREATION WAITING FOR REVELATION[1]

AND do they so? have they a sense
    Of aught but influence?
Can they their heads lift, and expect,
And groan too? why the Elect
    Can do no more; my volumes said
      They were all dull, and dead;
They judged them senseless, and their state
    Wholly inanimate.
      Go, go; Seal up thy looks,
        And burn thy books!

Sometimes I sit with Thee, and tarry
    An hour or so, then vary.
Thy other creatures in this scene
    Thee only aim, and mean;
Some rise to seek Thee, and with heads
    Erect, peep from their beds;
Others, whose birth[2] is in the tomb,
    And cannot quit the womb,
      Sigh there, and groan for Thee,
        Their liberty.

I would I were a stone, or tree,
    Or flower by pedigree,
Or some poor highway herb, or spring
    To flow, or bird to sing!
Then should I—tied to one sure state—
    All day expect my date[3];
But I am sadly loose, and stray
    A giddy blast each way;
      O let me not thus range!
        Thou canst not change.

[1] See Note   [2] *others, whose birth*, perhaps, gems, or crystals
[3] *date*, end of life

CXIX

RETIREMENT

FRESH fields and woods! the Earth's fair face!
   God's footstool! and man's dwelling-place!
I ask not why the first believer [1]
Did love to be a country liver?
Who to secure pious content
Did pitch by groves and wells his tent;
Where he might view his boundless sky,
And all those glorious lights on high:
With flying meteors, mists, and showers:
Subjected hills, trees, meads, and flowers:
And every minute bless the King
And wise Creator of each thing.

  I ask not why he did remove
To happy Mamre's holy grove,
Leaving the cities of the plain
To Lot and his successless train?
All various lusts in cities still
Are found; they are the thrones of ill;
The dismal sinks, where blood is spill'd,
Cages with much uncleanness fill'd:
But rural shades are the sweet sense [2]
Of piety and innocence;
They are the meek's calm region, where
Angels descend, and rule the sphere;
Where Heaven lies leiguer [3], and the Dove
Duly as dew comes from above.
If Eden be on Earth at all,
'Tis that which we the country call.

[1] Abraham   [2] May probably be *fence*
[3] *leiguer*, (for *lieger*), at rest; or (by confusion with *leaguer*), encamped

CXX

THE WATER-FALL

WITH what deep murmurs, through Time's silent stealth,
  Dost thy transparent, cool, and watery wealth
    Here flowing fall,
    And chide [1] and call,
As if his liquid, loose retinue [2] stay'd
Lingering, and were of this steep place afraid;—
    The common pass,
    As clear as glass,

All must descend
Not to an end,
But quicken'd by this deep and rocky grave,
Rise to a longer course, more bright and brave.

Dear stream! dear bank! where often I
Have sate, and pleased my pensive eye;
Why, since each drop of thy quick store
Runs thither where it flow'd before,
Should poor souls fear a shade or night,
Who came—sure—from a sea of light?
Or, since those drops are all sent back
So sure to thee that none doth lack,
Why should frail flesh doubt any more
That what God takes He'll not restore?

O useful element and clear!
My sacred wash and cleanser here;
My first consigner[3] unto those
Fountains of life, where the Lamb goes!
What sublime truths and wholesome themes
Lodge in thy mystical, deep streams!
Such as dull man can never find,
Unless that Spirit lead his mind,
Which first upon thy face did move
And hatch'd all with His quickening love.
As this loud brook's incessant fall
In streaming rings restagnates all,
Which reach by course the bank, and then
Are no more seen: just so pass men.
—O my invisible estate,
My glorious liberty, still late!
Thou art the channel my soul seeks,
Not this[4] with cataracts and creeks.

[1] *chide*, make a ringing sound   [2] *retinue*, the waters regarded as the Stream's troop or following   [3] *consigner*, in Baptism   [4] *Not this . . .* I look for the passage into heavenly freedom, not to glide down like the stream

CXXI

I WALK'D the other day, (to spend my hour),
     Into a field,
Where I sometimes had seen the soil to yield
     A gallant flower;
But Winter now had ruffled all the bower
     And curious store,
     I knew there heretofore,

Yet I, whose search loved not to peep and peer
    I' th' face of things,
Thought with myself, there might be other springs
    Besides this here,
Which, like cold friends, sees us but once a year;
    And so the flower
Might have some other bower.

Then taking up what I could nearest spy,
    I digg'd about
That place where I had seen him to grow out;
    And by and by
I saw the warm Recluse alone to lie,
    Where fresh and green
He lived of us unseen.

Many a question intricate and rare
    Did I there strow[1];
But all I could extort was, that he now
    Did there repair
Such losses as befell him in this air,
    And would ere long
Come forth most fair and young.

This past, I threw the clothes quite o'er his head;
    And stung with fear
Of my own frailty, dropp'd down many a tear
    Upon his bed;
Then sighing whisper'd 'Happy are the dead!
    What peace doth now
Rock him asleep below!'

And yet, how few believe such doctrine springs
    From a poor root,
Which all the Winter sleeps here underfoot,
    And hath no wings
To raise it to the truth and light of things;
    But is still trod
By every wandering clod[2].

—O Thou! Whose Spirit did at first inflame
    And warm the dead,
And by a sacred incubation, fed
    With life this frame,
Which once had neither being, form, nor name;
    Grant I may so
Thy steps track here below,

That in these Masques and shadows, I may see
    Thy sacred way;
And by those hid ascents climb to that day,
    Which breaks from Thee,
Who art in all things, though invisibly:—
    Shew me Thy peace,
    Thy mercy, love, and ease.

  [1] *strow*, put   [2] *clod*, countryman

CXXII

THE TIMBER

SURE thou didst flourish once! and many springs,
  Many bright mornings, much dew, many showers
Past o'er thy head; many light hearts and wings,
  Which now are dead, lodged in thy living bowers.

And still a new succession sings and flies;
  Fresh groves grow up, and their green branches shoot
Towards the old and still enduring skies,
  While the low violet thrives at their root.

But thou beneath the sad and heavy line
  Of death, doth waste all senseless, cold and dark;
Where not so much as dreams of light may shine,
  Nor any thought of greenness, leaf, or bark.

And yet—as if some deep hate and dissent,
  Bred in thy growth betwixt high winds and thee,
Were still alive—thou dost great storms resent[1]
  Before they come, and know'st how near they be.

Else all at rest thou liest, and the fierce breath
  Of tempests can no more disturb thy ease;
But this thy strange resentment after death
  Means only those who broke,—in life,—thy peace.

So murder'd man, when lovely life is done,
  And his blood freezed, keeps in the centre still
Some secret sense, which makes the dead blood run
  At his approach that did the body kill.

—And is there any murderer worse than sin?
  Or any storms more foul than a lewd life?
Or what resentient[2] can work more within,
  Than true remorse, when with past sins at strife?

  [1] *storms resent*, apparently means that the trunk groans or twists
      [2] *resentient*, sympathetic feeling

CXXIII

THE BIRD

HITHER thou com'st: the busy wind all night
  Blew through thy lodging, where thy own warm wing
Thy pillow was. Many a sullen storm
  —For which coarse man seems much the fitter born—
      Rain'd on thy bed
      And harmless head :—

And now as fresh and cheerful as the light
Thy little heart in early hymns doth sing
Unto that Providence, Whose unseen arm
  Curb'd them, and clothed thee well and warm.
        All things that be, praise Him; and had
        Their lesson taught them when first made.

So hills and valleys into singing break;
And though poor stones have neither speech nor tongue,
While active winds and streams both run and speak,
Yet stones are deep in admiration.
Thus praise and prayer here beneath the sun
Make lesser mornings, when the great are done.

CXXIV

THE SHOWER

'TWAS so; I saw thy birth :—That drowsy lake
    From her faint bosom breathed thee, the disease[1]
Of her sick waters, and infectious ease.
        But, now at even,
        Too gross for heaven,
Thou fall'st in tears, and weep'st for thy mistake.

Ah! it is so with me: oft have I prest
Heaven with a lazy breath; but fruitless this
Pierced not; Love only can with quick access
        Unlock the way;
        When all else stray,
The smoke and exhalations of the breast.

Yet, if as thou dost melt, and with thy train
Of drops make soft the Earth, my eyes could weep
O'er my hard heart, that's bound-up and asleep;
        Perhaps at last,
        —Some such showers past—
My God would give a Sun-shine after rain.

¹ The shower is here regarded as a stagnant and a lazy exhalation

CXXV

THE NIGHT

THROUGH that pure virgin shrine,
    That sacred veil drawn o'er Thy glorious noon,
That men might look and live, as glow-worms shine
      And face the moon :
  Wise Nicodemus saw such light
  As made him know his GOD by night.

    No mercy-seat of gold,
No dead and dusty cherub, nor carved stone,
But His own living works did my LORD hold
      And lodge alone ;
  Where trees and herbs did watch and peep
  And wonder, while the Jews did sleep.

    Dear Night! this world's defeat;
The stop to busy fools ; Care's check and curb;
The day of Spirits ; my soul's calm retreat
      Which none disturb!
  CHRIST's progress [1], and His prayer time ;
  The hours to which high Heaven doth chime.

    There is in GOD—some say—
A deep, but dazzling darkness ; as men here
Say it is late and dusky, because they
      See not all clear.
  O for that Night! where I in Him
  Might live invisible and dim!

        [1] See S. Mark i. 35 ; S. Luke xxi. 37

CXXVI

THE SHEPHERDS

SWEET, harmless lives!—[up]on whose holy leisure
    Waits Innocence and pleasure—
Whose leaders to those pastures and clear springs
  Were Patriarchs, Saints, and Kings :
How happen'd it that in the dead of night
  You, only, saw true light,
While Palestine was fast asleep, and lay
  Without one thought of Day?
Was it because those first and blesséd swains
  Were pilgrims on those plains

When they received the Promise, for which now
  'Twas there first shown to you?
'Tis true He loves that dust whereon they go
  That serve Him here below,
And therefore might, for memory of those,
  His love there first disclose;
But wretched Salem, once His love, must now
  No voice nor vision know:—
Her stately piles with all their height and pride,
  Now languishéd and died,
And Bethlem's humble cots above them stept,
  While all her seërs slept;
Her cedar, fir, hew'd stones and gold, were all
  Polluted through their fall,
And those once sacred mansions were now
  Mere emptiness and show.
This made the Angel call at reeds and thatch:—
  Yet where the shepherds watch,
And God's own lodging—though He could not lack—
  To be a common rack [1],
No costly pride, no soft-clothed luxury
  In those thin cells could lie;
Each stirring wind and storm blew through their cots,
  Which never harbour'd plots;
Only Content and Love and humble joys
  Lived there without all noise;
Perhaps some harmless cares for the next day
  Did in their bosoms play,
As where to lead their sheep, what silent nook,
  What springs or shades to look:
But that 'was all; And now with gladsome care
  They for the town prepare;
They leave their flock, and in a busy talk
  All towards Bethlem walk
To see their souls' great Shepherd, Who was come
  To bring all stragglers home;
Where now they find Him out, and, taught before,
  That Lamb of God adore,—
That Lamb Whose days great kings and 'prophets wish'd
  And long'd to see, but miss'd.
The first light they beheld was bright and gay,
  And turn'd their night to day;—
But to this later light they saw in Him,
  Their day was dark and dim.

[1] rack, manger: see Note

CXXVII

THE NATIVITY

THOU cam'st from Heaven to Earth, that we
    Might go from Earth to Heaven with Thee :
And though Thou found'st no welcome here,
Thou didst provide us mansions there.
A stable was Thy Court, and when
Men turn'd to beasts, beasts would be men :
They were Thy courtiers ; others none ;
And their poor manger was Thy throne.
No swaddling silks Thy limbs did fold,
Though Thou couldst turn Thy rags to gold.
No rockers waited on Thy birth,
No cradles stirr'd, nor songs of mirth ;
But Her chaste lap and sacred breast,
Which lodged Thee first, did give Thee rest.

CXXVIII

THE KNOT

BRIGHT Queen of Heaven ! God's Virgin Spouse !
    The glad world's blesséd Maid !
Whose beauty tied life to thy house [1],
    And brought us saving aid ;

Thou art the true Love's-Knot ; by thee
    God is made our ally ;
And man's inferior essence He
    With His did dignify.

For coalescent by that band
    We are His body grown,
Nourish'd with favours from His hand,
    Whom for our Head we own.

And such a knot, what arm dares loose,
    What life, what death can sever ?
Which us in Him, and Him in us,
    United keeps for ever.

[1] Apparently, whose beauty of soul caused the Life of mankind to dwell
in thee.

CXXIX

S. MARY MAGDALENE

DEAR, beauteous Saint! more white than Day,
    When in his naked, pure array;
Fresher than morning-flowers, which shew
As thou in tears dost, best in dew.
How art thou changed! how lively-fair,
Pleasing, and innocent an air,
Not tutor'd by thy glass, but free,
Native and pure, shines now in thee!
But since thy beauty doth still keep
Bloomy and fresh, why dost thou weep?
This dusky state of sighs and tears
Durst not look on those smiling years,
When Magdal-castle[1] was thy seat,
Where all was sumptuous, rare and neat.
Why lies this hair despiséd now
Which once thy care and art did show?
Who then did dress the much-loved toy,
In spires, globes, angry[2] curls and coy,
Which with skill'd negligence seem'd shed
About thy curious, wild, young head?
Why is this rich, this pistic[3] nard
Spilt, and the box quite broke and marr'd?
What pretty sullenness did haste
Thy easy hands to do this waste?
Why art thou humbled thus, and low
As earth thy lovely head dost bow?
Dear soul! thou knew'st flowers here on Earth
At their Lord's foot-stool have their birth;
Therefore thy wither'd self in haste
Beneath His blest feet thou didst cast,
That at the root of this green tree
Thy great decays restored might be.
Thy curious vanities and rare
Odorous ointments, kept with care
And dearly bought,—when thou didst see
They could not cure nor comfort thee—
Like a wise, early penitent,
Thou sadly didst to Him present,
Whose interceding, meek, and calm
Blood, is the world's all-healing balm.
This, this Divine Restorative
Call'd forth thy tears, which ran in live
And hasty drops, as if they had
—Their Lord so near—sense to be glad.

Learn, ladies, here the faithful cure
Makes [4] beauty lasting, fresh and pure;
Learn Mary's art of tears, and then
Say, you have got the day from men.
Cheap, mighty art! Her art of love,
Who loved much, and much more could move;
Her art! whose memory must last
Till truth through all the world be past;
Till His abused, despisèd flame [5]
Return to Heaven, from whence it came,
And send a fire down, that shall bring
Destruction on his ruddy wing.

Her art! whose pensive, weeping eyes,
Were once sin's loose and tempting spies;
But now are fixèd stars, whose light
Helps such dark stragglers to their sight.
Self-boasting Pharisee! how blind
A judge wert thou, and how unkind!
It was impossible, that thou,
Who wert all false, should'st true grief know.
Is 't just to judge her faithful tears
By that foul rheum thy false eye wears?

This woman—say'st thou—is a sinner:
And sate there none such at thy dinner?
Go, leper, go! wash till thy flesh
Comes like a child's, spotless and fresh;
He is still leprous that still paints:
Who saint themselves, they are no saints.

[1] See Note   [2] *angry*, defiant   [3] *pistic*, pure   [4] [which] *makes*
[5] *flame*, of Love

CXXX

THE ORNAMENT

THE lucky World shew'd me one day
     Her gorgeous mart and glittering store,
Where with proud haste the rich made way
     To buy, the poor came to adore.

Serious they seem'd, and bought up all
     The latest modes of pride and lust;
Although the first must surely fall,
     And the last is most loathsome dust.

But while each gay, alluring ware
　　With idle hearts and busy looks
They view'd,—for Idleness hath there
　　Laid up all her archives and books,—

Quite through their proud and pompous file,
　　Blushing, and in meek weeds array'd,
With native looks which knew no guile,
　　Came the sheep-keeping Syrian Maid[1].

Whom straight the shining row all faced,
　　Forced[2] by her artless looks and dress;
While one cried out, We are disgraced!
　　For She is bravest, you confess!

[1] *Syrian Maid*, the Church, under figure of Rachel　　　[2] *forced*, compelled

CXXXI

THE WORLD

I SAW Eternity the other night,
　　Like a great ring of pure and endless light,
　　　　All calm, as it was bright;
And round beneath it, Time, in hours, days, years,
　　　　Driven by the spheres,
Like a vast shadow moved; In which the world
　　　　And all her train were hurl'd.

The doting Lover in his quaintest strain
　　　　Did there complain;
Near him, his lute, his fancy, and his slights[1],
　　　　Wit's sour[2] delights;
With gloves and knots[3], the silly snares of pleasure;
　　　　Yet his dear treasure
All scatter'd lay, while he his eyes did pour
　　　　Upon a flower.

The darksome Statesman[4] hung with weights and woe,
Like a thick midnight-fog, moved there so slow,
　　　　He did not stay, nor go;
Condemning thoughts—like sad eclipses—scowl
　　　　Upon his soul,
And clouds of crying witnesses without
　　　　Pursued him with one shout;
Yet digg'd the mole, and lest his ways be found,
　　　　Work'd under ground,

Where he did clutch his prey; but One did see
  That policy;
Churches and altars fed him; perjuries
  Were gnats and flies;
It rain'd about him blood and tears, but he
  Drank them as free.

The fearful Miser on a heap of rust
Sate pining all his life there; did scarce trust
  His own hands with the dust;
Yet would not place one piece above, but lives
  In fear of thieves:
Thousands there were as frantic as himself,
  And hugg'd each one his pelf.
The down-right Epicure placed heaven in sense,
  And scorn'd pretence;
While others, slipt into a wide excess,
  Said little less;
The weaker sort, slight, trivial wares enslave,
  Who think them brave[3];
And poor, despiséd Truth sat counting by
  Their victory.

Yet some, who all this while did weep and sing,
And sing, and weep, soar'd up into the ring;
  But most would use no wing.
O fools—said I—thus to prefer dark night
  Before true light!
To live in grots, and caves, and hate the day
  Because it shews the way:—
The way, which from this dead and dark abode
  Leads up to God;
A way where you might tread the Sun, and be
  More bright than he!
But as I did their madness so discuss,
  One whisper'd thus,—
This ring the Bride-groom did for none provide,
  But for His Bride.

---

[1] *slights*, sleights, tricks [2] *sour*, perhaps, unsatisfying [3] *knots*, ribbons
[4] *the Statesman*, Pym's career, with O. Cromwell's by poetic insight, is here
(1650) unquestionably photographed [5] *brave*, magnificent

CXXXII

MAN

WEIGHING the steadfastness and state
    ·Of some mean things which here below reside,
Where birds, like watchful clocks, the noiseless date
    And intercourse of times divide;
Where bees at night 'get home and hive; and flowers,
        Early as well as late,
Rise with the sun, and set in the same bowers;—

    I would (said I) my GOD would give
The staidness of these things to Man! For these
To His divine appointments ever cleave,
    And no new business breaks their peace;
The birds nor sow nor reap, yet sup and dine;
        The flowers without clothes live;
Yet Solomon was never drest so fine.

    Man hath still either toys, or care;
He hath no root, nor to one place is tied,
But ever restless and irregular
    About this Earth doth run and ride.
He knows he hath a home, but scarce knows where;
        He says it is so far[1],
That he hath quite forgot how to go[1] there.

    He knocks at all doors, strays and roams,
Nay hath not so much wit as some stones[2] have,
Which in the darkest nights point to their homes,
    By some hid sense their Maker gave;
Man is the shuttle, to whose winding quest
        And passage[1] through these looms
GOD order'd motion, but ordain'd no rest.

[1] *far—how to go—passage*, misprinted *for—height—pastage* (1650)   [2] *some stones*, the magnet

CXXXIII

THE WORLD

THOU art not Truth! for he that tries
    Shall find thee all deceit and lies.
Thou art not Friendship! for in thee
'Tis but the bait of policy,
Which, like a viper lodged in flowers,
Its venom through that sweetness pours;

And when not so, then always 'tis
A fading paint, the short-lived bliss
Of air and humour[1]; out and in,
Like colours in a dolphin's skin:
But must not live beyond one day,
Or for convenience; then away.
  Thou art not Riches! for that trash,
Which one age hoards, the next doth wash
And so severely sweep away
That few remember where it lay.
So, rapid streams the wealthy land
About them have at their command;
And shifting channels here restore,
There break down, what they bank'd before.
  Thou art not Honour! for those gay
Feathers will wear and drop away;
And princes to some upstart line
Give new ones, that are full as fine.
  Thou art not Pleasure! for thy rose
Upon a thorn doth still repose;
Which, if not cropt, will quickly shed,
But soon as cropt, grows dull and dead.
  Thou art the sand, which fills one glass,
And then doth to another pass;
And could I put thee to a stay,
Thou art but dust! Then go thy way,
And leave me clean and bright, though poor:
Who stops thee doth but daub his floor;
And, swallow-like, when he hath done,
To unknown dwellings must be gone!

  Welcome, pure thoughts, and peaceful hours,
Enrich'd with sunshine and with showers;
Welcome fair hopes, and holy cares,
The not to be repented shares
Of Time and business: the sure road
Unto my last and loved abode!
    O supreme Bliss:
The Circle, Centre, and Abyss
Of blessings, never let me miss
Nor leave that path, which leads to Thee,
Who art alone all things to me!
I hear, I see, all the long day
The noise and pomp of the Broad Way:
I note their coarse and proud approaches,
Their silks, perfumes, and glittering coaches.
But in the Narrow Way to Thee
I observe only poverty,

And despised things; and all along
The ragged, mean, and humble throng
Are still on foot; and as they go
They sigh, and say, their LORD went so.

[1] *humour*, moisture

CXXXIV

AN ELEGY

THOU that know'st for whom I mourn,
　And why these tears appear,
That keep'st account till he return
　Of all his dust left here;
As easily Thou might'st prevent
　As now produce, these tears,
And add unto that day he went
　A fair supply of years.
But 'twas my sin that forced Thy hand
　To cull this primrose out,
That by Thy early choice forewarn'd
　My soul might look about.

O what a vanity is Man!
　How like the eye's quick wink
His cottage fails; whose narrow span
　Begins e'en at the brink!
Nine months Thy hands are fashioning us,
　And many years—alas!—
Ere we can lisp, or aught discuss
　Concerning Thee, must pass;
Yet have I known Thy slightest things,
　A feather, or a shell,
A stick, or rod, which some chance brings,
　The best of us excel;—
Yea, I have known these shreds outlast
　A fair compacted frame,
And for one twenty we have past[1]
　Almost outlive our name.
Yet had our pilgrimage been free,
　And smooth without a thorn,
Pleasures had foil'd[2] Eternity,
　And tares had choked the corn.
Thus by the Cross Salvation runs;
　Affliction is a mother,
Whose painful throes yield many sons,
　Each fairer than the other.

A silent tear can pierce Thy throne,
 When loud joys want a wing;
And sweeter airs stream from a groan,
 Than any arted[3] string.

Thus, LORD, I see my gain is great,
 My loss but little to it;
Yet something more I must entreat,
 And only Thou canst do it.
O let me—like him—know my end!
 And be as glad to find it:
And whatsoe'er Thou shalt commend
 Still let Thy servant mind it!
Then make my soul white as his own,
 My faith as pure and steady,
And deck me, LORD, with the same crown
 That has crown'd him already!

[1] See Note   [2] Or, *soil'd*: the first letter dubious
  [3] *arted*, played on skilfully

CXXXV

FRIENDS DEPARTED

THEY are all gone into the world of light!
 And I alone sit lingering here;
Their very memory is fair and bright,
 And my sad thoughts doth clear.

It glows and glitters in my cloudy breast,
 Like stars upon some gloomy grove,
Or those faint beams in which this hill is drest
 After the sun's remove.

I see them walking in an air of glory,
 Whose light doth trample[1] on my days:
My days, which are at best but dull and hoary,
 Mere glimmering and decays.

O holy Hope! and high Humility,
 High as the heavens above!
These are your walks, and you have shew'd them me,
 To kindle my cold love.

Dear, beauteous Death! the jewel of the Just,
 Shining no where, but in the dark;
What mysteries do lie beyond thy dust;
 Could man outlook that mark!

He that hath found some fledged bird's nest, may know
    At first sight, if the bird be flown;
But what fair well[2] or grove he sings in now,
    That is to him unknown.

And yet as Angels in some brighter dreams
    Call to the soul, when man doth sleep:
So some strange thoughts transcend our wonted themes,
    And into glory peep.

If a star were confined into a tomb,
    Her captive flames must needs burn there;
But when the hand that lock'd her up, gives room,
    She 'll shine through all the sphere.

O Father of eternal life, and all
    Created glories under Thee!
Resume Thy spirit[3] from this world of thrall
    Into true liberty.

Either disperse these mists, which blot and fill
    My perspective—still—as they pass:
Or else remove me hence unto that hill,
    Where I shall need no glass.

---

[1] *trample*, tread on and efface   [2] *well*, spring-head   [3] *Thy spirit*, unless a misprint for *my*, may mean, the Soul Thou hast placed here

CXXXVI

THE DAWNING

AH! what time wilt Thou come? when shall that cry,
    The Bridegroom 's coming! fill the sky?
Shall it in the evening run
When our words and works are done?
Or will Thy all-surprizing light
    Break at midnight,
When either sleep, or some dark pleasure
Possesseth mad Man without measure?
Or shall these early, fragrant hours
    Unlock Thy bowers?
And with their blush of light descry
Thy locks crown'd with eternity!
Indeed, it is the only time
That with Thy glory doth best chime;
All now are stirring, every field
    Full hymns doth yield;

The whole Creation shakes off night,
And for Thy shadow, looks[1] the light;
Stars now vanish without number,
Sleepy planets set, and slumber,
The pursy clouds disband, and scatter;
All expect some sudden matter;
Not one beam triumphs, but from far
    That Morning-star.

O at what time soever Thou,
—Unknown to us—the heavens wilt bow,
And, with Thy Angels in the van,
Descend to judge poor careless Man,—
Grant, I may not like puddle lie
In a corrupt security,
Where, if a traveller water crave,
He finds it dead, and in a grave;
But as this restless, vocal Spring
All day and night doth run, and sing,
And though here born, yet is acquainted[2]
Elsewhere, and flowing keeps untainted;
So let me all. my busy age
In Thy free services engage;
And though—while here—of force I must
Have commerce sometimes with poor dust,
And in my flesh, though vile and low,
As this doth in her channel, flow[3],
Yet let my course, my aim, my love,
And chief acquaintance be above;
So when that day and hour shall come,
In which Thyself will be the Sun,
Thou'lt find me drest, and on my way,
Watching the break of Thy great day.

[1] *looks* [for]   [2] *acquainted*, knows other regions   [3] *flow*, move

CXXXVII

THE THRONE

WHEN with these eyes, closed now by Thee,
    But then restored,
The great and white throne I shall see
    Of my dread LORD;
And lowly kneeling—for the most
    Stiff, then must kneel,—
Shall look on Him, at Whose high cost
    —Unseen—such joys I feel:—

Whatever arguments or skill
    Wise heads shall use,
Tears only and my blushes still
    I will produce.
And should those speechless beggars fail,
    Which oft have won,
Then taught by Thee I will prevail,
    And say, Thy will be done!

CXXXVIII

THE DAY OF JUDGMENT

O DAY of life, of light, of love!
    The only day dealt from above!
A day so fresh, so bright, so brave[1],
'Twill show us each forgotten grave,
And make the dead, like flowers, arise
Youthful and fair to see new skies.
All other days, compared to thee,
Are but Light's weak minority;
They are but veils and cypress[2] drawn
Like clouds, before thy glorious dawn.
O come! arise! shine! do not stay,
    Dearly loved Day!
The fields are long since white, and I
With earnest groans for freedom cry;
My fellow-creatures too say, Come!
And stones, though speechless, are not dumb.
When shall we hear that glorious voice
    Of life and joys?
That voice which to each secret bed
    Of my Lord's dead
Shall bring true day, and make dust see
The way to immortality?
When shall those first white pilgrims rise,
Whose holy, happy histories
—Because they sleep so long—some men
Count but the blots of a vain pen?
    Dear Lord! make haste!

---

[1] *brave*, splendid   [2] *cypress*, crape

CXXXIX

AT BETHLEHEM

COME, we shepherds, whose blest sight
   Hath met Love's noon in Nature's night;
Come, lift we up our loftier song,
And wake the Sun that lies too long.

Gloomy night embraced the place
  Where the noble Infant lay:
The Babe look'd up, and show'd His face;
  In spite of darkness, it was day:—
It was Thy day, Sweet! and did rise
Not from the East, but from Thine eyes.

We saw Thee in Thy balmy nest,
  Young dawn of our eternal Day;
We saw Thine eyes break from their East,
  And chase the trembling shades away:
We saw Thee, (and we blest the sight),
We saw Thee by Thine own sweet light.

Welcome, all wonders in one sight!
  Eternity shut in a span!
Summer in Winter! Day in Night!
  Heaven in Earth! and God in man!
Great Little One, Whose all-embracing birth,
Lifts Earth to Heaven, stoops Heaven to Earth.

R. Crashaw

CXL

AN ECSTASY

LORD, when the sense of Thy sweet grace
  Sends up my soul to seek Thy face,
Thy blesséd eyes breed such desire,
I die in Love's delicious fire.
    O Love, I am thy sacrifice;
Be still triumphant, blesséd eyes;
Still shine on me, fair suns! that I
Still may behold, though still I die.

  Though still I die, I live again,
Still longing so to be still slain;
So gainful is such loss of breath,
I die e'en in desire of death.

Still live in me this longing strife
Of living death and dying life;
For while Thou sweetly slayest me,
Dead to myself, I live in Thee.

CXLI

AN IDYLL OF CHRISTIAN LIFE

HAPPY me! O happy sheep!
    Whom my GOD vouchsafes to keep,
Ev'n my GOD, ev'n He it is
That points me to these paths of bliss;
On Whose pastures cheerful Spring,
All the year doth sit and sing,
And rejoicing, smiles to see
Their green backs wear His livery:
Pleasure sings my soul to rest,
Plenty wears me at her breast,
Whose sweet temper teaches me
Not wanton, nor in want to be.
At my feet the blubbering mountain
Weeping, melts into a fountain,
Whose soft silver-sweating streams
Make high-noon forget his beams:
When my wayward breath is flying,
He calls home my soul from dying,
Strokes and tames my rabid grief,
And does woo me into life:
When my simple weakness strays,
(Tangled in forbidden ways),
He (my Shepherd) is my guide;
He's before me, on my side;
And behind me, He beguiles
Craft in all her knotty wiles:
He expounds the weary wonder
Of my giddy steps, and under
Spreads a path clear as the day,
Where no churlish rub[1] says nay
To my joy-conducted feet,
Whilst they gladly go to meet
Grace and Peace, to learn new lays
Tuned to my great Shepherd's praise.

Come now, all ye terrors, sally,
Muster forth into the valley,
Where triumphant darkness hovers
With a sable wing, that covers

Brooding horror. Come, thou Death,
Let the damps of thy dull breath
Over-shadow e'en that shade,
And make Darkness' self afraid;
There my feet, e'en there, shall find
Way for a resolvéd mind.
Still my Shepherd, still my God,
Thou art with me; still Thy rod,
And Thy staff, whose influence
Gives direction, gives defence.
At the whisper of Thy word
Crown'd abundance spreads my board :
While I feast, my foes do feed
Their rank malice, not their need,
So that with the self-same bread
They are starved, and I am fed.
How my head in ointment swims!
How my cup o'er-looks her brims!
So, e'en so still may I move
By the line of Thy dear love ;
Still may Thy sweet mercy spread
A shady arm above my head,
About my paths; so shall I find
The fair centre of my mind,
Thy temple, and those lovely walls
Bright ever with a beam that falls
Fresh from the pure glance of Thine eye,
Lighting to Eternity.
There I 'll dwell for ever, there
Will I find a purer air
To feed my life with, there I 'll sup
Balm and nectar in my cup ;
And thence my ripe soul will I breathe
Warm into the arms of Death.

[1] rub, obstruction

CXLII

MORNING HYMN

WHAT's this Morn's bright eye to me,
    If I see not Thine and Thee,
Fairer Jesu; in whose Face
All my Heaven is spread !—Alas,
Still I grovel in dead Night,
Whilst I want Thy living Light;

Dreaming with wide open eyes
Fond fantastic vanities.

Shine, my only Day-Star, shine:
So mine eyes shall wake by Thine;
So the dreams I grope-in now
To clear visions all shall grow;
So my day shall measured be
By Thy Grace's clarity[1];
So shall I discern the Path
Thy sweet Law prescribéd hath;
For Thy ways cannot be shown
By any light but by Thine own.

J. Beaumont

[1] *clarity*, clear light

CXLIII

EVENING HYMN

NEVER yet could careless Sleep
  On Love's watchful eyelid creep:
Never yet could gloomy Night
Damp His Eye's immortal light:
Love is His own Day, and sees
Whatsoe'er Himself doth please:
Love His piercing look can dart
Thro' the shades of my dark heart,
And read plainer far than I
All the spots which there do lie.

Pardon then what thou dost see,
Mighty Love, in wretched me:
Let the sweet wrath of Thy ray
Chide my sinful Night to Day;
To the blesséd Day of Grace
Whose dear East smiles in Thy Face.
So no Powers of Darkness shall
In this Night my soul appal;
So shall I the sounder sleep,
'Cause my heart awake I keep;
Meekly waiting upon Thee,
Whilst Thou deign'st to watch for Me.

CXLIV

HOME

WHAT is House and what is Home,
    Where with freedom thou hast room,
And may'st to all tyrants say,
This you cannot take away?
'Tis no thing with doors and walls,
Which at every earthquake falls;
No fair towers, whose princely fashion
Is but Plunder's invitation;
No stout marble structure, where
Walls Eternity do dare;
No brass gates, no bars of steel,
Tho' Time's teeth they scorn to feel:
Brass is not so bold as Pride,
If on Power's wings it ride;
Marble's not so hard as Spite
Arm'd with lawless Strength and Might.
Right and just Possession, be
Potent names, when Laws stand free:
But if once that rampart fall,
Stoutest thieves inherit all:
To be rich and weak's a sure
And sufficient forfeiture.

    Seek no more abroad, say I,
House and Home, but turn thine eye
Inward, and observe thy breast;
There alone dwells solid Rest.
That's a close immuréd tower
Which can mock all hostile power.
To thyself a tenant be,
And inhabit safe and free.
Say not that this House is small,
Girt up in a narrow wall:
In a cleanly sober mind
Heaven itself full room doth find.
Th' Infinite CREATOR can
Dwell in it; and may not Man?
Here content make thy abode
With thyself and with thy GOD.
Here in this sweet privacy
May'st thou with thyself agree,
And keep House in peace, tho' all
Th' Universe's fabric fall.
No disaster can distress thee,
Nor no Fury dispossess thee:

Let all war and plunder come,
Still may'st thou dwell safe at Home.

Home is everywhere to thee,
Who can'st thine own dwelling be;
Yea, tho' ruthless Death assail thee,
Still thy lodging will not fail thee;
Still thy Soul's thine own; and she
To an House removed shall be;
An eternal House above,
Wall'd, and roof'd, and paved with Love.
There shall these mud-walls of thine,
Gallantly repair'd, out-shine
Mortal Stars;—No Stars shall be
In that Heaven but such as Thee.

CXLV

WHIT SUNDAY

FOUNTAIN of Sweets! Eternal Dove!
  Which leav'st Thy glorious perch above,
And hovering down, vouchsafest thus
To make Thy nest below with Us.

Soft as Thy softest feathers, may
We find Thy Love to us to-day;
And in the shelter of Thy wing
Obtain Thy leave and grace to sing.

CXLVI

THE ASCENSION

LIFT up your heads, great Gates, and sing,
  Now Glory comes, and Glory's King;
Now by your high all-golden way
The fairer Heaven comes home to-day.

Hark! now the Gates are ope, and hear
The tune of each triumphant sphere;
Where every Angel as he sings
Keeps time with his applauding wings,
And makes Heaven's loftiest roof rebound
The echoes of the noble sound.

CXLVII

RESOLUTION:

THE SONG OF HYLOBARIS CONCERNING
DIVINE PROVIDENCE

WHERE's now the object of thy fears;
　　Needless sighs and fruitless tears?
They be all gone like idle dream
Suggested from the body's steam.
O Cave of horror black as pitch!
Dark den of Spectres that bewitch
The weaken'd phansy, sore affright
With the grim shades of grisly Night.
What's Plague and Prison? Loss of friends?
War, Dearth, and Death that all things ends?
Mere bug-bears for the childish mind :
Pure panic terrors of the blind.

Collect thy soul into one sphere
Of light, and 'bove the earth it rear :
Those wild scatter'd thoughts that erst
Lay loosely in the World disperst
Call in : Thy spirit thus knit in one
Fair lucid orb; those fears be gone
Like vain impostures of the Night
That fly before the Morning bright.
Then with pure eyes thou shalt behold
How the first Goodness doth infold
All things in loving tender arms :
That deeméd mischiefs are no harms,
But sovereign salves, and skilful cures
Of greater woes the world endures;
That Man's stout soul may win a state
Far raised above the reach of Fate.

Then wilt thou say, GOD rules the World,
Though mountain over mountain hurl'd
Be pitch'd amid the foaming main,
Which busy winds to wrath constrain.
His fall doth make the billows start
And backward skip from every part,
Quite sunk; then o'er his senseless side
The waves in triumph proudly ride.
Though inward tempests fiercely rock
The tottering Earth, that with the shock
High spires and heavy rocks fall down
With their own weight drove into ground;

Though pitchy blasts from Hell up-borne
Stop the outgoings of the Morn,
And Nature play her fiery games
In this forced Night, with fulgurant[1] flames,
Baring by fits for more affright
The pale dead visages, ghastly sight
Of men astonish'd at the stoure[2]
Of Heaven's great rage, the rattling showers
Of hail, the hoarse bellowing of thunder,
Their own loud shrieks made mad with wonder:
All this confusion cannot move
The purgéd mind, freed from the love
Of commerce with her body dear,
Cell of sad thoughts, sole spring of fear.

Whate'er I feel or hear or see
Threats but these parts that mortal be.
Nought can the honest heart dismay
Unless the love of living clay,
And long acquaintance with the light
Of this Out-world, and what to sight
Those too officious beams discover
Of forms that round about us hover.

Power, Wisdom, Goodness sure did frame
This Universe, and still guide the same.
But thoughts from passions sprung, deceive
Vain mortals. No man can contrive
A better course than what's been run
Since the first circuit of the Sun.

He that beholds all from on high
Knows better what to do than I.
I'm not mine own : should I repine
If He dispose of what's not mine?
Purge but thy soul of blind self-will,
Thou straight shalt see GOD doth no ill.
The world He fills with the bright rays
Of His free goodness. He displays
Himself throughout: Like common air
That spirit of life through all doth fare.
Suck'd in by them as vital breath
That willingly embrace not death.
But those that with that living Law
Be unacquainted, cares do gnaw;
Mistrust of GOD's good providence
Doth daily vex their wearied sense.

                              H. More

----

[1] *fulgurant*, lightning   [2] *stoure*, tumult

CXLVIII

THE PHILOSOPHER'S DEVOTION:
THE SONG OF BATHYNOUS

SING aloud, His praise rehearse,
  Who hath made the Universe.
He the boundless Heavens has spread,
All the vital Orbs has kned[1];
He that on Olympus high
Tends His flocks[2] with watchful eye,
And this eye[3] has multiplied
Midst each flock for to reside:
Thus as round about they stray,
Toucheth each with out-stretch'd ray;
Nimble they hold on their way,
Shaping out their Night and Day.
Summer, Winter, Autumn, Spring,
Their inclinéd Axes bring.
Never slack they; none respires,
Dancing round their central fires.

In due order as they move,
Echoes sweet be gently drove
Thorough Heaven's vast hollowness,
Which unto all corners press:
Music that the heart of Jove[4]
Moves to joy and sportful love;
Fills the listening Sailors' ears
Riding on the wandering spheres.
Neither Speech nor Language is
Where their voice is not transmiss.[5]

God is Good, is Wise, is Strong,
Witness all the creature-throng,
Is confess'd by every tongue.
All things back from whence they sprung,
As the thankful rivers pay
What they borrow'd of the sea.

Now myself I do resign;
Take me whole, I all am thine.
Save me, God! from Self-desire,
Death's pit, dark Hell's raging fire,
Envy, Hatred, Vengeance, Ire:
Let not Lust my soul bemire.

Quit from these, Thy praise I'll sing.
Loudly sweep the trembling string.
Bear a part, O Wisdom's sons!
Freed from vain Religions.

Lo! from far I you salute,
Sweetly warbling on my lute,
Indie, Egypt, Araby,
Asia, Greece, and Tartary,
Carmel-tracts and Lebanon,
With the Mountains of the Moon,
From whence muddy Nile doth run;
Or where ever else you won [6]
Breathing in one vital air,
One we are, though distant far.

Rise at once let's sacrifice,
Odours sweet perfume the skies.
See how heavenly lightning fires
Hearts inflamed with high aspires!
All the substance of our souls
Up in clouds of incense rolls.
Leave we nothing to ourselves,
Save a voice, what need we else?
Or an hand to wear and tire
On the thankful lute or lyre.

Sing aloud, His praise rehearse
Who hath made the Universe.

[1] *kned*, knit for *Jehovah* [2] *flocks*, the stars [3] *eye*, sun [4] *Jove*, used
[5] *transmiss*, sent through [6] *won*, abide

CXLIX

THE ASPIRATION

HOW long, great GOD, how long must I
 Immured in this dark prison lie;
Where at the grates and avenues of sense,
My soul must watch to have intelligence;
Where but faint gleams of Thee salute my sight,
Like doubtful moonshine in a cloudy night:
 When shall I leave this magic sphere,
 And be all mind, all eye, all ear?

How cold this clime! And yet my sense
 Perceives e'en here Thy influence.
E'en here Thy strong magnetic charms I feel,
And pant and tremble like the amorous steel.
To lower good, and beauties less divine,
Sometimes my erroneous needle does decline,
 But yet, so strong the sympathy,
 It turns, and points again to Thee.

I long to see this excellence
Which at such distance strikes my sense.
My impatient soul struggles to disengage
Her wings from the confinement of her cage.
Wouldst thou, great Love, this prisoner once set free,
How would she hasten to be link'd to Thee!
She 'd for no angels' conduct stay,
But fly, and love-on, all the way.

J. Norris

CL

SERAPHIC LOVE

THROUGH Contemplation's optics I have seen
   Him Who is 'fairer than the sons of men':
The source of good, the light archetypal,
   Beauty in the original.
   'The fairest of ten thousand,' He,
   Proportion all and harmony;
   All mortal beauty 's but a ray
   Of His bright ever-shining day;
   A little, feeble, twinkling star,
Which, now the Sun 's in place, must disappear:—
There is but One that 's good, there is but One that 's fair.

To Thee, Thou only Fair, my soul aspires
With holy breathings, languishing desires.
To thee m' inamoured panting heart does move,
   By efforts of ecstatic love.
   How do Thy glorious streams of light
   Refresh my intellectual sight!
   Tho' broken, and strain'd through a screen
   Of envious flesh that stands between!
   When shall m' imprison'd soul be free,
That she Thy native uncorrected light may see,
And gaze upon Thy beatific face to all eternity?

CLI

THE BELOVED

E'EN like two little bank-dividing brooks,
   That wash the pebbles with their wanton streams,
And having ranged and search'd a thousand nooks,
   Meet both at length in silver-breasted Thames,
   Where in a greater current they conjoin:
So I my Best-beloved's am; so He is mine.

E'en so we met; and after long pursuit,
  E'en so we join'd: we both became entire;
No need for either to renew a suit,
  For I was flax and He was flames of fire:
    Our firm-united souls did more than twine;
So I my Best-beloved's am; so He is mine.

He is my Altar; I, His Holy Place;
  I am His guest; and He my living food;
I'm His by penitence; He mine by grace;
  I'm His by purchase; He is mine, by blood;
    He's my supporting elm; and I His vine;
Thus I my Best-beloved's am; thus He is mine.

If all those glittering Monarchs that command
  The servile quarters of this earthly ball,
Should tender, in exchange, their shares of land,
  I would not change my fortunes for them all:
    Their wealth is but a counter to my coin;
The world's but their's; but my Beloved's mine.

F. Quarles

CLII

QUIA AMORE LANGUEO

YOU holy Virgins, that so oft surround
  The city's sapphire walls; whose snowy feet
Measure the pearly paths of sacred ground,
  And trace the new Jerusalem's jasper street;
Ah, you whose care-forsaken hearts are crown'd
  With your best wishes; that enjoy the sweet
    Of all your hopes; if e'er you chance to spy
    My absent Love, O tell Him that I lie
Deep-wounded with the flames that furnaced from His eye.

I charge you, Virgins, as you hope to hear
  The heavenly music of your Lover's voice;
I charge you by the solemn faith ye bear
  To plighted vows, and to that loyal choice
Of your affections; or, if aught more dear
  You hold; by Hymen; by your marriage-joys;
    I charge you tell Him, that a flaming dart,
    Shot from His eye, hath pierced my bleeding heart;
And I am sick of love, and languish in my smart.

Tell Him, O tell Him, how my panting breast
  Is scorch'd with flames, and how my soul is pined;
Tell Him, O tell Him, how I lie opprest
  With the full torments of a troubled mind;
O tell Him, tell Him, that He loves in jest,   .
  But I in earnest; tell Him, He 's unkind:
    But if a discontented frown appears
    Upon His angry brow, accost His ears
With soft and fewer words, and act the rest in tears.

O, tell Him, that His cruelties deprive
  My soul of peace, while peace in vain she seeks;
Tell Him those damask roses, that did strive
  With white, both fade, upon my sallow cheeks;
Tell Him, no token doth proclaim I live,
  But tears, and sighs, and sobs, and sudden shrieks;
    Thus if your piercing words should chance to bore
    His harkening ear, and move a sigh, give o'er
To speak; and tell Him,—Tell Him that I could no more.

CLIII

GOOD NIGHT

CLOSE now thine eyes, and rest secure;
  Thy soul is safe enough; thy body sure;
    He that loves thee, He that keeps
And guards thee, never slumbers, never sleeps.
The smiling Conscience in a sleeping breast
    Has only peace, has only rest:
    The music and the mirth of kings
Are all but very discords, when she sings:
    Then close thine eyes and rest secure;
No sleep so sweet as thine, no rest so sure.

CLIV

MY glass is half unspent; Forbear t' arrest
  My thriftless day too soon: my poor request
Is that my glass may run but out the rest.

My time-devoured minutes will be done
Without Thy help; see, see how swift they run;
Cut not my thread, before my thread be spun.

The gain 's not great I purchase by this stay;
What loss sustain'st Thou by so small delay,
To whom ten thousand years are but a day!

My following eye can hardly make a shift
To count my wingéd hours; they fly so swift,
They scarce deserve the bounteous name of gift.

The secret wheels of hurrying Time do give
So short a warning, and so fast they drive,
That I am dead before I seem to live.

And what's a Life? a weary Pilgrimage,
Whose glory in one day doth fill the stage
With Childhood, Manhood, and decrepit Age.

And what's a Life? the flourishing array
Of the proud Summer meadow, which today
Wears her green plush, and is tomorrow hay.

And what's a Life? a blast sustain'd with clothing,
Maintain'd with food, retain'd with vile self-loathing;
Then weary of itself, again'd to nothing.

Read on this dial, how the shades devour
My short-lived winter's day; hour eats up hour,
Alas, the total's but from eight to four.

Behold these Lilies (which Thy hands have made
Fair copies of my life, and open laid
To view) how soon they droop, how soon they fade!

Shade not that dial, night will blind too soon;
My nonaged day already points to noon;
How simple is my suit! how small my boon!

Nor do I beg this slender inch, to while
The time away, or falsely to beguile
My thoughts with joy; here's nothing worth a smile:

No, no; 'tis not to please my wanton ears
With frantic mirth, I beg but hours, not years;
And what Thou giv'st me, I will give to tears.

Draw not that soul which would be rather led;
That Seed has yét not broke my Serpent's head;
O shall I die before my sins are dead?

Behold these rags; am I a fitting guest
To taste the dainties of Thy royal feast,
With hands and face unwash'd, ungirt, unblest?

First, let the Jordan streams, (that find supplies
From the deep fountain of my heart), arise,
And cleanse my spots, and clear my leprous eyes.

I have a world of sins to be lamented;
I have a sea of tears that must be vented:
O spare till then!—and then I die contented.

CLV

EVENING

BEHOLD the sun, that seem'd but now
  Enthronéd overhead,
Beginning to decline below
  The globe whereon we tread;
And he, whom yet we look upon
  With comfort and delight,
Will quite depart from hence anon,
  And leave us to the night.

Thus Time, unheeded, steals away
  The life which Nature gave;
Thus are our bodies every day
  Declining to the grave :
Thus from us all our pleasures fly
  Whereon we set our heart;
And when the night of death draws nigh,
  Thus will they all depart.

Lord! though the sun forsake our sight,
  And mortal hopes are vain;
Let still Thine everlasting light
  Within our souls remain!
And in the nights of our distress
  Vouchsafe those rays divine,
Which from the Sun of Righteousness
  For ever brightly shine!

G. Wither

CLVI

A LULLABY

SWEET baby, sleep! what ails my dear,
  What ails my darling thus to cry?
Be still, my child, and lend thine ear,
  To hear me sing thy lullaby :
My pretty lamb, forbear to weep;
Be still, my dear; sweet baby, sleep.

Thou blesséd soul, what canst thou fear?
  What thing to thee can mischief do?
Thy God is now thy Father dear,
  His holy Spouse, thy Mother too.
Sweet baby, then forbear to weep;
Be still, my babe; sweet baby, sleep.

Sweet baby, sleep, and nothing fear;
  For whosoever thee offends
By thy Protector threaten'd are,
  And GOD and Angels are thy friends.
Sweet baby, then forbear to weep;
Be still, my babe; sweet baby, sleep.

When GOD with us was dwelling here,
  In little babes He took delight;
Such innocents as thou, my dear,
  Are ever precious in His sight.
Sweet baby, then forbear to weep;
Be still, my babe; sweet baby, sleep.

A little infant once was He;
  And strength in weakness then was laid
Upon His Virgin Mother's knee,
  That power to thee might be convey'd.
Sweet baby, then forbear to weep;
Be still, my babe; sweet baby, sleep.

The King of kings, when He was born,
  Had not so much for outward ease;
By Him such dressings were not worn,
  Nor such-like swaddling-clothes as these.
Sweet baby, then forbear to weep;
Be still, my babe; sweet baby, sleep.

Within a manger lodged thy LORD,
  Where oxen lay, and asses fed:
Warm rooms we do to thee afford,
  An easy cradle or a bed.
Sweet baby, then forbear to weep;
Be still, my babe; sweet baby, sleep.

Thou hast, yet more, to perfect this,
  A promise and an earnest got
Of gaining everlasting bliss,
  Though thou, my babe, perceiv'st it not;
Sweet baby, then forbear to weep;
Be still, my babe; sweet baby, sleep.

CLVII

MY soul doth pant towards Thee,
    My GOD, source of eternal life:
      Flesh fights with me;
      Oh end the strife,
And part us, that in peace I may
      Unclay

My wearied spirit, and take
My flight to Thy eternal spring,
      Where, for His sake
      Who is my King,
I may wash all my tears away,
        That day.

Thou Conqueror of death,
Glorious triumpher o'er the grave,
      Whose holy breath
      Was spent to save
Lost mankind, make me to be styled
        Thy child,

And take me when I die
And go unto my dust; my soul
      Above the sky
      With saints enrol,
That in Thy arms, for ever, I
        May lie.

J. Taylor

CLVIII

HYMN FOR ADVENT

LORD, come away;
  Why dost Thou stay?
Thy road is ready; and Thy paths, made straight,
  With longing expectation wait
The consecration of Thy beauteous feet.
Ride on triumphantly: behold we lay
Our lusts and proud wills in thy way.
Hosannah! welcome to our hearts? LORD, here
Thou hast a temple too, and full as dear
As that of Sion; and as full of sin:
Nothing but thieves and robbers dwell therein:
Enter, and chase them forth, and cleanse the floor;
Crucify them, that they may never more
    Profane that holy place
  Where Thou hast chose to set Thy face.
  And then if our stiff tongues shall be
  Mute in the praises of Thy Deity,
  The stones out of the temple-wall
    Shall cry aloud, and call
Hosannah! and Thy glorious footsteps greet.

CLIX

L ORD, it belongs not to my care,
 Whether I die or live;
To love and serve Thee is my share,
 And this Thy grace must give.

If life be long I will be glad,
 That I may long obey;
If short—yet why should I be sad
 To soar to endless day?

CHRIST leads me through no darker rooms
 Than He went through before;
He that unto GOD's kingdom comes,
 Must enter by this door.

Come, LORD, when grace has made me meet
 Thy blessèd face to see;
For if Thy work on earth be sweet,
 What will Thy glory be!

Then I shall end my sad complaints,
 And weary, sinful days;
And join with the triumphant saints,
 To sing JEHOVAH's praise.

My knowledge of that life is small,
 The eye of faith is dim;
But 'tis enough that CHRIST knows all,
 And I shall be with Him.

       R. Baxter

CLX

I SAID sometimes with tears,
 Ah me! I'm loth to die!
LORD, silence Thou these fears:
My life's with Thee on high.
  Sweet truth to me!
   I shall arise,
   And with these eyes
  My Saviour see.

 My life's a shade, my days
 Apace to death decline;
 My LORD is Life; He'll raise
 My dust again, ev'n mine.

My peaceful grave shall keep
My bones till, that sweet day,
I wake from my long sleep
And leave my bed of clay.

My LORD His angels shall
Their golden trumpets sound;
At whose most welcome call
My grave shall be unbound.
     Sweet truth to me!
        I shall arise,
          And with these eyes
     My Saviour see.

S. Crossman

CLXI

SWEET place, sweet place alone!
     The court of GOD most High,
The Heaven of Heavens, the Throne
Of spotless majesty!
     O happy place!
        When shall I be,
          My GOD, with Thee,
     To see Thy face?

The stranger homeward bends,
And sigheth for his rest:
Heaven is my home, my friends
Lodge there in Abraham's breast.

Earth's but a sorry tent
Pitch'd for a few frail days,
A short-leased tenement;
Heaven's still my song, my praise.

No tears from any eyes
Drop in that holy quire;
But Death itself there dies,
And sighs themselves expire.

There should temptations cease,
My frailties there should end;
There should I rest in peace
In the arms of my best Friend.

Jerusalem on high
My song and City is,
My home whene'er I die,
The centre of my bliss.

Thy walls, sweet City, thine,
With pearls are garnishéd;
Thy gates with praises shine,
Thy streets with gold are spread;

No sun by day shines there,
Nor moon by silent night;
Oh no! these needless are;
The Lamb's the city's Light.

There dwells my LORD, my King,
Judged here unfit to live;
There Angels to Him sing,
And lowly homage give.

The Patriarchs of old
There from their travels cease;
The Prophets there behold
Their long'd-for Prince of Peace:

The Lamb's Apostles there
I might with joy behold,
The Harpers I might hear
Harping on harps of gold:

The bleeding Martyrs, they
Within those courts are found,
Clothéd in pure array,
Their scars with glory crown'd.

Ah me! Ah me! that I
In Kedar's tents here stay!
No place like this on high!
Thither, LORD! guide my way!
    O happy place!
      When shall I be,
     My GOD, with Thee,
   To see Thy face?

CLXII

BLEST be Thy love, dear LORD,
   That taught us this sweet way,
Only to love Thee for Thyself,
   And for that love obey.

O Thou, our souls' chief hope!
   We to Thy mercy fly;
Where'er we are, Thou canst protect,
   Whate'er we need, supply.

> Whether we sleep or wake,
> To Thee we both resign;
> By night we see, as well as day,
> If Thy light on us shine.
>
> Whether we live or die,
> Both we submit to Thee;
> In death we live, as well as life,
> If Thine in death we be.

J. Austin

CLXIII

FAIN would my thoughts fly up to Thee,
    Thy peace, sweet LORD, to find;
But when I offer, still the world
    Lays clogs upon my mind.

Sometimes I climb a little way
    And thence look down below;
How nothing, there, do all things seem,
    That here make such a show!

Then round about I turn my eyes
    To feast my hungry sight;
I meet with Heaven in every thing,
    In every thing delight.

When I have thus triumph'd awhile,
    And think to build my nest,
Some cross conceits come fluttering by,
    And interrupt my rest.

Then to the earth again I fall,
    And from my low dust cry,
'Twas not in my wing, LORD, but Thine,
    That I got up so high.

And now, my GOD, whether I rise,
    Or still lie down in dust,
Both I submit to Thy blest will;
    In both, on Thee I trust.

Guide Thou my way, who art Thyself
    My everlasting End,
That every step, or swift, or slow,
    Still to Thyself may tend!

To Father, Son, and Holy Ghost,
    One consubstantial Three,
All highest praise, all humblest thanks,
    Now and for ever be!

K 2.

CLXIV

HARK, my soul, how every thing
　　Strives to serve our bounteous King;
Each a double tribute pays;
Sings its part, and then obeys.

Nature's sweet and chiefest quire
Him with cheerful notes admire;
Chanting every day their lauds[1],
While the grove their song applauds.

Though their voices lower be,
Streams have too their melody;
Night and day they warbling run,
Never pause, but still sing on.

All the flowers that gild the spring
Hither their still music bring;
If Heaven bless them, thankful they
Smell more sweet, and look more gay.

Only we can scarce afford
This short office to our LORD;
We,—on whom His bounty flows,
All things gives, and nothing owes.

Wake, for shame, my sluggish heart,
Wake, and gladly sing thy part:
Learn of birds, and springs, and flowers,
How to use thy noble powers.

Call whole Nature to thy aid,
Since 'twas He whole Nature made;
Join in one eternal song,
Who to one GOD all belong.

Live for ever, glorious LORD,
Live, by all Thy works adored;
One in Three, and Three in One,
Thrice we bow to Thee alone.

[1] *lauds* here has reference to the Office, for which this hymn was written

CLXV

ALL SAINTS' DAY

WAKE, all my hopes, lift up your eyes,
　　And crown your heads with mirth;
See how they shine beyond the skies,
　　Who once dwelt on our earth!

Peace, busy thoughts, away, vain cares,
 That clog us here below;
Let us go up above the spheres,
 And to each Order bow.

Hail, glorious Angels, Heirs of Light,
 The high-born sons of Fire!
Whose hearts burn chaste, whose flames shine bright;
 All joy, yet all desire.

Hail, holy Saints, who long in hope,
 Long in the shadow 'sate,
Till our victorious LORD set ope
 Heaven's everlasting Gate.

Hail, great Apostles of the Lamb,
 Who brought that early ray
Which from our Sun reflected came,
 And made our first fair day.

Hail, generous Martyrs, whose strong hearts
 Bravely rejoiced to prove,
How weak, pale Death, are all thy darts,
 Compared to those of Love.

Hail, blesséd Confessors, who died
 A death too, Love did give;
Whilst your own flesh ye crucified,
 To make your Spirit live.

Hail, beauteous Virgins, whose chaste vows
 Renounced all fond desires:
Who wisely chose your LORD for Spouse,
 And burn'd with His pure fires.

Hail, all ye happy Spirits above,
 Who maké that glorious ring
About the sparkling Throne of Love,
 And there for ever sing.

Hail, and among your crowns of praise,
 Present this little wreath,
Which, while your lofty notes you raise,
 We humbly sing beneath.

All glory to the sacred Three,
 One ever-living LORD;
As at the first, still may He be
 Beloved, obey'd, adored.

CLXVI

BEHOLD we come, dear LORD, to Thee,
   And bow before Thy throne;
We come to offer on our knee
   Our vows to Thee alone.

Whate'er we have, whate'er we are,
   Thy bounty freely gave;
Thou dost us here in mercy spare,
   And wilt hereafter save.

Come then, my soul, bring all thy powers,
   And grieve thou hast no more,
Bring every day thy choicest hours,
   And thy great GOD adore.

But, above all, prepare thine heart
   On this, His own blest day,
In its sweet task to bear thy part,
   And sing, and love, and pray.

CLXVII

MY LORD, my Love, was crucified;
   He all the pains did bear;
But in the sweetness of His rest
   He makes His servants share.
How sweetly rest Thy saints above
   Which in Thy bosom lie!
The Church below doth rest in hope
   Of that felicity.

Thou, LORD, who daily feed'st Thy sheep,
   Mak'st them a weekly feast;
Thy flocks meet in their several folds
   Upon this day of rest:—
Welcome and dear unto my soul
   Are these sweet feasts of love:
But what a sabbath shall I keep
   When I shall rest above!

I bless Thy wise and wondrous love,
   Which binds us to be free;
Which makes us leave our earthly snares,
   That we may come to Thee!

I come, I wait, I hear, I pray!
  Thy footsteps, LORD, I trace!
I sing to think this is the way
  Unto my Saviour's face!

J. Mason

CLXVIII

THERE is a Stream, which issues forth
    From GOD's eternal Throne,
And from the Lamb,—a living stream
  Clear as the crystal stone.

The stream doth water Paradise;
  It makes the Angels sing;
One cordial drop revives my heart;
  Hence all my joys do spring.

Eye hath not seen, nor ear hath heard,
  From fancy 'tis conceal'd,
What Thou, LORD, hast laid up for Thine,
  And hast to me reveal'd.

CLXIX

HOW shall I sing that Majesty
    Which Angels do admire?
Let dust in dust and silence lie;
  Sing, sing, ye heavenly quire!
Thousands of thousands stand around
  Thy throne, O GOD most high;
Ten thousand times ten thousand sound
  Thy praise; but who am I?

Thy brightness unto them appears,
  Whilst I Thy footsteps trace;
A sound of GOD comes to my ears;
  But they behold Thy face.
They sing because Thou art their sun:
  LORD, send a beam on me;
For where heaven is but once begun,
  There hallelujahs be.

How great a being, LORD, is thine,
  Which doth all beings keep!
Thy knowledge is the only line
  To sound so vast a deep.

Thou art a sea without a shore,
  A sun without a sphere;
Thy time is now and evermore,
  Thy place is everywhere.

Who would not fear Thy searching eye,
  Witness to all that's true!
Dark Hell, and deep hypocrisy,
  Lie plain before Its view.
Motions and thoughts before they grow,
  Thy knowledge doth espy;
What unborn ages are to do,
  Is done before Thine eye.

CLXX

ALAS, my God, that we should be
  Such strangers to each other!
O that as friends we might agree,
  And walk and talk together!

May I taste that communion, Lord,
  Thy people have with Thee?
Thy Spirit daily talks with them,
  O let It talk with me!

Like Enoch, let me walk with God,
  And thus walk out my day,
Attended with the heavenly Guards,
  Upon the King's highway.

When wilt Thou come unto me, Lord?
  O come, my Lord most dear!
Come near, come nearer, nearer still:
  I'm well when Thou art near.

There's no such thing as pleasure here;
  My Jesus is my all:
As Thou dost shine or disappear,
  My pleasures rise and fall.

When wilt Thou come unto me, Lord?
  For, till Thou dost appear,
I count each moment for a day,
  Each minute for a year.

T. Shepherd

CLXXI

THE WAYS OF WISDOM

THESE sweeter far than lilies are,
 No roses may with these compare :
  How these excel,
  No tongue can tell
Which he that well and truly knows
 With praise and joy he goes!
How great and happy's he that knows his ways
 To be divine and heavenly joys :—
 To whom each city is more brave
Than walls of pearl, and streets which gold doth pave :—
  Whose open eyes
  Behold the skies;
 Who loves their wealth and beauty more
  Than kings love golden ore!

Who sees the heavenly ancient ways
Of GOD the LORD, with joy and praise
  More than the skies :—
  With open eyes
Doth prize them all; yea, more than gems,
 And regal diadems :
That more esteemeth mountains, as they are,
 Than if they gold and silver were :
 To whom the sun more pleasure brings,
Than crowns, and thrones, and palaces to kings;—
  That knows his ways
  To be the joys
And way of GOD. These things who knows
 With joy and praise he goes!
       Anon.

End of Book First

Book Second

CLXXII

REASON

THE Holy Book, like the Eighth Sphere[1], does shine
    With thousand lights of truth divine :
So numberless the stars, that to the eye
    It makes but all one galaxy :—
Yet Reason must assist too, for in seas
    So vast and dangerous as these,
Our course by stars above we cannot know,
    Without the compass too below.

Though Reason cannot through Faith's mysteries see,
    It sees that there and such they be ;
Leads to Heaven's-door, and there does humbly keep,
    And there through chinks and key-holes peep.
Though it, like Moses, by a sad command
    Must not come into th' Holy Land,
Yet thither it infallibly does guide,
    And from afar 'tis all descried.

A. Cowley

[1] *Eighth Sphere*, that of the fixed stars in old astronomy

CLXXIII

VENI CREATOR SPIRITUS

CREATOR Spirit, by whose aid
    The world's foundations first were laid,
Come, visit every pious mind ;
Come, pour Thy joys on human kind ;
From sin and sorrow set us free,
And make Thy temples worthy Thee.
    O source of uncreated light,
The Father's promised Paraclete !
Thrice holy fount, thrice holy fire,
Our hearts with heavenly love inspire ;
Come, and Thy sacred unction bring
To sanctify us, while we sing.

Plenteous of grace, descend from high,
Rich in Thy sevenfold energy!
Thou strength of His Almighty hand,
Whose power does heaven and earth command;
Proceeding Spirit, our defence,
Who dost the gift of tongues dispense,
And crown'st Thy gift with eloquence.
    Chase from our minds the infernal foe,
And Peace, the fruit of Love, bestow;
And lest our feet should step astray,
Protect and guide us in the way.
    Make us eternal truths receive,
And practise all that we believe:
Give us Thyself, that we may see
The Father and the Son by Thee.
    Immortal honour, endless fame,
Attend the Almighty Father's name:
The Saviour Son be glorified,
Who for lost man's redemption died:
And equal adoration be,
Eternal Paraclete, to Thee.

J. Dryden

CLXXIV

HOW are Thy servants blest, O Lord!
    How sure is their defence!
Eternal wisdom is their guide,
    Their help Omnipotence.

In foreign realms, and lands remote,
    Supported by Thy care,
Through burning climes I pass'd unhurt,
    And breathed in tainted air.

Thy mercy sweeten'd every soil,
    Made every region please;
The hoary Alpine hills it warm'd,
    And smoothed the Tyrrhene seas[1].

Think, O my soul, devoutly think,
    How, with affrighted eyes,
Thou saw'st the wide-extended deep
    In all its horrors rise!

Confusion dwelt in every face,
    And fear in every heart;
When waves on waves, and gulphs on gulphs,
    O'ercame the pilot's art.

Yet then from all my griefs, O Lord,
 Thy mercy set me free;
Whilst, in the confidence of prayer,
 My soul took hold on Thee.

For though in dreadful whirls we hung
 High on the broken wave,
I knew Thou wert not slow to hear,
 Nor impotent to save.

The storm was laid, the winds retired,
 Obedient to Thy will;
The sea that roar'd at Thy command,
 At Thy command was still.

In midst of dangers, fears, and death,
 Thy goodness I 'll adore;
And praise Thee for Thy mercies past,
 And humbly hope for more.

My life, if Thou preserv'st my life,
 Thy sacrifice shall be;
And death, if death must be my doom,
 Shall join my soul to Thee.

J. Addison

[1] See Note

CLXXV

WHEN all Thy mercies, O my God,
 My rising soul surveys;
Transported with the view, I 'm lost
 In wonder, love, and praise.

O how shall words with equal warmth
 The gratitude declare
That glows within my ravish'd heart!
 But Thou canst read it there.

Thy providence my life sustain'd,
 And all my wants redrest,
When in the silent womb I lay,
 Or hung upon the breast.

To all my weak complaints and cries
 Thy mercy lent an ear,
Ere yet my feeble thoughts had learnt
 To form themselves in prayer.

Unnumber'd comforts to my soul
  Thy tender care bestow'd,
Before my infant heart conceived
  From Whom those comforts flow'd.

When in the slippery paths of youth
  With heedless steps I ran,
Thine arm unseen convey'd me safe,
  And led me up to man;

Through hidden dangers, toils, and deaths,
  It gently clear'd my way,
And through the pleasing snares of vice,
  More to be fear'd than they.

When worn with sickness, oft hast Thou
  With health renew'd my face;
And when in sins and sorrows sunk,
  Revived my soul with grace.

Thy bounteous hand with worldly bliss
  Has made my cup run o'er,
And in a kind and faithful friend
  Has doubled all my store.

Ten thousand thousand precious gifts
  My daily thanks employ;
Nor is the least a cheerful heart,
  That tastes those gifts with joy.

Through every period of my life,
  Thy goodness I'll pursue;
And after death, in distant worlds,
  The glorious theme renew.

When nature fails, and day and night
  Divide Thy works no more,
My ever-grateful heart, O LORD,
  Thy mercy shall adore.

Through all eternity, to Thee
  A joyful song I'll raise;
For, oh! eternity's too short
  To utter all Thy praise.

CLXXVI

THE spacious firmament on high,
  With all the blue ethereal sky,
And spangled Heavens, a shining frame,
Their great Original proclaim.

Th' unwearied Sun from day to day
Does his Creator's power display;
And publishes, to every land,
The work of an Almighty hand.

Soon as the evening shades prevail,
The Moon takes up the wondrous tale;
And nightly, to the listening Earth,
Repeats the story of her birth:
Whilst all the stars that round her burn,
And all the planets in their turn,
Confirm the tidings as they roll,
And spread the truth from pole to pole.

What though, in solemn silence, all
Move round the dark terrestrial ball;
What though nor real voice, nor sound
Amidst their radiant orbs be found;
In reason's ear they all rejoice,
And utter forth a glorious voice;
For ever singing as they shine:
'The Hand that made us is divine.'

CLXXVII

MORNING HYMN

AWAKE, my Soul, and with the sun,
　　Thy daily stage of duty run;
Shake off dull sloth, and joyful rise,
To pay thy morning sacrifice.

Thy precious time misspent, redeem;
Each present day thy last esteem;
Improve thy talent with due care,
For the great day thyself prepare.

Let all thy converse be sincere,
Thy conscience as the noon-day clear;
Think how all-seeing God thy ways,
And all thy secret thoughts, surveys.

By influence of the light divine,
Let thy own light to others shine;
Reflect all heaven's propitious rays,
In ardent love, and cheerful praise.

Wake, and lift up thyself, my heart,
And with the Angels bear thy part,
Who all night long unwearied sing
High praise to the eternal King.

Awake, awake! ye heavenly choir,
May your devotion me inspire,
That I, like you, my age may spend;
Like you, may on my GOD attend.

May I, like you, in GOD delight,
Have all day long my GOD in sight,
Perform, like you, my Maker's will—
O, may I never more do ill!

Had I your wings, to heaven I'd fly;
But GOD shall that defect supply;
And my soul, wing'd with warm desire,
Shall all day long to heaven aspire.

Glory to Thee, who safe hast kept,
And hast refresh'd me whilst I slept :—
Grant, LORD, when I from death shall wake,
I may of endless light partake.

I would not wake, nor rise again,
E'en Heaven itself I would disdain,
Wert not Thou there to be enjoy'd,
And I in hymns to be employ'd.

Heaven is, dear LORD, where'er Thou art;
O never then from me depart;
For to my soul, 'tis hell to be,
But for one moment, without Thee.

LORD, I my vows to Thee renew,
Scatter my sins as morning dew;
Guard my first springs of thought and will,
And with Thyself my spirit fill.

Direct, control, suggest, this day,
All I design, or do, or say;
That all my powers, with all their might,
In Thy sole glory may unite.

Praise GOD, from whom all blessings flow,
Praise Him, all creatures here below;
Praise Him above, ye heavenly host,
Praise Father, Son, and Holy Ghost.

T. Ken

CLXXVIII

EVENING HYMN

GLORY to Thee, my GOD, this night,
  For all the blessings of the light!
Keep me, O keep me, King of kings,
Beneath Thy own almighty wings.

Forgive me, LORD, for Thy dear Son,
The ill that I this day have done;
That with the world, myself, and Thee,
I, ere I sleep, at peace may be.

Teach me to live, that I may dread
The grave as little as my bed;
Teach me to die, that so I may
Rise glorious at the awful day.

O! may my soul on Thee repose,
And with sweet sleep mine eyelids close—
Sleep, that may me more vigorous make,
To serve my GOD when I awake!

When in the night I sleepless lie,
My soul with heavenly thoughts supply:
Let no ill dreams disturb my rest,
No powers of darkness me molest.

Dull sleep!—of sense me to deprive;
I am but half my days alive.
Thy faithful lovers, LORD, are grieved,
To lie so long of Thee bereaved.

But though sleep o'er my frailty reigns,
Let it not hold me long in chains,
And now and then let loose my heart,
Till it an Hallelujah dart.

The faster sleep the sense doth bind,
The more unfetter'd is the mind:
O may my soul, from matter free,
Thy loveliness unclouded see!

O when shall I, in endless day,
For ever chase dark sleep away,
And hymns with the supernal choir
Incessant sing, and never tire!

You, my blest Guardian, whilst I sleep,
Close to my bed your vigils keep,
Divine Love into me instil,
Stop all the avenues of ill:

Thought to thought with my soul converse,
Celestial joys to me rehearse,
Or in my stead, all the night long,
. Sing to my GOD a grateful song.

Praise GOD, from whom all blessings flow,
Praise Him, all creatures here below;
Praise Him above, ye heavenly host,
Praise Father, Son, and Holy Ghost.

CLXXIX

MIDNIGHT HYMN

MY GOD, now I from sleep awake,
The sole possession of me take;
From midnight terrors me secure,
And guard my heart from thoughts impure.

Blest Angels! while we silent lie,
Your Hallelujahs sing on high;
You, ever wakeful near the Throne,
Prostrate adore the Three in One.

I with your choir celestial join,
In offering up a hymn divine:
With you in heaven I hope to dwell,
And bid the night and world farewell.

My soul, when I shake off this dust,
LORD! in Thy arms I will intrust:
O, make me Thy peculiar care,
Some mansion for my soul prepare.

Give me a place at Thy saints' feet,
Or some fall'n Angel's vacant seat:
I'll strive to sing as loud as they,
Who sit above in brighter day.

O may I always ready stand,
With my lamp burning in my hand;
May I in sight of heaven rejoice,
Whenc'er I hear the Bridegroom's voice!

Glory to Thee, in light array'd,
Who Light Thy dwelling-place hast made;
A boundless ocean of bright beams
From Thy all-glorious Godhead streams.

The sun in its meridian height
Is very darkness in Thy sight :
My soul, O lighten and inflame,
With thought and love of Thy great name.

Blest JESU! Thou, on heaven intent,
Whole nights hast in devotion spent ;
But I, frail creature, soon am tired,
And all my zeal is soon expired.

My soul!—how canst thou weary grow
Of antedating bliss, below,
In sacred hymns and heavenly love,
Which will eternal be above ?

Shine on me, LORD! new life impart,
Fresh ardours kindle in my heart ;
One ray of Thy all-quickening light
Dispels the sloth and clouds of night.

LORD! lest the tempter me surprise,
Watch over Thine own sacrifice ;
All loose, all idle, thoughts cast out,
And make my very dreams devout.

Praise GOD, from whom all blessings flow,
Praise Him, all creatures here below ;
Praise Him above, y' Angelic host,
Praise Father, Son, and Holy Ghost.

CLXXX

LIFE

O FOOL,—of short-lived goods possest,—
In mere uncertainties to rest ;
From your full barns and bags of gold,
To dream of slowly growing old ;—
Can you bribe death, with all your store,
To respite you one moment more ?

Tell me, my soul, is there no art,
To arm against death's sudden dart ?
Has gracious Heaven contrived no way
Of lengthening here our mortal stay,
Or, on this momentaneous stage,
In a short time to live an age ?

The infants from the font who fly,
Unsullied, to the joys on high,
Live longer than obdurate men,
Who sin to threescore years and ten :—
We those dear moments only live,
Which we to GOD devoutly give.

CLXXXI

GRATEFUL ASPIRATIONS

I OFT recal the moments dear,
   Enjoy'd in penitential tear :
A beam of pardon through me shined,
Diffusing sweetness o'er my mind;
Upon my knees, while that I felt,
I could eternally have dwelt.

LORD! while in view Thy love I keep,
The fruits of love I daily reap,
Grief with fresh consolations cheer'd,
Hope nearer towards assurance rear'd;
Of GOD beloved, more likeness gain'd,
Or frailty with fresh aids sustain'd :

To prayer some gracious answer sent,
Some meditation more intent,
Or sudden fervency devout,
Or heavenly guidance when in doubt—
Ah, what am I, great GOD should be
Thus wondrously benign to me!

CLXXXII

THE MISER

I SAW this day a miser old
   Receive and count a bag of gold;
    His spectacles he clear'd,
    And on his nostrils rear'd,
Then moved his table toward the light,
To gain an unobstructed sight.

The pieces one by one he took,
And fix'd on either side his look;
    The edge he search'd with care,
    To find deficience there;
Next to the touchstone it applied,
And by the current standard tried.

Then reach'd his balance nicely made,
Which smallest things minutely weigh'd;
    The piece which pass'd his view
    Into the scale he threw,
Accounting what he must abate
For every atom short of weight.

Soon from the wretch I turn'd away,
Idolater of shining clay;
    But Conscience me here check'd,
    And chid my self-neglect;
She back me on a sudden drew,
My observation to renew.

'You,' Conscience said, 'that wretch despise,
Who yet may teach you to be wise;
    He, with a mind full bent,
    On his own gain intent,
His short-lived riches tells and weighs—
You thus should number all your days.

'Blest JESUS warn'd that, here below,
Misers would in their conduct show
    More zeal for short-lived toys,
    Than saints for endless joys:
If saints and misers we compare,
The worldly-minded wisest are.'

My conscience then my thought improved,
And me to think of Judgment moved,
    When every act, word, thought,
    To GOD's tribunal brought,
The Searcher of our hearts will try,
More nicely than the miser's eye.

On my past time I then reflect,
Deploring sadly my neglect:
    Vast treasure I had heap'd,
    And should at death have reap'd,
Had I the minutes, as they roll'd,
Heeded, as that vile wretch his gold.

In vanity I spent my prime:
In age I wasted precious time—
    Time which I should employ
    To purchase endless joy—
Time which, when once away it flies,
I never, never can reprise.

I nothing should too dear esteem,
My heedless minutes to redeem :—
    O that I had the power
    To live a year each hour,
That I might, ere I breathed my last,
Retrieve my idle minutes past!

CLXXXIII

NOW

THE *Past* can be no more—
    Whose misemploying I deplore :
The *Future* is to me
An absolute uncertainty :
The *Now*, which will not with me stay,
Within a second flies away.

  I heard GOD often say,
Now, of salvation is the day,—
    But turn'd from heaven my view,
I still had something else to do ;
Till GOD a dream instructive sent,
To warn me timely to repent.

  Methought Death, with his dart,
Had mortally transfix'd my heart ;
    And devils round about,
To seize my spirit flying out,
Cried—' *Now*, of which you took no care,
Is turn'd to *Never* and despair!'

  I gave a sudden start,
And waked, with *Never* in my heart :
    Still I that *Never* felt,
Never upon my spirit dwelt ;—
A thousand thanks to GOD I paid,
That my sad Never was delay'd.

CLXXXIV

SIGHS

SIGHS—whether swift to Heaven they rise
    As morning gilds the skies—
Or GOD, by omnipresent car,
  When they are sigh'd, is near—
Since GOD vouchsafes what I desire,
  'Twere fruitless to inquire.

In Heaven accounts of sighs are kept,
  Of every tear that's wept;
Saints feel the blessing back they bring,
  Swift as angelic wing:
The humble what they beg obtain,—
  They never sigh in vain.

CLXXXV

AN ANODYNE

AS in the night I restless lie,
  I the watch-candle keep in eye;
The innocent I often blame,
For the slow wasting of its flame.
Sweet ease!—O whither are you fled!—
With one short slumber ease my head!

My curtain oft I draw away,
Eager to see the morning ray;
But when the morning gilds the skies,
The morning no relief supplies.
To me, alas! the morning light
Is as afflictive as the night.

My vigorous cries to GOD ascend,
Oh!—will not GOD my cries attend?
Can GOD paternal love forbear—
Can GOD reject a filial prayer?
Is there in Heaven for me no cure—
Why do I then such pains endure?

My flesh in torture oft repines
At what GOD for my good designs;
My spirit the repiner chides,
Submissive to GOD's will abides:
GOD my disease and temper weighs;
No pang superfluous on me lays.

Why should I then my pains decline,
Inflicted by pure love divine?
Let them run out their destined course,
And spend upon me all their force:
Short pains can never grievous be,
Which work a blest eternity.

See Note

CLXXXVI

LOVE STRONG AS DEATH

A SAINT, to few but God well known,
   Who seem'd in town to dwell alone :
With few but saints who e'er conversed,
His alms in secret who dispersed ;
Whose virtues lay so out of view,
That Satan ne'er his saintship knew—
Such was the Saint to Jesus dear,
Who often made him visits here.

   Jesus to Death commission gave,
To lay his body in the grave ;—
Death to confederate Hell reveal'd
For whom his warrant next was seal'd.
Death and Hell out together went,
On the saint's endless ruin bent :
They both approaching his sick-bed,
His watchful Angel o'er his head
Brandish'd his bright angelic blade,
That neither could the saint invade.

   His license Death began to plead :
'That,' said the Angel, 'you exceed ;
For, when his dying Heaven design'd,
You should have left your hell behind—
Hell, which Heaven damns to strict restraint,
From troubling a departed saint.'

   The Angel, with his two-edged fire,
Made the infernal Fiend retire ;
'Your dart,' said he, 'now on him try ;
In slumbers sweet you see him lie :
Truth says that Love as Death is strong,
To see the experiment I long—
Death ! what your strength is, fully say,
And I 'll his love against it weigh.'

   Grim Death replied—'What lovers dare
Weak Love with this strong arm compare ?
I, a crown'd king, this sceptre sway ;
All living creatures me obey :
I daily, round the heavenly arch,
Arm'd with ten thousand terrors, march :
My darts I at my pleasure fling,
At statesman, hero, prelate, king.'

'Blest Enoch and Elias flew
To heavenly rest in spite of you:
Love over dangers, tortures, pains,
Invincible, the conquest gains;
Contemns you when you, fierce, appear,
And never feels what 'tis to fear.'

'I vanquish'd your incarnate GOD,
And on His grave triumphant trod:
And can weak Love my force withstand,
When JESUS own'd my conquering hand?'

''Twas Love, not you, made GOD to die,
That lovers might your darts defy:
He down His life was pleased to lay,
A ransom for man's guilt to pay.

'Death! when to lovers you draw nigh,
You're forced to lay your terrors by;
When warrants are for lovers sign'd,
You leave sting, sceptre, crown, behind:
Love eyes dear JESUS on the tree,
And from your tyranny is free.
You force exert on brittle clay,
Which has no power to disobey.
Love fights with lust, the world, and hell,
Has foes unnumber'd to repel;
Love runs through life a dangerous course,
And must at last take Heaven by force.

'On dust you, like the serpent, feed;
By Love the soul from dust is freed:
You, sin-born, seize the baser part,
Love keeps for GOD the heaven-born heart.
—Death! you are mortal!—you'll at last
Into the fiery lake be cast:
Love will, immortal, still 'abide,
Eternally beatified.'

CLXXXVII

WHILE shepherds watch'd their flocks by night
    All seated on the ground,
The Angel of the LORD came down,
    And glory shone around.

'Fear not,' said he; (for mighty dread
    Had seized their troubled mind;)
'Glad tidings of great joy I bring
    To you and all mankind.

'To you, in David's town, this day
  Is born of David's line
The Saviour, Who is CHRIST the LORD;
  And this shall be the sign :—

'The heavenly Babe you there shall find
  To human view display'd,
All meanly wrapt in swathing-bands,
  And in a manger laid.'

Thus spake the Seraph; and forthwith
  Appear'd a shining throng
Of Angels, praising GOD, and thus
  Address'd their joyful song :—

'All glory be to GOD on high,
  And to the earth be peace;
Good-will henceforth from Heaven to men
  Begin, and never cease!'

N. Tate

CLXXXVIII

ANGELS' SONG

O HOLY, holy, holy LORD,
    Eternal GOD, Almighty One,
Be Thou for ever, and be Thou alone,
By all Thy creatures, constantly adored!
    Ineffable, co-equal Three,
    Who from non-entity gave birth
To angels and to men, to Heaven and to Earth,
Yet always wast Thyself, and wilt for ever be.
    But for Thy mercy, we had ne'er possest
    These thrones, and this immense felicity;
    Could ne'er have been so infinitely blest!
Therefore all glory, power, dominion, majesty,
    To Thee, O Lamb of GOD, to Thee,
For ever, longer than for ever, be!

J. Pomfret

CLXXXIX

FELICITY

NO; 'tis in vain to seek for bliss;
    For bliss can ne'er be found
Till we arrive where JESUS is,
    And tread on heavenly ground.

There 's nothing round these painted skies,
 Or round this dusty clod,
Nothing, my soul! that 's worth thy joys,
 Or lovely as thy God.

'Tis Heaven on Earth to taste His love,
 To feel His quickening grace;
And all the Heaven I hope above
 Is but to see His face.

I. Watts

CXC

THE NATIVITY

'SHEPHERDS, rejoice, lift up your eyes,
 And send your fears away;
News from the region of the skies!—
 Salvation 's born to-day.

'Jesus, the God whom Angels fear,
 Comes down to dwell with you;
To-day He makes His entrance here,
 But not as monarchs do.

'No gold, nor purple swaddling-bands,
 Nor royal shining things;
A manger for His cradle stands,
 And holds the King of kings.

'Go, shepherds, where the Infant lies,
 And see His humble throne :—
With tears of joy in all your eyes
 Go, shepherds, kiss the Son.'

Thus Gabriel sang: and straight around
 The heavenly armies throng;
They tune their harps to lofty sound,
 And thus conclude the song:

'Glory to God that reigns above,
 Let peace surround the Earth;
Mortals shall know their Maker's love,
 At their Redeemer's birth.'

Lord! and shall angels have their songs,
 And men no tunes to raise?
O may we lose these useless tongues,
 When they forget to praise!

Glory to God that reigns above,
 That pitied us forlorn!
We join to sing our Maker's love—
 For there's a Saviour born.

CXCI

FAIREST of all the lights above,
 Thou Sun, whose beams adorn the spheres,
And with unwearied swiftness move
To form the circles of our years:
Praise the Creator of the skies,
That dress'd thine orb in golden rays;
Or may the Sun forget to rise,
If. he forget his Maker's praise!

Thou reigning beauty of the night,
Fair queen of silence, silver Moon,
Whose gentle beams and borrow'd light
Are softer rivals of the noon,—
Arise, and to that Sovereign Power,
Waxing and waning, honours pay,
Who bade thee rule the dusky hour,
And half supply the absent day.

Ye twinkling Stars, who gild the skies
When darkness has its curtains drawn,
Who keep your watch, with wakeful eyes,
When business, cares, and day are gone:
Proclaim the glories of your Lord,
Dispersed through all the heavenly street,
Whose boundless treasures can afford
So rich a pavement for His feet.

CXCII

INFINITE Power, Eternal Lord,
 How sovereign is Thy hand!
All Nature rose t' obey Thy word,
 And moves at Thy command.

With steady course Thy shining Sun
 Keeps his appointed way;
And all the hours obedient run
 The circle of the day.

But ah! how wide my spirit flies
 And wanders from her God!
My soul forgets the heavenly prize,
 And treads the downward road.

Shall creatures of a meaner frame
  Pay all their dues to Thee,
—Creatures, that never knew Thy name,
  That never loved like me!

Great GOD, create my soul anew,
  Conform my heart to Thine;
Melt down my will, and let it flow,
  And take the mould divine.

Seize my whole frame into Thy hand;
  Here all my powers I bring:
Manage the wheels by Thy command,
  And govern every spring.

Then shall my feet no more depart,
  Nor wandering senses rove;
Devotion shall be all my heart,
  And all my passions, love.

Then not the Sun shall more than I
  His Maker's law perform,
Nor travel swifter through the sky,
  Nor with a zeal so warm.

CXCIII

WHERE'ER my flattering passions rove,
  I find a lurking snare;
'Tis dangerous to let loose our love
  Beneath the Eternal Fair.

Souls whom the tie of friendship binds,
  And partners of our blood,
Seize a large portion of our minds,
  And leave the less for GOD.

Nature has soft but powerful bands,
  And Reason she controls;
While children with their little hands
  Hang closest to our souls.

Thoughtless they act the old Serpent's part;
  What tempting things they be!
LORD, how they twine about our heart,
  And draw it off from Thee!

Dear Sovereign, break these fetters off,
  And set our spirits free ;
GOD in Himself is bliss enough ;
  For we have all in Thee.

See Note

CXCIV

O GOD, our help in ages past,
    Our hope for years to come,
Our shelter from the stormy blast,
  And our eternal home :

Under the shadow of Thy Throne
  Thy saints have dwelt secure;
Sufficient is Thine arm alone,
  And our defence is sure.

Before the hills in order stood,
  Or earth received her frame,
From everlasting Thou art GOD,
  To endless years the same.

A thousand ages in Thy sight
  Are like an evening gone ;
Short as the watch that ends the night
  Before the rising sun.

Time, like an ever-rolling stream,
  Bears all its sons away ;
They fly forgotten, as a dream
  Dies at the opening day.

Our GOD, our help in ages past;
  Our hope for years to come;
Be Thou our guard while troubles last,
  And our eternal home !

CXCV

HEAR what the voice from Heaven proclaims
    For all the pious dead,—
Sweet is the savour of their names,
  And soft their sleeping bed.

Why should we tremble to convey
  Their relics to the tomb ?
There the Redeemer's body lay,
  And left a long perfume.

The graves of all His saints He blest,
 And soften'd every bed ;
Where should the dying members rest,
 But with the dying Head?

CXCVI

THE EXAMPLES OF THE SAINTS

GIVE me the wings of faith, to rise
 Within the veil, and see
The Saints above, how great their joys,
 How bright their glories be !

Once they were mourning here below,
 And wet their couch with tears ;
They wrestled hard, as we do now,
 With sins, and doubts, and fears.

I ask them whence their victory came ;
 They, with united breath,
Ascribe their conquest to the Lamb,
 Their triumph to His death.

They mark'd the footsteps that He trod ;
 His zeal inspired their breast ;
And, following their incarnate God,
 Possess the promised rest.

Our glorious Leader claims our praise,
 For His own pattern given ;
While the long cloud of witnesses
 Show the same path to Heaven.

CXCVII

A CRADLE SONG

HUSH ! my dear, lie still and slumber,
 Holy Angels guard thy bed !
Heavenly blessings without number
 Gently falling on thy head.

Sleep, my babe ; thy food and raiment,
 House and home, thy friends provide ;
All without thy care or payment,
 All thy wants are well supplied.

How much better thou 'rt attended
  Than the Son of God could be,
When from heaven He descended,
  And became a child like thee!

Soft and easy is thy cradle:
  Coarse and hard thy Saviour lay:
When His birthplace was a stable,
  And His softest bed was hay.

See the kinder shepherds round Him,
  Telling wonders from the sky!
Where they sought Him, there they found Him,
  With His Virgin-Mother by.

See the lovely Babe a-dressing;
  Lovely Infant, how He smiled!
When He wept, the Mother's blessing
  Soothed and hush'd the holy Child.

Lo, He slumbers in His manger,
  Where the hornéd oxen fed;
—Peace, my darling, here 's no danger;
  Here 's no ox a-near thy bed!

May'st Thou live to know and fear Him,
  Trust and love Him all thy days;
Then go dwell for ever near Him,
  See His face, and sing His praise!

I could give thee thousand kisses,
  Hoping what I most desire;
Not a mother's fondest wishes
  Can to greater joys aspire.

See Note

CXCVIII

SURSUM

YE golden lamps of Heaven, farewell,
    With all your feeble light;
Farewell, thou ever-changing moon,
  Pale empress of the night.

And thou, refulgent orb of day,
  In brighter flames array'd;
—My soul, that springs beyond thy sphere,
  No more demands thine aid.

Ye stars are but the shining dust
  Of my Divine abode,
The pavement of those heavenly courts
  Where I shall reign with God.

The Father of eternal light
  Shall there His beams display;
Nor shall one moment's darkness mix
  With that unvaried day.

No more the drops of piercing grief
  Shall swell into mine eyes;
Nor the meridian sun decline
  Amidst those brighter skies.

P. Doddridge

CXCIX

AT THE SEPULCHRE

YE humble souls, that seek the Lord,
  Chase all your fears away;
And bow with pleasure down to see
  The place where Jesus lay.

Thus low the Lord of life was brought;
  Such wonders Love can do;
Thus cold in death that bosom lay,
  Which throbb'd and bled for you.

Then raise your eyes, and tune your songs;
  The Saviour lives again!
Not all the bolts and bars of death
  The Conqueror could detain:

High o'er the angelic bands He rears
  His once dishonour'd head;
And through unnumber'd years He reigns,
  Who dwelt among the dead.

CC

JESUS! I love Thy charming name;
  'Tis music to my ear:
Fain would I sound it out so loud
  That heaven and earth should hear!

Yes, Thou art precious to my soul,
  My transport, and my trust:
Jewels to Thee are gaudy toys,
  And gold is sordid dust.

All my capacious powers can wish
  In Thee most richly meet :
Nor to my eyes is life so dear,
  Nor friendship half so sweet.

I 'll speak the honours of Thy name
  With my last labouring breath :
Then speechless clasp Thee in my arms—
  The antidote of death.

CCI

HARK the glad sound ! The Saviour comes,
    The Saviour promised long ;
Let every heart prepare a throne,
  And every voice a song !

He comes the prisoners to release
  In Satan's bondage held ;
The gates of brass before Him burst,
  The iron fetters yield.

He comes, the broken heart to bind,
  The bleeding soul to cure,
And with the treasures of His grace
  T' enrich the humble poor.

Our glad Hosannas, Prince of Peace,
  Thy welcome shall proclaim,
And Heaven's eternal arches ring
  With Thy belovéd Name.

CCII

DESIDERIUM

MY spirit longeth for Thee,
    Within my troubled breast
Altho' I be unworthy
  Of so divine a Guest.

Of so divine a Guest,
  Unworthy tho' I be,
Yet has my heart no rest,
  Unless it come from Thee.

Unless it come from Thee,
  In vain I look around ;
In all that I can see,
  No rest is to be found.

M

No rest is to be found,
  But in Thy blessèd love;
O!. let my wish be crown'd,
  And send it from above!

J. Byrom

CCIII

A HYMN ON RECOVERY FROM SEVERE ILLNESS

WHEN Israel's ruler on the royal bed
  In anguish and in perturbation lay,
The down relieved not his anointed head,
  And rest gave place to horror and dismay.
Fast flow'd the tears, high heaved each gasping sigh,
When GOD's own prophet thunder'd—'Monarch, thou must die.'

'And must I go,' the illustrious mourner cried,
  'I who have served Thee still in faith and truth,
Whose snow-white conscience no foul crime has dyed
  From youth to manhood, infancy to youth;
Like David, who have still revered Thy word—
The sovereign of myself, and servant of the LORD.'

The Judge Almighty heard His suppliant's moan,
  Repeal'd his sentence, and his health restored;
The beams of mercy on his temples shone,
  Shot from that Heaven to which his sighs had soar'd;
The Sun retreated at his Maker's nod,
And miracles confirm the genuine work of GOD.

But, O Immortals!—What had I to plead
  When Death stood o'er me with his threatening lance,
When reason left me in the time of need,
  And sense was lost in terror or in trance?
My sinking soul was with my blood inflamed,
And the celestial image sunk, defaced and maim'd.

I sent back memory, in heedful guise,
  To search the records of preceding years;
Home, like the raven to the ark, she flies,
  Croaking bad tidings to my trembling ears:
O Sun, again that¹ thy retreat was made,
And threw my follies back into the friendly shade!

But soul-rejoicing health again returns,
  The blood meanders gentle in each vein;
The lamp of life renew'd with vigour burns,
  And exiled reason takes her seat again:—
Brisk leaps the heart, the mind's at large once more,
To love, to praise, to bless, to wonder and adore.

The virtuous partner of my nuptial bands
  Appear'd a widow to my frantic sight;
My little prattlers, lifting up their hands,
  Beckon me back to them, to life, and light;
I come, ye spotless sweets! I come again,
Nor have your tears been shed, nor have ye knelt in vain.

—All glory to the Eternal, to the Immense,
  All glory to the Omniscient and Good,
Whose power's uncircumscribed, Whose love's intense,
  But yet Whose justice ne'er could be withstood,
Except thro' Him—thro' Him, Who stands alone,
Of worth, of weight allow'd for all mankind to atone!

O Penitence!—to virtue near allied,
  Thou canst new joys e'en to the blest impart;
The listening Angels lay their harps aside
  To hear the music of thy contrite heart;
And Heaven itself wears a more radiant face,
When Charity presents thee to the Throne of grace!

Chief of metallic forms is regal gold;
  Of elements, the limpid fount that flows;
Give me 'mongst gems the brilliant to behold;
  O'er Flora's flock imperial is the rose:
Above all birds the sovereign eagle soars;
And monarch of the field the lordly lion roars.

What can with great Leviathan compare,
  Who takes his pastime in the mighty main?
What, like the Sun, shines thro' the realms of air,
  And gilds and glorifies th' ethereal plain?—
Yet what are these to man, who bears the sway?
For all was made for him—to serve and to obey.

Thus in high Heaven Charity is great,
  Faith, hope, devotion hold a lower place;
On her the Cherubs and the Seraphs wait,
  Her, every virtue courts, and every grace;
See! on the right, close by the Almighty's throne,
In Him she shines confess'd, Who came to make her known.

Deep-rooted in my heart then let her grow,
  That for the past the future may atone;
That I may act what Thou hast given to know,
  That I may live for Thee, and Thee alone,—
And justify those sweetest words from Heaven,
'That he shall love Thee most, to whom Thou 'st most forgiven.'

C. Smart

---

1 *again* [would] *that*

CCIV

SONG TO DAVID

HE sang of God—the mighty source
  Of all things—the stupendous force
    On which all strength depends;
From Whose right arm, beneath Whose eyes,
All period, power, and enterprise
    Commences, reigns, and ends.

Tell them, I AM, Jehovah said
To Moses; while earth heard in dread,
    And, smitten to the heart,
At once above, beneath, around,
All Nature, without voice or sound,
    Replied, O LORD, THOU ART.

The world,—the clustering spheres, He made,
The glorious light, the soothing shade,
    Dale, champaign, grove, and hill;
The multitudinous abyss,
Where Secrecy remains in bliss,
    And Wisdom hides her skill.

The pillars of the LORD are seven,
Which stand from earth to topmost heaven;
    His Wisdom drew the plan;
His Word accomplish'd the design,
From brightest gem to deepest mine;
    From CHRIST enthroned, to Man.

For Adoration all the ranks
Of Angels yield eternal thanks,
    And David in the midst;
With GOD's good poor, which, last and least
In man's esteem, Thou to Thy feast,
    O blesséd Bridegroom, bid'st!

For Adoration, David's Psalms
Lift up the heart to deeds of alms;
    And he, who kneels and chants,
Prevails his passions to control,
Finds meat and medicine to the soul,
    Which for translation pants.

For Adoration, in the dome
Of CHRIST, the sparrows find a home;
    And on His olives perch:
—The swallow also dwells with thee,
O man of GOD's humility,
    Within his Saviour's Church.

Sweet is the dew that falls betimes,
And drops upon the leafy limes;
    Sweet, Hermon's fragrant air:
Sweet is the lily's silver bell,
And sweet the wakeful tapers' smell
    That watch for early prayer.

Sweet the young nurse, with love intense,
Which smiles o'er sleeping innocence;
    Sweet, when the lost arrive:
Sweet the musician's ardour beats,
While his vague mind's in quest of sweets,
    The choicest flowers to hive.

Strong is the horse upon his speed;
Strong in pursuit the rapid glede [1],
    Which makes at once his game:
Strong the tall ostrich on the ground;
Strong through the turbulent profound
    Shoots Xiphias [2] to his aim.

Strong is the lion—like a coal
His eyeball,—like a bastion's mole
    His chest against the foes:
Strong the gier-eagle [3] on his sail;
Strong against tide the enormous whale
    Emerges as he goes.

But stronger still, in earth and air,
And in the sea, the man of prayer,
    And far beneath the tide:
And in the seat to faith assign'd,
Where ask is have, where seek is find,
    Where knock is open wide.

Precious the penitential tear;
And precious is the sigh sincere,
    Acceptable to God:
And precious are the winning flowers,
In gladsome Israel's feast of bowers
    Bound on the hallow'd sod.

Glorious the sun in mid career;
Glorious the assembled fires appear;
    Glorious the comet's train:
Glorious the trumpet and alarm;
Glorious the Almighty's stretch'd-out arm;
    Glorious the enraptured main:

Glorious the northern lights a-stream;
Glorious the song, when GOD's the theme;
Glorious the thunder's roar:
Glorious Hosannah from the den;
Glorious the catholic Amen;
Glorious the martyr's gore:

Glorious,—more glorious,—is the crown
Of Him that brought salvation down,
By meekness call'd Thy Son;
Thou that stupendous truth believed;—
And now the matchless deed's achieved,
Determined, Dared, and Done.

1 *glede*, hawk   2 *Xiphias*, sword-fish   3 *gier-eagle*, probably, circling

CCV

SIMEON WAITING

WHEN JESUS, by the Virgin brought,
(So runs the law of Heaven),
Was offer'd holy to the LORD,
And at the altar given;

Simeon the just and the devout,
Who frequent in the fane
Had for the Saviour waited long,
But waited still in vain,—

Came Heaven-directed at the hour
When Mary held her Son;
He stretchéd forth his aged arms,
While tears of gladness run:

With holy joy upon his face
The good old father smiled,
While fondly in his wither'd arms
He clasp'd the promised Child.

And then he lifted up to Heaven
An earnest asking eye;
'My joy is full, my hour is come;
LORD, let Thy servant die.

'At last my arms embrace my LORD;
Now let their vigour cease;
At last my eyes my Saviour see,
Now let them close In peace!

'The Star and Glory of the land
  Hath now begun to shine;
The morning that shall gild the globe
  Breaks on these eyes of mine!'

M. Bruce

CCVI

TRUST IN PROVIDENCE

ALMIGHTY Father of mankind,
  On Thee my hopes remain;
And when the day of trouble comes,
  I shall not trust in vain.

Thou art our kind Preserver, from
  The cradle to the tomb;
And I was cast upon Thy care,
  E'en from my mother's womb.

In early days Thou wast my guide,
  And of my youth the friend;
And as my days began with Thee,
  With Thee my days shall end.

In former times, when trouble came,
  Thou didst not stand afar;
Nor didst Thou prove an absent friend
  Amid the din of war.

My God, who caused'st me to hope,
  When life began to beat,
And when a stranger in the world
  Didst guide my wandering feet;

Thou wilt not cast me off, when age
  And evil days descend;
Thou wilt not leave me in despair,
  To mourn my latter end!

I know the Power in Whom I trust,
  The Arm on Which I lean;
He will my Saviour ever be,
  Who has my Saviour been.

CCVII

MESSIAH! at Thy glad approach
  The howling wilds are still;
Thy praises fill the lonely waste,
  And breathe from every hill.

The hidden fountains, at Thy call,
  Their sacred stores unlock;
Loud in the desert sudden streams
  Burst living from the rock.

The incense of the Spring ascends
  Upon the morning gale;
Red o'er the hill the roses bloom,
  The lilies in the vale.

The kingdom of Messiah come,
  Appointed times disclose;
And fairer in Emmanuel's land
  The new Creation glows:—

Renew'd, the earth a robe of light,
  A robe of beauty wears;
And in new Heavens a brighter Sun
  Leads on the promised years.

CCVIII

THE God of Abraham praise,
  Who reigns enthroned above,
Ancient of everlasting days,
  And God of love!
Jehovah! Great I AM!
  By earth and Heaven confest;
I bow and bless the sacred Name,
  For ever blest!

The God of Abraham praise!
  At Whose supreme command
From earth I rise, and seek the joys
  At His right hand:
I all on earth forsake,
  Its wisdom, fame, and power,
And Him my only portion make,
  My Shield and Tower.

He by Himself hath sworn;
  I on His oath depend:
I shall, on eagle's wings upborne,
  To Heaven ascend;
I shall behold His face,
  I shall His power adore,
And sing the wonders of His grace
  For evermore!

There dwells the Lord our King,
The Lord our Righteousness,
Triumphant o'er the world and sin,
    The Prince of Peace!
On Sion's sacred height
His kingdom still maintains,
And, glorious with His saints in light,
    For ever reigns!

Before the great Three-One
They all exulting stand,
And tell the wonders He hath done
    Through all their land;
The listening spheres attend
And swell the growing fame,
And sing, in songs which never end,
    The wondrous Name!

The God, who reigns on high,
The great Archangels sing,
And, ' Holy, holy, holy,' cry,
    ' Almighty King!
Who Was, and Is, the same,
And evermore shall be!
Jehovah! Father! Great I am!
    We worship Thee!'

Before the Saviour's face
The ransom'd nations bow,
O'erwhelm'd at His Almighty grace,
    For ever new:
He shows His prints of Love;
They kindle to a flame,
And sound, through all the worlds above,
    The slaughter'd Lamb!

The whole triumphant host
Give thanks to God on high;
' Hail! Father, Son, and Holy Ghost!'
    They ever cry:
Hail! Abraham's God, and mine!
I join the heavenly lays;
All might and majesty are Thine,
    And endless praise!

                    T. Olivers

CCIX

ROCK of Ages, cleft for me,
    Let me hide myself in Thee!
Let the water and the blood
From Thy riven side which flow'd,
Be of sin the double cure,
Cleanse me from its guilt and power.

Not the labours of my hands
Can fulfil Thy law's demands;
Could my zeal no respite know,
Could my tears for ever flow,
All for sin could not atone;
Thou must save, and Thou alone.

Nothing in my hand I bring;
Simply to Thy Cross I cling;
Naked, come to Thee for dress;
Helpless, look to Thee for grace;
Foul, I to the Fountain fly;
Wash me, Saviour, or I die!

While I draw this fleeting breath,
When my eyestrings break in death,
When I soar through tracts unknown,
See Thee on Thy Judgment-throne;
Rock of Ages, cleft for me,
Let me hide myself in Thee!

A. M. Toplady

CCX

AH! give me, LORD, the single eye,
    Which aims at nought but Thee:
I fain would live, and yet not I—
    But JESUS live in me.

Like Noah's dove, no rest I find
    But in Thy ark of peace;
Thy cross, the balance [1] of my mind;
    Thy wounds, my hiding-place.

In vain the tempter spreads the snare,
    If Thou my keeper art;
—Get thee behind me, GOD is near,
    My Saviour takes my part!

On Him my spirit I recline,
    Who put my nature on;
His light shall in my darkness shine,
    And guide me to His throne.

[1] *balance*, see Note

CCXI

LORD! it is not life to live,
     If Thy presence Thou deny;
Lord! if Thou Thy presence give,
     'Tis no longer death—to die.
Source and Giver of repose,
Singly from Thy smile it flows;
Peace and happiness are Thine,—
Mine they are, if Thou art mine.

CCXII

COMPARED with Christ, in all beside
     No comeliness I see;
The one thing needful, dearest Lord,
     Is to be one with Thee.
Whatever else Thy will withholds,
     Here grant me to succeed!
O let Thyself my portion be,
     And I am blest indeed!

Loved of my God, for Him again
     With love intense I burn:
Chosen of Thee ere time began,
     I choose Thee in return!
Less than Thyself will not suffice
     My comfort to restore;
More than Thyself I cannot have;
     And Thou canst give no more.

CCXIII

COME, Thou long-expected Jesus,
     Born to set Thy people free;
From our fears and sins release us,
     Let us find our rest in Thee:
Israel's strength and consolation,
     Hope of all the earth Thou art;
Dear desire of every nation,
     Joy of every longing heart.

Born Thy people to deliver;
     Born a Child, and yet a King;
Born to reign in us for ever,
     Now Thy gracious kingdom bring:

By Thine own eternal Spirit
  Rule in all our hearts alone;
By Thine all-sufficient merit,
  Raise us to Thy glorious throne.

                              C. Wesley

CCXIV

FOR A CHILD

LAMB of GOD, I look to Thee;
  Thou shalt my example be;
Thou art gentle, meek, and mild;
Thou wast once a little child.

Thou didst live to GOD alone;
Thou didst never seek Thine own;
Thou Thyself didst never please;
GOD was all Thy happiness.

Loving JESU, gentle Lamb,
In Thy gracious hands I am;
Make me, Saviour, what Thou art!
Live Thyself within my heart!

I shall then show forth Thy praise;
Serve Thee all my happy days;
Then the world shall always see
CHRIST, the Holy Child, in me.

CCXV

WRESTLING WITH THE ANGEL

COME, O Thou Traveller unknown,
  Whom still I hold, but cannot see,
My company before is gone,
  And I am left alone with Thee;
With Thee all night I mean to stay,
And wrestle till the break of day.

I need not tell Thee who I am,
  My misery or sin declare;
Thyself hast call'd me by my name;
  Look on Thy hands, and read it there!
But Who, I ask Thee, Who art Thou?
Tell me Thy Name, and tell me now.

In vain Thou strugglest to get free,
  I never will unloose my hold;
Art Thou the Man that died for me?
  The secret of Thy love unfold.
Wrestling, I will not let Thee go,
Till I Thy Name, Thy Nature know.

Wilt Thou not yet to me reveal
  Thy new, unutterable Name?
Tell me, I still beseech Thee, tell:
  To know it now, resolved I am:
Wrestling, I will not let Thee go,
Till I Thy Name, Thy Nature know.

What though my shrinking flesh complain,
  And murmur to contend so long?
I rise superior to my pain;
  When I am weak, then I am strong:
And when my all of strength shall fail,
I shall with the God-Man prevail.

My strength is gone; my nature dies;
  I sink beneath Thy weighty hand;
Faint to revive, and fall to rise;
  I fall, and yet by faith I stand:
I stand, and will not let Thee go,
Till I Thy Name, Thy Nature know.

Yield to me now, for I am weak,
  But confident in self-despair;
Speak to my heart, in blessings speak,
  Be conquer'd by my instant prayer!
Speak, or Thou never hence shalt move,—
And tell me, if Thy Name is Love?

—'Tis Love! 'tis Love! Thou diedst for me!
  I hear Thy whisper in my heart!
The morning breaks, the shadows flee;
  Pure universal Love Thou art!
To me, to all, Thy bowels move;
Thy Nature and Thy Name is Love!

My prayer hath power with God; the grace
  Unspeakable I now receive;
Through faith I see Thee face to face,
  I see Thee face to face, and live:
In vain I have not wept and strove;
Thy Nature and Thy Name is Love.

I know Thee, Saviour, Who Thou art;
 Jesus, the feeble sinner's Friend!
Nor wilt Thou with the night depart,
 But stay, and love me to the end!
Thy mercies never shall remove—
Thy Nature and Thy Name is Love!

The Sun of Righteousness on me
 Hath rose, with healing in His wings;
Wither'd my nature's strength, from Thee
 My soul its life and succour brings;
My help is all laid up above;
Thy Nature, and Thy Name, is Love.

Contented now upon my thigh
 I halt, till life's short journey end;
All helplessness, all weakness, I
 On Thee alone for strength depend;
Nor have I power from Thee to move;
Thy Nature, and Thy Name, is Love.

Lame as I am, I take the prey,
 Hell, earth, and sin, with ease o'ercome;
I leap for joy, pursue my way,
 And as a bounding hart fly home—
Through all eternity to prove,
Thy Nature and Thy Name is Love!

CCXVI

HARK! how all the welkin rings
 Glory to the King of kings!
Peace on earth and mercy mild,
God and sinners reconciled!
Joyful, all ye nations, rise,
Join the triumph of the skies;
Universal nature say,
Christ the Lord is born to-day!

Christ, by highest Heaven adored;
Christ, the Everlasting Lord;
Late in time behold Him come,
Offspring of a Virgin's womb:
Veil'd in flesh the Godhead see;
Hail, th' Incarnate Deity,
Pleased as man with men t' appear,
Jesus, our Immanuel here!

Hail! the heavenly Prince of Peace!
Hail the Sun of Righteousness!
Light and life to all He brings,
Risen with healing in His wings.
Mild He lays His glory by,
Born that man no more may die,
Born to raise the sons of earth,
Born to give them second birth.

CCXVII

MORNING

CHRIST, Whose glory fills the skies,
    CHRIST, the true, the only Light,
Sun of Righteousness, arise,
    Triumph o'er the shades of night!
Day-spring from on high, be near!
Day-star, in my heart appear!

Dark and cheerless is the morn
    Unaccompanied by Thee;
Joyless is the day's return,
    Till Thy mercy's beams I see;
Till they inward light impart,
Glad my eyes, and warm my heart.

Visit then this soul of mine,
    Pierce the gloom of sin and grief!
Fill me, Radiancy Divine,
    Scatter all my unbelief!
More and more Thyself display,
Shining to the perfect day!

CCXVIII

NIGHT

ALL praise to Him who dwells in bliss,
    Who made both day and night;
Whose throne is darkness, in th' abyss
    Of uncreated light!

Each thought and deed His piercing eyes
    With strictest search survey;
The deepest shades no more disguise
    Than the full blaze of day.

Whom Thou dost guard, O King of kings,
  No evil shall molest:
Under the shadow of Thy wings
  Shall they securely rest.

Thy Angels shall around their beds
  Their constant stations keep;
Thy faith and truth shall shield their heads,
  For Thou dost never sleep.

May we, with calm and sweet repose,
  And heavenly thoughts refresh'd,
Our eyelids with the morn unclose,
  And bless the Ever-bless'd!

CCXIX

TIMES without number have I pray'd,
    'This only once forgive';
Relapsing, when Thy hand was stay'd,
  And suffer'd me to live:—

Yet now the kingdom of Thy peace,
  LORD, to my heart restore;
Forgive my vain repentances,
  And bid me sin no more.

CCXX

COME, let us join our friends above,
    That have obtain'd the prize,
And on the eagle wings of Love
  To joy celestial rise.
Let all the saints terrestrial sing
  With those to glory gone,
For all the servants of our King,
  In Earth and Heaven, are one.

One family we dwell in Him,
  One Church, above, beneath,
Though now divided by the stream,
  The narrow stream of death.
One army of the living GOD,
  To His command we bow;
Part of His host hath cross'd the flood,
  And part is crossing now.

Our old companions in distress
  We haste again to see,
And eager long for our release
  And full felicity:—

Oh! that we now might grasp our Guide!
  Oh! that the word were given!
Come, LORD of hosts! the waves divide,
  And land us all in Heaven!

CCXXI

JESU, Lover of my soul,
  Let me to Thy bosom fly,
While the nearer waters roll,
  While the tempest still is high:
Hide me, O my Saviour, hide
  Till the storm of life is past,
Safe into the haven guide,
  O receive my soul at last!

Other refuge have I none;
  Hangs my helpless soul on Thee;
Leave, ah! leave me not alone,
  Still support and comfort me!
All my trust on Thee is stay'd,
  All my help from Thee I bring:
Cover my defenceless head
  With the shadow of Thy wing!

Wilt Thou not regard my call?
  Wilt Thou not accept my prayer?
Lo! I sink, I faint, I fall—
  Lo! on Thee I cast my care!
Reach me out Thy gracious hand:
  While I of Thy strength receive,
Hoping against hope I stand,
  Dying, and behold I live!

Plenteous grace with Thee is found,
  Grace to cover all my sin;
Let the healing streams abound;
  Make and keep me pure within:—
Thou of Life the Fountain art,
  Freely let me take of Thee;
Spring Thou up within my heart,—
  Rise to all eternity!

CCXXII

TO GOD, ye choir above, begin
  A hymn so loud and strong
That all the universe may hear
  And join the grateful song.

Praise Him, thou sun, Who dwells unseen
  Amidst transcendent light,
Where thy refulgent orb would seem
  A spot, as dark as night.

Thou silver moon, ye host of stars,
  The universal song
Through the serene and silent night
  To listening worlds prolong.

Sing Him, ye distant worlds and suns,
  From whence no travelling ray
Hath yet to us, through ages past,
  Had time to make its way.

Assist, ye raging storms, and bear
  On rapid wings His praise,
From north to south, from east to west,
  Through heaven, and earth, and seas.

Exert your voice, ye furious fires
  That rend the watery cloud,
And thunder to this nether world
  Your Maker's words aloud.

Ye works of God, that dwell unknown
  Beneath the rolling main ;
Ye birds, that sing among the groves,
  And sweep the azure plain ;

Ye stately hills, that rear your heads,
  And towering pierce the sky ;
Ye clouds, that with an awful pace
  Majestic roll on high ;

Ye insects small, to which one leaf
  Within its narrow sides
A vast extended world displays,
  And spacious realms provides ;

Ye race, still less than these, with which
  The stagnant water teems,
To which one drop, however small,
  A boundless ocean seems ;

—Whate'er ye are, where'er ye dwell,
  Ye creatures great or small,
Adore the Wisdom, praise the Power,
  That made and governs all.

                              P. Skelton

CCXXIII

CHILDREN of the Heavenly King,
    As ye journey, sweetly sing;
Sing your Saviour's worthy praise,
Glorious in His works and ways!

We are travelling home to GOD,
In the way the Fathers trod;
They are happy now; and we
Soon their happiness shall see.

Shout, ye little flock, and blest!
You on JESUS' Throne shall rest;
There your seat is now prepared,
There your kingdom and reward.

Lift your eyes, ye sons of Light!
Zion's city is in sight:
There our endless home shall be,
There our LORD we soon shall see.

Fear not, brethren; joyful stand
On the borders of your land;
JESUS CHRIST, your Father's Son,
Bids you undismay'd go on.

LORD! obediently we go,
Gladly leaving all below:
Only Thou our Leader be,
And we still will follow Thee.

J. Cennick

CCXXIV

A VISION OF LIFE IN DEATH

IN evil long I took delight,
    Unawed by shame or fear,
Till a new object struck my sight,
    And stopp'd my wild career:
I saw One hanging on a Tree
    In agonies and blood,
Who fix'd His languid eyes on me,
    As near His Cross I stood.

Sure never till my latest breath
    Can I forget that look:
It seem'd to charge me with His death,
    Though not a word He spoke:

N 2

My conscience felt and own'd the guilt,
 And plunged me in despair;
I saw my sins His Blood had spilt,
 And help'd to nail Him there.

Alas! I knew not what I did!
 But now my tears are vain:
Where shall my trembling soul be hid?
 For I the LORD have slain!
—A second look He gave, which said,
 'I freely all forgive;
This Blood is for thy ransom paid;
 I die, that thou may'st live.'

Thus, while His death my sin displays
 In all its blackest hue,
Such is the mystery of grace,
 It seals my pardon too.
With pleasing grief, and mournful joy,
 My spirit now is fill'd,
That I should such a life destroy,—
 Yet live by Him I kill'd!

         J. Newton

    See Note

CCXXV

APPROACH, my soul, the mercy-seat
 Where JESUS answers prayer;
There humbly fall before His feet,
 For none can perish there.

Thy promise is my only plea,
 With this I venture nigh;
Thou callest burden'd souls to Thee,
 And such, O LORD, am I.

Bow'd down beneath a load of sin,
 By Satan sorely prest,
By war without, and fears within,
 I come to Thee for rest:—

Be Thou my shield and hiding-place,
 That, shelter'd near Thy side,
I may my fierce accuser face,
 And tell him, Thou hast died!

CCXXVI

HOW sweet the Name of JESUS sounds
 In a believer's ear!
It soothes his sorrows, heals his wounds,
 And drives away his fear!

It makes the wounded spirit whole
  And calms the troubled breast;
'Tis manna to the hungry soul,
  And to the weary, rest.

Dear Name! the rock on which I build,
  My shield and hiding-place,
My never-failing treasury, fill'd
  With boundless stores of grace,—

By Thee my prayers acceptance gain,
  Although with sin defiled;
Satan accuses me in vain,
  And I am own'd a Child.

Weak is the effort of my heart,
  And cold my warmest thought;
But, when I see Thee as Thou art,
  I 'll praise Thee as I ought.

Till then, I would Thy love proclaim
  With every fleeting breath;
And may the music of Thy Name
  Refresh my soul in death!

CCXXVII

QUIET, Lord, my froward heart:
  Make me teachable and mild,
  Upright, simple, free from art,—
Make me as a weanéd child:
From distrust and envy free,
Pleased with all that pleases Thee.

What Thou shalt to-day provide,
Let me as a child receive;
What to-morrow may betide,
Calmly to Thy wisdom leave;
'Tis enough that Thou wilt care:
Why should I the burden bear?

As a little child relies
On a care beyond his own,
Knows he 's neither strong nor wise,
Fears to stir a step alone;
Let me thus with Thee abide,
As my Father, Guard, and Guide.

CCXXVIII

THE Lord will happiness divine
  On contrite hearts bestow;
Then tell me, gracious God, is mine
  A contrite heart, or no?

I hear, but seem to hear in vain,
  Insensible as steel;
If aught is felt, 'tis only pain,
  To find I cannot feel.

My best desires are faint and few,
  I fain would strive for more;
But when I cry, 'My strength renew!'
  Seem weaker than before.

Thy saints are comforted, I know,
  And love Thy house of prayer;
I therefore go where others go,
  But find no comfort there.

Oh make this heart rejoice or ache!
  Decide this doubt for me;
And if it be not broken, break,—
  And heal it if it be.

W. Cowper

CCXXIX

HARK, my soul! it is the Lord;
  'Tis thy Saviour,—hear His word;
Jesus speaks, and speaks to thee,
'Say, poor sinner, lov'st thou Me?

'I deliver'd thee when bound,
And when bleeding, heal'd thy wound;
Sought thee wandering, set thee right;
Turn'd thy darkness into light.

'Can a woman's tender care
Cease towards the child she bare?
Yes, she may forgetful be,
Yet will I remember thee.

'Mine is an unchanging love,
Higher than the heights above,
Deeper than the depths beneath,
Free and faithful, strong as death.

'Thou shalt see My glory soon,
When the work of grace is done;
Partner of My throne shalt be;—
Say, poor sinner, lov'st thou Me?'

Lord, it is my chief complaint,
That my love is weak and faint;
Yet I love Thee and adore,—
Oh! for grace to love Thee more!

CCXXX

O LORD, my best desire fulfil,
   And help me to resign
Life, health, and comfort to Thy will,
   And make Thy pleasure mine.

Why should I shrink at Thy command,
   Whose love forbids my fears?
Or tremble at the gracious hand
   That wipes away my tears?

No, rather let me freely yield
   What most I prize to Thee;
Who never hast a good withheld,
   Or wilt withhold from me!

CCXXXI

SOMETIMES a light surprises
   The Christian while he sings;
It is the Lord who rises
   With healing in His wings:
When comforts are declining,
   He grants the soul again
A season of clear shining,
   To cheer it after rain.

In holy contemplation,
   We sweetly then pursue
The theme of God's salvation,
   And find it ever new:
Set free from present sorrow,
   We cheerfully can say,
E'en let the unknown to-morrow
   Bring with it what it may!

It can bring with it nothing
  But He will bear us through;
Who gives the lilies clothing
  Will clothe His people too;
Beneath the spreading heavens
  No creature but is fed;
And He who feeds the ravens
  Will give His children bread.

Though vine nor fig-tree neither
  Their wonted fruit shall bear,
Though all the field should wither,
  Nor flocks nor herds be there:
Yet God the same abiding,
  His praise shall tune my voice;
For, while in Him confiding,
  I cannot but rejoice.

CCXXXII

TO keep the lamp alive,
  With oil we fill the bowl;
'Tis water makes the willow thrive,
  And grace that feeds the soul.

The Lord's unsparing hand
Supplies the living stream;
It is not at our own command,
  But still derived from Him.

Beware of Peter's word,
Nor confidently say,
'I never will deny Thee, Lord,'—
But,—'Grant I never may.'

Man's wisdom is to seek
His strength in God alone;
And e'en an Angel would be weak
Who trusted in his own.

CCXXXIII

FAR from the world, O Lord, I flee,
  From strife and tumult far;
From scenes where Satan wages still
  His most successful war.

The calm retreat, the silent shade,
 With prayer and praise agree;
And seem by Thy sweet bounty made
 For those who follow Thee.

There, if Thy Spirit touch the soul,
 And grace her mean abode,
Oh! with what peace, and joy, and love,
 She communes with her GOD!

There, like the nightingale, she pours
 Her solitary lays;
Nor asks a witness of her song,
 Nor thirsts for human praise.

Author and guardian of my life,
 Sweet source of light divine,
And—all harmonious names in one—
 My Saviour! Thou art mine!

What thanks I owe Thee, and what love,
 A boundless, endless store,
Shall echo through the realms above,
 When time shall be no more.
See Note

CCXXXIV

O THOU unknown, Almighty Cause
 Of all my hope and fear!
In Whose dread presence, ere an hour,
 Perhaps I must appear!

If I have wander'd in those paths
 Of life I ought to shun;
As something, loudly in my breast,
 Remonstrates I have done;

Thou know'st that Thou hast forméd me
 With passions wild and strong;
And listening to their witching voice
 Has often led me wrong.

Where human weakness has come short,
 Or frailty stept aside,
Do Thou, All-Good! for such Thou art,
 In shades of darkness hide.

Where with intention I have err'd,
 No other plea I have
But, Thou art good; and Goodness still
 Delighteth to forgive.
R. Burns

CCXXXV

CRADLE SONG

SWEET dreams, form a shade
　O'er my lovely infant's head!
Sweet dreams of pleasant streams
By happy, silent, moony beams!

Sweet sleep, with soft down
Weave thy brows an infant crown!
Sweet sleep, angel mild,
Hover o'er my happy child!

Sweet babe, in thy face
Holy image I can trace;
Sweet babe, once like thee
Thy Maker lay, and wept for me!

Wept for me, for thee, for all,
When He was an Infant small.
Thou His image ever see[1],
Heavenly face that smiles on thee!

Smiles on thee, on me, on all,
Who became an Infant small;
Infant smiles like His own smile
Heaven and earth to peace beguile.

W. Blake

[1] *ever* [dost] *see*

CCXXXVI

CAN I see another's woe,
　And not be in sorrow too?
Can I see another's grief,
And not seek for kind relief?

Can I see a falling tear,
And not feel my sorrow's share?
Can a father see his child
Weep, nor be with sorrow fill'd?

Can a mother sit and hear
An infant groan, an infant fear?
No, no! never can it be!
Never, never can it be!

And can He, who smiles on all,
Hear the wren, with sorrows small,
Hear the small bird's grief and care,
Hear the woes that infants bear?

And not sit beside the nest,
Pouring Pity in their breast?
And not sit the cradle near,
Weeping tear on infant's tear?

And not sit both night and day,
Wiping all our tears away?
Oh, no! never can it be!
Never, never can it be!

He doth give His joy to all:
He becomes an Infant small,
He becomes a Man of woe,
He doth feel the sorrow too.

Think not thou canst sigh a sigh,
And thy Maker is not by:
Think not thou canst weep a tear,
And thy Maker is not near.

Oh! He gives to us His joy,
That our griefs He may destroy:
Till our grief is fled and gone
He doth sit by us and moan.

CCXXXVII

THE LAMB

LITTLE lamb, who made thee?
 Dost thou know who made thee?
Gave thee life, and bade thee feed
By the stream and o'er the mead;
Gave thee clothing of delight,
Softest clothing, woolly, bright;
Gave thee such a tender voice,
Making all the vales rejoice?
 Little lamb, who made thee?
 Dost thou know Who made thee?

 Little lamb, I 'll tell thee;
 Little lamb, I 'll tell thee:
He is calléd by thy name,
For He calls Himself a Lamb.
He is meek, and He is mild,
He became a little child.
I a child, and thou a lamb,
We are calléd by His name.
 Little lamb, God bless thee!
 Little lamb, God bless thee!

CCXXXVIII

THE door of death is made of gold,
  That mortal eyes cannot behold :—
But when the mortal eyes are closed,
And cold and pale the limbs reposed,
The Soul awakes, and, wondering, sees
In her mild hand the golden keys.
—The grave is Heaven's golden gate,
And rich and poor around it wait.

CCXXXIX

FOR ever with the LORD!
  Amen! so let it be!
Life from the dead is in that word,
  And immortality!

Here in the body pent,
  Absent from Him I roam,
Yet nightly pitch my moving tent
  A day's march nearer home.

My Father's house on high,
  Home of my soul! how near,
At times, to Faith's foreseeing eye,
  Thy golden gates appear!

Ah! then my spirit faints
  To reach the land I love,
The bright inheritance of saints,
  Jerusalem above!

Yet clouds will intervene,
  And all my prospect flies;
Like Noah's dove, I flit between
  Rough seas and stormy skies.

Anon the clouds depart,
  The winds and waters cease;
While sweetly o'er my gladden'd heart
  Expands the bow of peace!

Beneath its glowing arch,
  Along the hallow'd ground,
I see cherubic armies march,
  A camp of fire around.

I hear at morn and even,
At noon and midnight hour,
The choral harmonics of Heaven
Earth's Babel tongues o'erpower.

Then, then I feel, that He,
Remember'd or forgot,
The LORD, is never far from me,
Though I perceive Him not.

J. Montgomery

CCXL

TO Thy temple I repair;
LORD, I love to worship there,
When, within the veil, I meet
CHRIST before the mercy-seat.

Thou, through Him, art reconciled;
I, through Him, became Thy child;
Abba! Father! give me grace
In Thy courts to seek Thy face!

While Thy glorious praise is sung,
Touch my lips, unloose my tongue;
Hear me, for Thy SPIRIT pleads;
Hear, for JESUS intercedes!

From Thy house when I return,
May my heart within me burn;
And at evening let me say,
—I have walk'd with GOD to-day!

CCXLI

PRAYER is the soul's sincere desire,
Utter'd, or unexpress'd;
The motion of a hidden fire
That trembles in the breast.

Prayer is the burden of a sigh,
The falling of a tear;
The upward glancing of an eye,
When none but GOD is near.

Prayer is the simplest form of speech
That infant lips can try;
Prayer, the sublimest strains that reach
The Majesty on high.

Prayer is the contrite sinner's voice
  Returning from his ways;
While Angels in their songs rejoice,
  And cry, Behold, he prays!

Prayer is the Christian's vital breath,
  The Christian's native air;
His watch-word at the gates of death;
  He enters Heaven with prayer.

The saints, in prayer, appear as one
  In word, and deed, and mind;
While with the Father and the Son
  Sweet fellowship they find.

Nor prayer is made on earth, alone:
  The Holy SPIRIT pleads;
And JESUS, on the eternal Throne,
  For mourners intercedes.

O Thou, by Whom we come to GOD,
  The Life, the Truth, the Way!
The path of prayer Thyself hast trod:
  LORD! teach us how to pray!

CCXLII

WHEN gathering clouds around I view,
  And days are dark and friends are few,
On Him I lean, Who not in vain
Experienced every human pain;
He sees my wants, allays my fears,
And counts and treasures up my tears.

If aught should tempt my soul to stray
From heavenly wisdom's narrow way;
To fly the good I would pursue,
Or do the sin I would not do;
Still He, Who felt temptation's power,
Shall guard me in that dangerous hour.

If wounded love my bosom swell,
Deceived by those I prized too well;
He shall His pitying aid bestow,
Who felt on earth severer woe,—
At once betray'd, denied, or fled,
By those who shared His daily bread.

If vexing thoughts within me rise,
And, sore dismay'd, my spirit dies;
Still He, Who once vouchsafed to bear
The sickening anguish of despair,
Shall sweetly soothe, shall gently dry,
The throbbing heart, the streaming eye.

When sorrowing o'er some stone I bend,
Which covers what was once a friend,
And from his voice, his hand, his smile,
Divides me for a little while;
Thou, Saviour, mark'st the tears I shed—
For Thou didst weep o'er Lazarus dead!

And O! when I have safely past
Through every conflict but the last;
Still, still unchanging, watch beside
My painful bed, for Thou hast died!
Then point to realms of cloudless day,
And wipe the latest tear away!

R. Grant

CCXLIII

SAVIOUR, when in dust to Thee
    Low we bend the adoring knee;
When repentant to the skies
Scarce we lift our weeping eyes;
Oh! by all the pains and woe
Suffer'd once for man below,
Bending from Thy throne on high,
Hear our solemn Litany!

By Thy helpless infant years,
By Thy life of want and tears,
By Thy days of sore distress
In the savage wilderness;
By the dread mysterious hour
Of the insulting tempter's power;
Turn, oh! turn a favouring eye,—
Hear our solemn Litany!

By the sacred griefs that wept
O'er the grave where Lazarus slept;
By the boding tears that flow'd
Over Salem's loved abode;
By the anguish'd sigh that told
Treachery lurk'd within Thy fold;
From Thy seat above the sky,
Hear our solemn Litany!

By Thine hour of dire despair;
By Thine agony of prayer;
By the cross, the nail, the thorn,
Piercing spear, and torturing scorn;
By the gloom that veil'd the skies
O'er the dreadful Sacrifice;
Listen to our humble cry,
Hear our solemn Litany!

By Thy deep expiring groan;
By the sad sepulchral stone;
By the vault, whose dark abode
Held in vain the rising God;
Oh! from earth to heaven restored,
Mighty re-ascended Lord,
Listen, listen to the cry
Of our solemn Litany!

CCXLIV

PRAISE to God, immortal praise,
    For the love that crowns our days!
Bounteous source of every joy,
Let Thy praise our tongues employ.

For the blessings of the field,
For the stores the gardens yield;
For the vine's exalted juice,
For the generous olive's use:

Flocks that whiten all the plain;
Yellow sheaves of ripen'd grain;
Clouds that drop their fattening dews,
Suns that temperate warmth diffuse:

All that Spring with bounteous hand
Scatters o'er the smiling land;
All that liberal Autumn pours
From her rich o'erflowing stores:

These to Thee, my God, we owe,—
Source whence all our blessings flow;
And for these my soul shall raise
Grateful vows and solemn praise.

Yet, should rising whirlwinds tear
From its stem the ripening ear;
Should the fig-tree's blasted shoot
Drop her green untimely fruit;

Should the vine put forth no more,
Nor the olive yield her store;
Though the sickening flocks should fall,
And the herds desert the stall;

Should Thine alter'd hand restrain
The early and the latter rain;
Blast each opening bud of joy,
And the rising year destroy;

Yet to Thee my soul should raise
Grateful vows and solemn praise;
And, when every blessing's flown,
Love Thee for Thyself alone!

A. L. Barbauld

CCXLV

VENI, SEQUERE ME

AWAKE, my soul, lift up thine eyes,
    See where thy foes against thee rise,
In long array, a numerous host;
Awake, my soul, or thou art lost!

Here giant Danger threatening stands,
Mustering his pale terrific bands;
There Pleasure's silken banners spread,
And willing souls are captive led.

See where rebellious passions rage,
And fierce desires and lusts engage;
The meanest foe of all the train
Has thousands and ten thousands slain!

Thou tread'st upon enchanted ground,
Perils and snares beset thee round;
Beware of all, guard every part,
But most, the traitor in thy heart.

Come then, my soul, now learn to wield
The weight of thine immortal shield;
Put on the armour from above
Of heavenly Truth and heavenly Love.

The terror and the charm repel,
And powers of earth, and powers of hell;
The Man of Calvary triumph'd here:
Why should His faithful followers fear?

End of Book Second

Book Third

CCXLVI

BRIGHTEST and best of the Sons of the morning!
  Dawn on our darkness and lend us thine aid!
Star of the East, the horizon adorning,
  Guide where our Infant Redeemer is laid!

Cold on His cradle the dew-drops are shining,
  Low lies His head with the beasts of the stall;
Angels adore Him in slumber reclining,
  Maker and Monarch and Saviour of all!

Say, shall we yield Him, in costly devotion,
  Odours of Edom and offerings divine?
Gems of the mountain and pearls of the ocean,
  Myrrh from the forest, or gold from the mine?

Vainly we offer each ample oblation;
  Vainly with gifts would His favour secure:
Richer by far is the heart's adoration;
  Dearer to GOD are the prayers of the poor.

Brightest and best of the Sons of the morning!
  Dawn on our darkness and lend us thine aid!
Star of the East, the horizon adorning,
  Guide where our Infant Redeemer is laid!

R. Heber

CCXLVII

THE HOLY INNOCENTS

OH weep not o'er thy children's tomb,
  Oh Rachel, weep not so!
The bud is cropt by martyrdom,
  The flower in Heaven shall blow!

Firstlings of faith! the murderer's knife
  Has miss'd its deadliest aim:
The GOD for Whom they gave their life,
  For them to suffer came!

Though feeble were their days and few,
    Baptized in blood and pain,
He knows them, Whom they never knew,
    And they shall live again.

Then weep not o'er thy children's tomb,
    Oh Rachel, weep not so!
The bud is cropt by martyrdom,
    The flower in Heaven shall blow!

CCXLVIII

L ORD of mercy and of might,
    Of mankind the life and light,
Maker, Teacher infinite,
    Jesus! hear and save!

Who, when Sin's tremendous doom
Gave creation to the tomb,
Didst not scorn the Virgin's womb,
    Jesus! hear and save!

Mighty Monarch! Saviour mild!
Humbled to a mortal child,
Captive, beaten, bound, reviled,
    Jesus! hear and save!

Throned above celestial things,
Borne aloft on Angels' wings,
Lord of Lords, and King of kings,
    Jesus! hear and save!

Who shalt yet return from high,
Robed in might and majesty,
Hear us! help us when we cry!
    Jesus! hear and save!

CCXLIX

H OLY, holy, holy, LORD GOD Almighty!
    Early in the morning our song shall rise to Thee;
Holy, holy, holy! merciful and mighty!
    GOD in Three Persons, blesséd TRINITY!

Holy, holy, holy! all the saints adore Thee,
    Casting down their golden crowns around the glassy sea;
Cherubim and Seraphim falling down before Thee,
    Which wert and art and evermore shalt be!

Holy, holy, holy! Though the darkness hide Thee,
　Though the eye of sinful man Thy glory may not see,
Only Thou art holy, there is none beside Thee,
　Perfect in power, in love, and purity!

Holy, holy, holy, LORD GOD Almighty!
　All Thy works shall praise Thy Name in earth and sky
　　and sea :—
Holy, holy, holy! Merciful and mighty!
　GOD in Three Persons, blesséd TRINITY!

CCL

I PRAISED the Earth, in beauty seen
　With garlands gay of various green;
I praised the Sea, whose ample field
Shone glorious as a silver shield;
And Earth and Ocean seem'd to say
'Our beauties are but for a day!'

I praised the Sun, whose chariot roll'd
On wheels of amber and of gold;
I praised the Moon, whose softer eye
Gleam'd sweetly through the summer sky :—
And Moon and Sun in answer said,
'Our days of light are numberéd!'

O GOD! O Good beyond compare!
If thus Thy meaner works are fair;
If thus Thy bounties gild the span
Of ruin'd earth and sinful man;
How glorious must the mansion be
Where Thy redeem'd shall dwell with Thee!

CCLI

BY cool Siloam's shady rill
　How sweet the lily grows!
How sweet the breath beneath the hill
　Of Sharon's dewy rose!

Lo, such the child whose early feet
　The paths of peace have trod;
Whose secret heart, with influence sweet,
　Is upward drawn to GOD.

By cool Siloam's shady rill
　The lily must decay;
The rose that blooms beneath the hill
　Must shortly fade away.

And soon, too soon, the wintry hour
 Of man's maturer age
Will shake the soul with sorrow's power,
 And stormy passion's rage.

O Thou, Whose infant feet were found
 Within Thy Father's shrine!
Whose years, with changeless virtue crown'd,
 Were all alike Divine;

Dependant on Thy bounteous breath,
 We seek Thy grace alone,
In childhood, manhood, age, and death,
 To keep us still Thine own!

CCLII

—*AGAINST PRINCIPALITIES, AGAINST POWERS, AGAINST THE RULERS OF THE DARKNESS OF THIS WORLD*—

THE sound of war! In earth and air
 The volleying thunders roll:
Their fiery darts the Fiends prepare,
And dig the pit, and spread the snare,
 Against the Christian's soul.
The Tyrant's sword, the rack, the flame,
 The scorner's serpent-tone,
Of bitter doubt the barbéd aim,
All, all conspire his heart to tame:
Force, fraud, and hellish fires assail
The rivets of his heavenly mail,
 Amidst his foes alone.

Gods of the world! ye warrior host
 Of darkness and of air,
In vain is all your impious boast,
In vain each missile lightning tost,
 In vain the Tempter's snare!
Though fast and far your arrows fly,
 Though mortal nerve and bone
Shrink in convulsive agony,
The Christian can your rage defy:
Towers o'er his head Salvation's crest,
Faith, like a buckler, guards his breast,
 Undaunted, though alone.

—'Tis past! 'tis o'er! in foul defeat
  The Demon host are fled!
Before the Saviour's mercy-seat,
(His live-long work of faith complete,)
  Their conqueror bends his head.
' The spoils Thyself hast gain'd, [O] Lord!
  I lay before Thy throne :
Thou wert my rock, my shield, my sword;
My trust was in Thy name and word :
'Twas in Thy strength my heart was strong;
Thy spirit went with mine along;
  How was I then alone?'

CCLIII

IN TIMES OF DISTRESS AND DANGER

OH God that madest earth and sky, the darkness and
     the day,
Give ear to this Thy family, and help us when we pray!
For wide the waves of bitterness around our vessel roar,
And heavy grows the pilot's heart to view the rocky shore!

The Cross our Master bore for us, for Him we fain would bear;
But mortal strength to weakness turns, and courage to despair!
Then mercy on our failings, Lord! our sinking faith renew !
And when Thy sorrows visit us, Oh send Thy patience too!

CCLIV

EVENING HYMN

GOD that madest Earth and Heaven,
    Darkness and light!
Who the day for toil hast given,
  For rest the night!
May Thine Angel-guards defend us,
Slumber sweet Thy mercy send us,
Holy dreams and hopes attend us,
  This livelong night!

CCLV

THE HOLY FIELD

BENEATH our feet and o'er our head
  Is equal warning given;
Beneath us lie the countless dead,
  Above us is the Heaven!

Their names are graven on the stone,
 Their bones are in the clay;
And ere another day is done,
 Ourselves may be as they.

Death rides on every passing breeze,
 He lurks in every flower;
Each season has its own disease,
 Its peril every hour.

Our eyes have seen the rosy light
 Of youth's soft cheek decay,
And Fate descend in sudden night
 On manhood's middle day.

Our eyes have seen the steps of age
 Halt feebly towards the tomb;
And yet shall earth our hearts engage,
 And dreams of days to come!

Turn, mortal, turn! thy danger know;
 Where'er thy foot can tread
The earth rings hollow from below,
 And warns thee of her dead!

Turn, Christian, turn! thy soul apply
 To truths divinely given;
The bones that underneath thee lie
 Shall live for Hell or Heaven!

CCLVI

OH help us, Lord! each hour of need
 Thy Heavenly succour give;
Help us in thought, and word, and deed,
 Each hour on Earth we live.

Oh help us, when our spirits bleed
 With contrite anguish sore;
And when our hearts are cold and dead,
 O help us, Lord, the more.

Oh help us, through the prayer of faith,
 More firmly to believe;
For still the more the servant hath,
 The more shall he receive.

Oh help us, Jesus! from on high,
 We know no help but Thee;
Oh! help us so to live and die
 As Thine in Heaven to be!

       H. H. Milman

CCLVII

WHEN our heads are bow'd with woe,
  When our bitter tears o'erflow;
When we mourn the lost, the dear,
Gracious Son of Mary, hear!

Thou our throbbing flesh hast worn,
Thou our mortal griefs hast borne,
Thou hast shed the human tear:
Gracious Son of Mary, hear!

When the sullen death-bell tolls
For our own departed souls;
When our final doom is near,
Gracious Son of Mary, hear!

Thou hast bow'd the dying head;
Thou the blood of life hast shed;
Thou hast fill'd a mortal bier:
Gracious Son of Mary, hear!

When the heart is sad within
With the thought of all its sin;
When the spirit shrinks with fear,
Gracious Son of Mary, hear!

Thou the shame, the grief hast known,
Though the sins were not Thine own;
Thou hast deign'd their load to bear—
Gracious Son of Mary, hear!

CCLVIII

THE PRIMROSE OF THE ROCK

A ROCK there is whose homely front
  The passing traveller slights;
Yet there the glow-worms hang their lamps
  Like stars, at various heights;
And one coy Primrose to that Rock
  The vernal breeze invites.

What hideous warfare hath been waged,
  What kingdoms overthrown,
Since first I spied that Primrose-tuft
  And mark'd it for my own;
A lasting link in Nature's chain
  From highest Heaven let down.

The flowers, still faithful to the stems,
  Their fellowship renew;
The stems are faithful to the root,
  That worketh out of view;
And to the rock the root adheres
  In every fibre true.

Close clings to earth the living rock,
  Though threatening still to fall;
The earth is constant to her sphere;
  And GOD upholds them all;
So blooms this lonely Plant, nor dreads
  Her annual funeral.

—Here closed the meditative strain;
  But air breathed soft that day,
The hoary mountain-heights were cheer'd,
  The sunny vale look'd gay;
And to the Primrose of the Rock
  I gave this after-lay :—

Sin-blighted though we are, we too,
  The reasoning Sons of Men,
From one oblivious winter call'd
  Shall rise, and breathe again;
And in eternal summer lose
  Our threescore years and ten.

To humbleness of heart descends
  This prescience from on high,
The Faith that elevates the just,
  Before and when they die;
And makes each soul a separate heaven,
  A court for Deity.

W. Wordsworth

CCLIX

DEVOTIONAL INCITEMENTS

WHERE will they stop, those breathing Powers,
    The Spirits of the new-born flowers?
They wander with the breeze, they wind
Where'er the streams a passage find;
Up from their native ground they rise
In mute aërial harmonies;
From humble violet, modest thyme,
Exhaled, the essential odours climb,

As if no space below the sky
Their subtle flight could satisfy :
Heaven will not tax our thoughts with pride,
If like ambition be their guide.

Roused by this kindliest of May-showers,
The spirit-quickener of the flowers,
That with moist virtue softly cleaves
The buds, and freshens the young leaves,
The birds pour forth their souls in notes
Of rapture from a thousand throats—
Here check'd by too impetuous haste,
While there the music runs to waste
With bounty more and more enlarged,
Till the whole air is overcharged ;
—Give ear, O Man ! to their appeal,
And thirst for no inferior zeal,
Thou, who canst think, as well as feel !

Mount from the earth ; aspire ! aspire !
So pleads the town's cathedral quire,
In strains that from their solemn height
Sink, to attain a loftier flight ;
While incense from the altar breathes
Rich fragrance in embodied wreaths ;
Or, flung from swinging censer, shrouds
The taper-lights, and curls in clouds
Around angelic Forms, the still
Creation of the Painter's skill,
That on thé service wait conceal'd
One moment, and the next reveal'd.
—Cast off your bonds, awake, arise,
And for no transient ecstasies !
What else can mean the visual plea
Of still or moving imagery—
The iterated summons loud,
Not wasted, on the attendant crowd,
Nor wholly lost upon the throng
Hurrying the busy streets along ?

Alas ! the sanctities combined
By art to unsensualise the mind,
Decay and languish ; or, as creeds
And humours change, are spurn'd like weeds :
The priests are from their altars thrust ;
Temples are levell'd with the dust ;
And solemn rites and awful forms
Founder amid fanatic storms.

Yet evermore, through years renew'd
In undisturb'd vicissitude
Of seasons balancing their flight
On the swift wings of day and night,
Kind Nature keeps a heavenly door
Wide open for the scatter'd Poor.
Where flower-breathed incense to the skies
Is wafted in mute harmonies;
And ground fresh-cloven by the plough
Is fragrant with a humbler vow;
Where birds and brooks from leafy dells
Chime forth unwearied canticles,
And vapours magnify and spread
The glory of the sun's bright head :—
Still constant in her worship, still
Conforming to the eternal Will,
Whether men sow or reap the fields,
Divine monition Nature yields,
That not by bread alone we live,
Or what a hand of flesh can give;
That every day should leave some part
Free for a sabbath of the heart:
So shall the seventh be truly blest,
From morn to eve, with hallow'd rest.

CCLX

IN CATHOLIC SWITZERLAND

DOOM'D as we are our native dust
 To wet with many a bitter shower,
It ill befits us to disdain
The altar, to deride the fane,
Where simple Sufferers bend, in trust
To win a happier hour.

I love, where spreads the village lawn,
Upon some knee-worn cell to gaze :
Hail to the firm unmoving Cross,
Aloft, where pines their branches toss!
And to the chapel far withdrawn,
That lurks by lonely ways!

Where'er we roam,—along the brink
Of Rhine,—or by the sweeping Po;
Through Alpine vale, or champain wide,
Whate'er we look on, at our side
Be Charity!—to bid us think,
And feel, if we would know.

CCLXI

HOLY BAPTISM

DEAR be the Church, that, watching o'er the needs
    Of Infancy, provides a timely shower
Whose virtue changes to a Christian Flower
A Growth from sinful Nature's bed of weeds!—

Fitliest beneath the sacred roof proceeds
The ministration; while parental Love
Looks on, and Grace descendeth from above
As the high service pledges now, now pleads.

There, should vain thoughts outspread their wings and fly
To meet the coming hours of festal mirth,
The tombs—which hear and answer that brief cry,
The Infant's notice of his Second Birth,—
Recal the wandering Soul to sympathy
With what man hopes from Heaven, yet fears from Earth.

CCLXII

WITHIN KING'S COLLEGE CHAPEL

TAX not the royal Saint with vain expense,
    With ill-match'd aims the Architect who plann'd—
Albeit labouring for a scanty band
Of white-robed Scholars only—this immense
And glorious Work of fine intelligence!
Give all thou canst; high Heaven rejects the lore
Of nicely-calculated less or more;
—So deem'd the man who fashion'd for the sense
These lofty pillars, spread that branching roof
Self-poised, and scoop'd into ten thousand cells,
Where light and shade repose, where music dwells
Lingering—and wandering on as loth to die;
Like thoughts whose very sweetness yieldeth proof
That they were born for immortality.

CCLXIII

A LESSON

GLORY to GOD! and to the Power Who came
    In Filial duty, clothed with love divine,
That made His human tabernacle shine
Like Ocean burning with purpureal flame;

Or like the Alpine Mount, that takes its name
From roseate hues, far kenn'd at morn and even,
In hours of peace, or when the storm is driven
Along the nether region's rugged frame!

Earth prompts,—Heaven urges; let us seek the light,
Studious of that pure intercourse begun
When first our infant brows their lustre won;

So, like the Mountain, may we grow more bright
From unimpeded commerce with the Sun,
At the approach of all-involving night.

CCLXIV

IT is a beauteous evening, calm and free;
 The holy time is quiet as a Nun
Breathless with adoration; the broad sun
Is sinking down in its tranquillity;

The gentleness of heaven is on the Sea:
Listen! the mighty Being is awake,
And doth with his eternal motion make
A sound like thunder—everlastingly.

Dear Child! dear Girl! that walkest with me here,
If thou appear untouch'd by solemn thought,
Thy nature is not therefore less divine:

Thou liest in Abraham's bosom all the year,
And worship'st at the Temple's inner shrine,
GOD being with thee when we know it not.

CCLXV

NOT seldom, clad in radiant vest,
 Deceitfully goes forth the Morn;
Not seldom Evening in the west
Sinks smilingly forsworn.

The smoothest seas will sometimes prove
To the confiding Bark, untrue;
And if she trust the stars above,
They can be treacherous too.

But Thou art true, incarnate LORD,
Who didst vouchsafe for man to die;
Thy smile is sure, Thy plighted word
No change can falsify!

I bent before Thy gracious throne,
And ask'd for peace on suppliant knee;
And peace was given,—nor peace alone,
But Faith sublimed to ecstasy!

CCLXVI

THE TWO WORLDS

THERE is a book, who runs may read,
　　Which heavenly truth imparts,
And all the lore its scholars need,
　　Pure eyes and Christian hearts.

The works of GOD above, below,
　　Within us and around,
Are pages in that book, to show
　　How GOD Himself is found.

The glorious sky embracing all
　　Is like the Maker's love,
Wherewith encompass'd, great and small
　　In peace and order move.

The Moon above, the Church below,
　　A wondrous race they run,
But all their radiance, all their glow,
　　Each borrows of its Sun.

The Saviour lends the light and heat
　　That crowns His holy hill;
The saints, like stars, around His seat,
　　Perform their courses still.

The saints above are stars in Heaven—
　　What are the saints on earth?
Like trees they stand whom GOD has given,
　　Our Eden's happy birth.

Faith is their fix'd unswerving root,
　　Hope their unfading flower,
Fair deeds of charity their fruit,
　　The glory of their bower.

The dew of Heaven is like Thy grace,
　　It steals in silence down;
But where it lights, the favour'd place
　　By richest fruits is known.

One Name above all glorious names
    With its ten thousand tongues
The everlasting sea proclaims,·
    Echoing angelic songs.

The raging Fire, the roaring Wind,
    Thy boundless power display :
But in the gentler breeze we find
    Thy SPIRIT's viewless way.

Two worlds are ours : 'tis only Sin
    Forbids us to descry
The mystic heaven and earth within,
    Plain as the sea and sky.

Thou, Who hast given me eyes to see
    And love this sight so fair,
Give me a heart to find out Thee,
    And read Thee every where.

J. Keble

See Note

CCLXVII

WHERE is Thy favour'd haunt, eternal Voice,
    The region of Thy choice,
Where, undisturb'd by sin and earth, the soul
    Owns Thy entire control ?—
'Tis on the mountain's summit dark and high,
    When storms are hurrying by :
'Tis 'mid the strong foundations of the earth,
    Where torrents have their birth.

No sounds of worldly toil ascending there
    Mar the full burst of prayer;
Lone Nature feels that she may freely breathe,
    And round us and beneath
Are heard her sacred tones : the fitful sweep
    Of winds across the steep,
Through wither'd bents—romantic note and clear,
    Meet for a hermit's ear,—

The wheeling kite's wild solitary cry,
    And, scarcely heard so high,
The dashing waters when the air is still
    From many a torrent rill
That winds unseen beneath the shaggy fell,
    Track'd by the blue mist well :
Such sounds as make deep silence in the heart
    For Thought to do her part.

'Tis then we hear the voice of GOD within,
    Pleading with care and sin :
'Child of My love! how have I wearied thee?
    Why wilt thou err from Me?
Have I not brought thee from the house of slaves,
    Parted the drowning waves,
And set My saints before thee in the way,
    Lest thou shouldst faint or stray?

'What? was the promise made to thee alone?
    Art thou th' excepted one?
An heir of glory without grief or pain?
    O vision false and vain!
There lies thy cross; beneath it meekly bow;
    It fits thy stature now:
Who scornful pass it with averted eye,
    'Twill crush them by-and-by.

'Raise thy repining eyes, and take true measure
    Of thine eternal treasure;
The Father of thy LORD can grudge thee nought,—
    The world for thee was bought;
And as this landscape broad—earth, sea, and sky,—
    All centres in thine eye,
So all GOD does, if rightly understood,
    Shall work thy final good.'

CCLXVIII

CITY AND COUNTRY

YE hermits blest, ye holy maids,
    The nearest Heaven on earth,
Who talk with GOD in shadowy glades,
    Free from rude care and mirth;
To whom some viewless teacher brings
The secret lore of rural things,
The moral of each fleeting cloud and gale,
The whispers from above, that haunt the twilight vale:

Say, when in pity ye have gazed
    On the wreathed smoke afar,
That o'er some town, like mist upraised,
    Hung hiding sun and star,—
Then as ye turn'd your weary eye
To the green earth and open sky,
Were ye not fain to doubt how Faith could dwell
Amid that dreary glare, in this world's citadel?

But Love's a flower that will not die
   For lack of leafy screen,
And Christian Hope can cheer the eye
   That ne'er saw vernal green;
Then be ye sure that Love can bless
E'en in this crowded loneliness,
Where ever-moving myriads seem to say,
Go—thou art nought to us, nor we to thee—away!

CCLXIX

WHAT went ye out to see
   O'er the rude sandy lea,
Where stately Jordan flows by many a palm,
   Or where Gennesaret's wave
   Delights the flowers to lave,
That o'er her western slope breathe airs of balm?

   All through the summer night,
   Those blossoms red and bright [1]
Spread their soft breasts, unheeding, to the breeze
   Like hermits watching still
   Around the sacred hill,
Where erst our Saviour watch'd upon His knees.

   The Paschal moon above
   Seems like a saint to rove,
Left shining in the world with CHRIST alone;
   Below, the lake's still face
   Sleeps sweetly in th' embrace
Of mountains terraced high with mossy stone.

   Here may we sit, and dream
   Over the heavenly theme,
Till to our soul the former days return;
   Till on the grassy bed,
   Where thousands once He fed,
The world's incarnate Maker we discern.

   O cross no more the main [1],
   Wandering so wild and vain,
To count the reeds that tremble in the wind,
   On listless dalliance bound,
   Like children gazing round,
Who on GOD's works no seal of Godhead find:—

Bask not in courtly bower,
Or sun-bright hall of power,
Pass Babel quick, and seek the holy land—
From robes of Tyrian dye
Turn with undazzled eye
To Bethlehem's glade, or Carmel's haunted strand.

Or choose thee out a cell
In Kedron's storied dell,
Beside the springs of Love, that never die;
Among the olives kneel
The chill night-blast to feel,
And watch the Moon that saw thy Master's agony.

Then rise at dawn of day,
And wind thy thoughtful way,
Where rested once the Temple's stately shade,—
With due feet tracing round
The city's northern bound,
To th' other holy garden, where the LORD was laid.

—Who thus alternate see
His death and victory,
Rising and falling as on angel wings,
They, while they seem to roam,
Draw daily nearer home,—
Their heart untravell'd still adores the King of kings.

¹ See Note

CCLXX

'TIS true, of old th' unchanging sun
His daily course refused to run,
The pale moon hurrying to the west
Paused at a mortal's call, to aid
Th' avenging storm of war, that laid
Seven guilty realms at once on earth's defiléd breast.

But can it be, one suppliant tear
Should stay the ever-moving sphere?
A sick man's lowly-breathéd sigh,
When from the world he turns away,
And hides his weary eyes to pray,
Should change your mystic dance, ye wanderers of the sky?

We too, O LORD, would fain command,
As then, Thy wonder-working hand,
And backward force the waves of Time,
That now so swift and silent bear
Our restless bark from year to year;
Help us to pause and mourn to Thee our tale of crime.

Bright hopes, that erst the bosom warm'd,
And vows, too pure to be perform'd,
 And prayers blown wide by gales of care;—
These, and such faint half-waking dreams,
Like stormy lights on mountain streams,
Wavering and broken all, athwart the conscience glare.

How shall we 'scape th' o'erwhelming Past?
Can spirits broken, joys o'ercast,
 And eyes that never more may smile:—
Can these th' avenging bolt delay,
Or win us back one little day
The bitterness of death to soften and beguile?

Father and Lover of our souls!
Though darkly round Thine anger rolls,
 Thy sunshine smiles beneath the gloom,—
Thou seek'st to warn us, not confound;
Thy showers would pierce the harden'd ground,
And win it to give out its brightness and perfume.

Thou smil'st on us in wrath, and we,
E'en in remorse, would smile on Thee;
 The tears that bathe our offer'd hearts
We would not have them stain'd and dim,
But dropp'd from wings of seraphim,
All glowing with the light accepted love imparts.

Time's waters will not ebb, nor stay,
Power cannot change them, but Love may;
 What cannot be, Love counts it done.
Deep in the heart, her searching view
Can read where Faith is fix'd and true,
Through shades of setting life can see Heaven's work begun.

O Thou, who keep'st the Key of Love,
Open Thy fount, eternal Dove,
 And overflow this heart of mine,
Enlarging as it fills with Thee,
Till in one blaze of charity
Care and remorse are lost, like motes in light divine;

Till, as each moment wafts us higher,
By every gush of pure desire,
 And high-breathed hope of joys above,
By every secret sigh we heave,
Whole years of folly we outlive,
In His unerring sight, who measures Life by Love.

CCLXXI

I MARK'D a rainbow in the north,
    What time the wild autumnal sun
From his dark veil at noon look'd forth,
    As glorying in his course half done,
Flinging soft radiance far and wide
Over the dusky heaven and bleak hill-side.

It was a gleam to Memory dear,—
    And as I walk and muse apart,
When all seems faithless round and drear
    I would revive it in my heart,
And watch how light can find its way
To regions farthest from the fount of day.

Light flashes in the gloomiest sky,
    And Music in the dullest plain,—
For there the lark is soaring high
    Over her flat and leafless reign,
And chanting in so blithe a tone,
It shames the weary heart to feel itself alone.

Brighter than rainbow in the north,
    More cheery than the matin lark,
Is the soft gleam of Christian worth,
    Which on some holy house we mark;
Dear to the pastor's aching heart
To think, where'er he looks, such gleam may have a part;

May dwell, unseen by all but Heaven,
    Like diamond blazing in the mine;
For, ever, where such grace is given,
    It fears in open day to shine,
Lest the deep stain it owns within
Break out, and Faith be shamed by the believer's sin.

In silence and afar they wait,
    To find a prayer their LORD may hear:
Voice of the poor and-desolate,
    You best may bring it to His ear!
Your grateful intercessions rise
With more than royal pomp, and pierce the skies.

Happy the soul, whose precious cause
    You in the Sovereign Presence plead—
'This is the lover of Thy laws,
    The friend of Thine in fear and need'—
For to the poor Thy mercy lends
That solemn style, 'Thy nation and Thy friends.'

He too is blest, whose outward eye
  The graceful lines of art may trace,
While his free spirit, soaring high,
  Discerns the glorious from the base;
Till out of dust his magic raise
A home for prayer and love, and full harmonious praise,

Where far away and high above,
  In maze on maze the trancéd sight
Strays, mindful of that heavenly love
  Which knows no end in depth or height,
While the strong breath of Music seems
To waft us ever on, soaring in blissful dreams.

What though in poor and humble guise
  Thou here didst sojourn, cottage-born?
Yet from Thy glory in the skies
  Our earthly gold Thou dost not scorn :—
For Love delights to bring her best,
And where Love is, that offering evermore is blest.

Love on the Saviour's dying head
  Her spikenard drops unblamed may pour,
May mount His cross, and wrap Him dead
  In spices from the golden shore;
Risen, may embalm His sacred name
With all a Painter's art, and all a Minstrel's flame.

Worthless and lost our offerings seem,—
  Drops in the ocean of His praise;
But Mercy with her genial beam
  Is ripening them to pearly blaze,
To sparkle in His crown above,
Who welcomes here a child's as there an angel's love.

CCLXXII

RED o'er the forest peers the setting sun,
  The line of yellow light dies fast away
That crown'd the eastern copse : and chill and dun
  Falls on the moor the brief November day.

Now the tired hunter winds a parting note,
  And Echo bids good-night from every glade;
Yet wait awhile, and see the calm leaves float
  Each to his rest beneath their parent shade.

How like decaying life they seem to glide!
　And yet no second spring have they in store,
But where they fall, forgotten to abide
　Is all their portion, and they ask no more.

Soon o'er their heads blithe April airs shall sing,
　A thousand wild-flowers round them shall unfold,
The green buds glisten in the dews of Spring,
　And all be vernal rapture as of old.

Unconscious they in waste oblivion lie,—
　In all the world of busy life around
No thought of them; in all the bounteous sky
　No drop, for them, of kindly influence found.

Man's portion is to die and rise again—
　Yet he complains, while these unmurmuring part
With their sweet lives, as pure from sin and stain,
　As his when Eden held his virgin heart.

And haply half unblamed his murmuring voice
　Might sound in Heaven, were all his second life
Only the first renew'd—the heathen's choice,
　A round of listless joy and weary strife.

For dreary were this earth, if earth were all,
　Tho' brighten'd oft by dear Affection's kiss;—
Who for the spangles wears the funeral pall?
　But catch a gleam beyond it, and 'tis bliss.

Heavy and dull this frame of limbs and heart,
　Whether slow creeping on cold earth, or borne
On lofty steed, or loftier prow, we dart
　O'er wave or field: yet breezes laugh to scorn

Our puny speed, and birds, and clouds in heaven,
　And fish, like living shafts that pierce the main,
And stars that shoot through freezing air at even—
　Who but would follow, might he break his chain?

And thou shalt break it soon; the grovelling worm
　Shall find his wings, and soar as fast and free
As his transfigured LORD with lightning form
　And snowy vest—such grace He won for thee,

When from the grave He sprang at dawn of morn,
　And led through boundless air thy conquering road,
Leaving a glorious track, where saints, new-born,
　Might fearless follow to their blest abode.

But first, by many a stern and fiery blast
  The world's rude furnace must thy blood refine,
And many a gale of keenest woe be pass'd,
  Till every pulse beat true to airs divine,

Till every limb obey the mounting soul,—
  The mounting soul, the call by JESUS given : —
He Who the stormy heart can so control,
  The laggard body soon will waft to Heaven.

See Note

CCLXXIII

THE REDEMPTION OF NATURE

SIN is with man at morning-break,
    And through the live-long day
Deafens the ear that fain would wake
    To Nature's simple lay.

But when eve's silent foot-fall steals
    Along the eastern sky,
And one by one to earth reveals
    Those purer fires on high,

When one by one each human sound
    Dies on the awful ear,
Then Nature's voice no more is drown'd,
    She speaks, and we must hear.

Then pours she on the Christian heart
    That warning still and deep,
At which high spirits of old would start
    E'en from their Pagan sleep,

Just guessing, through their murky blind,
    —Few, faint, and baffling sight—
Streaks of a brighter heaven behind,
    A cloudless depth of light.

Such thoughts, the wreck of Paradise,
    Through many a dreary age,
Upbore whate'er of good and wise
    Yet lived in bard or sage :

They mark'd what agonizing throes
    Shook the great mother's womb;
But Reason's spells might not disclose
    The gracious Birth to come;

Nor could th' enchantress Hope forecast
　　God's secret love and power;
The travail pangs of Earth must last
　　Till her appointed hour;

The hour that saw from opening heaven
　　Redeeming glory stream,
Beyond the summer hues of even,
　　Beyond the mid-day beam.

Thenceforth, to eyes of high desire,
　　The meanest things below,
As with a seraph's robe of fire
　　Invested, burn and glow:

The rod of Heaven has touch'd them all,
　　The word from Heaven is spoken;
' Rise, shine, and sing, thou captive thrall:
　　Are not thy fetters broken?

' The God Who hallow'd thee and blest,
　　Pronouncing thee all good—
Hath He not all thy wrongs redrest,
　　And all thy bliss renew'd?

' Why mourn'st thou still as one bereft,
　　Now that th' eternal Son
His blesséd home in Heaven hath left
　　To make thee all His own?'

CCLXXIV

WHEN Nature tries her finest touch,
　　Weaving her vernal wreath,
Mark ye, how close she veils her round,
Not to be traced by sight or sound,
　　Nor soil'd by ruder breath?

Who ever saw the earliest rose
　　First open her sweet breast?
Or, when the summer sun goes down,
The first soft star in evening's crown
　　Light up her gleaming crest?

Fondly we seek the dawning bloom
　　On features wan and fair,—
The gazing eye no change can trace,
But look away a little space,
　　Then turn, and lo! 'tis there.

But there 's a sweeter flower than e'er
 Blush'd on the rosy spray—
A brighter star, a richer bloom
Than e'er did western heaven illume
 At close of summer day.

'Tis Love, the last best gift of Heaven;
 Love gentle, holy, pure;
But tenderer than a dove's soft eye,
The searching sun, the open sky,
 She never could endure.

So still and secret is her growth,
 Ever the truest heart,
Where deepest strikes her kindly root
For hope or joy, for flower or fruit,
 Least knows its happy part.

E'en human Love will shrink from sight
 Here in the coarse rude earth :
How then should rash intruding glance
Break in upon *her* sacred trance
 Who boasts a heavenly birth?

No—let the dainty rose awhile
 Her bashful fragrance hide—
Rend not her silken veil too soon,
But leave her, in her own soft noon,
 To flourish and abide.

CCLXXV

O LORD my GOD, do Thou Thy holy will—
  I will lie still—
I will not stir, lest I forsake Thine arm,
  And break the charm,
Which lulls me, clinging to my Father's breast,
  In perfect rest.

 Come, Self-devotion, high and pure,
Thoughts that in thankfulness endure,
Though dearest hopes are faithless found,
And dearest hearts are bursting round.
Come, Resignation, spirit meek,
And let me kiss thy placid cheek,
And read in thy pale eye serene
Their blessing, who by faith can wean
Their hearts from sense, and learn to love
GOD only, and the joys above.

They say[1], who know the life divine,
And upward gaze with eagle eyne,
That by each golden crown on high,
Rich with celestial jewelry,
Which for our LORD's redeem'd is set,
There hangs a radiant coronet,
All gemm'd with pure and living light,
Too dazzling for a sinner's sight,
Prepared for virgin souls, and them
Who seek the martyr's diadem.

Nor deem, who to that bliss aspire,
Must win their way through blood and fire.
The writhings of a wounded heart
Are fiercer than a foeman's dart.
Oft in Life's stillest shade reclining,
In Desolation unrepining,
Without a hope on earth to find
A mirror in an answering mind,
Meek souls there are, who little dream
Their daily strife an Angel's theme,
Or that the rod they take so calm
Shall prove in Heaven a martyr's palm.

And there are souls that seem to dwell
Above this earth—so rich a spell
Floats round their steps, where'er they move,
From hopes fulfill'd and mutual love.
Such, if on high their thoughts are set,
Nor in the stream the source forget,
If prompt to quit the bliss they know,
Following the Lamb where'er He go,
By purest pleasures unbeguiled
To idolize or wife or child;
Such wedded souls our GOD shall own
For faultless virgins round His throne.

[1] See Note

CCLXXVI

SEMPER IDEM

STRANGE to our ears the church-bells of our home;
   The fragrance of our old paternal fields
May be forgotten; and the time may come
   When the babe's kiss no sense of pleasure yields
E'en to the doting mother: but Thine own
Thou never canst forget, nor leave alone.

There are who sigh that no fond heart is theirs,
  None loves them best—O vain and selfish sigh!
Out of the bosom of His love He spares—
  The Father spares the Son, for thee to die:
For thee He died—for thee He lives again:
O'er thee He watches in His boundless reign.

Thou art as much His care, as if beside
  Nor man nor angel lived in Heaven or earth:
Thus sunbeams pour alike their glorious tide
  To light up worlds, or wake an insect's mirth:
They shine and shine with unexhausted store—
Thou art thy Saviour's darling—seek no more.

CCLXXVII

CHRISTO CONSOLATORI

LORD of my heart, by Thy last cry,
  Let not Thy blood on earth be spent—
Lo, at Thy feet I fainting lie,
  Mine eyes upon Thy wounds are bent,
Upon Thy streaming wounds my weary eyes
Wait like the parchéd earth on April skies.

Wash me, and dry these bitter tears,—
  O let my heart no further roam,
'Tis Thine by vows, and hopes, and fears,
  Long since—O call Thy wanderer home;
To that dear home, safe in Thy wounded side,
Where only broken hearts their sin and shame may hide.

See Note

CCLXXVIII

EPHPHATHA

THE Son of God in doing good
  Was fain to look to Heaven and sigh:
And shall the heirs of sinful blood
  Seek joy unmix'd in charity?
God will not let Love's work impart
Full solace, lest it steal the heart;
Be thou content in tears to sow,
Blessing, like Jesus, in thy woe.

The deaf may hear the Saviour's voice,
  The fetter'd tongue its chain may break;
But the deaf heart, the dumb by choice,
  The laggard soul, that will not wake,
The guilt that scorns to be forgiven;—
These baffle e'en the spells of Heaven;
In thought of these, His brows benign
Not e'en in healing cloudless shine.

No eye but His might ever bear
  To gaze all down that drear abyss,
Because none ever saw so clear
  The shore beyond of endless bliss:
The giddy waves so restless hurl'd,
The vex'd pulse of this feverish world,
He views and counts with steady sight,
Used to behold the Infinite.

But that in such communion high
  He hath a fount of strength within,
Sure His meek heart would break and die,
  O'erburthen'd by His brethren's sin:
—Lord, by Thy sad and earnest eye,
When Thou didst look to Heaven and sigh;
Thy voice, that with a word could chase
The dumb, deaf spirit from his place;

As Thou hast touch'd our ears, and taught
  Our tongues to speak Thy praises plain,
Quell Thou each thankless godless thought
  That would make fast our bonds again.
From worldly strife, from mirth unblest,
Drowning Thy music in the breast,
From foul reproach, from thrilling fears,
Preserve, good Lord, Thy servants' ears.

From idle words, that restless throng
  And haunt our hearts when we would pray,
From Pride's false chime, and jarring wrong,
  Seal Thou my lips, and guard the way:
For Thou hast sworn, that every ear,
Willing or loth, Thy trump shall hear,
And every tongue unchainéd be
To own no hope, no God, but Thee.

CCLXXIX

WISH not, dear friends, my pain away—
  Wish me a wise and thankful heart,
With God, in all my griefs, to stay,
  Nor from His loved correction start.

The dearest offering He can crave
  His portion in our souls to prove,
What is it to the gift He gave,
  The only Son of His dear love?

But we, like vex'd unquiet sprights,
  Will still be hovering o'er the tomb,
Where buried lie our vain delights,
  Nor sweetly take a sinner's doom.

In Life's long sickness evermore
  Our thoughts are tossing to and fro :
We change our posture o'er and o'er[1],
  But cannot rest, nor cheat our woe:

Were it not better to lie still,
  Let Him strike home and bless the rod,
Never so safe as when our will
  Yields undiscern'd by all but God?

Thy precious things, whate'er they be,
  That haunt and vex thee, heart and brain,
Look to the Cross, and thou shalt see
  How thou may'st turn them all to gain.

Lovest thou praise? the Cross is shame :
  Or ease? the Cross is bitter grief:
More pangs than tongue or heart can frame
  Were suffer'd there without relief.

We of that Altar would partake,
  But cannot quit[2] the cost—no throne
Is ours, to leave for Thy dear sake—
  We cannot do as Thou hast done.

We cannot part with Heaven for Thee—
  Yet guide us in Thy track of love :
Let us gaze on where light should be,
  Though not a beam the clouds remove.

So wanderers ever fond and true
  Look homeward through the evening sky,
Without a streak of heaven's soft blue
  To aid Affection's dreaming eye.

The wanderer·seeks his native bower,
  And we will look and long for Thee,
And thank Thee for each trying hour,
  Wishing, not struggling, to be free.

¹ See Note   ² *quit*, pay

CCLXXX

WHY should we faint and fear to live alone,
  Since all alone, so Heaven has will'd, we die,
Nor e'en the tenderest heart, and next our own,
  Knows half the reasons why we smile and sigh!

Each in his hidden sphere of joy or woe
  Our hermit spirits dwell, and range apart,
Our eyes see all around in gloom or glow—
  Hues of their own, fresh borrow'd from the heart.

And well it is for us our GOD should feel
  Alone our secret throbbings : so our prayer
May readier spring to Heaven, nor spend its zeal
  On cloud-born idols of this lower air.

For if one heart in perfect sympathy
  Beat with another, answering love for love,
Weak mortals, all entranced, on earth would lie,
  Nor listen for those purer strains above.

Or what if Heaven for once its searching light
  Lent to some partial eye, disclosing all
The rude bad thoughts, that in our bosom's night
  Wander at large, nor heed Love's gentle thrall!

Who would not shun the dreary uncouth place?
  As if, fond leaning where her infant slept,
A mother's arm a serpent should embrace :
  So might we friendless live, and die unwept.

Then keep the softening veil in mercy drawn,
  Thou Who canst love us, tho' Thou read us true;
As on the bosom of th' aërial lawn
  Melts in dim haze each coarse ungentle hue.

Thou know'st our bitterness—our joys are Thine—
  No stranger Thou to all our wanderings wild :
Nor could we bear to think, how every line
  Of us, Thy darken'd likeness and defiled,

Stands in full sunshine of Thy piercing eye,
  But that Thou call'st us Brethren : sweet repose
Is in that word—the LORD who dwells on high
  Knows all, yet loves us better than He knows.

CCLXXXI

B. V. M.

AVE Maria! blessèd Maid!
   Lily of Eden's fragrant shade,
     Who can express the love
That nurtured thee so pure and sweet,
Making thy heart a shelter meet
     For JESUS' holy Dove?

Ave Maria! Mother blest,
To whom, caressing and caress'd,
     Clings the Eternal Child;
Favour'd beyond Archangels' dream,
When first on thee with tenderest gleam
     Thy new-born Saviour smiled :—

Ave Maria! thou whose name
All but adoring love may claim,
     Yet may we reach thy shrine;
For He, thy Son and Saviour, vows
To crown all lowly lofty brows
     With love and joy like thine.

Bless'd is the womb that bare Him—bless'd
The bosom where His lips were press'd;
     But rather bless'd are they
Who hear His word and keep it well,
The living homes where CHRIST shall dwell,
     And never pass away.

CCLXXXII

THE PURIFICATION

BLESS'D are the pure in heart,
   For they shall see our GOD;
The secret of the LORD is theirs,
   Their soul is CHRIST's abode.

   —Might mortal thought presume
   To guess an angel's lay,
Such are the notes that echo through
   The courts of Heaven to-day.

   Such the triumphal hymns
   On Sion's Prince that wait,
In high procession passing on
   Towards His temple-gate.

Give ear, ye kings—bow down
 Ye rulers of the earth—
This, this is He; your Priest by grace,
 Your God and King by birth.

No pomp of earthly guards
 Attends with sword and spear,
And all-defying, dauntless look,
 Their monarch's way to clear;

Yet are there more with Him
 Than all that are with you—
The armies of the highest Heaven,
 All righteous, good and true.

Spotless their robes and pure,
 Dipp'd in the sea of light,
That hides the unapproachéd shrine
 From men's and angels' sight.

His throne, thy bosom blest,
 O Mother undefiled—
That throne, if aught beneath the skies,
 Beseems the sinless child.

Lost in high thoughts, 'whose son
 The wondrous Babe might prove,'
Her guileless husband walks beside,
 Bearing the hallow'd dove;

Meet emblem of His vow,
 Who, on this happy day,
His dove-like soul—best sacrifice—
 Did on God's altar lay.

But who is he, by years
 Bow'd, but erect in heart,
Whose prayers are struggling with his tears?
 'Lord, let me now depart.

'Now hath Thy servant seen
 Thy saving health, O Lord;
'Tis time that I depart in peace,
 According to Thy word.'

Yet swells the pomp: one more
 Comes forth to bless her God:
Full fourscore years, meek widow, she
 Her heaven-ward way hath trod.

She who to earthly joys
So long had given farewell,
Now sees, unlook'd for, Heaven on earth,
CHRIST in His Israel.

Wide open from that hour
The temple-gates are set,
And still the saints rejoicing there
The holy Child have met.

—Now count His train to-day,
And who may meet Him, learn :
Him child-like sires, meek maidens find,
Where pride can nought discern.

Still to the lowly soul
He doth Himself impart,
And for His cradle and His throne
Chooseth the pure in heart.

CCLXXXIII

BEATI QUI NON VIDERUNT

WE were not by when JESUS came;
But round us, far and near,
We see His trophies, and His name
In choral echoes hear.
In a fair ground our lot is cast,
As in the solemn week that past,
While some might doubt, but all adored,
Ere the whole widow'd Church had seen her risen LORD.

Then, gliding through th' unopening door,
Smooth without step or sound,
' Peace to your souls,' He said—no more—
They own Him, kneeling round.
Eye, ear, and hand, and loving heart,
Body and soul in every part,
Successive made His witnesses that hour,
Cease not in all the world to shew His saving power.

—Is there, on earth, a spirit frail,
Who fears to take their word,
Scarce daring, through the twilight pale,
To think he sees the LORD?
With eyes too tremblingly awake
To bear with dimness for His sake?
Read and confess the Hand Divine
That drew thy likeness here so true in every line.

For all thy rankling doubts so sore,
  Love thou thy Saviour still,
Him for thy LORD and GOD adore,
  And ever do His will.
Though vexing thoughts may seem to last,
Let not thy soul be quite o'ercast;—
Soon will He shew thee all His wounds, and say,
'Long have I known thy name—know thou My face alway.'

CCLXXXIV

THE CONVERSION OF S. PAUL

THE mid-day sun, with fiercest glare,
    Broods o'er the hazy, twinkling air;
  Along the level sand
The palm-tree's shade unwavering lies,
Just as thy towers, Damascus, rise
  To greet yon wearied band.

The leader of that martial crew
Seems bent some mighty deed to do,
  So steadily he speeds,
With lips firm closed and fixéd eye,
Like warrior when the fight is nigh,
  Nor talk nor landscape heeds.

What sudden blaze is round him pour'd,
As though all Heaven's refulgent hoard
  In one rich glory shone?
One moment—and to earth he falls:
What voice his inmost heart appals?—
  Voice heard by him alone;—

For to the rest both words and form
Seem lost in lightning and in storm,
    While Saul, in wakeful trance,
Sees deep within that dazzling field
His persecuted LORD reveal'd
    With keen yet pitying glance:

And hears the meek upbraiding call
As gently on his spirit fall,
    As if th' Almighty Son
Were prisoner yet in this dark earth,
Nor had proclaim'd His royal birth,
    Nor His great power begun.

'Ah! wherefore persecut'st thou Me?'
He heard and saw, and sought to free
 His strain'd eye from the sight:
But Heaven's high magic bound it there,
Still gazing, though untaught to bear
 Th' insufferable light.

'Who art Thou, Lord?' he falters forth:—
So shall Sin ask of heaven and earth
 At the last awful day.
'When did we see Thee suffering nigh,
And pass'd Thee with unheeding eye?
 Great God of judgment, say!'

Ah! little dream our listless eyes
What glorious presence they despise,
 While, in our noon of life,
To power or fame we rudely press:—
Christ is at hand, to scorn or bless,
 Christ suffers in our strife.

And though heaven-gate long since have closed,
And our dear Lord in bliss reposed,
 High above mortal ken,
To every ear in every land
(Though meek ears only understand)
 He speaks as He did then.

'Ah! wherefore persecute ye Me?
'Tis hard, ye so in love should be
 With your own endless woe.
Know, though at God's right hand I live,
I feel each wound ye reckless give
 To the least saint below.

'I in your care My brethren left,
Not willing ye should be bereft
 Of waiting on your Lord.
The meanest offering ye can make—
A drop of water—for love's sake,
 In Heaven, be sure, is stored.'

O by those gentle tones and dear,
When Thou hast stay'd our wild career,
 Thou only hope of souls,
Ne'er let us cast one look behind,
But in the thought of Jesus find
 What every thought controls.

As to Thy last Apostle's heart
Thy lightning glance did then impart
  Zeal's never-dying fire,
So teach us on Thy shrine to lay
Our hearts, and let them day by day
  Intenser blaze and higher.

And as each mild and winning note
(Like pulses that round harp-strings float
  When the full strain is o'er)
Left lingering on his inward ear
Music, that taught, as death drew near,
  Love's lesson more and more :

So, as we walk our earthly round,
Still may the echo of that sound
  Be in our memory stored :
'Christians! behold your happy state :
Christ is in these, who round you wait;
  Make much of your dear Lord !'

CCLXXXV

HOLY BAPTISM

WHERE is it mothers learn their love !—
    In every Church a fountain springs
  O'er which th' eternal Dove
  Hovers on softest wings.

What sparkles in that lucid flood
  Is water, by gross mortals eyed :
    But seen by Faith, 'tis blood
    . Out of a dear Friend's side.

A few calm words of faith and prayer,
  A few bright drops of holy dew,
    Shall work a wonder there
      Earth's charmers never knew.

O happy arms, where cradled lies,
  And ready for the Lord's embrace,
    That precious sacrifice,
      The darling of His grace !

Blest eyes, that see the smiling gleam
  Upon the slumbering features glow,
    When the life-giving stream
      Touches the tender brow :

Or when the holy cross is sign'd,
  And the young soldier duly sworn
    With true and fearless mind
      To serve the Virgin-born.

But happiest ye, who seal'd and blest
  Back to your arms your treasure take,
    With JESUS' mark impress'd
      To nurse for JESUS' sake:

To whom—as if in hallow'd air
  Ye knelt before some awful shrine—
    His innocent gestures wear
      A meaning half divine:

By whom Love's daily touch is seen
  In strengthening form and freshening hue,
    In the fix'd brow serene,
      The deep yet eager view.—

Who taught thy pure and even breath
  To come and go with such sweet grace!
    Whence thy reposing Faith,
      Though in our frail embrace?

O tender gem, and full of Heaven!
  Not in the twilight stars on high,
    Not in moist flowers at even
      See we our GOD so nigh.

Sweet one, make haste and know Him too,
  Thine own adopting Father love,
    That like thine earliest dew
      Thy dying sweets may prove.

CLXXXVI

CATECHISM

OH! say not, dream not, heavenly notes
    To childish ears are vain,
That the young mind at random floats,
  And cannot reach the strain.

Dim or unheard, the words may fall,
    And yet the heaven-taught mind
May learn the sacred air, and all
  The harmony unwind.

Was not our Lord a little child,
    Taught by degrees to pray,
By father dear and mother mild
    Instructed day by day?

And loved He not of Heaven to talk
    With children in His sight,
To meet them in His daily walk,
    And to His arms invite?

What though around His throne of fire
    The everlasting chant
Be wafted from the seraph choir
    In glory jubilant?

Yet stoops He, ever pleased to mark
    Our rude essays of love,
Faint as the pipe of wakening lark,
    Heard by some twilight grove:

Yet is He near us, to survey
    These bright and order'd files,
Like spring-flowers in their best array,
    All silence and all smiles.

Save that each little voice in turn
    Some glorious truth proclaims,
What sages would have died to learn,
    Now taught by cottage dames.

And if some tones be false or low,
    What are all prayers beneath
But cries of babes, that cannot know
    Half the deep thought they breathe?

In His own words we Christ adore,
    But angels, as we speak,
Higher above our meaning soar
    Than we o'er children weak:

And yet His words mean more than they,
    And yet He owns their praise:
Why should we think, He turns away
    From infants' simple lays?

CCLXXXVII

CONFIRMATION

DRAW, Holy Ghost, Thy seven-fold veil
    Between us and the fires of youth;
Breathe, Holy Ghost, Thy freshening gale,
Our fever'd brow in age to soothe.

And oft as sin and sorrow tire,
  The hallow'd hour do Thou renew,
When beckon'd up the awful choir
  By pastoral hands, toward Thee we drew;

When trembling at the sacred rail
  We hid our eyes and held our breath,
Felt Thee how strong, our hearts how frail,
  And long'd to own Thee to the death.

For ever on our souls be traced
  That blessing dear, that dove-like hand,
A sheltering rock in Memory's waste,
  O'er-shadowing all the weary land.

CCLXXXVIII

MORNING

HUES of the rich unfolding morn,
  That, ere the glorious sun be born,
By some soft touch invisible
Around his path are taught to swell;—

Thou rustling breeze so fresh and gay,
That dancest forth at opening day,
And brushing by with joyous wing,
Wakenest each little leaf to sing;—

Ye fragrant clouds of dewy steam,
By which deep grove and tangled stream
Pay, for soft rains in season given,
Their tribute to the genial heaven;—

Why waste your treasures of delight
Upon our thankless, joyless sight;
Who day by day to sin awake,
Seldom of Heaven and you partake?

Oh! timely happy, timely wise,
Hearts that with rising morn arise!
Eyes that the beam celestial view,
Which evermore makes all things new!

New every morning is the love
Our wakening and uprising prove;
Through sleep and darkness safely brought,
Restored to life, and power, and thought.

New mercies, each returning day,
Hover around us while we pray;
New perils past, new sins forgiven,
New thoughts of God, new hopes of Heaven.

If on our daily course our mind
Be set to hallow all we find,
New treasures still, of countless price,
God will provide for sacrifice.

Old friends, old scenes, will lovelier be,
As more of Heaven in each we see:
Some softening gleam of love and prayer
Shall dawn on every cross and care.

As for some-dear familiar strain
Untired we ask, and ask again,
Ever, in its melodious store,
Finding a spell unheard before;

Such is the bliss of souls serene,
When they have sworn, and stedfast mean,
Counting the cost, in all t' espy
Their God, in all themselves deny.

O could we learn that sacrifice,
What lights would all around us rise!
How would our hearts with wisdom talk
Along Life's dullest dreariest walk!

We need not bid, for cloister'd cell,
Our neighbour and our work farewell,
Nor strive to wind ourselves too high
For sinful man beneath the sky:

The trivial round, the common task,
Would furnish all we ought to ask;
Room to deny ourselves; a road
To bring us, daily, nearer God.

Seek we no more; content with these,
Let present Rapture, Comfort, Ease,
As Heaven shall bid them, come and go:—
The secret this of Rest below.

Only, O Lord, in Thy dear love
Fit us for perfect Rest above;
And help us, this and every day,
To live more nearly as we pray.

CCLXXXIX

EVENING

'TIS gone, that bright and orbéd blaze,
 Fast fading from our wistful gaze;
Yon mantling cloud has hid from sight
The last faint pulse of quivering light.

In darkness and in weariness
The traveller on his way must press,
No gleam to watch on tree or tower,
Whiling away the lonesome hour.

Sun of my soul! Thou Saviour dear,
It is not night if Thou be near:
Oh! may no earth-born cloud arise
To hide Thee from Thy servant's eyes.

When round Thy wondrous works below
My searching rapturous glance I throw,
Tracing out Wisdom, Power, and Love,
In earth or sky, in stream or grove;—

Or by the light Thy words disclose
Watch Time's full river as it flows,
Scanning Thy gracious Providence,
Where not too deep for mortal sense :—

When with dear friends sweet talk I hold,
And all the flowers of life unfold;
Let not my heart within me burn,
Except in all I Thee discern.

When the soft dews of kindly sleep
My wearied eyelids gently steep,
Be my last thought, how sweet to rest
For ever on my Saviour's breast.

Abide with me from morn till eve,
For without Thee I cannot live:
Abide with me when night is nigh,
For without Thee I dare not die.

Thou Framer of the light and dark,
Steer through the tempest Thine own ark:
Amid the howling wintry sea
We are in port if we have Thee.

The Rulers of this Christian land,
'Twixt Thee and us ordain'd to stand,—
Guide Thou their course, O Lord, aright,
Let all do all as in Thy sight.

Oh! by Thine own sad burthen, borne
So meekly up the hill of scorn,
Teach Thou Thy Priests their daily cross
To bear as Thine, nor count it loss!

If some poor wandering child of Thine
Have spurn'd, to-day, the voice divine,
Now, Lord, the gracious work begin;
Let him no more lie down in sin.

Watch by the sick: enrich the poor
With blessings from Thy boundless store:
Be every mourner's sleep to-night
Like infants' slumbers, pure and light.

Come near and bless us when we wake,
Ere through the world our way we take;
Till in the ocean of Thy love
We lose ourselves in Heaven above.

CCXC

THE KINGDOM OF GOD

I SAY to thee, do thou repeat
 To the first man thou mayest meet
In lane, highway, or open street—

That he and we and all men move
Under a canopy of love,
As broad as the blue sky above;

That doubt and trouble, fear and pain
And anguish, all are shadows vain,
That death itself shall not remain;

That weary deserts we may tread,
A dreary labyrinth may thread,
Through dark ways underground be led;

Yet, if we will one Guide obey,
The dreariest path, the darkest way
Shall issue out in heavenly day;

And we, on divers shores now cast,
Shall meet, our perilous voyage past,
All in our Father's house at last.

R. C. Trench

CCXCI

WHAT, many times I musing ask'd, is Man,
        If grief and care
Keep far from him? he knows not what he can,
        What cannot bear.

He, till the fire hath proved him, doth remain
        The main part dross:
To lack the loving discipline of pain
        Were endless loss.

Yet when my LORD did ask me on what side
        I were content
The grief, whereby I must be purified,
        To me were sent,

As each imagined anguish did appear,
        Each withering bliss,
Before my soul, I cried, 'Oh! spare me here;
        Oh no, not this!'—

Like one that having need of, deep within,
        The surgeon's knife,
Would hardly bear that it should graze the skin,
        Though for his life :—

Till He at last, Who best doth understand
        Both what we need,
And what can bear, did take my case in hand,
        Nor crying heed.

CCXCII

OH thou of dark forebodings drear,
        Oh thou of such a faithless heart,
    Hast thou forgotten what thou art,
That thou hast ventured so to fear?

No weed on ocean's bosom cast,
    Borne by its never-resting foam
    This way and that, without a home,
Till flung on some bleak shore at last :

But thou the lotus, which above
    Sway'd here and there by wind and tide,
    Yet still below doth fix'd abide,
Fast rooted in the eternal Love.

CCXCIII

DUST TO DUST

OH blessing, wearing semblance of a curse,
　　We fear thee, thou stern sentence!—yet to be
Link'd to immortal bodies were far worse
　　　Than thus to be set free.

For mingling with the life-blood through each vein
　　The venom of the serpent's bite has run,
And only thus might be expell'd again—
　　　Thus only health be won.

Shall we not then a gracious sentence own,
　　Now since the leprosy has fretted through
The entire house, that Thou wilt take it down,
　　　And build it all anew?

Build it this time (since Thou wilt build again),
　　A holy house, where righteousness may dwell;
And we, though in the unbuilding there be pain,
　　　Will still affirm,—'tis well.

CCXCIV

THIS did not once so trouble me,
　　That better I could not love Thee;
　　But now I feel and know
That only when we love, we find
How far our hearts remain behind
　　The love they should bestow.

While we had little care to call
On Thee, and scarcely pray'd at all,
　　We seem'd enough to pray:
But now we only think with shame,
How seldom to Thy glorious Name
　　Our lips their offerings pay.

And when we gave yet slighter heed
Unto our brother's suffering need,
　　Our hearts reproach'd us then
Not half so much as now, that we
With such a careless eye can see
　　The woes and wants of men.

In doing is this knowledge won,
To see what yet remains undone;
  With this our pride repress,
And give us grace, a growing store,
That day by day we may do more,
  And may esteem it less.

CCXCV

THE GUESTEN HOUSE

LORD, weary of a painful way,
    All night our heads we would not lay
  Under the naked sky;
But ask, who worthiest? who will best
Entreat a tired and lowly guest
  With promptest courtesy?

And Thou art worthiest; there will not
One loving usage be forgot
  By Thee; Thy kiss will greet
Us entering; Thou wilt not disdain
To wash away each guilty stain
  From off our soiléd feet.

We enter, from this time to prove
Thy hospitality and love
  Shown tow'rd Thy meanest guest:
From house to house we would not stray,
For whither should we go away?
  With Thee is perfect rest.

CCXCVI

PRAYER

IF we with earnest effort could succeed
    To make our life one long connected prayer,
As lives of some perhaps have been and are:
If never leaving Thee, we had no need
Our wandering spirits back again to lead
Into Thy presence, but continued there,
Like angels standing on the highest stair
Of the sapphire throne,—this were to pray indeed.

But if distractions manifold prevail,
And if in this we must confess we fail,

Grant us to keep at least a prompt desire,
Continual readiness for prayer and praise,
An altar heap'd and waiting to take fire
With the least spark, and leap into a blaze.

CCXCVII

HERE AND HEREAFTER

TO leave unseen so many a glorious sight,
　To leave so many lands unvisited,
To leave so many worthiest books unread,
Unrealized so many visions bright;—

Oh! wretched yet inevitable spite
Of our brief span, that we must yield our breath,
And wrap us in the unfeeling coil of death,
So much remaining of unproved delight!

But hush, my soul, and vain regrets, be still'd;
Find rest in Him who is the complement
Of whatsoe'er transcends our mortal doom,
Of baffled hope and unfulfill'd intent;
In the clear vision and aspéct of Whom
All longings and all hopes shall be fulfill'd.

CCXCVIII

THOU inevitable Day,
　When a voice to me shall say—
'Thou must rise and come away;

'All thine other journeys past,
Gird thee, and make ready fast
For thy longest and thy last':—

Day deep-hidden from our sight
In impenetrable night,
Who may guess of thee aright?

Art thou distant, art thou near?
Wilt thou seem more dark or clear?
Day with more of hope or fear?

Wilt thou come, unseen before
Thou art standing at the door,
Saying, light and life are o'er?

Or with such a gradual pace,
As shall leave me largest space
To regard thee face to face?

Shall I lay my drooping head
On some loved lap,—round my bed
Prayer be made and tears be shed?

Or at distance from mine own,
Name and kin alike unknown,
Make my solitary moan?

Will there yet be things to leave,
Hearts to which this heart must cleave,
From which parting it must grieve?

Or shall life's best ties be o'er,
And all loved ones gone before
To that other happier shore?

Shall I gently fall on sleep,
Death, like slumber, o'er me creep,
Like a slumber sweet and deep?

Or the soul long strive in vain,
To escape, with toil and pain,
From its half-divided chain?

Little skills it where or how,
If thou comest then or now,
With a smooth or angry brow;

Come thou must, and we must die—
Jesus! Saviour! stand Thou by,
When that last sleep seals our eye!

CCXCIX

AT THE FONT

IN token that thou shalt not fear
  Christ Crucified to own,
We print the Cross upon thee here,
  And stamp thee His alone.

In token that thou shalt not blush
  To glory in His Name,
We blazon here upon thy front
  His glory and His shame.

In token that thou shalt not flinch
  Christ's quarrel to maintain,
But 'neath His banner manfully
  Firm at thy post remain;

In token that thou too shalt tread
  The path He travell'd by,
Endure the cross, despise the shame,
  And sit thee down on high;

Thus, outwardly and visibly,
  We seal thee for His own;
And may the brow that wears His Cross
  Hereafter share His Crown!

H. Alford

CCC

BE not afraid to pray—to pray is right.
  Pray, if thou canst, with hope; but ever pray,
Though hope be weak, or sick with long delay;
Pray in the darkness, if there be no light.

Far is the time, remote from human sight,
When war and discord on the earth shall cease;
Yet every prayer for universal peace
Avails the blessèd time to expedite.

Whate'er is good to wish, ask that of Heaven,
Though it be what thou canst not hope to see;
Pray to be perfect, though material leaven
Forbid the spirit so on earth to be:

But if for any wish thou darest not pray,
Then pray to God to cast that wish away.

H. Coleridge

CCCI

MULTUM DILEXIT

SHE sat and wept beside His feet; the weight
  Of sin oppress'd her heart; for all the blame,
And the poor malice of the worldly shame,
To her was past, extinct, and out of date:

Only the sin remain'd,—the leprous state;
She would be melted by the heat of love,
By fires far fiercer than are blown to prove
And purge the silver ore adulterate.

She sat and wept, and with her untress'd hair
Still wiped the feet she was so blest to touch;
And He wiped off the soiling of despair
From her sweet soul, because she loved so much.

I am a sinner, full of doubts and fears,—
Make me a humble thing of love and tears!

CCCII

OF SUCH IS THE KINGDOM OF GOD

IN stature perfect, and with every gift
   Which GOD would on His favourite work bestow,
Did our great Parent his pure form uplift,
And sprang from earth, the lord of all below.

But Adam fell before a child was born,
And want and weakness with his fall began;
So his first offspring was a thing forlorn,
In human shape, without the strength of man.

So, Heaven has doom'd that all of Adam's race,
Naked and helpless, shall their course begin,—
E'en at their birth confess their need of grace—
And weeping, wail the penalty of sin.

Yet sure the babe is in the cradle blest,
Since GOD Himself a baby deign'd to be—
And slept upon a mortal Mother's breast,
And steep'd in baby tears His Deity.

—O sleep, sweet infant, for we all must sleep,
And wake like babes, that we may wake with Him,
Who watches still His own from harm to keep,
And o'er them spreads the wings of Cherubim.

CCCIII

THE LAND O' THE LEAL

I'M wearin' awa', John,
   Like snaw-wreaths in thaw, John,
I'm wearin' awa'
     To the land o' the leal.
There's nae sorrow there, John,
There's neither cauld nor care, John,
The day's aye fair
     I' the land o' the leal.

Our bonnie bairn's there, John,
She was baith gude and fair, John,
And, oh! we grudged her sair
     To the land o' the leal.
But sorrow's sel' wears past, John,
And joy's comin' fast, John,
The joy that's aye to last
     In the land o' the leal.

Sae dear's that joy was bought, John,
Sae free the battle fought, John,
That sinfu' man e'er brought[1]
      To the land o' the leal.
Oh! dry your glist'ning ee, John,
My saul langs to be free, John,
And Angels beckon me
      To the land o' the leal.

Oh, haud[2] ye leal and true, John,
Your day it's wearin' thro', John,
An' I 'll welcome you
      To the land o' the leal.
Now fare ye weel, my ain John,
This world's cares are vain, John,
We 'll meet and aye be fain[3]
      I' the land o' the leal.

C. Lady Nairn

[1] See Note　　　[2] *haud*, keep　　　[3] *fain*, happy

CCCIV

MORNING THOUGHTS

AGAIN, O LORD, I ope my eyes
  Thy glorious light to see,
And share the gifts so largely lent
  To thankless man by Thee.

And why has GOD o'er me this night
  The watch so kindly kept?
And why have I so safely waked,
  And why so sweetly slept?

And wherefore do I live and breathe?
  And wherefore have I still
The mind to know, the sense to choose,
  The strength to do Thy will?

Is it, to waste another day
  In folly, sin, and shame?
To give to these my heart and hand,
  And spurn my Maker's claim?

Is it, for honour, wealth, or power
  My heavenly hopes to sell?
Is it, to grasp at pleasure's flower
  Upon the brink of hell?

Is it, to grow unto the world,
 As glides the world from me;
Be one day nearer to the grave,
 And further, LORD, from Thee?

No! thus too many days I've spent!
 To Thee, then, this be given:
Teach what I owe to Man below,
 And to Thyself in heaven.

H. F. Lyte

CCCV

THE ALPS

HAIL, scenes of holy grandeur! hail!
 Where mortal sense stands hush'd and awed:—
Oh, who could gaze on such, and fail
 To think of Thee, my GOD?

Alone and dread Thou dwellest here,
 The Source and Soul of all I see.
I look around in joy and fear,
 And feel I am with Thee!

I see Thee on the mountain sit,
 At summer's noon, sublime and still;
Or, in the giant shadows flit
 Along from hill to hill.

I read Thy presence and Thy power
 In each eternal rock I meet;
I trace Thy love in every flower
 That blossoms at my feet.

Thou speakest from each rolling cloud
 That pours its stormy mirth on high,
When cliff to cliff is shouting loud,
 Responsive to the sky:—

Thy voice at night is in the sound
 Of sinking glaciers, rushing rills,
And avalanches thundering round
 Among the startled hills:—

The mountain-mists in all their moods,
 The snows by earthly feet untrod,—
The fells, the forests, and the floods,
 Are all instinct with GOD.

CCCVI

THE LORD hath builded for Himself
   He needs no earthly dome;
The universe His dwelling is,
   Eternity His home.

Yon glorious sky His temple stands,
   So lofty, bright, and blue,
All lamp'd with stars, and curtain'd round
   With clouds of every hue.

Earth is His altar: Nature there
   Her daily tribute pays;
The elements upon Him wait;
   The seasons roll His praise.

Where shall I see Him? How describe
   The Dread, Eternal One?
His foot-prints are in every place,
   Himself is found in none.

He call'd the world, and it arose;
   The heavens, and they appear'd:
His hand pour'd forth the mighty deep;
   His arm the mountains rear'd.

He sets His foot upon the hills,
   And earth beneath Him quakes;
He walks upon the hurricane,
   And in the thunder speaks.

—I search the rounds of space and time,
   Nor find His semblance there:
Grandeur has nothing so sublime,
   Nor Beauty half so fair.

CCCVII

A FALLEN SISTER

SHE is not dead—she only sleeps:
   Life in her soul its vigil keeps:
Though dark the cloud, though strong the chain,
Speak, LORD, and she shall live again!

She is not dead:—it cannot be
That one, whose soul so glow'd to Thee,
Should all that's past renounce, forget:
Oh, speak, and she will hear Thee yet!

I know, I know how once she felt,
Have seen her spirit mount and melt;
Have join'd with her in praise and prayer;
And cannot, dare not, yet despair.

She that has fed on heavenly food,
Conversed with all that 's great and good,
Can she descend from heights like these
To the poor worldling's husks and lees?

She, that has bent at Heaven's high throne,
And claim'd its glories for her own,
An earthworm here again to crawl?—
She cannot long so deeply fall.

I know how many for her feel,
And plead with Thee to come and heal:
I know the power of faith and prayer,
And cannot, will not, yet despair.

Sunk as she is in thoughtless sin,
Thou hast a still, small voice within—
A silent hold—a hidden plea—
That needs but quickening, LORD, from Thee.

A look of Thine can life impart;
A tone of Thine can touch the heart:
The very grave Thy voice must hear:
Oh, bid it reach our sister's ear!

Press on her soul each pang and scorn,
Which Thou for her of old hast borne;
And ask how she will dare to meet
Thy face upon a Judgment-seat.

Talk to her heart, and bid her feel;
Send forth Thy word to wound and heal;
Melt off her spirit's icy chain,
And bid her rise and live again.

She is not dead :—Thy voice Divine
Can still revive, and seal her Thine;
And 'neath Thy wing she yet may dwell,
More meek, more safe, than ere she fell.

CCCVIII

THE song of GOD, so nobly sung
    By Angels in a higher sphere,
Shall my unworthy heart and tongue
    Attempt its numbers here?

With spirit cleaving to the dust,
  How should I hope to glow and soar?
How speak of heavenly joy and trust,
    Till I have felt them more?

An heir of guilt, a child of sin,
  An exile in a world like this,
What should I find without, within,
    To match with Him and His?

In vain I spread my flickering wings;
  In vain I strive aloft to flee:
Great LORD of lords, and KING of kings,
    I cannot sing of Thee!

I want a Seraph's lofty voice,
  I want a Seraph's soaring wing,
Before I make such themes my choice,
    And GOD's dread glories sing.

Thou needest not a note of mine
  To swell the triumphs of Thy throne,
Where myriads round Thee bend and shine,
    And Heaven is all Thy own!

No, rather let me sit and sigh,
  And drop contrition's silent tear:
Praise is the task of saints on high;
    But prayer of sinners here.

The song of GOD, that glorious song,—
  From me in such a world as this?—
O no! a worthier heart and tongue
    Must speak of Him and His!

CCCIX

WHY do I sigh to find
    Life's evening shadows gathering round my way?
The keen eye dimming, and the buoyant mind
  Unhinging day by day?

  Is it the natural dread
Of that stern lot, which all who live must see?
The worm, the clay, the dark and narrow bed,—
  Have these such awe for me?

As nears my soul the verge
Of this dim continent of woe and crime,
Shrinks she to hear Eternity's long surge
    Break on the shores of Time!

I want not vulgar fame—
I seek not to survive in brass or stone;
Hearts may not kindle when they hear my name,
    Nor tears my value own—

But might I leave behind
Some blessing for my fellows, some fair trust
To guide, to cheer, to elevate my kind,
    When I was in the dust;—

Within my narrow bed
Might I not wholly mute or useless be;
But hope that they, who trampled o'er my head,
    Drew still some good from me;—

Might verse of mine inspire
One virtuous aim, one high resolve impart;
Light in one drooping soul a hallow'd fire,
    Or bind one broken heart;—

Death would be sweeter then,
More calm my slumber 'neath the silent sod,—
Might I thus live to bless my fellow-men,
    Or glorify my God!

—Why do we ever lose
As judgment ripens, our diviner powers?
Why do we only learn our gifts to use
    When they no more are ours?

O Thou! whose touch can lend
Life to the dead, Thy quickening grace supply,
'And grant me, swanlike, my last breath to spend
    In song that may not die[1]!

[1] See Note

CCCX

ABIDE with me! Fast falls the eventide;
    The darkness deepens: LORD, with me abide!
When other helpers fail, and comforts flee,
Help of the helpless, O abide with me!

Swift to its close ebbs out life's little day;
Earth's joys grow dim; its glories pass away:
Change and decay in all around I see;
O Thou, who changest not, abide with me!

Not a brief glance I beg, a passing word,
But as Thou dwell'st with Thy disciples, Lord,
Familiar, condescending, patient, free,
Come, not to sojourn, but abide, with me!

Come not in terrors, as the King of kings;
But kind and good, with healing in Thy wings:
Tears for all woes, a heart for every plea :—
Come, Friend of sinners, and thus bide with me!

Thou on my head in early youth didst smile,
And, though rebellious and perverse meanwhile,
Thou hast not left me, oft as I left Thee.
On to the close, O Lord, abide with me!

I need Thy presence every passing hour :
What but Thy grace can foil the Tempter's power?
Who like Thyself my guide and stay can be?
Through cloud and sunshine, O abide with me!

I fear no foe with Thee at hand to bless :
Ills have no weight, and tears no bitterness.
Where is Death's sting? where, Grave, thy victory?
—I triumph still, if Thou abide with me.

Hold Thou Thy Cross before my closing eyes;
Shine through the gloom, and point me to the skies :
Heaven's morning breaks, and earth's vain shadows flee :—
In life and death, O Lord, abide with me!

CCCXI

PLEASANT are Thy courts above
In the land of light and love;
Pleasant are Thy courts below
In this land of sin and woe.
O, my spirit longs and faints
For the converse of Thy Saints,
For the brightness of Thy face,
For Thy fullness, God of grace!

Happy birds that sing and fly
Round Thy altars, O Most High!
Happier souls that find a rest
In a Heavenly Father's breast!

Like the wandering dove, that found
No repose on earth around,
They can to their ark repair,
And enjoy it ever there.

Happy souls! their praises flow
Even in this vale of woe;
Waters in the desert rise,
Manna feeds them from the skies:
On they go from strength to strength,
Till they reach Thy throne at length,
At Thy feet adoring fall,
Who hast led them safe through all.

CCCXII

LIFTING UP TO THE CROSS

OFT have I read of sunny realms, where skies are pure at
   even,
And sight goes deep in lucid air, and earth seems nearer Heaven,
And wheresoe'er you lift your eyes, the holy Cross, they say,
Stands guardian of your journey, by lone or crowded way;
And I have mused how awfully its shadows and its gleams
Might haply fall on infants' eyes, and mingle with their dreams,
And draw them up by silent power of its o'ershading arm,
And deepen on the tender brow CHRIST's seal and saintly charm.

—Upon a verdant hillock the sacred sign appears,
A damsel on no trembling arm an eager babe uprears,
With a sister's yearning love, and an elder sister's pride,
She lifts the new-baptized, to greet the Friend Who for him died.
Who may the maiden's thought divine, performing thus in sight
Of all the heavenly Watchers her pure unbidden rite?
While fearless to those awful Lips her treasure she would raise,
I see her features shrink, as though she fain would downward gaze.

Perchance a breath of self-reproach is. fluttering round her
   heart :—
'Thou, darling, in our Saviour may'st for certain claim thy part:
The dews baptismal bright and keen are glistening on thy brow,
He cannot choose but own thee, in His arms received e'en now.
But much I've sinn'd and little wept: will He not say, "Be-
   gone"?
I dare not meet His searching eye; my penance is undone.
But thou and thy good Angel, who nerves mine arm to bear
And lift thee up so near Him, will strive for me in prayer.'

Or chanced the Thorny Crown her first upseeking glance to
   win,
And the deep lines of agony traced by the whole world's sin?
Oh, deeply in her bosom went the thought, 'Who draw so nigh
Unto those awful Lips, and share the Lord's departing sigh,—
Who knoweth what mysterious pledge upon their souls is bound,
To copy in their own hearts' blood each keen and bitter Wound?
If of the dying Jesus we the Kiss of Peace receive,
How but in daily dying thenceforward dare we live?

'And was it meet, thou tender flower, on thy young life to lay
Such burden, pledging thee to vows thou never canst unsay?
What if the martyrs' fire some day thy dainty limbs devour?
What if beneath the scourge they writhe, or in dull famine
   cower?
What if thou bear the cross within, all aching and decay?—
And 'twas I that laid it on thee:—what if thou fall away?'
Such is Love's deep misgiving, when stronger far than Faith,
She brings her earthly darlings to the Cross for life or death.

O, be Thou present in that hour, high Comforter, to lead
Her memory to th' eternal Law, by the great King decreed,
What time the highly favour'd one who on His bosom lay,
And he who of the chosen twelve first trode the martyrs' way,
Taught by their mother, craved the boon next to Thy throne
   to be,
For her dreams were of the Glory, but the Cross she could
   not see.
O well for that fond mother, well for her beloved, that they,
When th' hour His secret meaning told, did by their promise
   stay!

'Thy baptism and Thy cup be ours: for both our hearts are
   strong.'
Learn it, ye babes, at matin prime, repeat it all day long.
Ev'n as the mother's morning kiss is token of delight
Through all the merry hours of day, and at fall of dewy night
Her evening kiss shall to her babe the softest slumbers seal,
So Thy first greeting life imparts, Thy last shall cheer and
   heal.—
Then, maiden, trust thy nursling here! thou wilt not choose
   amiss
For his sweet soul; here let him dwell; here is the gate of
   bliss.

See Note

CCCXIII

WHEN travail hours are spent and o'er,
   And genial hours of joy
In cradle songs and nursery lore
   All the glad home employ,

Full busy in her kindly mood
   Is Fancy, to descry
The welcome notes of fatherhood,
   In form, and lip, and eye.

And elder brethren's hearts are proud,
   And sisters blush and smile,
As round the babe by turns they crowd
   A brief and wondering while.

With eager speed they ready make
   Soft bosom and safe arm,
As though such burthen once to take
   A blessing were and charm.

And ever as with hastening wing
   His little life glides on,
By power of that first wondrous spring
   To all but babes unknown,

Easier each hour the task will grow,
   To name the unfolding flower,
By plumage and by song to know
   The nestling in his bower.—

Oh, while your hearts so blithely dance
   With frail fond hopes of earth,
Will ye not cast one onward glance
   To the true heavenly birth?

Will ye not say, 'God speed the time
   When Spirits pure, to trace
The hues of a more glorious prime,
   Shall lean from their high place,

'And mark, too keen for earthly day,
   The Father's stamp and seal,
Christ in the heart, the Living Ray,
   Its deepening light reveal?'

—Oh, well the denizens of Heaven
   Their Master's children know,
By filial yearnings sweet and even,
   By patient smiles in woe,

By gaze of meek inquiry, turn'd
　Towards th' informing Eye,
By tears that to obey have learn'd,
　By claspéd hands on high!

CCCXIV

GIVE me a tender spotless child,
　　Rehearsing or at eve or morn
His chant of glory undefiled,
　The Creed that with the Church was born:—

Down be his earnest forehead cast,
　His slender fingers join'd for prayer,
With half a frown his eye seal'd fast
　Against the world's intruding glare.

Who,—while his lips so gently move,
　And all his look is purpose strong,
Can say what wonders, wrought above,
　Upon his unstain'd fancy throng?

The world new-framed, the CHRIST new-born,
　The Mother-Maid, the cross and grave,
The rising sun on Easter morn,
　The fiery tongues sent down to save,—

The gathering Church, the Font of Life,
　The saints and mourners kneeling round,
The Day to end the body's strife,
　The Saviour in His people crown'd,—

All in majestic march and even
　To the veil'd eye by turns appear,
True to their time as stars in heaven,—
　No morning dream so still and clear.

CCCXV

EXAMPLE

WE scatter seeds with careless hand,
　And dream we ne'er shall see them more:
　　But for a thousand years
　　　Their fruit appears,
　　In weeds that mar the land,
　　　Or healthful store.

The deeds we do, the words we say,—
Into still air they seem to fleet,
    We count them ever past;
    But they shall last,
    In the dread judgment they
    And we shall meet!

—I charge thee by the years gone by,
For the love's sake of brethren dear,
    Keep thou the one true way
    In work and play,
    Lest in that world their cry
    Of woe thou hear!

CCCXVI

I MARK'D when vernal meads were bright,
    And many a primrose smiled,
I mark'd her, blithe as morning light,
    A dimpled three years' child.

A basket on one tender arm
    Contain'd her precious store
Of spring-flowers in their freshest charm,
    Told proudly o'er and o'er.

The other wound with earnest hold
    About her blooming guide,
A maid who scarce twelve years had told:
    So walk'd they side by side.

One a bright bud, and one might seem
    A sister flower half blown.
Full joyous on their loving dream
    The sky of April shone.

The summer months swept by: again
    That loving pair I met.
On russet heath, and bowery lane,
    Th' autumnal sun had set:

And chill and damp that Sunday eve
    Breathed on the mourners' road
That bright-eyed little one to leave
    Safe in the Saints' abode.

Behind, the guardian sister came,
    Her bright brow dim and pale—
O cheer thee, maiden! in His Name,
    Who still'd Jairus' wail!

Thou mourn'st to miss the fingers soft
    That held by thine so fast,
The fond appealing eye, full oft
    Tow'rd thee for refuge cast.

Sweet toils, sweet cares, for ever gone!
    No more from stranger's face
Or startling sound, the timid one
    Shall hide in thine embrace.

Thy first glad earthly task is o'er,
    And dreary seems thy way.
But what if nearer than before
    She watch thee e'en to-day?

What if henceforth by Heaven's decree
    She leave thee not alone,
But in her turn prove guide to thee
    In ways to Angels known?

O yield thee to her whisperings sweet:
    Away with thoughts of gloom!
In love the loving spirits greet,
    Who wait to bless her tomb.

In loving hope with her unseen
    Walk as in hallow'd air.
When foes are strong and trials keen,
    Think, 'What if she be there?'

CCCXVII

ELIJAH AT SAREPTA

LO, cast at random on the wild sea sand
    A child low wailing lies;
Around, with eye forlorn and feeble hand,
    Scarce heeding its faint cries,
The widow'd mother in the wilderness
Gathers dry boughs, their last sad meal to dress.

But who is this that comes with mantle rude
    And vigil-wasted air,
Who to the famish'd cries, 'Come give me food,
    I with thy child would share?'
She bounteous gives: but hard he seems of heart,
Who of such scanty store would crave a part.

Haply the child his little hand holds forth,
  That all his own may be.—
Nay, simple one, thy mother's faith is worth
  Healing and life to thee.
That handful given, for years ensures thee bread:
That drop of oil shall raise thee from the dead.

For in yon haggard form He begs unseen,
  To Whom for life we kneel:
One little cake He asks with lowly mien,
  Who blesses every meal.
Lavish for Him, ye poor, your children's store,
So shall your cruse for many a day run o'er.

And thou, dear child, though hungering, give glad way
  To JESUS in His need:
So thy blest mother at the awful day
  Thy name in Heaven may read;
So by His touch for ever may'st thou live,
Who asks our alms, and lends a heart to give.

See Note

CCCXVIII

AT MATINS

HEAVEN in the depth and height is seen;
    On high among the stars, and low
In deep clear waters: all betveen
    Is earth, and tastes of earth: ev'n so
    The Almighty One draws near
To strongest seraphs there, to weakest infants here.

  GOD's Angels keep the eternal round
    Of praise on high, and never tire.
  His lambs are in His Temple found
    Early, with all their hearts' desire.
    They boast not to be free,—
They grudge not to their LORD meek ear and bended knee.

CCCXIX

'TIS only our dull hearts that tire so soon
    Of CHRIST's repeated call; while they in Heaven,
Unwearied basking in the eternal noon,
Still sound the note, by the first Seraph given,
What time the Morning Stars around their King
Began for evermore to shine and sing.

And you, ye gentle babes, true image here
Of such as walk in white before the Throne,
Ye weary not of Love, how oft soe'er
Her yearnings she repeat in unchanged tone.
To tale familiar, to remember'd strain,
To frolic ten times tried, ye cry, Again.

How have I seen you, when the unpleasing time
Came for some kindly guest to pass away,
Cling round his skirts! how mark'd the playful chime
Of earnest voices, pledged to make him stay!
O deeply sink, and with a tearful spell,
The memories of such welcome and farewell.

Nor wants in elder love the like soft charm.
The Mother tires not of one little voice,
Ev'n as she fain all day with patient arm
Would bear one burthen.　O frail heart, rejoice!
Love trains thee now by repetition sweet
The unwasting and unvarying bliss to greet.

CCCXX

CHILDREN'S CHRISTMAS EVE

REJOICE in God alway,
　　With stars in Heaven rejoice,
Ere dawn of Christ's own day
　　Lift up each little voice.
Look up with glad pure eye,
　And count those lamps on high.
Nay, who may count them? on our gaze
They from their deeps come out in ever widening maze.

　　Each in his stand aloof
　　　Prepares his keenest beam,
　　Upon that hovel roof,
　　　In at that door, to stream,
　　Where meekly waits her time
　.　The whole earth's Flower and Prime :—
Where in few hours the Eternal One
Will make a clear new day, rising before the sun.

　　Rejoice in God alway,
　　　With each green leaf rejoice,
　　Of berries on each spray
　　　The brightest be your choice.

From bower and mountain lone
The autumnal hues are gone,
Yet gay shall be our Christmas wreath,
The glistening beads above, the burnish'd leaves beneath.

Rejoice in God alway,
    With Powers rejoice on high,
Who now with glad array
    Are gathering in the sky,
His cradle to attend,
And there all lowly bend.
But half so low as He hath bow'd
Did never highest Angel stoop from brightest cloud.

Rejoice in God alway,
    All creatures, bird and beast,
Rejoice, again I say,
    His mightiest and His least;
From ox and ass that wait
Here on His poor estate,
To the four living Powers, decreed
A thousand ways at once His awful car to speed.

Rejoice in God alway:
    With Saints in Paradise
Your midnight service say,
    For vigil glad arise.
Ev'n they in their calm bowers
Too tardy find the hours
Till He reveal the wondrous Birth:
How must we look and long, chain'd here to sin and earth!

Ye babes, to Jesus dear,
    Rejoice in Him alway.
Ye whom He bade draw near,
    O'er whom He loved to pray,
Wake and lift up the head
Each in his quiet bed.
Listen: His voice the night-wind brings:
He in your cradle lies, He in our carols sings.

CCCXXI

'NURSE, let me draw the baby's veil aside,
    I want to see the Cross upon her brow.
Nay, maiden dear, that seal may not abide
    In sight of mortals' ken; 'tis vanish'd now.

'Alas, for pity! when the holy man
  Said even now, *I sign thee with the cross*,
What joy to think that I at home should scan
  The bright, clear lines! O, sad and sudden loss!'

—Complain not so, my child: no loss is here,
  But endless gain. If thou wilt open wide
Faith's inward eye, soon shall to thee appear
  What now by wondering angels is descried,

Thy LORD's true token, seen not, but believed,
  And therefore doubly blest. O, mark it well;
And be this rule in thy young heart received—
  Blest, who content with Him in twilight dwell.

Thy saints, O LORD, and Thine own Mother dear
  Are round Thee as a glory-cloud: we see
The general glow, not each in outline clear,
  Or several station: all are hid in Thee.

In prayer we own Thee, Father, at our side,
  Not always feel or taste Thee; and 'tis well.
So, hour by hour, courageous faith is tried;
  So, gladlier will the morn all mists dispel.

See Note

CCCXXII

HARVEST

LORD, in Thy Name Thy servants plead,
  And Thou hast sworn to hear;
Thine is the harvest, Thine the seed,
  The fresh and fading year:

Our hope, when Autumn winds blew wild,
  We trusted, LORD, with Thee;
And still, now Spring has on us smiled,
  We wait on Thy decree.

The former and the latter rain,
  The summer sun and air,
The green ear, and the golden grain,—
  All Thine, are ours by prayer.

Thine too by right, and ours by grace,
  The wondrous growth unseen,
The hopes that soothe, the fears that brace,
  The love that shines serene.

So grant the precious things brought forth
  By sun and moon below,
That Thee in Thy new heaven and earth
  We never may forego.

CCCXXIII

ANTIPODES

FAR, far on other isles,
    Where other stars are beaming,
Where the bright rose on Christmas smiles,
    And Whitsun lights with frost are gleaming,
Yon kindly Moon, and glorious Sun
Their race, as here, unwearying run.

What if all else be strange?
  The two great lights of heaven
Know neither error, stay, nor change.
  By them all else to sight is given;
And with them duly, fresh and bright,
Home thoughts return both day and night.

 Glory to our true Sun,
  Who shineth far and near;
Who for His duteous Spouse hath won
  A place as of a lunar sphere;
And by their light, where'er she roam,
Faith finds a safe, familiar home.

CCCXXIV

THE GATHERING OF THE CHURCH

WHEREFORE shrink, and say, ''Tis vain';
    In their hour hell-powers must reign;
Vainly, vainly would we force
Fatal error's torrent course;
Earth is mighty, we are frail;
Faith is gone, and hope must fail.'

Yet along the Church's sky
Stars are scatter'd, pure and high;
Yet her wasted gardens bear
Autumn violets, sweet and rare—
Relics of a spring-time clear,
Earnest of a bright new year.

Israel yet hath thousands seal'd,
Who to Baal never kneel'd;
Seize the banner, spread its fold!
Seize it with no faltering hold!
Spread its foldings high and fair,
Let all see the Cross is there!

What if to the trumpet's sound
Voices few come answering round?
Scarce a votary swell the burst,
When the anthem peals at first?
GOD hath sown, and He will reap;
Growth is slow when roots are deep;—

He will aid the work begun,
For the love of His dear Son;
He will breathe in their true breath,
Who, serene in prayer and faith,
Would our dying embers fan
Bright as when their glow began.

CCCXXV

DRAW near as early as we may,
  Grace, like an angel, goes before.
  The stone is roll'd away,
  We find an open door.

O, wondrous chain! where aye entwine
  Our human wills, a tender thread,
    With the strong will divine:—
    We run as we are led.

We, did I say? 'tis all Thine own;
  Thou in the dark dost Mary guide:
    Thine angel moves the stone;
    ·Love feels Thee at her side.

CCCXXVI

THE COMMUNION OF THE SICK

HOLY is the sick man's room:—
  Temper'd air, and curtain'd gloom,
Measured steps, and tones as mild
As the breath of new-born child,
Postures lowly, waitings still,
Looks subdued to duty's will,

Reverent, thoughtful, grave and sweet:
These to wait on CHRIST are meet.
These may kneel where He lies low,
In His members suffering woe.
Nor in other discipline
Train we hearts, that to His shrine
May unblamed draw near, and be
With His favour'd two or three:—
Therefore in its silent gloom
Holy is the sick man's room.

CCCXXVII

I THOUGHT to meet no more, so dreary seem'd
  Death's interposing veil, and thou so pure,
      Thy place in Paradise
      Beyond where I could soar;

Friend of this worthless heart! but happier thoughts
Spring like unbidden violets from the sod,
      Where patiently thou tak'st
      Thy sweet and sure repose.

The shadows fall more soothing : the soft air
Is full of cheering whispers like thine own;
      While Memory, by thy grave,
      Lives o'er thy funeral day;

The deep knell dying down, the mourners' pause,
Waiting their Saviour's welcome at the gate.—
      Sure with the words of Heaven
      Thy spirit met us there,

And sought with us along th' accustom'd way
The hallow'd porch, and entering in, beheld
      The pageant of sad joy
      So dear to Faith and Hope.

O! hadst thou brought a strain from Paradise
To cheer us, happy soul, thou hadst not touch'd
      The sacred springs of grief
      More tenderly and true,

Than those deep-warbled anthems, high and low,
Low as the grave, high as th' Eternal Throne,
      Guiding through light and gloom
      Our mourning fancies wild,

Till gently, like soft golden clouds at eve
Around the western twilight, all subside
  Into a placid faith,
  That even with beaming eye

Counts thy sad honours, coffin, bier, and pall;
So many relics of a frail love lost,
  So many tokens dear
  Of endless love begun.

Listen! it is no dream : th' Apostles' trump
Gives earnest of th' Archangel's ;—calmly now,
  Our hearts yet beating high
  To that victorious lay,

(Most like a warrior's, to the martial dirge
Of a true comrade), in the grave we trust
  Our treasure for awhile :
  And if a tear steal down,

If human anguish o'er the shaded brow
Pass shuddering, when the handful of pure earth
  Touches the coffin-lid ;
  If at our brother's name,

Once and again the thought, 'for ever gone,'
Come o'er us like a cloud ; yet, gentle spright,
  Thou turnest not away,
  Thou know'st us calm at heart.

One look, and we have seen our last of thee,
Till we too sleep and our long sleep be o'er.
  O cleanse us, ere we view
  That countenance pure again,

Thou, who canst change the heart, and raise the dead!
As Thou art by to soothe our parting hour,
  Be ready when we meet,
  With Thy dear pardoning words.

See Note

CCCXXVIII

LORD Jesus, loving hearts and dear
 Are resting in Thy shadow here;
In life Thou wast their hope, and we
In death would trust them, Lord, with Thee.

See Note

CCCXXIX

BETHLEHEM, above all cities blest!
  Th' Incarnate Saviour's earthly rest,
Where in His manger safe He lay,
By angels guarded night and day.

Bethlehem, of cities most forlorn,
Where in the dust sad mothers mourn,
Nor see the heavenly glory shed
On each pale infant's martyr'd head.

—'Tis ever thus: who CHRIST would win,
Must in the school of woe begin;
And still the nearest to His grace,
Know least of their own glorious place.

CCCXXX

AVE, GRATIA PLENA

MOTHER of GOD! O, not in vain
  We learn'd of old thy lowly strain.
Fain in thy shadow would we rest,
And kneel with thee, and call thee blest;
With thee would ' magnify the LORD,'—
And if thou art not here adored,
Yet seek we, day by day, the love and fear
Which bring thee, with all saints, near and more near.

What glory thou above hast won,
By special grace of thy dear Son,
We see not yet, nor dare espy
Thy crownéd form with open eye.
Rather beside the manger meek
Thee bending with veil'd brow we seek;
Or where the angel in the thrice-great Name
Hail'd thee, and JESUS to thy bosom came.

Yearly since then with bitterer cry
Man hath assail'd the Throne on high,
And sin and hate more fiercely striven
To mar the league 'twixt earth and heaven.
But the dread tie, that pardoning hour,
Made fast in Mary's awful bower,
Hath mightier proved to bind than we to break:—
None may that work undo, that Flesh unmake.

Thenceforth, Whom thousand worlds adore,
He calls thee Mother evermore;
Angel nor Saint His face may see
Apart from what He took of thee.
How may we choose but name thy name,
Echoing below their high acclaim
In holy Creeds? Since earthly song and prayer
Must keep faint time to the dread anthem there.

How, but in love, on thine own days,
Thou blissful one, upon thee gaze?
Nay every day, each suppliant hour,
Whene'er we kneel in aisle or bower,
Thy glories we may greet unblamed,
Nor shun the lay by seraphs framed,
'Hail, Mary, full of grace!' O, welcome sweet,
Which daily in all lands all saints repeat!.

Therefore as kneeling day by day
We to our Father duteous pray,
So unforbidden may we speak
An Ave to CHRIST's Mother meek:
(As children with 'good morrow' come
To elders in some happy home :)
Inviting so the saintly host above
With our unworthiness to pray in love.

See Note

CCCXXXI

VO'K A-COMÈN INTO CHURCH

THE church do zeem a touchèn zight,
   When vo'k, a-comèn in at door,
      Do softly tread the long-ailed vloor
Below the pillar'd arches' height,
      Wi' bells a-pealèn,
      Vo'k a-kneelèn,
Hearts a-healèn, wi' the love
An' peáce a-zent[1] em vrom above.

An' there, wi' mild an' thoughtvul feáce,
      Wi' downcast eyes, an' vaïces dum',
      The wold an' young do slowly come,
An' teáke in stillness each his pleáce,
      A-zinkèn slowly,
      Kneelèn lowly,
Seekèn holy thoughts alwone[2],
In pray'r avore their Meáker's throne.

An' there be sons in youthvul pride,
     An' fathers weak, wi' years an' païn,
     An' daughters in their mother's traïn,
The tall wi' smaller at their zide;
        Heads in murnèn[3]
        Never turnèn,
Cheäks a-burnèn, wi' the het
O' youth, an' eyes noo tears do wet.

There friends do settle, zide by zide,
     The knower speechless to the known;
     Their vaïce is there vor GOD alwone,
To flesh an' blood their tongues be tied.
        Grief a-wringèn,
        Jaÿ[4] a-zingèn,
Pray'r a-bringèn welcome rest
So softly to the troubled breast.

                     W. Barnes

---

[1] *a-zent*, sent   [2] *alwone*, alone   [3] *murnen*, mourning   [4] *jay*, joy

CCCXXXII

READEN OV A HEAD-STWONE

AS I wer readèn ov a stwone
     In Grenley church-yard all alwone,
A little maïd ran up, wi' pride
To zee me there, an' push'd a-zide
A bunch o' bennets[1] that did hide
     A verse her father, as she zaïd,
     Put up above her mother's head,
        To tell how much he loved her.

The verse wer short, but very good,
I stood an' larn'd en where I stood :—
'Mid[2] GOD, dear Meäry, gi'e me greäce
To vind, lik' thee, a better pleäce,
Where I woonce mwore mid zee thy feäce;
     An' bring thy childern up to know
     His word, that they mid come an' show
        Thy soul how much I loved thee.'

'Where 's father, then,' I zaid, 'my chile?'
'Dead too,' she answer'd wi' a smile;
'An' I an' brother Jim do bide
At Betty White's, o' tother zide

O' road.' 'Mid He, my chile,' I cried,
  'That 's father to the fatherless,
  Become thy father now, an' bless,
    An' keep, an' leäd, an' love thee.'

Though she 've a-lost, I thought, so much,
Still He don't let the thoughts o't touch
Here litsome heart by day or night;
An' zoo[3], if we could teäke it right,
Do show He 'll meäke His burdens light
    To weaker souls, an' that His smile
    Is sweet upon a harmless chile,
      When they be dead that loved it.

[1] *bennets*, coarse flowering grasses   [2] *mid*, may   [3] *zoo*, so

CCCXXXIII

THE CHILD'S GREÄVE

AVORE the time when zuns went down
    On zummer's green a-turn'd to brown,
When sheädes o' swayèn wheat-eärs vell[1]
Upon the scarlet pimpernel;
The while you still mid[2] goo, an' vind
    'Ithin the geärden's mossy wall,
    Sweet blossoms, low or risèn[3] tall,
To meäke a tutty[4] to your mind,
In churchyard heaved, wi' grassy breast,
The greäve-mound ov a beäby's rest.

An' when a high day broke, to call
A throng 'ithin the churchyard wall,
The mother brought, wi' thoughtvul mind,
The feärest buds her eyes could vind,
To trim the little greäve, an' show
    To other souls her love an' loss,
    An' meäde a Seävior's little cross
O' brightest flow'rs that then did blow,
A-droppèn tears a-sheenèn[5] bright,
Among the dew, in mornèn light.

An woone sweet bud her han' did pleäce
Up where did droop the Seävior's feäce;
An' two she zet a-bloomèn bright,
Where reach'd His hands o' left an' right;

Two mwore feäir blossoms, crimson dyed,
   Did mark the pleäces ov His veet,
   An' woone did lie, a-smellèn sweet,
Up where the spear did wound the zide
Ov Him that is the life ov all
Greäve sleepers, whether big or small.

The mother that in faïth could zee
The Seävior on the high cross tree
Mid be a-vound[6] a-grievèn sore,
But not to grieve vor evermwore,
Vor He shall show her faithvul mind,
   His chaïce is all that she should choose,
   An' love that here do grieve to lose,
Shall be, above, a jay[7] to vind,
Wi' Him that evermwore shall keep
The souls that He do lay asleep.

[1] *vell*, fell   [2] *mid*, may   [3] *risèn*, rising   [4] *tutty*, nosegay
    [5] *a-sheenèn*, shining   [6] *vound*, found   [7] *jay*, joy

CCCXXXIV

THE CHURCH AN' HAPPY ZUNDAY

AH! ev'ry day mid bring a while
   O' eäse vrom all woone's[1] ceäre an' tweil[2],
The welcome evenèn, when 'tis sweet
Vor tired friends wi' weary veet,
But litsome hearts o' love, to meet:
An' yet while weekly times do roll,
The best vor body an' vor soul
      'S the church an' happy Zunday.

Vor then our loosen'd souls do rise
Wi' holy thoughts beyond the skies,
As we do think o' Him that shed
His blood vor us, an' still do spread
His love upon the live an' dead;
An' how He gi'ed a time an' pleäce
To gather us, an' gi'e us greäce,—
      The church an' happy Zunday.

There, under leänen[3] mossy stwones,
Do lie, vorgot, our fathers' bwones,
That trod this groun' vor years agoo,
When things that now be wold wer new;

An' comely maïdens, mild an' true,
That meäde their sweet-hearts happy brides,
An' come to kneel down at their zides
　　At church o' happy Zundays.

'Tis good to zee woone's naïghbours come
Out drough[4] the church-yard, vlockèn[5] hwome,
As woone do nod, an' woone do smile,
An' woone do toss another's chile;
An' zome be sheäken han's, the while
Poll's uncle, chuckèn her below
Her chin, do tell her she do grow,
　　At church o' happy Zundays.

Zoo while our blood do run in vaïns
O' livèn souls in theäsum[6] plaïns,
Mid happy housen smoky round
The church an' holy bit o' ground;
An' while their weddèn bells do sound,
Oh! mid em have the meäns o' greäce,
The holy day an' holy pleäce,
　　The church an' happy Zunday.

[1] *woone*, one　　　[2] *tweil*, toil　　　[3] *leänèn*, leaning　　　[4] *drough*, through
　　　[5] *vlockèn*, flocking　　　[6] *theäsum*, these

CCCXXXV

WITHSTANDERS

WHEN weakness now do strive wi' might
　　In struggles ov' an e'thly[1] trial,
Might mid overcome the right,
　An' truth be turn'd by might's denial;
Withstanders we ha' mwost[2] to feär,
If selfishness do wring us here,
Be souls a-holdèn in their hand
The might an' riches o' the land.

But when the wicked, now so strong,
　Shall stan' vor judgment, peäle as ashes,
By the souls that rued their wrong,
　Wi' tears a-hangèn on their lashes—
Then withstanders they shall deäre[3]
The leäst ov' all to meet wi' there,
Mid be the helpless souls that now
Below their wrongvul might mid bow.

Sweet childern o' the dead, bereft
  Ov all their goods by guile an' forgèn[4];
Souls o' driven sleäves that left
  Their weäry limbs a-mark'd by scourgèn;
They that God ha' call'd to die
Vor a truth ageän the worold's lie,
An' they that groan'd an' cried in vain,
A-bound by foes' unrighteous chain.

The maid that selfish craft led on
  To sin, an' left wi' hope a-blighted;
Starvèn workmen, thin an' wan,
  Wi' hopeless leäbour ill requited;
Souls a-wrong'd, an' call'd to vill
Wi' dread, the men that used em ill,—
When might shall yield to right as pliant
As a dwarf avore a giant.

When there, at last, the good shall glow
  In starbright bodies lik' their Seäviour,
Vor all their flesh noo mwore mid show,
  The marks o' man's unkind beheäviour:
Wi' speechless tongue, an' burnèn cheak,
The strong shall bow avore the weäk,
An' vind that helplessness, wi' right,
Is strong beyond all e'thly might.

[1] *e'thly*, earthly   [2] *ha mwost*, have most   [3] *deäre*, dare
                            [4] *forgen*, forgery

CCCXXXVI

THE MOTHER'S DREAM

I 'D a dream to-night
  As I fell asleep,
Oh! the touching sight
Makes me still to weep:
Of my little lad,
Gone to leave me sad,
Aye, the child I had,
But was not to keep.

As in heaven high,
I my child did seek,
There, in train, came by
Children fair and meek,

Each in lily-white,
With a lamp alight;
Each was clear to sight,
But they did not speak.

Then, a little sad,
Came my child in turn,
But the lamp he had,   ·
Oh! it did not burn;
He, to clear my doubt,
Said, half turn'd about,
'Your tears put it out;
Mother, never mourn.'

CCCXXXVII

PER PACEM AD LUCEM

I DO not ask, O Lord, that life may be
    A pleasant road;
I do not ask that Thou wouldst take from me
    Aught of its load:

I do not ask that flowers should always spring
    Beneath my feet;
I know too well the poison and the sting
    Of things too sweet.

For one thing only, Lord, dear Lord, I plead:
    Lead me aright—
Though strength should falter and though heart should
      bleed,
    Through Peace to Light.

I do not ask, O Lord, that Thou shouldst shed
    Full radiance here:
Give but a ray of peace, that I may tread
    Without a fear.

I do not ask my cross to understand,
    My way to see;
Better in darkness just to-feel Thy hand,
    And follow Thee.

A. A. Procter

CCCXXXVIII

THIS Advent moon shines cold and clear,
    These Advent nights are long;
Our lamps have burn'd year after year
    And still their flame is strong.

'Watchman, what of the night?' we cry
  Heart-sick with hope deferr'd:
'No speaking signs are in the sky,'
  Is still the watchman's word.

The Porter watches at the gate,
  The servants watch within;
The watch is long betimes and late,
  The prize is slow to win.
'Watchman, what of the night?' but still
  His answer sounds the same:
'No daybreak tops the utmost hill,
  Nor pale our lamps of flame.'

One to another hear them speak
  The patient Virgins wise:
'Surely He is not far to seek'—
  'All night we watch and rise.'
'The days are evil looking back,
  The coming days are dim;
Yet count we not His promise slack,
  But watch and wait for Him.'

One with another, soul with soul,
  They kindle fire from fire:
'Friends watch us who have touch'd the goal.'
  'They urge us, come up higher.'
'With them shall rest our waysore feet,
  With them is built our home,
With CHRIST.'—'They sweet, but He most sweet,
  Sweeter than honeycomb.'

There no more parting, no more pain,
  The distant ones brought near,
The lost so long are found again,—
  Long lost but longer dear:
Eye hath not seen, ear hath not heard,
  Nor heart conceived that rest,
With them our good things long deferr'd,
  With JESUS CHRIST our Best.

We weep because the night is long,
  We laugh, for day shall rise;
We sing a slow contented song,
  And knock at Paradise.
Weeping we hold Him fast, Who wept
  For us, we hold Him fast;
And will not let Him go except
  He bless us first or last.

Weeping we hold Him fast to-night;
  We will not let Him go
Till daybreak smite our wearied sight
  And summer smite the snow:
Then figs shall bud, and dove with dove
  Shall coo the livelong day;
Then He shall say, 'Arise, My love,
  My fair one, come away.'

C. G. Rossetti

CCCXXXIX

A CHRISTMAS CAROL

IN the bleak mid-winter
    Frosty wind made moan,
Earth stood hard as iron,
    Water like a stone;
Snow had fallen, snow on snow,
    Snow on snow,
In the bleak mid-winter
        Long ago.

Our GOD, Heaven cannot hold Him,
    Nor earth sustain;
Heaven and earth shall flee away
    When He comes to reign:
In the bleak mid-winter
    A stable-place sufficed
The LORD GOD Almighty
        JESUS CHRIST.

Enough for Him Whom cherubim
    Worship night and day,
A breastful of milk
    And a mangerful of hay;
Enough for Him Whom angels
    Fall down before,
The ox and ass and camel
        Which adore.

Angels and archangels
    May have gather'd there,
Cherubim and seraphim
    Throng'd the air,—
But only His Mother
    In her maiden bliss
Worshipp'd the Belovéd
        With a kiss.

What can I give Him
   Poor as I am !
If I were a shepherd
   I would bring a lamb ;
If I were a wise man
   I would do my part ;
Yet what I can I give Him,—
   Give my heart.

CCCXL

DESPISED AND REJECTED

MY sun has set, I dwell
      In darkness as a dead man out of sight ;
And none remains, not one, that I should tell
To him mine evil plight
This bitter night.
I will make fast my door
That hollow friends may trouble me no more.

' Friend, open to Me.'—Who is this that calls ?
Nay, I am deaf as are my walls :
Cease crying, for I will not hear
Thy cry of hope or fear.
Others were dear,
Others forsook me : what art thou indeed
That I should heed
Thy lamentable need ?
Hungry, should feed,
Or. stranger, lodge thee here ?

' Friend, My Feet bleed.
Open thy door to Me and comfort Me.'
I will not open, trouble me no more.
Go on thy way footsore,
I will not rise and open unto thee.
' Then is it nothing to thee ? Open, see
Who stands to plead with thee.
Open, lest I should pass thee by, and thou
One day entreat My Face
And howl for grace,
And I be deaf as thou art now.
Open to Me.'

Then I cried out upon him : Cease,
Leave me in peace :
Fear not that I should crave
Aught thou may'st have.

Leave me in peace, yea trouble me no more,
Lest I arise and chase thee from my door.
What, shall I not be let
Alone, that thou dost vex me yet!

But all night long that voice spake urgently:
'Open to Me.'
Still harping in mine ears:
'Rise, let Me in.'
Pleading with tears:
'Open to Me, that I may come to thee.'
While the dew dropp'd, while the dark hours were cold:
'My Feet bleed, see my Face,
See My Hands bleed that bring thee grace,
My Heart doth bleed for thee,—
Open to Me.'

So till the break of day:
Then died away
That voice, in silence as of sorrow;
Then footsteps echoing like a sigh
Pass'd me by,
Lingering footsteps slow to pass.
On the morrow
I saw upon the grass
Each footprint mark'd in blood, and on my door
The mark of blood for evermore.

CCCXLI

GIVE me the lowest place: not that I dare
Ask for that lowest place, but Thou hast died
That I might live and share
Thy glory by Thy side.

Give me the lowest place: or if for me
That lowest place too high, make one more low
Where I may sit and see
My God, and love Thee so.

CCCXLII

FOR THE DESOLATE

WHEN thy lone dreams sweet visions see,
And loving looks upon thee shine,
And loving lips speak joys to thee
That never, never may be thine;

Then press thy hand hard on thy side,
 And force down all the swelling pain;
Trust me, the wound, however wide,
 Shall close at last, and heal again.

Think not of what is from thee kept;
 Think, rather, what thou hast received:
Thine eyes have smiled, if they have wept;
 Thy heart has danced, if it has grieved.
Rich comforts yet shall be thine own;
 Yea, GOD Himself shall wipe thine eyes;
And still His love alike is shown
 In what He gives, and what denies.

H. S. Sutton

CCCXLIII

HOW beautiful it is to be alive!
 To wake each morn as if the Maker's grace
Did us afresh from nothingness derive
That we might sing 'How happy is our case!
How beautiful it is to be alive!'

To read in GOD's great Book, until we feel
Love for the love that gave it; then to kneel
Close unto Him Whose truth our souls will shrive,
While every moment's joy doth more reveal
How beautiful it is to be alive.

Rather to go without what might increase
Our worldly standing, than our souls deprive
Of frequent speech with GOD, or than to cease
To feel, through having wasted health or peace,
How beautiful it is to be alive.

Not to forget, when pain and grief draw nigh,
Into the ocean of time past to dive
For memories of GOD's mercies, or to try
To bear all sweetly, hoping still to cry
'How beautiful it is to be alive!'

Thus ever towards man's height of nobleness
Strive still some new progression to contrive;
Till, just as any other friend's, we press
Death's hand; and, having died, feel none the less
How beautiful it is to be alive.

CCCXLIV

A PREACHER'S SOLILOQUY

WHAT wealth to earth our God hath given!
　　What growing increment for heaven!
Men, women, youth, and children small,
I thank the good God for you all!

Not always was it mine to give
Such high regard to all who live;
Time was, I know, when I could go
　Along the streets and scarcely see
The presences my God did show
　So lavishly to me.
Around my steps,—before, behind,—
　They His creative power declared;
I only heeded them, to find
　The easiest path, as on I fared.
And ev'n the innocent little ones,
Of value high o'er stars and suns,—
Evangelists, by Heaven's decree,
Commission'd truths to teach to me
　That elsewise I had never known,—
They seem'd young foreigners to be,
　They never seem'd mine own.
How could I be so dull and blind?
How dared I slight God's humankind?

I know ye nothing care for me;—
　Each to each deep mysteries,
We cannot guess what we may be
　Except by what a glance can seize.
Perchance we never met before,
　Meet now the first and final time,
Yet are ye mine, over and o'er,
　That, haply, I may help you climb
To Jesus, up the mount divine.
Oh might such high success be mine!
Fain would I couch your vision dim;
Fain would I lead you up to Him!

Nay, nay, I cannot yield up one—
　No little child, no youth, no man;
I cannot say, Depart from me;
　I cannot say, Begone, begone,
　　I have no part in thee.

No part? But how? Do I not love you?
  Is not this title still more strong
Than if I'd bought you all with gold?—
Love strenuous flies, a spirit above you;
  Try to escape, it will outfly you,
  It will embrace, ay, and defy you
To break away its gentle hold.
Because God's love is swift and strong,
Therefore ye all to me belong.

Why do I dare love all mankind?
'Tis not because each face, each form
  Is comely, for it is not so;
Nor is it that each soul is warm
  With any Godlike glow.
Yet there's no one to whom's not given
Some little lineament of heaven,
Some partial symbol, at the least, in sign
Of what should be, if it is not, within,
Reminding of the death of sin
  And life of the Divine.
There was a time, full well I know,
  When I had not yet seen you so;
Time was, when few seem'd fair;
But now, as through the streets I go,
There seems no face so shapeless, so
  Forlorn, but that there's something there
That, like the heavens, doth declare
  The glory of the great All-Fair;
And so mine own each one I call;
And so I dare to love you all.

Glory to God, who hath assign'd
To me this mixture with mankind!
Glory to God, that I am born
  Into a world, whose palace-gates
So many royal ones adorn!
  Heaven's possible novitiates,
With self-subduing freedom free,
Princely ye are, each one, to me,
  Each of secret kingly blood,
Though not inheritors as yet
  Of all your own right royal things;
For it were folly to forget
  That they alone are queens and kings
    Who are the truly good.
Yet are ye angels in disguise,
  Angels who have not found your wings;

> I see more in ye than ye are
>   As yet, while earth so closely clings;
> As through a cloud that hides the skies
>   Undoubting science hails a star
> Not to be seen by other eyes,
>   Yet surely among things that are,—
> So the dense veil of your deformities
>   Love gives me power away to pull.
> —Alas! why will ye not from sin arise,
>   And be Christ's beautiful?

CCCXLV

THE TOYS

My little son, who look'd from thoughtful eyes,
    And moved and spoke in quiet grown-up wise,
Having my law the seventh time disobey'd,
I struck him, and dismiss'd
With hard words and unkiss'd;
His Mother, who was patient, being dead.
Then, fearing lest his grief should hinder sleep,
I visited his bed,
But found him slumbering deep,
With darken'd eyelids, and their lashes yet
From his late sobbing wet.
And I, with moan,
Kissing away his tears, left others of my own;
For, on a table drawn beside his head,
He had put, within his reach,
A box of counters and a red-vein'd stone,
A piece of glass abraded by the beach
And six or seven shells,
A bottle with bluebells,
And two French copper coins, ranged there with careful art,
To comfort his sad heart.

So when that night I pray'd
To God, I wept, and said:
Ah, when at last we lie with trancéd breath,
Not vexing Thee in death,
And Thou rememberest of what toys
We made our joys,
How weakly understood
Thy great commanded good,—
Then, Fatherly not less
Than I whom Thou hast moulded from the clay,
Thou'lt leave Thy wrath, and say,
'I will be sorry for their childishness.'

C. Patmore

CCCXLVI

QUI LABORAT ORAT

O ONLY Source of all our light and life,
  Whom as our truth, our strength, we see and feel,
But whom the hours of mortal moral strife
  Alone aright reveal!

Mine inmost soul, before Thee inly brought,
  Thy presence owns ineffable, divine;
Chastised each rebel self-encenter'd thought,
  My will adoreth Thine.

With eye down-dropt, if then this earthly mind
  Speechless remain, or speechless e'en depart;
Nor seek to see—for what of earthly kind
  Can see Thee as Thou art?—

If well-assured 'tis but profanely bold
  In thought's abstractest forms to seem to see,
It dare not dare the dread communion hold
  In ways unworthy Thee:—

O not unown'd, Thou shalt unnamed forgive;
  In worldly walks the prayerless heart prepare;
And if in work its life it seem to live,
  Shalt make that work be prayer.

Nor times shall lack, when while the work it plies,
  Unsummon'd powers the blinding film shall part,
And scarce by happy tears made dim, the eyes
  In recognition start.

But, as Thou willest, give or e'en forbear
  The beatific supersensual sight;—
So, with Thy blessing blest, that humbler prayer
  Approach Thee morn and night.

A. H. Clough

CCCXLVII

WHO seeketh finds: what shall be his relief
  Who hath no power to seek, no heart to pray,
No sense of GOD, but bears as best he may,
A lonely incommunicable grief?

What shall he do? One only thing he knows,
That his life flits a frail uneasy spark
In the great vast of universal dark,
And that the grave may not be all repose.

Be still, sad soul! lift thou no passionate cry,
But spread the desert of thy being bare
To the full searching of the All-seeing eye:

Wait—and through dark misgiving, blank despair,
God will come down in pity, and fill the dry
Dead place with light, and life, and vernal air.

J. C. Shairp

CCCXLVIII

SAINTS DEPARTED

WHILE they here sojourn'd, their presence drew us
 By the sweetness of their human love;
Day by day good thoughts of them renew us,
 Like fresh tidings from the world above;

Coming, like the stars at gloamin' glinting
 Through the western clouds, when loud winds cease,
Silently of that calm country hinting,
 Where they with the angels are at peace.

Not their own, ah! not from earth was flowing
 That high strain to which their souls were tuned,
Year by year we saw them inly growing
 Liker Him with Whom their hearts communed.

Then to Him they pass'd; but still unbroken,
 Age to age, lasts on that goodly line,
Whose pure lives are, more than all words spoken,
 Earth's best witness to the life divine.

Subtlest thought shall fail, and learning falter,
 Churches change, forms perish, systems go,
But our human needs, they will not alter,
 Christ no after age shall e'er outgrow.

Yea, Amen! O changeless One, Thou only
 Art life's guide and spiritual goal,
Thou the Light across the dark vale lonely,—
 Thou the eternal haven of the soul!

CCCXLIX

I HAVE a life with Christ to live,
 But, ere I live it, must I wait
Till learning can clear answer give
 Of this and that book's date?

I have a life in CHRIST to live,
I have a death in CHRIST to die;—
And must I wait, till science give
 All doubts a full reply?

Nay rather, while the sea of doubt
Is raging wildly round about,
Questioning of life and death and sin,
 Let me but creep within
Thy fold, O CHRIST, and at Thy feet
 Take but the lowest seat,
And hear Thine awful voice repeat
In gentlest accents, heavenly sweet,
 Come unto Me, and rest:
 Believe Me, and be blest.

CCCL

'TWIXT gleams of joy and clouds of doubt
 Our feelings come and go;
Our best estate is toss'd about
 In ceaseless ebb and flow.

No mood of feeling, form of thought,
 Is constant for a day;
But Thou, O LORD! Thou changest not;
 The same Thou art alway.

I grasp Thy strength, make it mine own,
 My heart with peace is blest;
I lose my hold, and then comes down
 Darkness and cold unrest.

Let me no more my comfort draw
 From my frail hold of Thee,—
In this alone rejoice with awe;
 Thy mighty grasp of me.

Out of that weak unquiet drift
 That comes but to depart,
To that pure Heaven my spirit lift
 Where Thou unchanging art.

Lay hold of me with Thy strong grasp,
 Let Thy Almighty arm
In its embrace my weakness clasp,
 And I shall fear no harm.

Thy purpose of eternal good
  Let me but surely know;
On this I'll lean, let changing mood
  And feeling come or go;

Glad when Thy sunshine fills my soul;
  Not lorn when clouds o'ercast;
Since Thou within Thy sure control
  Of Love dost hold me fast.

CCCLI

THE POWERS THAT BE ARE ORDAINED OF GOD

YES, mark the words, deem not that Saints alone
    Are Heaven's true servants, and His laws fulfil
Who rules o'er just and wicked. He from ill
Culls good, He moulds the Egyptian's heart of stone

To do him honour, and e'en Nero's throne
    Claims as His ordinance; before Him still
    Pride bows unconscious, and the rebel will
Most does His bidding, following most its own.

Then grieve not at their high and palmy state,
    Those proud bad men, whose unrelenting sway
    Has shatter'd holiest things, and led astray
CHRIST's little ones: they are but tools of Fate,
Duped rebels, doom'd to serve a POWER they hate,
    To earn a traitor's guerdon, yet obey.

                              R. H. Froude

CCCLII

A THANKSGIVING

LORD, in this dust Thy sovereign voice
    First quicken'd love divine;
I am all Thine,—Thy care and choice,
    My very praise is Thine.

I praise Thee, while Thy providence
    In childhood frail I trace,
For blessings given, ere dawning sense
    Could seek or scan Thy grace;

Blessings in boyhood's marvelling hour,
    Bright dreams, and fancyings strange;
Blessings, when reason's awful power
    Gave thought a bolder range;

Blessings of friends, which to my door
    Unask'd, unhoped, have come;
And, choicer still, a countless store
    Of eager smiles at home.

Yet, LORD, in memory's fondest place
    I shrine those seasons sad,
When, looking up, I saw Thy face
    In kind austereness clad.

I would not miss one sigh or tear,
    Heart-pang, or throbbing brow;
Sweet was the chastisement severe,
    And sweet its memory now.

Yes! let the fragrant scars abide,
    Love-tokens in Thy stead,
Faint shadows of the spear-pierced side
    And thorn-encompass'd head.

And such Thy tender force be still,
    When self would swerve or stray,
Shaping to truth the froward will
    Along Thy narrow way.

Deny me wealth; far, far remove
    The lure of power or name;
Hope thrives in straits, in weakness love,
    And faith in this world's shame.

J. H. Newman

CCCLIII

IN childhood, when with eager eyes
    The season-measured year I view'd,
    All, garb'd in fairy guise,
      Pledged constancy of good.

Spring sang of heaven; the summer flowers
    Bade me gaze on, and did not fade;
      Ev'n suns o'er autumn's bowers
        Heard my strong wish, and stay'd.

They came and went, the short-lived four;
    Yet, as their varying dance they wove,
      To my young heart each bore
        Its own sure claim of love.

Far different now;—the whirling year
    Vainly my dizzy eyes pursue;
      And its fair tints appear
        All blent in one dusk hue.

Then what this world to thee, my heart?
  Its gifts nor feed thee nor can bless.
    Thou hast no owner's part
      In all its fleetingness.

The flame, the storm, the quaking ground,
  Earth's joy, earth's terror, nought is thine;
    Thou must but hear the sound
      Of the still Voice Divine.

CCCLIV

THE SAINT AND THE HERO

O AGED Saint! far off I heard
    The praises of thy name;—
Thy deed of power, thy prudent word,
    Thy zeal's triumphant flame.

I came and saw; and, having seen,
    Weak heart, I drew offence
From thy prompt smile, thy simple mien,
    Thy lowly diligence.

The Saint's is not the Hero's praise;—
    This I have found, and learn
Nor to malign Heaven's humblest ways,
    Nor its least boon to spurn.

CCCLV

TRANSFIGURATION

I SAW thee once, and nought discern'd
    For stranger to admire;
A serious aspect, but it burn'd
    With no unearthly fire.

Again I saw, and I confess'd
    Thy speech was rare and high;
And yet it vex'd my burden'd breast,
    And scared, I knew not why.

I saw once more, and awe-struck gazed
    On face, and form, and air;
God's living glory round thee blazed—
    A Saint—a Saint was there!

CCCLVI

PERSECUTION

SAY, who is he in deserts seen,
  Or at the twilight hour?
Of garb austere, and dauntless mien,
Measured in speech, in purpose keen,
Calm as in Heaven he had been,
  Yet blithe when perils lower.

My Holy Mother made reply,
  'Dear child, it is my Priest.
The world has cast me forth, and I
Dwell with wild earth and gusty sky;
He bears to men my mandates high,
  And works my sage behest.

'Another day, dear child, and thou
  Shalt join his sacred band.
Ah! well I deem, thou shrinkest now
From urgent rule and severing vow;
Gay hopes flit round, and light thy brow:
  Time hath a taming hand!'

CCCLVII

ST. PHILIP NERI IN HIS SCHOOL

THIS is the Saint of gentleness and kindness,
  Cheerful in penance, and in precept winning;
Patiently healing of their pride and blindness
    Souls that are sinning.

This is the Saint, who, when the world allures us,
  Cries her false wares, and opes her magic coffers,
Points to a better city, and secures us
    With richer offers.

Love is his bond, he knows no other fetter,
  Asks not our all, but takes whate'er we spare him,
Willing to draw us on from good to better,
    As we can bear him.

When he comes near to teach us and to bless us,
  Prayer is so sweet, that hours are but a minute;
Mirth is so pure, though freely it possess us,
    Sin is not in it.

Thus he conducts by holy paths and pleasant,
   Innocent souls, and sinful souls forgiven,
Towards the bright palace where our GOD is present,
   Throned in high heaven.

CCCLVIII

THE CALL OF DAVID

LATEST born of Jesse's race,
   Wonder lights thy bashful face,
While the Prophet's gifted oil
Seals thee for a path of toil.
We, thy Angels, circling round thee,
Ne'er shall find thee as we found thee,
When thy faith first brought us near
To quell the lion and the bear.

Go! and mid thy flocks awhile
At thy doom of greatness smile;
Bold to bear GOD's heaviest load,
Dimly guessing of the road,—
Rocky road, and scarce ascended,
Though thy foot be angel-tended.

Twofold praise thou shalt attain,
In royal court and battle plain;
Then comes heart-ache, care, distress,
Blighted hope, and loneliness;
Wounds from friend and gifts from foe,
Dizzied faith, and guilt, and woe;
Loftiest aims by earth defiled,
Gleams of wisdom sin-beguiled,
Sated power's tyrannic mood,
Counsels shared with men of blood;
Sad success, parental tears,
And a dreary gift of years.

Strange, that guileless face and form
To lavish on the scarring storm!
Yet we take thee in thy blindness,
And we buffet thee in kindness;
Little chary of thy fame,—
Dust unborn may bless or blame,—
But we mould thee for the root
Of man's promised healing Fruit,
And we mould thee hence to rise,
As our brother, to the skies.

CCCLIX

JAMES AND JOHN

TWO brothers freely cast their lot
    With David's royal Son;
The cost of conquest counting not,
    They deem the battle won.

Brothers in heart, they hope to gain
    An undivided joy;
That man may one with man remain,
    As boy was one with boy.

Christ heard; and will'd that James should fall,
    First prey of Satan's rage;
John linger out his fellows all,
    And die in bloodless age.

Now they join hands once more above,
    Before the Conqueror's throne;
Thus God grants prayer, but in His love
    Makes times and ways His own.

CCCLX

FAITH AGAINST SIGHT

THE world has cycles in its course, when all
    That once has been, is acted o'er again:—
Not by some fated law, which need appal
    Our faith, or binds our deeds as with a chain;
But by men's separate sins, which, blended still,
    The same bad round fulfil.

Then fear ye not, though Gallio's scorn ye see,
    And soft-clad nobles count you mad, true hearts!
These are the fig-tree's signs;—rough deeds must be,
    Trials and crimes: so learn ye well your parts.
Once more to plough the earth it is decreed,
    And scatter wide the seed.

CCCLXI

SACRILEGE

THE Church shone brightly in her youthful days
    Ere the world on her smiled;
So now, an outcast, she would pour her rays
    Keen, free, and undefiled:
Yet would I not that arm of force were mine,
Which thrusts her from her awful ancient shrine.

'Twas duty bound each convert-king to rear
        His Mother from the dust,
And pious was it to enrich, nor fear
        CHRIST for the rest to trust;
And who shall dare make common or unclean
What once has on the Holy Altar been?

Dear brothers!—hence, while ye for ill prepare,
        Triumph is still your own;
Blest is a pilgrim Church!—yet shrink to share
        The curse of throwing down.
So will we toil in our old place to stand,
Watching, not dreading, the despoiler's hand.

CCCLXII

VEXATIONS

EACH trial has its weight; which, whoso bears
        Knows his own woe, and need of succouring grace;
The martyr's hope half wipes away the trace
Of flowing blood; the while life's humblest cares
Smart more, because they hold in Holy Writ no place.

This be my comfort, in these days of grief,
    Which is not CHRIST's, nor forms heroic tale.
Apart from Him, if not a sparrow fail,
May not He pitying view, and send relief
When foes or friends perplex, and peevish thoughts prevail?

Then keep good heart, nor take the niggard course
    Of Thomas, who must see ere he would trust.
Faith will fill up GOD's word, not poorly just
To the bare letter, heedless of its force,
But walking by its light amid Earth's sun and dust.

CCCLXIII

AT MESSINA

WHY, wedded to the LORD, still yearns my heart
        Towards these scenes of ancient heathen fame?
Yet legend hoar, and voice of bard that came
Fixing my restless youth with its sweet art,

And shades of power, and those who bore a part
In the mad deeds that set the world in flame,
So fret my memory here,—ah! is it blame?—
That from my eyes the tear is fain to start.

Nay, from no fount impure these drops arise;
'Tis but that sympathy with Adam's race
Which in each brother's history reads its own :—

So let the cliffs and seas of this fair place
Be named man's tomb and splendid record-stone,
High hope, pride-stain'd, the course without the prize.

CCCLXIV

TAORMINI

SAY, hast thou track'd a traveller's round,
 Nor visions met thee there,
Thou couldst but marvel to have found
 This blighted world so fair?

And feel an awe within thee rise,
 That sinful man should see
Glories far worthier Seraph's eyes
 Than to be shared by thee

Store them in heart! thou shalt not faint
 'Mid coming pains and fears,
As the third heaven once nerved a Saint
 For fourteen trial-years.

See Note

CCCLXV

THE PATH OF THE JUST

WHEN I look back upon my former race,
 Seasons I see, at which the Inward Ray
 More brightly burn'd, or guided some new way;
Truth, in its wealthier scene and nobler space
Given for my eye to range, and feet to trace.
 And next I mark, 'twas trial did convey,
 Or grief, or pain, or strange eventful day,
To my tormented soul such larger grace.

So now, whenc'er, in journeying on, I feel
The shadow of the Providential Hand,
 Deep breathless stirrings shoot across my breast,
Searching to know what He will now reveal,
What sin uncloak, what stricter rule command,
 And girding me to work His full behest.

U

CCCLXVI

THE WRATH TO COME

WHEN first GOD stirr'd me, and the Church's word
    Came as a theme of reverent search and fear,
It little cost to own the lustre clear
O'er rule she taught, and rite, and doctrine, pour'd;

For conscience craved, and reason did accord.
    Yet one there was that wore a mien austere,
    And I did doubt, and, troubled, ask'd to hear
Whose mouth had force to edge so sharp a sword.

My Mother oped her trust, the holy Book;
And heal'd my pang. She pointed, and I found
CHRIST on Himself, considerate Master, took
The utterance of that doctrine's fearful sound.
The Fount of Love His servants sends to tell
Love's deeds; Himself reveals the sinner's hell.

See Note

CCCLXVII

FLOWERS WITHOUT FRUIT

PRUNE thou thy words, the thoughts control
    That o'er thee swell and throng;
They will condense within thy soul,
    And change to purpose strong.

But he who lets his feelings run
    In soft luxurious flow,
Shrinks when hard service must be done,
    And faints at every woe.

Faith's meanest deed more favour bears,
    Where hearts and wills are weigh'd,
Than brightest transports, choicest prayers,
    Which bloom their hour and fade.

CCCLXVIII

THE TWO WORLDS

UNVEIL, O LORD, and on us shine
    In glory and in grace;
This gaudy world grows pale before
    The beauty of Thy face.

Till Thou art seen, it seems to be
  A sort of fairy ground,
Where suns unsetting light the sky,
  And flowers and fruits abound.

But when Thy keener, purer beam
  Is pour'd upon our sight,
It loses all its power to charm,
  And what was day is night;

Its noblest toils are then the scourge
  Which made Thy blood to flow;
Its joys are but the treacherous thorns
  Which circled round Thy brow.

And thus, when we renounce for Thee
  Its restless aims and fears,
The tender memories of the past,
  The hopes of coming years,

Poor is our sacrifice, whose eyes
  Are lighted from above;
We offer what we cannot keep,
  What we have ceased to love.

CCCLXIX

ZEAL AND PATIENCE

St. Paul in Prison

O COMRADE bold, of toil and pain!
  Thy trial how severe,
When sever'd first by prisoner's chain
  From thy loved labour-sphere!

Say, did impatience first impel
  The heaven-sent bond to break?
Or, couldst thou bear its hindrance well,
  Loitering for Jesu's sake!

O might we know! for sore we feel
  The languor of delay,
When sickness lets our fainter zeal,
  Or foes block up our way.

Lord! Who Thy thousand years dost wait
  To work the thousandth part
Of Thy vast plan, for us create
  With zeal, a patient heart.

CCCLXX

TEMPTATION

O HOLY Lord, who with the Children Three
    Didst walk the piercing flame,
Help, in those trial-hours, which, save to Thee,
    I dare not name;
Nor let these quivering eyes and sickening heart
Crumble to dust beneath the Tempter's dart.

Thou, who didst once Thy life from Mary's breast
    Renew from day to day,
O might her smile, severely sweet, but rest .
    On this frail clay!
Till I am Thine with my whole soul; and fear,
Not feel a secret joy, that Hell is near.

CCCLXXI

SENSITIVENESS

TIME was, I shrank from what was right
    From fear of what was wrong;
I would not brave the sacred fight,
    Because the foe was strong.

But now I cast that finer sense
    And sorer shame aside;
Such dread of sin was indolence,
    Such aim at Heaven was pride.

So, when my Saviour calls, I rise
    And calmly do my best;
Leaving to Him, with silent eyes
    Of hope and fear, the rest.

I step, I mount where He has led;
    Men count my haltings o'er;—
I know them; yet, though self I dread,
    I love His precept more.

CCCLXXII

THE ELEMENTS

A Tragic Chorus

MAN is permitted much
        To scan and learn
      In Nature's frame;
Till he well-nigh can tame
Brute mischiefs, and can touch
Invisible things, and turn
All warring ills to purposes of good.
    Thus, as a god below,
        He can control,
And harmonize, what seems amiss to flow
    As sever'd from the whole
    And dimly understood.

    But o'er the elements
        One Hand alone
        One Hand has sway.
    What influence day by day
    In straiter belt prevents
    The impious Ocean, thrown
Alternate o'er the ever-sounding shore?
    Or who has eye to trace
        How the Plague came?
Forerun the doublings of the Tempest's race?
    Or the Air's weight and flame
    On a set scale explore?

        Thus God has will'd
    That man, when fully skill'd,
    Still gropes in twilight dim;
    Encompass'd all his hours
        By fearfullest powers
        Inflexible to him.
    That so he may discern
        His feebleness,
    And e'en for earth's success
    To Him in wisdom turn,
Who holds for us the keys of either home,—
    Earth and the world to come.

See Note

CCCLXXIII

THE GUARDIAN ANGEL

O LORD, how wonderful in depth and height,
　　But most in man, how wonderful Thou art!
With what a love, what soft persuasive might
　Victorious o'er the stubborn fleshly heart,
Thy tale complete of saints Thou dost provide,
To fill the throne which Angels lost through pride!

O man, strange composite of heaven and earth!
　Majesty dwarf'd to baseness! fragrant flower
Running to poisonous seed! and seeming worth
　Cloking corruption! weakness mastering power!
Who never art so near to crime and shame,
As when thou hast achieved some deed of name;—

How should ethereal natures comprehend
　A thing made up of spirit and of clay,
Were we not task'd to nurse it and to tend,
　Link'd one to one throughout its mortal day?
More than the Seraph in his height of place,
The Angel-guardian knows and loves the ransom'd race.

CCCLXXIV

CONSOLATIONS IN BEREAVEMENT

DEATH was full urgent with thee, Sister dear,
　　And startling in his speed;—
Brief pain, then languor till thy end came near—
　　Such was the path decreed,
　　　The hurried road
To lead thy soul from earth to thine own God's abode.

Death wrought with thee, sweet maid, impatiently :—
　　　Yet merciful the haste
That baffles sickness;—dearest, thou didst die,
　　　Thou wast not made to taste
　　　Death's bitterness,
Decline's slow-wasting charm, or fever's fierce distress.

Death came unheralded :—but it was well ;·
   · For so thy Saviour bore
Kind witness, thou wast meet at once to dwell
   On His eternal shore;
     All warning spared,
For none He gives where hearts are for prompt change prepared.

Death wrought in mystery; both complaint and cure
   To human skill unknown :—
God put aside all means, to make us sure
   It was His deed alone;
     Lest we should lay
Reproach on our poor selves, that thou wast caught away.

Death urged as scant of time :—lest, Sister dear,
   We many a lingering day
'Had sicken'd with alternate hope and fear,—
   The ague of delay;
     Watching each spark
Of promise quench'd in turn, till all our sky was dark.

Death came and went :—that so thy image might
   Our yearning hearts possess,
Associate with all pleasant thoughts and bright,
   With youth and loveliness;
     Sorrow can claim,
Mary, nor lot nor part in thy soft soothing name.

Joy of sad hearts, and light of downcast eyes!
   Dearest, thou art enshrined
In all thy fragrance in our memories;
   For we must ever find
     Bare thought of thee
Freshen this weary life, while weary life shall be.

See Note

CCCLXXV

A VOICE FROM AFAR

WEEP not for me ;—
   Be blithe as wont, nor tinge with gloom
The stream of love that circles home,
   Light hearts and free!
Joy in the gifts Heaven's bounty lends ;
   Nor miss my face, dear friends!

    I still am near;—
Watching the smiles I prized on earth,
Your converse mild, your blameless mirth;
    Now too I hear
Of whisper'd sounds the tale complete,
    Low prayers, and musings sweet.

    A sea before
The Throne is spread;—its pure still glass
Pictures all earth-scenes as they pass.
    We, on its shore,
Share, in the bosom of our rest,
    GOD's knowledge, and are blest.

CCCLXXVI

A MARTYR-CONVERT

THE number of Thine own complete,
    Sum up and make an end;
Sift clean the chaff, and house the wheat;
    And then, O LORD, descend.

Descend, and solve by that descent
    This mystery of life;
Where good and ill, together blent,
    Wage an undying strife.

For rivers twain are gushing still,
    And pour a mingled flood;
Good in the very depths of ill,
    Ill in the heart of good.

The last are first, the first are last,
    As angel eyes behold;
These from the sheep-cote sternly cast,
    Those welcomed to the fold.

No Christian home, no pastor's eye,
    No preacher's vocal zeal,
Moved Thy dear Martyr to defy
    The prison and the wheel.

Forth from the heathen ranks she stept,
    The forfeit crown to claim
Of Christian souls who had not kept
    Their birthright and their name.

Grace form'd her out of sinful dust;
 She knelt a soul defiled,
She rose in all the faith, and trust,
 And sweetness of a child.

And in the freshness of that love
 She preach'd, by word and deed,
The mysteries of the world above,
 Her new-found, glorious creed.

And running, in a little hour,
 Of life the course complete,
She reach'd the Throne of endless power,
 And sits at JESU's feet.

CCCLXXVII

HORA NOVISSIMA

WHENE'ER goes forth Thy dread command,
 And my last hour is nigh,
LORD, grant me in a Christian land,
 As I was born, to die.

I pray not, LORD, that friends may be,
 Or kindred, standing by,—
Choice blessing! which I leave to Thee
 To grant me or deny.

But let my failing limbs beneath
 My Mother's smile recline;
And prayers sustain my labouring breath
 From out her sacred shrine.

And let the Cross beside my bed
 In its due emblems rest;
And let the absolving words be said,
 To ease a laden breast.

Thou, LORD, where'er we lie, canst aid:
 But He, who taught His own
To live as one, will not upbraid
 The dread to die alone.

CCCLXXVIII

A SOUL'S CRY

TAKE me away, and in the lowest deep
      There let me be,
And there in hope the lone night-watches keep,
      Told out for me.
There, motionless and happy in my pain,
      Lone, not forlorn,—
There will I sing my sad perpetual strain,
      Until the morn.
There will I sing, and soothe my stricken breast,
      Which ne'er can cease
To throb, and pine, and languish, till possest
      Of its Sole Peace.
There will I sing my absent LORD and Love :—
      Take me away,
That sooner I may rise, and go above,
And see Him in the truth of everlasting day.

CCCLXXIX

PRAISE to the Holiest in the height,
      And in the depth be praise :
In all His words most wonderful;
      Most sure in all His ways!

Woe to thee, man! for he was found
      A recreant in the fight;
And lost his heritage of heaven,
      And fellowship with light.

Above him now the angry sky,
      Around the tempest's din;
Who once had Angels for his friends,
      Had but the brutes for kin.

O man! a savage kindred they;
      To flee that monster brood
He scaled the seaside cave, and clomb
      The giants of the wood.

With now a fear, and now a hope,
      With aids which chance supplied,
From youth to eld, from sire to son,
      He lived, and toil'd, and died.

He dreed his penance age by age;
  And step by step began
Slowly to doff his savage garb,
  And be again a man.

And quicken'd by the Almighty's breath
  And chasten'd by His rod,
And taught by angel-visitings,
  At length he sought his GOD;

And learn'd to call upon His Name,
  And in His faith create
A household and a father-land,
  A city and a state.

Glory to Him who from the mire,
  In patient length of days,
Elaborated into life
  A people to His praise!

CCCLXXX

PRAISE to the Holiest in the height,
    And in the depth be praise:
In all His words most wonderful;
  Most sure in all His ways!

O loving wisdom of our GOD!
  When all was sin and shame,
A second Adam to the fight
  And to the rescue came.

O wisest love! that flesh and blood
  Which did in Adam fail,
Should strive afresh against their foe,
  Should strive and should prevail;

And that a higher gift than grace
  Should flesh and blood refine,
GOD's Presence and His very Self,
  And Essence all-divine.

O generous love! that He who smote
  In man for man the foe,
The double agony in man
  For man should undergo;

And in the garden secretly,
  And on the cross on high,
Should teach His brethren and inspire
  To suffer and to die.

CCCLXXXI

A MORNING PRAYER

I RISE and raise my claspéd hands to Thee!
  Henceforth, the darkness hath no part in me,
    Thy sacrifice this day;
Abiding firm, and with a freeman's might
Stemming the waves of passion in the fight;—
    Ah, should I from Thee stray,
My hoary head, Thy table where I bow,
Will be my shame, which are mine honour now.
Thus I set out;—LORD! lead me on my way!

See Note

CCCLXXXII

AN EVENING CONFESSION

O HOLIEST Truth! how have I lied to Thee!
  I vow'd this day Thy sacrifice to be;
    But I am dim ere night.
Surely I made my prayer, and I did deem
That I could keep in me Thy morning beam,
    Immaculate and bright.
But my foot slipp'd; and, as I lay, he came,
My gloomy foe, and robb'd me of heaven's flame.
Help Thou my darkness, LORD, till I am light.

CCCLXXXIII

THE PILLAR OF THE CLOUD

LEAD, Kindly Light, amid the encircling gloom,
    Lead Thou me on!
The night is dark, and I am far from home—
    Lead Thou me on!
Keep Thou my feet; I do not ask to see
The distant scene,—one step enough for me.

I was not ever thus, nor pray'd that Thou
    Shouldst lead me on.
I loved to choose and see my path; but now
    Lead Thou me on!
I loved the garish day, and, spite of fears,
Pride ruled my will: remember not past years.

So long Thy power hath blest me, sure it still
    Will lead me on,
O'er moor and fen, o'er crag and torrent, till
    The night is gone;
And with the morn those angel faces smile
Which I have loved long since, and lost awhile.

CCCLXXXIV

FOR TIRED WORKERS

WE look around, the murky sky is still;
    No answering sunbeam pierces. Clouds lie curl'd
Upon the dull horizon. Dark is His will
Who yet hath made us, and His ensigns furl'd.

Ah, if His speaking thunders were but hurl'd
Adown the sullen silence! but we stand,
Holding our puny thread with faithless hand
Pull'd from the grand disorder of the world.

What use, what use to hold so small a thing,
Loosed from the tangled web of giant wrong?
Let purpose perish and dear hope take wing!
So cry we. But the angels say, 'Be strong!
None other threads than these go weave the hem
Of GOD's own garment; so He treasures them!'

C. C. Fraser-Tytler

CCCLXXXV

AN INTERCESSION

WHY they have never known the way before—
    Why hundreds stand outside Thy mercy's door—
I know not: but I ask, dear LORD, that Thou
    Wouldst lead them now!

Why in the hard and thorny way they press
Unloved, uncomforted, with none to bless,
In living death, I know not: but spare Thou,
    And lead them now!

Saviour, be pitiful: their hell is here;
Dull parchéd sorrow that can shed no tear
Is theirs. They need indeed no further loss,—
    They bear their cross!

Eternal death to live away from Thee,
Eternal loss apart from Thee to be:
Eternal gain to have in Thee some part—
    To know Thou art!

Dawn for us here, thou bright undying day;
So in no dark and sudden-ending way
Life's timorous steps shall falter, but straight on
    Where CHRIST is gone:—

To wake and know the new life throbbing, find
Doubt and disquietude are left behind,
Eyes open'd, ears attuned to heavenly sound,
    Is Heaven found.

CCCLXXXVI

CROSSING THE RIVER

IN some lone walk through sunburnt fields,
    By sandy path and dusty road,
Hast thou not cast thine eyes abroad,
Seen afar off a water'd scene,
A grove of deep and tender green,
And found a river flows between!

There is a stream whose waves divide
Life from the shady shores beyond;
And we on this sad side are found,
Toiling on sandy flats, I ween,
Sighs our one moisture, tears our sheen,
While the still river flows between.

And yet, when our belovéd rise
To gird them for the ford, and pass
From wilderness to springing grass,
From barren waste to living green,
We weep that they no more are seen,
And that the river flows between.

Ah, could we follow where they go
And pierce the holy shade they find,
One grief were ours—to stay behind!
One hope—to join the Blest Unseen,—
To plant our steps where theirs have been,
And find no river flows between!

CCCLXXXVII

THE night is come, and all the world is still.
　　Men say it is a time for sleep and dreams;
But now she throws no pall upon the space
That spreads above me, like the God-like face
　　Of Him Who looms behind it all.　Meseems
This is the hour for man to bend the knee
Of the full soul to the Divinity.

Above, below, on every side there hang
　　These circling orbs.　And out of keenest sight
A myriad more pursue their pathless way
Unerring, through the awful space, where day
　　Is not, but an unending fearful night
Shrouds the immensity.　My GOD! the soul
Of man should faint could he but see the whole!

Sublimest silence.　Yet 'tis broke, for near
　　Some sparrow stirs the ivy on the wall,
Calling me back to take account of this
We little folk call 'life': to ask if bliss
　　For us or sparrow be not all too small
For Him to take account of, where He stands
Holding the boundless heavens in His hands?

Only, for Thee is neither great nor small!
　　'Tis human weakness but to count Thee so
As I, poor mortal, find myself: the slave
Of Time, himself but hastening to the grave.
　　And Thou canst teach the tender blade to grow
On this small world,—and with an equal might
Guide the low sweeping of the swallow's flight,

Or hurl new systems from Thee.　Thou art great,
　　But smallness is a word of human ken!
Trembling, my soul remembers this, and dares
To breathe into the universe its prayers.
　　For Thou art in the night, Thou Sun! and when
We dwell in darkness of the mind, 'tis we
That turn our faces from Thy radiancy.

Seeing Thee there, I cannot lose the way
　　Even in trackless places, where the soul
Shivers to feel itself imprison'd here
In the least part of some least rolling sphere.
　　Whither we rush[1], we know not; but the goal
To Thee is known.　Hold Thou me up, as Thou
Holdest the universe above me now!

Yet nearer. Come Thou nearer than to them!
　Blindly they follow Thy behest, but I
Yearn for Thee strongly through my fleshly frame.
And so, encompass'd with our flesh, He came,
　Thy Son, Thyself—to make less far and high
The distant Godhead. Now Thy heavens declare
No far Creator, but a Father there!

[1] See Note

CCCLXXXVIII

L ORD, I have wrestled through the livelong night;
　　　Do not depart,
Nor leave me thus in sad and weary plight,
　　　Broken in heart;
Where shall I turn, if Thou shouldst go away,
And leave me here in this cold world to stay?

I have no other help, no food, no light,
　　　No hand to guide;
The night is dark, my Home is not in sight,
　　　The path untried;
I dare not venture in the dark alone,—
I cannot ·find my way, if Thou be gone.

I cannot yet discern Thee as Thou art;
　　　More let me see;
I cannot bear the thought that I must part
　　　Away from Thee :
I will not let Thee go, except Thou bless;
Oh! help me, LORD, in all my helplessness!

J. Sharp

CCCLXXXIX

THE PASSION

L ORD, when I lift mine eyes to Thee,
　And see Thy bitter woe,
I ask, Why should the Holy One
　Such sorrows undergo?

LORD, who are they that thus inflict ,
　Those oft-repeated blows
Upon Thy virgin Form, that still
　No human sin-stain knows?

Who are the foes that drag Thee on
  To undeservéd woe,—
That will not, or for shame, or fear,
  One vengeance-stroke forego?

The first of all, Thy boundless Love,
  That could not rest within
While man remain'd apart from GOD;—
  The next, my own deep sin.

These two, dear LORD, have drawn Thee on
  Through all Thou didst endure;
Let not Thy Love be spent in vain,
  The curse of sin to cure.

Oh! never let me wound again
  The Love that set me free;
Nor ever crucify afresh
  The GOD Who died for me!

CCCXC

LIGHT IN THE WOOD

WHAT is it that amid some earthly home,
    Where all have equal nurture, and the care
Of loving hearts forbids all harm to come
  Within the limits of its sacred lair,
Makes difference in those who dwell therein;—
Some unrefined by grace, while others brightness win?

All seem alike within the sacred bound,
  And freely blend throughout the livelong day;
But ever and anon some traits are found
  In one or other, which define the way
Of closer walk with GOD well sought and found,
While others linger more on lower earthly ground.

As 'mid the thickness of some leafy wood
  The sunbeams find a passage here and there,
And light some spot which erst in shadow stood,
  Making each leaflet look more bright and fair,
While other patches, that lie round it, miss
The ray of radiant Light that fills itself with bliss,—

So is it in the tangled wood of life:
  Some souls there are that keep the open way,
Free from the boughs of earthly hindrance, rife
  For every advent of the Heavenly ray;—
Ready to catch it as in love it comes
To seek the loving souls that are its willing homes.

x

And as it shines it points them out to view
  As diverse from the rest, then flits away,
And leaves them each their duties to pursue,
  Like other men, in common light of day;—
Lest they should think themselves so much God's choice
That they have only need to linger and rejoice.

—Force not thy upward growth, but first of all
  Deepen thy roots, then may'st thou well sustain
The rays of sunlight that upon thee fall,
  And, without withering, all' thy strength retain.
Plants that have little else but leaf and flower,
However bright their hue, live but their little hour.

CCCXCI

YOUTH'S BRIGHTNESS GONE

THE flash of youthful light is past and gone;
    Not as of yore
Earth's joys abound; but I am left alone
    Still more and more,
As one by one the little sparks go out
From this world's stubble, that lies round about.

One hope remains, and that, as others fade,
    Grows brighter still
As shadows lengthen o'er this earthly glade,
    And up the hill
We higher mount towards the final Home,
To which in God's good time we hope to come.

And even here, where darkness gathers round,
    All is not dark,
There is, 'midst all, one spot of holy ground
    Which bears Heaven's mark—
The Place which God has chosen for His own,
That He may come and make His Presence known.

To that I cling the more as eventide
    Creeps on and on,
Scattering its sable shadows far and wide,
    And, one by one,
Bidding the weary lay them down to rest,
In trust and love upon their FATHER's Breast.

CCCXCII

L IGHT of the lonely pilgrim's heart,
   Star of the coming day!
Arise, and with Thy morning beams
   Chase all our griefs away!

Come, blessèd Lord! let every shore
   And answering island sing
The praises of Thy royal name,
   And own Thee as their King.

Bid the whole earth, responsive now
   To the bright world above,
Break forth in sweetest strains of joy
   In memory of Thy love.

Jesus! Thy fair creation groans,
   The air, the earth, the sea,
In unison with all our hearts,
   And calls aloud for Thee.

Thine was the Cross, with all its fruits
   Of grace and peace divine :
Be Thine the Crown of glory now,
   The palm of Victory, Thine!

E. Denny

CCCXCIII

T HY way, not mine, O Lord,
   However dark it be!
Lead me by Thine own hand,
   Choose out the path for me.

Smooth let it be or rough,
   It will be still the best;
Winding or straight, it leads
   Right onward to Thy rest.

I dare not choose my lot;
   I would not, if I might;
Choose Thou for me, my God;
   So shall I walk aright.

The kingdom that I seek
   Is Thine; so let the way
That leads to it be Thine;
   Else I must surely stray.

Take Thou my cup, and it
  With joy or sorrow fill,
As best to Thee may seem;
  Choose Thou my good and ill;

Choose Thou for me my friends,
  My sickness or my health;
Choose Thou my cares for me,
  My poverty or wealth.

Not mine, not mine the choice,
  In things or great or small;
Be Thou my guide, my strength,
  My wisdom, and my all!

H. Bonar

CCCXCIV

I HEARD the voice of Jesus say,
  Come unto Me and rest;
Lay down, thou weary one, lay down
  Thy head upon My breast.
I came to Jesus as I was,
  Weary and worn and sad,
I found in Him a resting-place,
  And He has made me glad.

I heard the voice of Jesus say,
  I am this dark world's light,
Look unto Me, thy morn shall rise,
  And all thy day be bright.
I look'd to Jesus, and I found
  In Him my Star, my Sun;
And in that light of life I'll walk,
  Till travelling days are done.

I heard the voice of Jesus say,
  Behold, I freely give
The living water, thirsty one,
  Stoop down and drink and live.
I came to Jesus, and I drank
  Of that life-giving stream,
My thirst was quench'd, my soul revived,
  And now I live in Him.

CCCXCV

HE is gone—beyond the skies,
    A cloud receives Him from our eyes;
Gone beyond the highest height
Of mortal gaze or angel's flight;
Through the veils of Time and Space,
Pass'd into the Holiest Place;
All the toil, the sorrow done,
All the battle fought and won.

He is gone—and we return,
And our hearts within us burn;
Olivet no more shall greet
With welcome shout His coming feet;
Never shall we track Him more
On Gennesareth's glistening shore;
Never in that look or voice
Shall Zion's hill again rejoice.

He is gone—and we remain
In this world of sin and pain;
In the void which He has left,
On this earth of Him bereft,
We have still His work to do,
We can still His path pursue;
Seek Him both in friend and foe,
In ourselves His image show.

He is gone—we heard Him say,
'Good that I should go away.'
Gone is that dear Form and Face,
But not gone His present grace;
Though Himself no more we see,
Comfortless we cannot be:
No, His Spirit still is ours,
Quickening, freshening all our powers.

He is gone—towards their goal,
World and Church must onwards roll:
Far behind we leave the past;
Forwards are our glances cast:
Still His words before us range
Through the ages, as they change:
Wheresoe'er the Truth shall lead,
He will give whate'er we need.

He is gone—but we once more
Shall behold Him as before;
In the Heaven of Heavens the same,
As on earth He went and came.
In the many mansions there,
Place for us will He prepare:
In that world, unseen, unknown,
He and we may yet be one.

A. P. Stanley

CCCXCVI

HOLD NOT THY PEACE AT MY TEARS

WHAT is the saddest sweetest lowest sound
  Nearest akin to perfect silence? Not
The delicate whisper sometimes in the hot
Autumnal morning heard the cornfields round;
Nor yet to lonely man, now almost bound
 By slumber, near his house a murmuring river
 Buzzing and droning o'er the stones for ever.
Not such faint voice of Autumn oat-encrown'd,
And not such liquid murmur, O my heart!
 But tears that drop o'er graves, and sins, and fears,
 A sound the very weeper scarcely hears,
A music in which silence hath some part.
—O Thou, all gentle, Who all-hearing art,
 Hold not Thy peace, sweet Saviour, at my tears!

W. Alexander

CCCXCVII

THE golden gates are lifted up,
 The doors are open'd wide;
The King of Glory is gone in
 Unto His FATHER's side.

Thou art gone up before us, LORD,
 To make for us a place,
That we may be where now Thou art,
 And look upon GOD's Face.

And ever on our earthly path
 A gleam of glory lies;
A light still breaks behind the cloud
 That veil'd Thee from our eyes.

Lift up our hearts, lift up our minds,
  Let Thy dear grace be given,
That, while we wander here below,
  Our treasure be in Heaven :—

That, where Thou art, at God's right hand,
  Our hope, our love, may be :—
Dwell Thou in us, that we may dwell
  For evermore in Thee.

C. F. Alexander

CCCXCVIII

HARK, the sound of holy voices, chanting at the crystal sea,
  Hallelujah ! Hallelujah ! Hallelujah ! Lord, to Thee.
Multitude, which none can number, like the stars in glory stand,
Clothed in white apparel, holding palms of Victory in their hand.

They have come from tribulation, and have wash'd their robes
  in Blood,
Wash'd them in the Blood of Jesus; tried they were, and firm
  they stood :
Gladly, Lord, with Thee they suffer'd; gladly, Lord, with Thee
  they died,
And by Death to Life immortal they were born and glorified.

Now they reign in heavenly glory, now they walk with
  golden light,
Now they drink as from a river, holy bliss and infinite;
Love and Peace they taste for ever; and all Truth and Knowledge
  see
In the beatific vision of the Blesséd Trinity.

God of God, the One-begotten, Light of Light, Emmanuel,
In Whose Body join'd together all the Saints for ever dwell,
Pour upon us of Thy fulness, that we may for evermore
God the Father, God the Son, and God the Holy Ghost adore.

C. Wordsworth

CCCXCIX

GOD of the living, in Whose eyes
  Unveil'd Thy whole creation lies;
All souls are Thine; we must not say
That those are dead who pass away;
From this our world of flesh set free,
We know them living unto Thee.

Released from earthly toil and strife,
With Thee is hidden still their life;
Thine are their thoughts, their works, their powers,
All Thine, and yet most truly ours;
For well we know, where'er they be,
Our dead are living unto Thee.

Not spilt like water on the ground,
Not wrapp'd in dreamless sleep profound,
Not wandering in unknown despair
Beyond Thy voice, Thine arm, Thy care;
Not left to lie like fallen tree;
Not dead, but living unto Thee.

Thy word is true, Thy will is just;
To Thee we leave them, Lord, in trust;
And bless Thee for the love which gave
Thy Son to fill a human grave,
That none might fear that world to see,
Where all are living unto Thee.

J. Ellerton

CCCC

GO not far from me, O my Strength,
  Whom all my times obey;
Take from me anything Thou wilt,
  But go not Thou away;
And let the storm that does Thy work
  Deal with me as it may.

On Thy compassion I repose,
  In weakness and distress;
I will not ask for greater ease,
  Lest I should love Thee less;
O 'tis a blessèd thing for me
  To need Thy tenderness!

There is no death for me to fear,
  For Christ, my Lord, hath died;
There is no curse in this my pain,
  For He was crucified;
And it is fellowship with Him
  That keeps me near His side.

A. L. Waring

CCCCI

THE CRY OF THE LOST ANSWERED

THAT was the Shepherd of the flock; He knew
   The distant voice of one poor sheep astray;
It had forsaken Him, but He was true,
   And listen'd for its bleating night and day.
Lost in a pitfall, yet alive it lay,
   To breathe the faint sad call that He would know;
But now the slighted fold was far away,
   And no approaching footstep soothed its woe.

A thing of life and nurture from above
   Sunk under earth where all was cold and dim,
With nothing in it to console His love,
   Only the miserable cry for Him.
His was the wounded heart, the bleeding limb
   That safe and sound He would have joy'd to keep;
And still, amidst the flock at home with Him,
   He was the Shepherd of that one lost sheep.

Oh! would He now but come and claim His own,
   How more than precious His restoring care!
How sweet the pasture of His choice alone,
   How bright the dullest path if He were there!
How well the pain of rescue it could bear,
   Held in the shelter of His strong embrace!
With Him it would find herbage anywhere,
   And springs of endless life in every place.

And so He came and raised it from the clay,
   While evil beasts went disappointed by.
He bore it home along the fearful way
   In the soft light of His rejoicing eye.
And *thou* fallen soul, afraid to live or die
   In the deep pit that will not set thee free,
Lift up to Him the helpless homeward cry,
   For all that tender love is seeking thee.

CCCCII

THE PAIN OF LOVE

JESUS! why dost Thou love me so?
   What hast Thou seen in me
To make my happiness so great,
   So dear a joy to Thee?

Wert Thou not God, I then might think
  Thou hadst no eye to read
The badness of that selfish heart,
  For which Thine own did bleed.

But Thou art God, and knowest all;
  Dear Lord! Thou knowest me;
And yet Thy knowledge hinders not
  Thy love's sweet liberty.

Ah, how Thy grace hath woo'd my soul
  With persevering wiles!
Now give me tears to weep; for tears
  Are deeper joy than smiles.

Each proof renew'd of Thy great love
  Humbles me more and more,
And brings to light forgotten sins,
  And lays them at my door.

The more I love Thee, Lord! the more
  I hate my own cold heart;
The more Thou woundest me with love,
  The more I feel the smart.

What shall I do, then, dearest Lord!
  Say, shall I fly from Thee,
And hide my poor unloving self
  Where Thou canst never see?

Or shall I pray that Thy dear love
  To me might not be given?
Ah no! love must be pain on earth,
  If it be bliss in Heaven.

F. W. Faber

CCCCIII

SELF-LOVE

OH I could go through all life's troubles singing,
  Turning earth's night to day,
If self were not so fast around me, clinging
  To all I do or say.

My very thoughts are selfish, always building
  Mean castles in the air;
I use my love of others for a gilding
  To make myself look fair.

I fancy all the world engross'd with judging
  My merit or my blame;
Its warmest praise seems an ungracious grudging
  Of praise which I might claim.

In youth or age, by city, wood, or mountain,
  Self is forgotten never;
Where'er we tread, it gushes like a fountain,
  And its waters flow for ever.

Alas! no speed in life can snatch us wholly
  Out of self's hateful sight ;
And it keeps step, whene'er we travel slowly,
  And sleeps with us at night.

O miserable omnipresence, stretching
  Over all time and space,
How have I run from thee, yet found thee reaching
  The goal in every race!

The opiate balms of grace may haply still thee,
  Deep in my nature lying;
For I may hardly hope, alas! to kill thee,
  Save by the act of dying.

O Lord! that I could waste my life for others,
  With no ends of my own,
That I could pour myself into my brothers,
  And live for them alone!

Such was the life Thou livedst; self abjuring,
  Thine own pains never easing,
Our burdens bearing, our just doom enduring,
  A life without self-pleasing!

CCCCIV

SWEETNESS IN PRAYER

WHY dost thou beat so quick, my heart?
    Why struggle in thy cage?
What shall I do for thee, poor heart!
    Thy throbbing heat to swage?

What spell is this come over thee,
  My soul! what sweet surprise?
And wherefore these unbidden tears
  That start into mine eyes?

' How great, how good does GOD appear,
  How dear our holy faith,
How tasteless life's best joys have grown;
  How I could welcome death!

—Would that Thou mightest stay with me,
  Or else that I might die
While heart and soul are still subdued
  With Thy sweet mastery.

Thy home is with the humble, LORD!
  The simple are Thy rest;
Thy lodging is in child-like hearts;
  Thou makest there Thy nest.

Dear Comforter! Eternal Love!
  If Thou wilt stay with me,
Of lowly thoughts and simple ways
  I'll build a nest for Thee.

Who made this beating heart of mine,
  But Thou, my heavenly Guest?
Let no one have it then but Thee,
  And let it be Thy nest.

CCCCV

THE WILL OF GOD

I WORSHIP Thee, sweet Will of GOD!
  And all Thy ways adore,
And every day I live, I seem
  To love Thee more and more.

Thou wert the end, the blessèd rule
 . Of our Saviour's toils and tears;
Thou wert the passion of His Heart
  Those Three-and-thirty years.

And He hath breathed into my soul
  A special love of Thee,
A love to lose my will in His,
  And by that loss be free.

He always wins who sides with GOD,
  To him no chance is lost;
GOD's Will is sweetest to him, when
  It triumphs at his cost.

When obstacles and trials seem
  Like prison-walls to be,
I do the little I can do,
  And leave the rest to Thee.

CCCCVI

VIA CRUCIS

FROM pain to pain, from woe to woe,
  With loving hearts and footsteps slow,
To Calvary with CHRIST we go.
  See how His Precious Blood
    At every Station pours!
  Was ever grief like His?
    Was ever sin like ours?

See Note

CCCCVII

JESUS CRUCIFIED

OH come and mourn with me awhile!
  See, Mary calls us to her side;
Oh come and let us mourn with her;
Jesus, our Love, is crucified!

Have we no tears to shed for Him,
While soldiers scoff and Jews deride?
Ah! look how patiently He hangs;
Jesus, our Love, is crucified!

His Mother cannot reach His Face;
She stands in helplessness beside;
Her heart is martyr'd with her Son's;
Jesus, our Love, is crucified!

Seven times He spoke, seven words of love,
And all three hours His silence cried
For mercy on the souls of men;
Jesus, our Love, is crucified!

What was Thy crime, my dearest LORD?
By earth, by heaven, Thou hast been tried,
And guilty found of too much love;
Jesus, our Love, is crucified!

Death came, and JESUS meekly bow'd;
His falling eyes He strove to guide
With mindful love to Mary's face;
JESUS, our Love, is crucified!

Oh break, oh break, hard heart of mine!
Thy weak self-love and guilty pride
His Pilate and His Judas were;
JESUS, our Love, is crucified!

Come, take thy stand beneath the Cross,
And let the Blood from out that Side
Fall gently on thee drop by drop;
JESUS, our Love, is crucified!

A broken heart, a fount of tears,
Ask, and they will not be denied;
A broken heart Love's cradle is;
JESUS, our Love, is crucified!

O Love of GOD! O Sin of man!
In this dread act your strength is tried;
And victory remains with Love;
For He, our Love, is crucified!

See Note

CCCCVIII

STARLIGHT

AT midnight, when yon azure fields on high
   Sparkle and glow without one cloudy bar,
   The radiance of some 'bright particular star'
Attracts, perchance, and holds my watching eye.

That star may long have vanish'd from the sky;
   Yet still its unspent rays, borne from afar,
   Come darting downwards in their golden car—
Proof it once glitter'd in the galaxy.

So in my heart I feel a healing ray
   Sweetly transmitted from a Star divine,
   Which once illumed the coasts of Palestine:
And though its beauty beams not there to-day,
   I know that Star of old did truly shine,
   Because its cheering radiance now is mine.

R. Wilton

CCCCIX

IONA

I LANDED on Iona's holy isle,
 And wandêr'd through its ancient ruins bare,
And felt the great Columba's self was there.
Thirteen long centuries seem'd 'a little while'

Before the unchanging sea and sky, whose smile
 He knew. He trod these paths; he breathed this air;
 These waves once roll'd responsive to his prayer,
Whose murmuring ripples now my ear beguile.

Nor to the Saint alone closer I stand,
 Nearer the Lord I seem, upon this shore;
The solid rock of this historic strand
 Helps me to bridge Time's waste of waters o'er,
And grasp His feet, and feel His loving hand
 In Whom all saints are one for evermore!

CCCCX

AN INCIDENT

AT the Lord's Table waiting, robed and stoled,
 Till all had knelt around, I saw a sign!
In the full chalice sudden splendours shine,
Azure and crimson, emerald and gold.

I stoop'd to see the wonder, when, behold!
 Within the cup a Countenance Divine
 Look'd upwards at me through the trembling wine,
Suffused with tenderest love and grief untold.

The comfort of that sacramental token
 From Memory's page Time never can erase;
The glass of that rich window may be broken,
 But not the mirror'd image of His grace,
Through which my dying Lord to me has spoken,
 At His own Holy Table, face to face!

See Note

CCCCXI

SONG OF AN ANGEL

AT noon a shower had fallen, and the clime
 Breathed sweetly, and upon a cloud there lay
 One more sublime in beauty than the Day,
Or all the Sons of Time;

A gold harp had he, and was singing there
  Songs that I yearn'd to hear; a glory shone
  Of rosy twilights on his cheeks—a zone
Of amaranth on his hair.

He sang of joys to which the earthly heart
  Hath never beat; he sang of deathless Youth,
  And by the throne of Love, Beauty and Truth
Meeting, no more to part;

He sang lost Hope, faint Faith, and vain Desire
  Crown'd there; great works, that on the earth began,
  Accomplish'd; towers impregnable to man
Scaled with the speed of fire;

Of Power, and Life, and wingéd Victory
  He sang—of bridges strown 'twixt star and star—
  And hosts all arm'd in light for bloodless war
Pass, and repass on high;

Lo! in the pauses of his jubilant voice
  He leans to listen: answers from the spheres,
  And mighty paeans thundering he hears
Down the empyreal skies:

Then suddenly he ceased—and seem'd to rest
  His goodly-fashion'd arm upon a slope
  Of that fair cloud, and with soft eyes of hope
He pointed towards the West;

And shed on me a smile of beams, that told
  Of a bright World beyond the thunder-piles,
  With blesséd fields, and hills, and happy isles,
And citadels of gold.

F. Tennyson

CCCCXII

O GOD, impart Thy blessing to my cries,
  Tho' I trust deeply, yet I daily err;
The waters of my heart are oft astir :—
An Angel's there! and yet I cannot rise!

  I wish that CHRIST were here among us still,
Proffering His bosom to his servant's brow;
But oh! that holy voice comes o'er us now
Like twilight echoes from a distant hill:

We long for His pure looks and words sublime;
His lowly-lofty innocence and grace;
The talk sweet-toned, and blessing all the time;
The mountain sermon and the ruthful gaze;
The cheerly credence gather'd from His face;
His voice in village-groups at eve or prime!

C. T. Turner

CCCCXIII

THE LATTICE AT SUNRISE

AS on my bed at dawn I mused and pray'd,
 I saw my lattice prankt upon the wall,
The flaunting leaves and flitting birds withal—
A sunny phantom interlaced with shade;

'Thanks be to heaven,' in happy mood I said,
'What sweeter aid my matins could befall
Than this fair glory from the East hath made?
What holy sleights hath GOD, the LORD of all,

To bid us feel and see! We are not free
To say we see not, for the glory comes
Nightly and daily, like the flowing sea;
His lustre pierceth through the midnight glooms;
And, at prime hour, behold! He follows me
With golden shadows to my secret rooms!'

. CCCCXIV

OUR MARY AND THE CHILD-MUMMY

WHEN the four quarters of the world shall rise,
 Men, women, children, at the Judgment-time,
Perchance this Memphian girl, dead ere her prime,
Shall drop her mask, and with dark new-born eyes

Salute our English Mary, loved and lost;
The Father knows her little scroll of prayer,
And life as pure as His Egyptian air;
For, though she knew not JESUS, nor the cost

At which He won the world, she learn'd to pray;
And though our own sweet babe on CHRIST's good name
Spent her last breath, premonish'd and advised
Of Him, and in His glorious Church baptized,
—She will not spurn this old-world child away,
Nor put her poor embalméd heart to shame.

See Note

Y

CCCCXV

THE HARVEST MOON

HOW peacefully the broad and golden moon
    Comes up to gaze upon the reaper's toil!
That they who own the land for many a mile,
May bless her beams, and they who take the boon

Of scatter'd ears; Oh! beautiful! how soon
The dusk is turn'd to silver without soil,
Which makes the fair sheaves fairer than at noon,
And guides the gleaner to his slender spoil;

So, to our souls, the LORD of love and might
Sends harvest-hours, when daylight disappears;
When age and sorrow, like a coming night,
Darken our field of work with doubts and fears,
He times the presence of His heavenly light
To rise up softly o'er our silver hairs.

CCCCXVI

ANASTASIS

THO' death met love upon thy dying smile,
    And staid him there for hours, yet the orbs of sight
So speedily resign'd their aspect bright,
That Christian hope fell earthward for awhile,
Appall'd by dissolution:—But on high
A record lives of thine identity!
Thou shalt not lose one charm of lip or eye;
The hues and liquid lights shall wait for thee,
And the fair tissues, wheresoe'er they be!
—Daughter of heaven! our grieving hearts repose
On the dear thought that we once more shall see
Thy beauty—like Himself our Master rose—
So shall that beauty its old rights maintain,
And thy sweet spirit own those eyes again.

See Note

CCCCXVII

MORNING HYMN

FOR BOYS IN THE GORDON HOME

THY servants pray, O hear us, LORD!
   Be Thou our shield, be Thou our sword,
Be Thou our guard against all sin,
From foes without, from foes within.

O make us loving brothers all,
Forgetting self at duty's call:
Bless Thou the guardians of our land,
And keep our dear ones in Thy hand.

E. Lady Tennyson

CCCCXVIII

EVENING HYMN

GREAT GOD Who knowest each man's need,
   Bless Thou our watch and guard our sleep;
Forgive our sins of thought and deed,
   And in Thy peace Thy servants keep.

We thank Thee for the day that 's done,
   We trust Thee for the days to be;
Thy love we learn in CHRIST Thy Son—
   O may we all His glory see!

CCCCXIX

LATE, late, so late! and dark the night and chill!
   Late, late, so late! but we can enter still.
Too late, too late! ye cannot enter now.

No light had we: for that we do repent;
And learning this, the Bridegroom will relent.
Too late, too late! ye cannot enter now.

No light: so late! and dark and chill the night!
O let us in, that we may find the light!
Too late, too late: ye cannot enter now.

Have we not heard the Bridegroom is so sweet!
O let us in, tho' late, to kiss His feet!
No, no, too late! ye cannot enter now.

A. Lord Tennyson

Y 2

CCCCXX

WHEN Lazarus left his charnel-cave,
    And home to Mary's house return'd,
    Was this demanded—if he yearn'd
To hear her weeping by his grave?

'Where wert thou, brother, those four days?'
    There lives no record of reply,
    Which telling what it is to die
Had surely added praise to praise.

From every house the neighbours met,
    The streets were fill'd with joyful sound,
    A solemn gladness even crown'd
The purple brows of Olivet.

Behold a man raised up by CHRIST!
    The rest remaineth unreveal'd;
    He told it not; or something seal'd
The lips of that Evangelist.

CCCCXXI

HER eyes are homes of silent prayer,
    Nor other thought her mind admits
    But, he was dead, and there he sits,
And He that brought him back is there.

Then one deep love doth supersede
    All other, when her ardent gaze
    Roves from the living brother's face,
And rests upon the Life indeed.

All subtle thought, all curious fears,
    Borne down by gladness so complete,
    She bows, she bathes the Saviour's feet
With costly spikenard and with tears.

Thrice blest whose lives are faithful prayers,
    Whose loves in higher love endure;
    What souls possess themselves so pure,
Or is there blessedness like theirs?

CCCCXXII

O MAN, forgive thy mortal foe,
    Nor ever strike him blow for blow;
For all the souls on earth that live
To be forgiven must forgive.
Forgive him seventy times and seven :
For all the blessèd souls in Heaven
Are both forgivers and forgiven !

CCCCXXIII

IN THE CHILDREN'S HOSPITAL

Emmie

OUR doctor had call'd in another, I never had seen him
      before,
But he sent a chill to my heart when I saw him come in at
      the door,
Fresh from the surgery-schools of France and of other lands—
Harsh red hair, big voice, big chest, big merciless hands !
Wonderful cures he had done, O yes, but they said too of him
He was happier using the knife than in trying to save the limb,
And that I can well believe, for he look'd so coarse and so red,
I could think he was one of those who would break their jests
      on the dead,
And mangle the living dog that had loved him and fawn'd at
      his knee—
Drench'd with the hellish oorali—that ever such things should
      be !

Here was a boy—I am sure that some of our children would
      die
But for the voice of Love, and the smile, and the comforting
      eye—
Here was a boy in the ward, every bone seem'd out of its
      place—
Caught in a mill and crush'd—it was all but a hopeless case :
And he handled him gently enough ; but his voice and his face
      were not kind,
And it was but a hopeless case, he had seen it and made up
      his mind,

And he said to me roughly 'The lad will need little more of
     your care.'
'All the more need,' I told him, 'to seek the Lord Jesus in
     prayer;
They are all His children here, and I pray for them all as my
     own:'
But he turn'd to me, 'Ay, good woman, can prayer set a
     broken bone?'
Then he mutter'd half to himself, but I know that I heard
     him say
'All very well—but the good Lord Jesus has had His day.'

Had? has it come? It has only dawn'd. It will come by and
     by.
O how could I serve in the wards if the hope of the world
     were a lie?
How could I bear with the sights and the loathsome smells of
     disease
But that He said 'Ye do it to Me, when ye do it to these'?

So he went. And we past to this ward where the younger
     children are laid:
Here is the cot of our orphan, our darling, our meek little
     maid;
Empty you see just now! We have lost her who loved her so
     much—
Patient of pain tho' as quick as a sensitive plant to the touch;
Hers was the prettiest prattle, it often moved me to tears,
Hers was the gratefullest heart I have found in a child of her
     years—
Nay you remember our Emmie; you used to send her the
     flowers;
How she would smile at 'em, play with 'em, talk to 'em hours
     after hours!
They that can wander at will where the works of the Lord
     are reveal'd
Little guess what joy can be got from a cowslip out of the
     field;
Flowers to these 'spirits in prison' are all they can know of
     the spring,
They freshen and sweeten the wards like the waft of an
     Angel's wing;
And she lay with a flower in one hand and her thin hands
     crost on her breast—
Wan, but as pretty as heart can desire, and we thought her
     at rest,

Quietly sleeping—so quiet, our doctor said 'Poor little dear,
Nurse, I must do it to-morrow; she 'll never live thro' it, I fear.'

I walk'd with our kindly old Doctor as far as the head of the
        stair,
Then I return'd to the ward; the child didn't see I was there.

Never since I was nurse, had I been so grieved and so vext!
Emmie had heard him. Softly she call'd from her cot to the
        next,
'He says I shall never live thro' it, O Annie, what shall I do?'
Annie consider'd. 'If I,' said the wise little Annie, 'was you,
I should cry to the dear LORD JESUS to help me, for, Emmie,
        you see,
It 's all in the picture there: *Little children should come to Me.'*
(Meaning the print that you gave us, I find that it always can
        please
Our children, the dear LORD JESUS with children about His
        knees.)
'Yes, and I will,' said Emmie, 'but then if I call to the LORD,
How should He know that it 's me? such a lot of beds in the
        ward!'
That was a puzzle for Annie. Again she consider'd, and said:
'Emmie, you put out your arms, and you leave 'em outside on
        the bed—
The LORD has so *much* to see to! but, Emmie, you tell it Him
        plain,
It's the little girl with her arms lying out on the counterpane.

I had sat three nights by the child—I could not watch her for
        four—
My brain had begun to reel—I felt I could do it no more.
That was my sleeping-night, but I thought that it never would
        pass.
There was a thunderclap once, and a clatter of hail on the
        glass,
And there was a phantom cry that I heard as I tost about,
The motherless bleat of a lamb in the storm and the darkness
        without;
My sleep was broken besides with dreams of the dreadful knife
And fears for our delicate Emmie who scarce would escape
        with her life;

Then in the gray of the morning it seem'd she stood by me
    and smiled,
And the doctor came at his hour, and we went to see to the
    child.

He had brought his ghastly tools: we believed her asleep
    again—
Her dear, long, lean, little arms lying out on the counterpane;
Say that His day is done! Ah why should we care what they
    say?
The Lord of the children had heard her, and Emmie had
    past away.

See Note

End of Book Third

NOTES

EXPLANATORY AND BIOGRAPHICAL

INTRODUCTION TO BOOK I

ENGLISH lyrical religious poetry is less easily divisible than our secular verse into well-marked periods, whether in regard to matter or to manner. Throughout its long course it has in great measure the groundwork of a common Book, a common Faith, and a common Purpose. And although incidents from human life and aspects of nature are not excluded (and have in this selection, when possible, been specially gathered, with the view of varying the garland here presented)—yet meditation, prayer, and praise will ever be the three great keys, successively rising in order of lyrical intensity, through which this music of the heart of Christianity expresses itself. Certain differing waves of feeling and expression may however be traced, and have suggested the tripartite division which will here be followed;—whilst yet we may say, as was said of the blessed Spirits met by Dante as he entered Paradise,

> . . . tutti fanno bello il primo giro,
> E differentemente han dolce vita,
> Per sentir più e men l' eterno spiro.

If we take our First Book as covering about the space between 1500 and 1680, we begin with a preliminary or tentative period, when the joyous and picturesque mediaevalism of Dunbar's *Nativity* passes at once into the sombre style characteristic of the thirty agitated and painful years which were the birth-throes of the Reformation. This was an ungenial atmosphere for sacred song. Yet the reign of Elizabeth was hardly more fertile—the Renaissance movement in our poetry led English writers into the pleasant paths of a revived and (with them) innocent classicalism : whilst the unsettled elements in the religious sphere, the dominance of Genevan doctrine—fervid indeed, but narrow, ultra-dogmatic, and rarely blessed by the smile of the Muses—were conditions equally disfavourable.

When the tide begins to flow more freely, our sacred poetry was enriched by such splendid outbursts of pure lyrical enthusiasm as the odes by Spenser and Milton, with which the Elizabethan age may be said almost to begin and to close. But lyrics of this class are only too rare ; and our religious verse tends to fall into that didactic vein which seems characteristic of the English genius ; it is meditative, introspective, personal, yet seldom in the modern more subtly analytical manner. And as the seventeenth century advances, it is varied by some singular and attractive specimens of mystical poetry, in which we may perceive at once the wide literary scholarship of that age and the effect of the evil days of the Commonwealth Usurpation, driving men for peace into the solitude of their own bosoms.

Our first period, it will be seen, is, however, by far most richly indebted to two writers, trained in the school of doctrine and practice which found its earliest great teacher in Richard Hooker. With this spirit, gradually systematized and widened, until it became the genuine and enduring representative of the mind of the English Church, Herbert and Vaughan were deeply imbued— with its broad scholarly learning, its liberal acceptance of art and culture, its faith at once rational, deeply founded, and fervent,

—The gracious creed that knows how to forgive,—

its strong and living sense of the underlying unity of the Christian Church through all her centuries of change or development. —But Theology, as such, is not within the purpose of this little book. In the City of God are many mansions ; and whichever may be ours, the religious elements just enumerated, it is undeniable, made powerfully towards poetry : they may be easily traced throughout as inspiring Herbert in his quiet Wiltshire valley and Vaughan among the wild hills of Brecon.—The difference between the respective poetical gifts of these two men—gifts which a just criticism must rate very high—may be best left to the reader's discrimination and enjoyment. Only this need here be noted, that both are instinct with the fervour, with the strangeness, of the Celtic sensitive imagination ; concealed indeed in some degree by Herbert's academical training, but everywhere pervading his disciple's work with a certain fascinating intensity.

Vaughan long over-lived the Restoration : after which date the condensed style, not free from overstrained fancy and ' conceit,' popular hitherto in the seventeenth century, gradually gave way to a greater simplicity of thought and language, a less imaginative colouring ;—to what, in a word, we might call the modern manner. To this time naturally belongs the beginning of religious song for public use. Perhaps the specimens here given might have been ranged with the hymns of the next hundred years. But they are placed in our first book because in style and in thought they are yet closely allied to the preceding period : they unite our own hymnology, looked at as a whole, with the last echoes of the Elizabethan age.

PAGE NO.

I   I   William Dunbar, 'a poet,' said Sir Walter Scott, 'un-
          rivalled by any that Scotland has ever produced,' was
          educated at the University of S. Andrews, entered the
          Franciscan Order, but seems to have lived much about
          the Scottish Court, or employed on secular business.
          He was the last great representative of Chaucer's
          School in Scotland; he stands on the boundary be-
          tween the world of the Middle Ages and the world of
          the Renaissance. Like the rich and lovely architecture
          of his time, Dunbar's poetry is the fine flower of ex-
          piring Mediaevalism.
             The graceful hymn here given is reprinted from
          Mr. H. M. Fitzgibbon's excellent little Selection of
          Early English Poetry (W. Scott, 1887). The spelling
          has been modernized; a process without which, small
          as are the substantial deviations from modern usage,
          the early Scottish orthography has, at first sight, the
          aspect of an unknown tongue.

2   II   Thomas, second Lord Vaux of Harrowden, held state
          appointments under Henry VIII, and was among the
          first of those high-born and high-educated writers with
          whom our modern literature begins.
             II and III, published in the *Paradise of Dainty Devices*,
          1576, reflect the gloom of that unhappy period between
          the middle of the reigns of Henry VIII and Elizabeth.
          Great is the contrast between their tone and the joyous
          brilliancy of Spenser's noble ode—published 1596—
          which follows.

5   IV   l. 15 *trinal triplicities*: A treatise on the Heavenly
          Hierarchy (erroneously ascribed to Dionysius the
          Areopagite, but of early date), which was held as an
          authority for many centuries, ranks the Angels in three
          main Orders, each subdivided into three. 'The names'
          (Dictionary of Christian Biography, 1877), 'appear to
          have been obtained by combining with the more ob-
          vious Seraphim, Cherubim, Archangels, and Angels, the
          five deduced from two passages of S. Paul, Eph. i. 21,
          and Col. i. 16.'
             Compare Milton, Par. Lost, v. 748:—
                        the mighty regencies
             Of Seraphim and Potentates and Thrones
             In their triple degrees.

10   V   To this deeply-felt sonnet (which forms a fit com-
          parison to Shakespeare's *Poor Soul*), the noble author
          has added the words :—
             Splendidis Longum Valedico Nugis:

with obvious reference to his romantic or amorous writings, *Arcadia* or *Astrophel*.

11   VII   Humfrey Gifford, ' Gentleman,' probably from a Devonshire family in the Bideford country, published his one book, (preserved now in a single copy), *A Posie of Gilloflowers*, in 1580. His verse is fresh, simple, spirited, and singularly modern in style.

12   VIII   Printed as prefatory to a Bible of 1594.

13   IX   Edmund Bolton, a critic and historian, published his main work in 1624. But the *Carol* appears in the great Elizabethan Anthology, *England's Helicon*, 1600.

14   X   Robert Southwell, of Horsham S. Faith's, Norfolk, was trained at Douai and Paris : at Rome, in 1578, entered the Society of Jesus : in 1586 returned to England : by 1590, for performance of his religious duties as a priest was imprisoned, thirteen times racked, and judicially murdered by the Elizabethan Government in 1595.

Ben Jonson said to the poet Drummond at Hawthornden (1618–9) that 'so he had written that piece, the *Burning Babe*, he would have been content to destroy many of his.' Fervour and sincerity of devotion, passionate intensity of faith in the Lord and Master under Whose name he served, has never received more beautiful expression than in this and the following poem, which their martyr-author probably thought out or (if the thirteen torturings of the persecutors left him the power), wrote down during his imprisonment.

15   XII   Taken, with several other inedited or little known early hymns, charming through their simplicity and depth of feeling, from the 'Illustrative Poems' appended by Mr. W. T. Brooke to his edition of *Christ's Victory and Triumph* (Griffith & Co., 1888). It has been ascribed mainly to Dr. Nicholas Postgate, Missioner in the Roman Communion, 'who, for baptizing a child, and exercising other priestly functions, was executed at York' in 1679, at 82 years of age.

16   XIII   Of Barnabe Barnes, says Dr. Grosart, who has edited his poems with his usual loving diligence, little is known but that he was son to Richard, Bishop of Durham, studied at Oxford, and served under Lord Essex in his expedition to France. His sonnets show truth of

feeling and freedom from ingenious 'conceits': he seems to have formed his style upon that of Sir P. Sidney, to whose *Astrophel* he makes reference.

17   XVI   Printed 1601; signed F. B. P. in a British Museum manuscript. 'Founded upon Cardinal Peter Damiani's *Ad perennis vitae fontem*' (W. T. Brooke).

19   XVII   John Donne was educated at Hart Hall, Oxford, and Trinity, Cambridge: admitted at Lincoln's Inn, travelled widely in Europe, and accompanied Lord Essex on his expeditions in 1596 and 1597. Took Holy Orders in 1614: in 1620 was appointed Dean of S. Paul's.

Donne's poems were first collected in 1633: they cover an extraordinary range in subject, and are throughout marked with a strange originality almost equally fascinating and repellent. It is possible that his familiarity with Italian and Spanish literatures, both at that time deeply coloured by fantastic and far-fetched thought, may have in some degree influenced him in that direction. His poems were probably written mainly during youth. There is a strange solemn passionate earnestness about them, a quality which underlies the fanciful 'conceits' of all his work. Donne, like Herbert and Vaughan, who show the same intensity and quaintness, was of Welsh descent.

20   XXI   The details of Thomas Campion's life share in the darkness which covers almost all our Elizabethan poets. By profession he was a Doctor of Medicine. His first English songs appeared in 1601; but we may reasonably suppose that he had practised poetry, as well as music, for some years previously. Campion's songs are admirable for their union of melodious simplicity, beauty, and strong common sense. So rare are the music-books in which they appeared, that they were practically rediscovered for us by Mr. A. H. Bullen, who has published the best in his charming selection of Lyrics (Nimmo, 1889).—No. XXVII, originally printed 1606, is from Mr. Bullen's volume. This is a song of great force and originality. The unknown writer saw deep into human nature.

24   XXX   William Drummond: educated at the High School and (newly founded) University of Edinburgh. On the Continent 1606-9; settled for life at 'classic Haw-

thornden' 1610. His letters, journal, and library show
a very wide and well-chosen range of study: they
perhaps present the first detailed picture we have of a
man of literature in the modern sense. Drummond's
(published 1616 and 1623) is the only Scottish poetry
which reflects the finest features of the English Elizabethan Renaissance: he has exquisite feeling, meditative grace, charm of form and style. In the troubles of
Scotland during the reign of Charles I he used all his
influence towards peace, moderation, culture, rational
loyalty and unfanatical religion; but his counsels were
far too wise for acceptance by either party of the day.

25 XXXII   l. 3 *In silence*: So Menander—ἅπαντα σιγῶν ὁ θεὸς
ἐξεργάζεται.

26 XXXV   This rendering (5 stanzas, of 8 in the Roman Breviary
text), appears to have been written by Drummond for
a translation of the *Primer or Office of the Blessed Virgin
Mary*: a copy of which, dated 1615, is in the British
Museum (W. T. Brooke).

25 XXXVII   George Herbert was born in Montgomery Castle, son
to Richard and Magdalen Newport (descended in the
female line from Bleddyn, Prince of Powys, and
Gwenllian, daughter to Gruffydd, Prince of North
Wales), an admirable woman, whose loving care (the
father dying early) trained her son's early years. He
was educated at Westminster School and Trinity,
Cambridge, and soon distinguished for varied and sound
study. Elected Public Orator 1620: made enduring
friendship with Dr. Donne, Bishop Andrewes, and
Francis Bacon. His interests were divided between
entering a profession, and the Court; where he seems
to have been in favour with James I. But by 1627
Herbert's hopes of royal advancement ended. After
much inward conflict, he decided on Holy Orders:
retired from Cambridge, his health beginning to fail;
married, and in 1630, at the request of his kinsman
Philip, Lord Pembroke, was presented with the cure of
Bemerton, a village between Salisbury and Wilton.
There the little road-side church, almost as in his
days, still

.... stands
Crouching entrench'd in slopes of daisy sod,
And duly deck'd by Herbert-honouring hands:—

And here—suffering also from advancing consumption
—he lived that saintly life of 'detachment' which his
poems reveal—say rather, embody. When no longer

able to walk to Salisbury Cathedral he would take his
lute and play : *The Sundays of Man's Life* (XLIII), being
the lines which he chose for his last song here—
Singing on earth, as Izaak Walton says, such hymns
and anthems as the Angels and he, and his holy friend
N. Ferrar now sing in Heaven. He lies nameless
beneath the altar in his little church at Bemerton.

For many details in this sketch, as in those of
Marvell, Vaughan, and others, the writer is indebted
to those careful editions of their works by which
Dr. A. Grosart has conferred services of high value
upon our literature.

This sonnet, (to which a title has been prefixed, whilst
for the rest of Herbert's his own have been retained),
was sent by him to his Mother as a New Year's gift in
1608—Herbert's first year at Cambridge—in order,
he says, to declare his resolution 'That my poor
abilities in poetry shall be all and ever consecrated to
God's glory.'

30 XLI The idea here is that costly monuments keep the dust
of the body artificially apart from its natural companion,
the dust of the earth ; and that tombs will at the Last
Day fall and do homage to the dead. Dust is the head
of man's *stem* or pedigree; his life, like the sand
contained in the hour-glass, is destined in its turn to
dust.

The appearance of a church interior, in the early
seventeenth century, is admirably characterized in
this and the following poem.

32 XLV Herbert seems to have written this curious auto-
biographical poem when in ill-health or low spirits,
and in remembrance of a time of morbid depression
(St. vi).

33 — l. 1 *My flesh began* . . . appears equivalent to *challenged.*
l. 17 *cross-bias* : an image from bowling, when a ball
sent on a curve strikes the opponent's aside. The
'conceit' in the last line may mean; Although forgotten
of God, unless my love to Him still continues in my
desolation, let me never be able to love Him.

35 XLIX Deep thought, simple yet subtle ideas, manly lucid
language, give a very high rank among our serious
lyrics to this and to No. LX.

40 LV St. i 'The aspects of the planets were their apparent
positions in regard to one another as seen' and cal-
culated beforehand 'from the earth' (Grosart). Upon
these *aspects* astronomy greatly relied for its predictions.
St. iii The chemist analyses *the creature*, the substance

before him,—until he discovers its *callow*, simple, unclothed, elements; which are only seen by ordinary spectators dressed out and disguised within the composite substance presented to the senses. In this poem we trace Herbert's friendship and co-operation with Francis Bacon.

46 LXI This lovely poem, which, as the reader will find, must have been studied as a model by Vaughan, was clearly written after a time of depression—due, perhaps, to the increasing ill-health of Herbert's later years; the 'consumption' alluded to by Izaak Walton in his *Life*. St. i, l. 3 *demesne*: seemingly used for *property*; the flowers, beside what their spot of earth grants them, gain joy through the contrast of Spring after frost. To the metrical skill and beauty of l. 4 S. T. Coleridge draws attention. St. iii *chiming* . . . *bell*: calling to prayer. St. iv *Offering at Heaven*: compare Vergil's equally charming phrase on a young tree's growth,

Exiit ad caelum ramis felicibus . . .

St. vii l. 6 *Swelling through store*: puffed up by wealth or place.

49 LXVII Archbishop Leighton, as quoted by Dr. Grosart, has a remark which appears tacitly to refer to this poem, and explains its title. 'Whatsoever be the matter of [human actions], the spiritual mind hath that alchemy indeed of turning base metals into gold, earthly employments into heavenly.'—*Tincture* (p. 50, St. i) may refer to the *Elixir*, regarded as a cleansing or transmuting liquid. But the more obvious sense will be, 'if coloured or tinged with this thought, *For God's sake.*'

51 LXXI Christopher Harvey's *Synagogue*, intended as a 'shadow' or sequel to Herbert's *Temple*, was published 1640. The writer was educated at Brasenose, Oxford; and died Vicar of Clifton in Warwickshire.

52 LXXII William Habington, son to a country gentleman, was educated in the Jesuit College of S. Omer and at Paris, and married Lucy Herbert (daughter to the first Baron Powys);—the *Castara* to whose honour his poems are inscribed.

58 LXXIX 'This Hymn was made by Sir H. Wotton, when he was an Ambassador at Venice, in the time of a great sickness.' Quitting diplomacy, he became Provost of Eton: whence in 1638 he wrote to Milton, then in his youth, an admirable letter, congratulating him on the beauty of *Comus,* and giving counsel, derived from his own experience, for Milton's Italian journey.

59 LXXX   Much in the style of Chidiock Tychbourne's pathetic little Elegy, *My prime of youth* . . . , printed in Dr. Hannah's valuable *Poems by Raleigh, Wotton, &c.* 1875.

60 LXXXI   Milton imagined this magnificent Ode at dawn of Christmas 1629,—having then lately passed his 21st birthday.   He here treats Nature (p. 61, st. ii, iii) as guilty,—as representing a fallen world.   The heathen religions of antiquity are similarly regarded as demon-worship, rather than the corruptions of, or the efforts to reach, divine truth : and the tradition that the power of the pagan Gods ended at the Nativity is worked out at length.   He begins with the deities of Greece and Rome, passing thence to Syria and Egypt.

64 —   *Lars and Lemures :* Household Gods, Spirits of the Dead.   *Flamens :* Roman priests.

65 —   *twice batter'd god :* Dagon.—*Libyc Hammon :* as worshipped in the Libyan Oasis.—In the legend of *Osiris,*—blended here with *Apis,*—he was described as shut up in a carved chest and cast upon the Nile.—But it is the mythological scholarship of his day, before the authentic Egyptian authorities were deciphered, which Milton here offers.

66 LXXXII·l. 6 *if, sad share* . . . If you, the Seraphim, desire to sympathize with us, but are through your fiery nature unable to give tears, give burning sighs.—Milton's earlier poetry has several of these elaborate fancies.

68 LXXXVI Sir William Davenant, dramatist, poet, and adherent of Charles I during the Civil War.   His poetry belongs mainly to the thoughtful style of his century; but he has left some excellent pieces in a lighter vein.

69 LXXXVII Sir Thomas Browne was educated at Winchester and Broadgate Hall, (now Pembroke College), Oxford.   Became M.D. at Leyden, and settled as a physician in Norwich.   The *Religio Medici,* (whence the hymn printed is taken), his most famous work, was first published 1642. Passages in this and in his *Hydriotaphia* are amongst the very finest efforts of English prose.   He was honoured by Dr. Johnson with a short biography.

69 LXXXVIII Thomas Pestel was a Chaplain to Charles I.   Mr. W. T. Brooke, (see note on XII), publishes this from his

Sermons.   The next he dates 1660 : It makes us wish, he justly observes, that ' more of Pestel's work had survived.'

71   XC   Of Robert Herrick's life, again, very little has survived. Probably trained in Westminster School, he went thence to S. John's and Trinity Hall, Cambridge. Some years he then seems to have spent in London : in 1629 becoming Vicar of Dean Prior, a sequestered Devon village not far from Totnes.   Ejected thence for the heresy or ' malignity' (as triumphant Puritanism named it) of remaining loyal to his Church and King, he published his one volume of sacred and secular song : was restored to his Vicarage in 1662, and lies buried at Dean Prior.
   Herrick is in the first rank of English lyric poets.   In virtue of his airy touch, his fluent melody, his simple directness of style, his graceful lucidity, he may be called an Elizabethan born out of his age.   But his range of subjects, his exquisite pictures of country life (see XCIV), his union of humour with seriousness (XCV), mark the gradual development of our lyrical poetry, and its enfranchisement from Renaissance limitations, during the Stuart period.

75   XCVI   Mildmay Fane, second Earl of Westmoreland, was friend of Herrick, who dedicated to him his beautiful *Harvest Home* picture, *The Hock-cart*, and begged the Earl to publish his own verses : which were privately printed in 1648.

76   XCVII   This and the next are republished by Mr. W. T. Brooke from an Anthology of 1677.

77   XCIX   *apples* (p. 78, l. 17) pine-apples (Grosart).—These emigrants are apparently supposed to be flying westward beyond the reach of Laud's ecclesiastical administration.   But Marvell, at least in youth, held so equable an attitude between the contentions of his day, remaining, indeed, a lover of the Monarchy at heart, that the motive of the poem was probably only chosen to gratify his intense feeling for natural scenery and imaginative hyperbole by this lovely picture.
   Andrew Marvell was of Trinity, Cambridge : made the ' grand tour' of those days : in 1650-2 taught the little Mary, daughter to General Lord Fairfax.   In 1657 he

was employed with Milton (at his recommendation) as a secretary in the Foreign Department of the Protectorate. He entered the House of Commons as Member for Hull, 1659, and sate there till his death :—in 1663 accompanying the first (Howard) Earl of Carlisle on his embassy to ' Muscovy,' and writing much political verse. This is of very small value as poetry. But Marvell, when he is great, is among our greatest poets in felicity of touch and vividness of penetrative imagination. Of this the *Coronet* (c) is a fine example. Here Marvell seems allegorically to shadow forth how hard it is to offer human gifts,—such as Poetry,—to Heaven, in a truly disinterested and devotional spirit.

79 CI The selection from Vaughan's poetry here given will probably be the largest mass of unfamiliar verse to most readers. It is also so condensed in style, filled with such strokes of penetrative imagination, not without fantastic touches, that it will require the careful study which it eminently repays. Rather full notes have been therefore added.

Henry Vaughan was descended from the branch of that ancient and noble family settled in Breconshire, which in Roman days formed part of the region Siluria : whence the Poet always signs himself *Silurist*. He was born at Scethrog (properly *Ysgythrog*, peaked, or craggy), near Usk, between Crickhowel and Brecon : in 1638 entered Jesus College, Oxford : thence went to London, where he was familiar with men of letters : took the degree of Doctor of Medicine : by 1647 practised at Scethrog or Newton, where his *Silex Scintillans* (Spark-giving Flintstone), published 1650 and 1655, *Thalia Rediviva*, 1678, and other books were written. Except that he married and had children nothing is known of the poet-physician's long life in his native place : only the tombstone in his parish church-yard of Llansantfraed records— 'Henricus Vaughan M.D. | Siluris: | Servus inutilis | Peccator maximus | Hic jaceo | Gloria! + miserere.'— To this good man's humble confession let us, however, allow ourselves to add his ancient family motto : ' Safe is the owner of a clear Conscience.'

80 CII Wordsworth, who owned a copy of the very rare *Silex Scintillans*, may have had this poem before him when writing his Ode upon *Intimations of Immortality*.— Vaughan's *my glorious train* answering to the *trailing clouds of glory* . . . of the later Poet.

PAGE NO.

82 CV An excellent example of the writer's skill in blending natural scenery with moral and religious thought :— It may be compared with the power of uniting figure-subjects with landscape which a few painters, (notably our own G. Mason), have shown.

The omnipresence of God in Nature is almost more constant and consistent in Vaughan's poetry than in Wordsworth's. Equally characteristic is the intensely imaginative picture of the higher heavens, the wide sweep of Vaughan's brush in painting them, exemplified in St. iv, l. 5, 6.

83 CVI *Man . . . flowers ;*—so in the only original text of 1650. Ingenious conjecture has here read *and . . . flowers, Angels . . .* But the phrase as it stands is quite in Vaughan's manner and gives sense. On the principles of safe emendatory criticism, it should therefore be left undisturbed.

84 CIX l. 16 *cheap book :* probably for *chap-book.*—P. 85, l. 4 : the sense may be, ' I strove long against the purifying and conscience-awakening doctrines of Holy Scripture.'

89 CXVI It is obviously against the persecutions and grinding tyranny, (stigmatized by Hallam with honest wrath, but disingenuously extenuated by more than one writer of our day), suffered by the country at the hand of the Puritans and Cromwell, that Vaughan (1655) makes this beautiful protest.

91 CXVIII The original title is—Rom. Cap. 8. ver. 19. *Etenim res Creatæ exerto Capite observantes expectant revelationem Filiorum Dei.* This seems to be a version framed by Vaughan to suit the imagery of this eminently characteristic poem;—the Vulgate giving *Nam expectatio creaturæ, revelationem filiorum Dei expectat.*

95 CXXII What breadth of sympathy,—what a strange power of living (as it were) the very life of Nature,—what eager tenderness and humanity,—in this most original poem !—It should be compared with the singular history of a Book, given in CVIII.—*Realism,* in Vaughan, is penetrated, or, rather, identified, with *Idealism.*

98 CXXVI l. 17–20 *This . . . rack :* some confusion or misreading must be here. The syntax becomes clearer if we place l. 19, 20 after l. 16, and suppose *made* understood after the *were now* of l. 15. Yet this transposition seems to weaken the contrast drawn between the fall of Salem and the glorification of Bethlem.

100 CXXIX   *Magdal-castle:* the Magdala whence Mary has been called was probably the Migdol (Tower) near Tiberias, where the remains of a watch-tower still exist. The name Magdalene may however mean ' the twiner or platter of hair,' and this interpretation possibly induced Vaughan to dwell so fully on the point. He returned to the subject in some lovely lines of his *Thalia Rediviva* (1678), where, in the description of a Beauty, he says

> Her hair laid out in curious setts
> And twists, doth show like silken nets,
> Where—since he play'd at hit or miss—
> The god of Love her pris'ner is,
> And fluttering with his skittish wings
> Puts all her locks in curls and rings.

It should be remembered that the identification whether of Mary of Magdala or Mary of Bethany with the Sinner of S. Luke vii is only conjectural, if not improbable.—Whether Vaughan was aware or not of this, he has left us no more curious and original poem than his *Mary Magdalen*, a figure as vivid, life-like, and quaint as one in a mediaeval missal.

106 CXXXIV   *for one twenty* . . . Possibly, common insensate things may outlast one who has lived twenty years ; referring to the life-time of the unknown youth lamented in this pathetic poem :—to which, as to the following, Vaughan has prefixed no title.

108 CXXXV   St. i. l. 3 *well: dell* has been conjectured, but the Welsh *ffynnon* stands for fountain or for spring-head, and may have influenced Vaughan to use *well* in the sense of *watery recess.*

111 CXXXIX   From Crashaw to Norris (CL) we are in the strange, attractive, remote region of mysticism and ecstasy, having its origin in Plato, but probably drawing more from Philo, Plotinus, and later sources. Oxford in the fifteenth century had her Renaissance move-ment, which has profoundly affected England ever since. The Cambridge Platonist movement was less diffused, less enduring :—yet it deserves study, not only as a singular exhibition of a phase which constantly recurs in the human mind, but from the merit of the literature which it has left.

Richard Crashaw, from the lately-founded Charter House, entered Cambridge in 1631, passing from Pembroke to Peterhouse : was ejected in 1644 with many more who refused to bow down before the

Scottish Covenant :—that transient idol which the Presbyterian party had set up and was trying to force upon reluctant England. He joined the Roman Communion about 1646, in which year his little volume of English poetry was published : Soon retired to France; thence to Rome: was made Canon in the Basilica Church of our Lady in Loreto, where he presently died and was buried.

Crashaw represents sensuous Mysticism, as the three poets who follow are intellectual mystics. Like Quarles, (though not to the same degree), he quits the ideal point of view, the high Platonic aether. We cannot say of him, as has been said of that ' Son of Light,' Origen, the great founder of Christian Mysticism, that he ' is never betrayed into the imagery of earthly passion used by the monastic writers,' and which also marked the style of the Italian Marino, from whose *Herod* Crashaw has left a brilliant paraphrase.

Yet this mode of feeling has its place ; it also demands and deserves its compartment in a Sacred Anthology. Crashaw's work in poetry, as a whole. is incomplete and irregular ; Pope, whilst praising him, was correct in recognizing that he was an amateur rather than an artist. It was the same with Marvell :—neither, one would say, did justice to his fine natural gift. But Crashaw has a charm so unique, an imagination so nimble and subtle, phrases of such sweet and passionate felicity, that readers who may be tempted by the very scanty specimens which alone it has been here possible to offer, to turn to his little book, will find themselves surprised and delighted, in proportion to their sympathetic sense of Poetry, when touched to its rarer and finer issues.

St. i. l. 4 *wake the Sun :* So in the popular mediaeval hymn *Verbum bonum* . . . the Blessed Virgin is addressed

> Ave, Solem genuisti,
> Ave, Solem protulisti.

113 CXLII Joseph Beaumont, born of that Leicestershire family which rivals the Tennysons of Lincolnshire in poetical fertility, was educated at Peterhouse, Cambridge, where he began that immense range of study which was characteristic of the ' Polymaths ' of the seventeenth century. With his friend Crashaw thrust forth in 1644, he retired to Hadleigh, where he

wrote his *Psyche, or Love's Mystery,*—an allegory of Life filling between thirty and forty thousand lines. Beaumont's later years, despite the political troubles of his time, were prosperous: he made a happy marriage (1650), and after 1660 became Head of Jesus and of his old College successively: Regius Professor of Divinity in 1674. Thenceforward he seems to have lived and worked at Peterhouse, where his epitaph in the Chapel still commemorates him as

Poeta, Orator, Theologus præstantissimus.

The pieces here printed, (which do not represent the mystical style of the *Psyche*), belong to 1652: CXLIV was doubtless suggested by the contrast of Beaumont's home-happiness in quiet Hadleigh, and the wretched state of England under the Commonwealth, and is a lesson as true for the nineteenth century as the seventeenth.

117 CXLVII   Henry More, the most interesting figure among our poetical mystics, went from Eton to Christ's, Cambridge, where he lived an ideal student's life among books, friends, and disciples, yet distinguished also for charitable deeds.

In youth he passed through a stage of bewildered thought, accompanied with the common miseries of scepticism, which he described in a few powerful lines,—till he reached clear vision;

Νῦν δέ τ' Ἔρως με πτεροῖσι θεόσσυτος ἐξυπερείδει·
Νύξ ἀπέβη μὲν ὄναρ τε . . .

—blessed henceforward with a firm happy philosophic Christian faith,—which in mode of expression was influenced not only by Plato and his later mystical followers, but by the mediaeval *Theologia Germanica*, by Ficino of Florence,—(probably in his *Theologia Platonica*)—and Descartes, then the leading thinker in Europe. But he moved through this labyrinth of speculation, safe in the singleness of heart, the *Monocardia*, as he terms it,—the faithfulness to the 'Good and the True,'—to the Sincerity which, (as on his death-bed 'he professed with tears' to the friend who watched by him), had been his lifelong pursuit. More's 'unwavering allegiance to reason,' which he held 'the glory and adornment of all true religion, and the special prerogative of Christianity' was 'the counterbalancing principle' in his mind to his mystical theories: (J. H. Overton, *The Church in the Eighteenth Century*).

R. Southey remarks on More that 'as a poet,—
strange and sometimes unreadably uncouth as he is,
there are lines and passages of the highest feeling and
most exquisite beauty.' His many poems cannot in
·his own age have been popular, and will never be so.
Yet it is impossible to glance at them without an
impression of strange imaginative force, of singular
and delightful depth of mystical conviction.

The two remarkable philosophical flights here
chosen are briefer, not lower, than More's more
sustained poems. Difficult at first sight from their
weight of condensed thought, from the remoteness
of the ideas presented, they remind of the passionate
power, the imaginative fury, of Lucretius :—but their
Christian Platonism lifts them in tone into a larger
aether, regions happier and higher, than could be
reached by the pupil of Empedocles and Epicurus.

120 CXLIX   In st. i. the order of l. 3 and 4 has been conjec-
turally transposed.

John Norris was educated at Winchester and Exeter
College, and Fellow of All Souls, Oxford. He held the
living of Bemerton, formerly G. Herbert's, (1691).
'That old and tranquil parsonage was to him a happy
hiding place :' and *Bene latuit* is his fitting epitaph.—
Norris wrote much and ably on metaphysical subjects :
was greatly influenced by the Cambridge Platonists,
More and Cudworth. His poems were published 1684,
and passed through a tenth edition by 1730 :—one
proof, out of many, how exaggerated is the criticism
which describes that period as devoid of inner life
and spiritual aspiration.

Norris may be reckoned the last among our Christian
Platonists of the seventeenth century. He has 'the
same noble tone of spiritualised thought and wistful,
imaginative, speculation, and a like *golden haze* over
it all' (C. J. Abbey) :—not without some share in
the fancifulness and overstrain prevalent in his day.

121 CLI   Francis Quarles, son to a country gentleman of
Romford : educated at Christ's, Cambridge : studied
at Lincoln's Inn : was for a time secretary to Archbishop Usher in Ireland, but lived mainly as an
author, publishing much in verse and prose from
1620 onward. He was a devoted royalist, and
suffered accordingly :—dying of grief, it is said, at
the robbery and destruction of his library.

The inconstancy of Fame has no better example than Quarles. He moralizes his song too much; his work is marred by fantastical lapses from good taste; by a fatal facility. Yet,—unless indeed a man's performance, when he has had free play, is always the measure of his natural gift,—Quarles has written so well, so sincerely, sometimes, (see CLI), so fervently,—that had he remembered how, in Poetry, Matter, however good, is of no ultimate avail without adequate Art, he might, we may easily believe, have deserved to retain some part of that immense popularity which he enjoyed among his contemporaries.

125 CLV   George Wither, educated at Magdalen, Oxford, was a lawyer; served on both sides in the Civil War; made a Major General by Cromwell, but was deprived of his spoils after the Restoration.—'His best poems,' says Hallam, 'were published in 1622, with the title of *Mistress of Philarete.* Some of them are highly beautiful . . . I think there is hardly anything in our lyric poetry of [that] period equal to his lines on his Muse.' But this promise was swamped by false fluency and the 'grovelling puritanism into which he afterwards fell.'

126 CLVII   Jeremy Taylor: Educated at Caius, Cambridge: made Fellow of All Souls, Oxford, by favour of Archbishop Laud: was imprisoned for his support of Charles I: lived poor and retiredly in Wales, but was once or twice more imprisoned:—moved to Lisburn and in 1660 was made Bishop of Down and Connor,—with Dromore, where he was buried, in addition. He united learning and fervent eloquence perhaps more than any other English writer.

128 CLIX   Richard Baxter: A man eminent for candour, charity, and goodness, but inconsistent and wavering in his public career during the evil days of the Civil War, Protectorate, and Restoration. He was a very voluminous polemical writer, but best known in his own day and since through his excellent manuals of practical piety. 'Read any of his works; they are all good,' said Dr. Johnson to Boswell.

— CLX   Samuel Crossman: Educated at Pembroke, Oxford: was ejected from his rectory in Essex for nonconformity in 1662: returned to the Church, and died

INTRODUCTION TO BOOK II

The changes which occur in poetical style, as we have noticed, are marked less strongly upon our religious than on our secular song.   Yet something of the clear diction and the easy metrical flow of Pope is traceable in the hymns of Addison: whilst the plain, even the prosaic, manner of De Foe has a counterpart in Ken's writing.   But the didactic tone, the repressed undercurrent of feeling, which in many ways colour our secular poetry during the second and third quarters of the eighteenth century, in religious verse soon gave way before what is generally known as the Evangelical movement.   This in some degree was doubtless a reaction towards warmth, enthusiasm, and (as we might say) Nature, from the argumentative habit, the constant appeal to reason and common sense, the studied moderation of tone, which were the general tendencies of the time.—But the motives and the men by whom the religious school in question was led from Watts, Toplady, and the Wesleys, to Cowper,—its strength and its weakness—need not here be dwelt on.   Suffice it to note that the poetry of the full-charged heart now found vent and relief, not in imaginative ode or didactic meditation, but in the form of hymns; amongst which many of the most beautiful, not less than the most practically precious, poems of that class existing in any literature, are found. These hymns indeed have often, to modern eyes, a conventional style, due to two causes : the phraseology common to the Evangelical school, and the general literary manner of the time. But the manner of one age is always the conventionality of the next : and they to whom this quality is repulsive in our eighteenth-century writers should remember that the styles which seem natural to us will probably, under the same law, seem artificial to those who live in the ' summers that we shall not see.'

PAGE NO.

138 CLXXII Abraham Cowley, of Westminster School and Trinity, Cambridge : a supporter of Charles I and his Queen :— by his contemporaries (and Milton's) held the greatest poet of his time. But cleverness and sense, both of which he has to a very high degree, when wanting good taste and that indescribable something which eternally severs poetry from verse, have long since placed him amongst those writers who are rarely read, but never read without profit.

139 CLXXIV *the Tyrrhene seas* : Addison here obviously refers to a violent storm by which, when sailing from Marseille to Italy during December 1699, he was assailed in the bay of Genoa. His vessel was driven back to Monaco, whence he took boat to Savona.

142 CLXXVII Thomas Ken was Scholar of Winchester 1652, Fellow of New College, Oxford, by election from school : studied music and physical science in addition to the ordinary subjects. Was chosen Fellow of Winchester, and Prebendary (1669) : resided there for some years and wrote his famous *Manual of Prayers* (1675`. Chaplain at the Hague to Princess Mary : consecrated Bishop of Bath and Wells 1685, at the special choice of Charles II, who honoured the courage of ' the little black fellow who would not give poor Nelly [Gwyn] a lodging' in his house at Winchester.

After Monmouth's invasion Ken saved the lives of many rebels : as Bishop he gave away his whole income, and was unbounded in kindness and aid to the poor. In 1688 he was one of the Seven Bishops who resisted James II : but, with much hesitation, found himself unable to take the Oath required by William III, and was deprived of his See in 1691. Henceforth he lived mostly in personal poverty at Longleat ; troubled often by Nonjuring disputants and failing health ; yet comforted by many friendships with old and young : for, childless himself, like Watts and Keble, he was distinguished by love for children. He received unfailing and reverent kindness from Lord Weymouth, under whose roof he died, and was buried at Frome Selwood, the nearest village in his old diocese.

Poetry more absolutely sincere, more high-minded than Bishop Ken's, does not exist. But heaviness of style, prolixity, want of charm and of variety, has sunk most of his work irretrievably. It is but the selection of a selection which is here offered. Three justly-famous Hymns have, however, been printed in full. The curious textual questions connected with them have been discussed by Dean Plumptre of Wells in his admirable Life of Ken (1888) :—a book which puts the man and his age before us with singular vividness. The text given in Ken's *Manual* for Winchester College, 1695, has here been mainly followed, with a few alterations from his revised edition of 1709.

150 CLXXXV Ken for many years before his death suffered grievously from rheumatism and other disorders, resorting to Bath and Clifton for relief. But disease grew upon him, and his latter days were over-shadowed by terrible tortures. This poem,—beauti-ful from its simplicity and depth of pathos, (as CLXXXVI through its dramatic straightforwardness`, —with others is ascribed by Dean Plumptre to that melancholy period. Ken says himself :—

> I some remission of my woes
> Feel, while I hymns compose.

152 CLXXXVII Nahum Tate : at Trinity, Dublin : Poet Laureate after Shadwell ; friend of Dryden. He translated the Psalms in conjunction with Dr. Brady, and has been criticized too severely for failing of success in a task where to succeed was impossible.

153 CLXXXVIII John Pomfret : of Queen's, Cambridge, and Rector of Malden, Bedfordshire. This little song is an oasis in a wilderness of commonplace.

— CLXXXIX Isaac Watts received a thorough classical educa-tion, and entered the 'Independent' ministry. His health failed in 1712 and the rest of his life he passed in Sir T. Abney's house ; dying there of old age ; after long and devoted work to his flock and in literature. He was buried in Bunhill Fields.

Watts may be counted (if we exclude Milton), as one 'of the earliest well-read and scholarly students among the nonconformists. His views as an Independent were modified and enlarged by his sweet devout temper; may we not add,—by his gift in poetry? And 'every Christian church,' as Dr. Johnson finely remarked, 'would rejoice to have adopted' one so fervently devout, so faithful to his duty;—we may add, so much more truly gifted by nature as a poet, than common Fame has recognized. As with C. Wesley and other good men, fluency, want of taste and finish, the sacrifice, in a word, of Art to direct usefulness, have probably lost them those honours in literature to which they were born. But they have their reward.

156 CXCIII The Calvinism within which the tender-hearted Watts was bound captive is doubtless too perceptible in this beautiful lyric. A similar vein of feeling may, however, be traced, centuries before, in that 'apathy' which S. Clement of Alexandria ascribes to the perfect Christian, who is 'so absorbed in the Divine Love that he can no longer be said to love his fellow-creatures, in the ordinary sense of the word.' Yet as we learn, (Bigg, *The Christian Platonists of Alexandria*), how 'there were many in Clement's own time who shrank from that too ethereal ideal, which, to use his own phrase, *touches earth with but one foot,*' so in this hymn the gracious spirit of Poetry seems to soften the grim atmosphere of Geneva.

158 CXCVII The admirable author of this hymn almost apologized for publishing it. Yet few child-pictures have been drawn in words or colours of more perfect tenderness.

159 CXCVIII Philip Doddridge: a nonconformist minister of much and varied reading: Head of a theological College at Northampton: a greatly esteemed and popular author of his day: died and was buried at Lisbon.

151 CCII John Byrom: trained at Merchant Taylors' and Trinity, Cambridge: his first publication was a Pastoral in the *Spectator*. After early poverty, he lived a retired blameless literary life on his property by Manchester. One of the many men of strong feeling in whom faith burned like 'a hidden flame' through the eighteenth century.

162 CCIII   Christopher Smart: student and fellow of Pembroke Hall, Cambridge: His life was one of literature actively followed as a profession; didactic, satirical, and religious. But his work is singularly unequal: only under the stress of illness and mental over-excitement did he reach the level of serious genius shown in our two specimens. Smart was eminent for wit, conviviality, kindliness, and carelessness: valued as a friend by men like Johnson and Garrick :— a type of one who has 'no enemy but himself.'

During a severe illness (1754-1756) Smart's mind partially failed: whilst in confinement he is believed to have written the 'Song to David' which he published in 1763 :—the Hymn on his Recovery has been dated about 1756. It seems that he never regained full sanity, although the disease was rather eccentricity than madness : and despite hard labour, he died under confinement for debt.

'My poor friend Smart,' Dr. Johnson said to Boswell, in 1763, 'showed the disturbance of his mind, by falling upon his knees, and saying his prayers in the street. . . . Now although, rationally speaking, it is greater madness not to pray at all, than to pray as Smart did, I am afraid there are so many who do not pray, that their understanding is not called in question.'

Some traces of Smart's excited spirit are visible in cciii :—far more in cciv, which may be described in a phrase of C. Lamb's as 'a kind of medley between inspiration and possession'; and in its noble wildness and transitions from grandeur to tenderness, from Earth to Heaven, is unique in our Poetry. It has been greatly abridged as here printed.

166 CCV   Michael Bruce: born and bred near Lochleven in Fifeshire : well educated in the village school, where he was a typical specimen of the poor, brave, Scottish student of those days, who could find in Latin literature lifelong strength and enlightenment and culture. Bruce was next at the University of Edinburgh (1762) in company with John Logan: teaching during his vacations, and after in the country schools of his native district. But this life was too hard for him : consumption set in, and he died in his sleep at twenty-one :—his copy of Holy Scripture,—turned down at the text *Weep ye not for the dead* . . . beside him.

Immediately after the death of Bruce, Logan secured all his papers. What followed has been the subject of much controversy. But the Editor cannot resist the conclusion that Logan, (whose after career was unsatisfactory), managed to gain himself credit for the authorship of most of his fellow-student's poems;—publishing them with more or less verbal alteration, and destroying all the original manuscripts. Yet, even as we have them, their grace, music, fine descriptive skill, and spiritual feeling, sufficiently prove that, had longer years been granted him, Michael Bruce might have fulfilled the renown of which his youth gave promise so remarkable.

168 CCVIII   Thomas Olivers : A shoemaker by trade; converted from a dissolute life by Whitefield's preaching, he became, first, a zealous assistant of John Wesley, and then was employed in his printing-office.

The musical service in a Synagogue at Westminster suggested to Olivers the noble Ode here printed : (C. J. Abbey).

170 CCIX   Augustus Montague Toplady: of Westminster School and Trinity, Dublin : sometime Vicar of Broadhembury, Devon : published his hymns in 1776. A zealous Calvinist; studied and wrote much: powerfully and bitterly opposing John Wesley. But his fervour of nature, when directed to worthier purpose, inspired Toplady with this splendid Lyric; which, in beauty and intensity of feeling, has a rival in CCXII,—a hymn truly sublime through the simplicity of its absolute self-surrender.

— CCX   *the balance* : Toplady seems here to have had in view a phrase from the famous hymn, *Vexilla Regis*, by Fortunatus the sixth-century poet,—who describes the Cross, whilst bearing the Saviour's Body, as *Statera facta saeculi* :—' His Body there in balance lay,' in J. Keble's version.

172 CCXV   Charles Wesley : younger brother to John : At Westminster School; Student of Christ Church, Oxford, where he worked diligently: was ordained; went on a short mission to the Indians of Georgia : afterwards, a Methodist preacher in England.

The dramatic vividness and fervour of this lyrical Monologue (founded upon Genesis xxxii)—the music and consoling sweetness of faith in CCXXI, may justify the opinion on the Hymnist's natural gift expressed in the previous Note upon Watts; who, with the charming candour natural to him, said, ' It was worth all the works he himself had written.'

In the *strove* and *rose* (St. ix and xi) for *striven* and *risen*, Wesley, as Archbishop Trench has remarked, adopts a usage found in Shakespeare and Milton.

177 CCXXII   Philip Skelton : Scholar in Trinity, Dublin : worked as clergyman at Monaghan and elsewhere ; being always distinguished for good sense, devotedness, self-denial, and success : published much ; mostly on religious subjects. Retired in old age to Dublin ; published his hymns in 1784.

This poem,—much indebted for its beauty to its scientific accuracy,—is an interesting example of the practical, the positive, spirit for which the eighteenth century has been often inconsiderately and indiscriminately censured.

179 CCXXIII   John Cennick : For a time, a Calvinistic Methodist ; afterwards a Moravian preacher :—To this period the hymn printed doubtless belongs.

— CCXXIV   John Newton : Began life as a sailor ; was employed in the African slave-trade ; profligate and miserable, yet worked perseveringly at Latin and mathematics. He awoke to the sense of Sin and of Mercy : left the sea : studied for Holy Orders : was ordained to the curacy of Olney (1765), and became friend of William Cowper. In 1779 Newton was made rector of a City church ; He had the generosity of a large heart, grateful for his conversion to piety and happiness ; and hence, doubtless, a singular gift in winning his hearers.

Mere bare simplicity and sincerity suffice to range this hymn amongst the most powerful in our Anthology : John Bunyan, or the great twelfth-century religious poet, Jacopone of Todi, who wrote the Canzone *Mirami, Sposa, un poco In sulla Croce ignudo*, might have been proud, or thankful, to own it.

182 CCXVIII-CCXXXII   These hymns were written at Olney in North Buckinghamshire between 1771-1779, at the suggestion and under the influence of John Newton. That influence was not wholly for good ; Assurance of Salvation—a cardinal point in the creed of his

Calvinist friend,—was physically and morally impossible to Cowper's tremulous, sensitive, nature. The Hymnal was not far advanced, when he again fell beneath the insanity of ten years before. His mind gradually recovered its proper tone:—and the jointly-written book, about one-fourth of which is by Cowper, was the first by which (1779) he became known as an author.

183 CCXXXI Mr. Abbey, in the excellent *Church in the Eighteenth Century*, assigns this brilliant lyric to J. Newton. It is however, marked C. in the first edition of the *Olney Hymns*,—the sign placed to distinguish Cowper's work:—to which, in point of style, it also clearly belongs.

184 CCXXXIII This beautiful poem was written in 1765, at the moment when Cowper, after his earliest fit of derangement, was deciding to quit London as his home, for ever. That the country, however, could not give lasting peace to that delicate and troubled spirit, is shown by the companion poem, of at least equal beauty, *O happy shades* . . ., written in 1773;—apparrently whilst the second attack (above noticed) was approaching.

186 CCXXXV William Blake : Mr. A. Gilchrist has well recounted the story of this singularly attractive poet and painter. A long life could hardly have fewer events; only a sixty years' cheerful and happy struggle against starvation : but the beautiful soul of the man, devoted to his art and his loving wife and his God, gives it an unique interest,—a fascination, rarely raised by any biography. And in Blake, more than most, the man is identified with the artist; the spell which the life holds over the sympathetic reader is renewed and confirmed by the poet-painter's designs and verses. The drawing may be often faulty; the syntax imperfect; yet there is a subtle simplicity, a tenderness springing equally from the heart and the imagination, —sometimes a sublimity of idea, which give the best work of Blake's youth a peculiar place of its own, high up amongst our ' treasures for ever.'

The soul of that child-like and celestial painter Fra Angelico, might have entered into Blake, (who in 1789 can have known nothing of the monastic Italian artist)—when writing this and the two following pieces for his *Songs of Innocence*.

The work of each was in truth irradiated by mystic

INTRODUCTION TO BOOK III

Our Second Book ranges from about 1680 to 1820. By this
latter date that fertile outburst of poetry, which gave a brilliancy
to the first half of this century, second only to that of the Elizabethan age, had fully established itself. And already also the
dominant schools of religious thought and practice familiar to us
all, (from whatever angle of view we may estimate them), were
working their way to the surface. There is now sufficient general
acquiescence in regard to the character of the Evangelical movement to render discussion of it here unnecessary. An opposite
reason dispenses with any critical sketch of the modes of thought
upon religion which are represented in this Third Book. Attention may however be called to the close parallelism between
the impulses which, respectively, supplied their wealth of poetic
material and inspiration to Herbert and Vaughan, and, in our own
day, to the two admirable writers who hold a place similar to
theirs in this section of our anthology.

194 CCLVI   Henry Hart Milman, of Eton and Brasenose, Oxford:
author of several plays, poems and histories, ably
written in a somewhat artificial style.   Professor of
Poetry at Oxford, 1821.   Canon of Westminster and
Dean of S. Paul's.—The hymns here given were
published, together with those by Bishop Heber, in
1827.

200 CCLVIII   All the poems selected from Wordsworth belong to
the later half of his life, with exception of CCLXIV,
which was 'composed on the beach near Calais,'
1802.

207 CCLXVII–CCLXXXIX are from the *Christian Year*, published 1827.
John Keble, educated by his father, before his
fifteenth birthday was elected Scholar of Corpus,
Oxford: First Class in the Classical and Mathematical
Schools, 1810: Fellow of Oriel, 1811: ordained
Priest 1816, when he asked a friend to 'pray for me
that I may free myself from all pride, all ambition, all
uncharitableness':—The prayer was granted, and it
may form the motto for Keble's long, useful, and
saintly life.   He was chosen unanimously Professor
of Poetry at Oxford 1831: settled as Vicar at Hurs-
ley near Winchester 1835, where his days henceforth
were passed, divided between prose and poetry and
the devout performance of duty: resting by his beloved wife at last in the peace of his own green
churchyard, beside the church rebuilt by him from
the proceeds of the *Christian Year*.
Keble's work as a co-operator with J. H. (Cardinal)
Newman, Dr. Pusey, and others, in the religious
movement to which his poetry gave its earliest
definite character is, perhaps, sufficiently illustrated
in the selection here offered.

209 CCLXIX   St. ii l. 2 *blossoms red and bright*: the original note
says, 'Rhododendrons': but was afterwards cor-
rected to 'Oleanders.'—St. v, vi, vii: the meaning
is, Turn from the world to Christ.

213 CCLXXII   In refinement of feeling for nature, in the human,
sympathetic attitude towards things inanimate, and
again, in the sense how often these are more happily
gifted than mankind, we are here closely reminded
of Vaughan.   Yet it is hardly probable that his very
rare little books should have fallen in Keble's way
by 1827.
No essay on Keble as a poet would be in place here.
Yet it may be noticed that, like Vaughan, his work

if not always clear either in its main lines or its phrases, is filled with admirable imaginative touches, with true and tender felicities, which deserve and reward readers,—careful, devoted, it might almost be said, microscopic.

218 CCLXXV   *They say . . . crown*: the author here refers in a note to Bishop Jeremy Taylor, *Holy Living*, c. xi, sect. 3.

219 CCLXXVII These beautiful stanzas, said Mr. Keble's wife, on the day of his death, 'I know were in his dying thoughts.'   She survived him but a few weeks.

221 CCLXXIX St. iv *We change our posture*: so Dante (*Purg.* vi, 149) compares Florence, in her sick state, to

> quella inferma
> Che non può trovar posa in su le piume,
> Ma con dar volta suo dolore scherma.

234 CCXC   Richard Chenevix Trench : Born at Dublin, educated at Trinity, Cambridge.   Theological Professor at King's College : Dean of Westminster, 1856 : Archbishop of Dublin, 1864.   In Philology and Biblical exegesis he ranks high amongst our prose-writers, and his poetry is penetrated by the high purity and nobility of his character.

239 CCXCIX   Henry Alford : Educated at Ilmington School, and Trinity, Cambridge : of which College he became Fellow.   A learned Greek Scholar ; edited the New Testament.   Dean of Canterbury, 1857.

240 CCC   Hartley Coleridge : eldest son to Samuel Taylor : Scholar of Merton, Oxford, and Fellow of Oriel. Lived mostly in the Lake Country, a gentle, dreamy man, who from feeble health and want of will failed to fulfil the promise of his youth ; whilst, in Wordsworth's beautiful phrase, Nature preserved for him throughout 'a young lamb's heart among the full-grown flocks.'

241 CCCIII   Carolina Baroness Nairn : Born (daughter to L. Oliphant) and died at Gask in Perthshire.   A high-minded woman, whose 'heart was in every good and Christian work of her time.'
   The Leal, Faithful. P. 242 *sae dear's* . . . It is a hard-fought and dearly-won battle, by which sinful man may reach Heaven.

242 CCCIV   Henry Francis Lyte : Of Trinity, Dublin : left Ireland for Brixham, Devonshire, through ill-health, and died at Nice.   Published his *Poems* 1833.

244 CCCVII   *The maid is not dead, but sleepeth*, is the Author's motto for these very tender and original lines. · Mr. Lyte's book has other lyrics, not within the scope of this selection, similarly distinguished by pathetic delicacy. His style often unites the characteristic merits of Addison and of Cowper.

247 CCCIX   *song that may not die*: cccx is dated, Berryhead, September, 1847. The writer died in the following November.

249 CCCXII–CCCXX From the *Lyra Innocentium*, published 1846: cccxxi–cccxxx, from the *Miscellaneous Poems*, written at many different dates.

254 CCCXVII Prefixed are the words ' Make me thereof a little cake first, and bring it unto me, and after make for thee and for thy son.'

257 CCCXXI   Dated 1854.

261 CCCXXVII Originally written for the *Christian Year*, from admission to which its personal character probably excluded it. This poem may be placed beside the beautiful *Ode to Evening* by Collins, as one of the rare successes of English poetry in the unrhymed lyric.

262 CCCXXVIII Composed ' for the Tomb of the old Biddlecombes, May 24, 1861.'

263 CCCXXX   Dated ' Dec. 8, *in Conceptione B.M.V.*, 1844.' The hymn ' was written for the *Lyra Innocentium*, but withheld from publication at the time, with Mr. Keble's consent but against his wish.'

264 CCCXXXI William Barnes, of a family who had held lands in Dorset for centuries, was born in a farmhouse within that beautiful Vale of Blackmore upon which his poems love to dwell. Educated in the country: at first placed in a lawyer's office; then conducted schools at Mere and Dorchester: made himself master of many languages, ancient and modern; obtained a degree from S. John's, Cambridge. By study and love of the Dorset folk and their ancient speech was led to write poems in hope of preserving the dialect. Ordained in 1847; in 1862 Rector of Winterbourne Came near Dorchester. And there, strenuously to the last doing his duty from cottage to cottage, yet studying and writing much on many subjects, Barnes' years passed quickly and happily on, till, in full Christian hope and peace, he was laid to rest within his little tree-shadowed churchyard.

    The poetry of Barnes, like that of Burns, is inseparable from the dialect. This, however, (easily as it may be mastered), has barred the lyrics of Barnes from their due place amongst the most varied in subject, the most perfect in form, the purest and sweetest in tone, which our literature contains. Humour and pathos, character and landscape, within the limits of the local sphere which he scarcely quits, each is at his command : of all modern poets he is the most truly and delightfully Idyllic.—The few specimens here given, it is hoped, may tempt genuine lovers of poetry to test this criticism for themselves :—the writer does not fear their verdict.

269 CCCXXXVI From *Poems . . . in common English*, 1868.   It is worthy of Blake at his best in its sweet picturesque simplicity.

270 CCCXXXVII Adelaide Anne Procter : daughter to a poet best known as ' Barry Cornwall.'   Her poems appeared in 1858, 1861, 1862.

274 CCCXLII From *Poems*, D. M. Main, Glasgow, 1886 :—a volume marked by delicate and original thought, expressed with simple grace.   For his acquaintance with the book, the Editor is indebted to Miss C. G. Rossetti.

279 CCCXLVI Published 1849.—Arthur Hugh Clough was educated at Rugby, Scholar of Balliol and Fellow of Oriel (1842), Oxford : afterwards in the Education Office : died and was buried at Florence.

— CCCXLVII John Campbell Shairp : born at Houstoun, Linlithgowshire, of an old Lowland Scottish family : trained at Edinburgh, Glasgow University, and Balliol, Oxford.   Worked as Master at Rugby, and afterwards as Professor of Humanity at S. Andrews : was there chosen Principal of the United Colleges ; Elected Professor of Poetry at Oxford (1877).

282 CCCLI Richard Hurrell Froude : At Eton and Oriel, Oxford : friend and co-operator with John Keble and John Henry (Cardinal) Newman in their movement for religious revival.

282 CCCLII The editor trusts that he has here dealt with the free permission of reprinting graciously given him, in a mode which will not be disapproved by one to whom, in company with millions, he owes a gratitude best expressed by silence,—a reverence such, *che nol diria sermone.*

bridge. Master of Harrow: Bishop of Lincoln, 1869. Eminent for scholarship and integrity of life.

313 CCCCII   Frederick William Faber: of Harrow School and University, Oxford: entered the Roman Church in 1845 and established the Oratory of S. Philip Neri in London: labouring zealously till his early death. His hymns were first published complete in 1862.

317 CCCCVI   'Verse sung at the Way of the Cross at the Oratory.'
— CCCCVII   *Jesus, our Love*: see note on CLXVII.

318 CCCCVIII   The poetry of Mr. Richard Wilton, (of S. Catherine's, Cambridge: Rector of Londesborough), *Woodnotes*, 1873, and *Lyrics*, 1878, deserves wider acceptance than it has hitherto received.

319 CCCCX   'The East window of Kirkby Wharfe or Grimston Church is filled with stained glass, . . . the subject being the Crucifixion.'

— CCCCXI   From *Days and Hours* by Frederick Tennyson, 1854 :—another noteworthy and too-neglected book.

320 CCCCXII   Charles Tennyson, born at Somersby, Lincolnshire, next brother to Frederick and senior to Alfred, was educated at Louth and Trinity, Cambridge: ordained 1835; married a sister of Emily, Lady Tennyson, and spent most of his life as Vicar of Grasby in the Wolds,—taking the surname of Turner under the will of a relation. His, as his nephew Hallam Tennyson truly writes, was an *alma beata e bella* :—a man of noble simplicity, tenderness, purity of heart, 'at once childlike and heroic.' The devoted love of his brother Alfred is expressed in the beautiful stanzas dated *Midnight*, June 30, 1879.

This poet was master of what may be termed the Idyllic sonnet; under which form he gave many pictures of his country and its indwellers, with his thoughts upon this and the other life. These Sonnets, (published collectively in 1880), have the charm of a singular humanity; of an originality which sometimes touches upon quaintness. No verse more sincere, more tender, more worthy of study, is contained in our Anthology.

321 CCCCXIV   *scroll of prayer*: 'The extract from the *Book of the Dead*, which was put into the hands of the deceased.'

322 CCCCXVI   *Thou shalt not lose*: so Petrarch, in one of those passages whose ethereal beauty reminds us of the

Paradise scenes by Fra Angelico, speaking of the souls in Heaven;

> Tanti volti che 'l Tempo e Morte han guasti
> Torneranno al lor più fiorito stato.

325 CCCCXXIII L. 10 *oorali*: a drug extracted from *Strychnos toxi-fera*; It acts by paralysing the nerves of motion, whilst those of sensation are left unimpaired.

Readers should remember that this poem forms in truth a little drama, wherein it is not the Poet, but the Hospital Nurse, who speaks throughout. The two little girls, whose story was published in a magazine, are the only characters here drawn from actual life.

.   .   .   .   .   .

307 CCCXCII This hymn, often printed as *Anonymous*, and so classed in former issues by the Editor, is by Sir Edward Denny, and was originally published in his *Hymns and Poems*, 1848 (W. T. Brooke).

The writer was educated at Exeter, Oxford, and died whilst this book was in the press.

May, 1890

INDEX OF WRITERS

WITH DATES OF BIRTH AND DEATH

* See page 361

INDEX OF FIRST LINES

THE END